Ju
F
H86   Hubner, Carol.
          The tattered tallis and
       other Devora Doresh
       mysteries.

The Tattered Tallis
and other
Devora Doresh Mysteries

The Tattered Tallis

and other
Devora Doresh Mysteries

by

Carol Korb Hubner

Illustrated by

Yochanan Jones

Judaica Press • 1979
New York

ISBN 0-910818-19-3

Contents

This book is dedicated to
My Mother
Mrs. Devorah Korb Gartenberg
my inspiration

The Mummy's Hand

The Mummy's Hand

errible," Rebbe Doresh exclaimed, turning off the radio. Mrs. Doresh was preparing Chaim's breakfast and watched her husband shake his head from side to side, sighing.

"Just terrible," he repeated, washing out his cereal bowl in the sink. "Every time I turn on the radio, all I hear are reports about robberies. Bank robberies, home robberies, and now museum robberies. We live in a society with too many dissatisfied customers. Everyone wants what the other has. Terrible."

"What happened?" Asked Mrs. Doresh. "Some paintings were stolen from the museum?"

"I don't think they were paintings," replied Rebbe Doresh. "The newsman said something about ancient jewels worth over two million dollars."

Devora walked into the kitchen, yawning. She took a cereal bowl from the cabinet and joined the others. As she sat down, Chaim looked at her amusedly.

"What's so funny, Chaim?" Asked Devora, pouring the cereal into the bowl.

"We were just talking about robberies," replied Chaim. "And all of a sudden, here you are!"

"Robberies?" Devora exclaimed. "Where? Who?"

"You seem more hungry for mysteries to solve than for breakfast," Mrs. Doresh remarked. "We were just discussing how you always hear about robberies every time you turn on the radio. *Abba*[1] just heard that the museum was robbed last night of over two million dollars' worth of ancient Jewels."

"Wow!" Devora said. "I wonder if O'Malley was assigned to this case."

"I doubt it," said Rebbe Doresh, "it's too big."

Devora finished her breakfast and recited the *borey nefoshos*.[2] She then rose from her chair and said goodbye to Chaim and to her mother. Rebbe Doresh led her out of the house and both climbed into the old Chevy for the trip to the yeshiva. As they rode, Devora spoke about the robbery and questioned her father for more information.

"Were they Egyptian jewels?" Devora asked.

"Egyptian jewels? What makes you think that?" Rebbe Doresh said.

"Doesn't the museum have a big exhibition right now from Egypt? Our history teacher mentioned something about that. We're studying middle-eastern history."

"Well," Rebbe Doresh said, pulling the car up to the curb in front of the Yocheved High School. "I don't remember the radio announcer saying anything about

1. Father.
2. A brief prayer of gratitude recited after most light snacks and drinks.

Egypt. I'm sure he would have mentioned it, if the jewels had anything to do with the exhibit you're talking about."

Devora stepped out of the car and waved to her father as he drove off to a nearby yeshiva where he was a *Rebbe*.[3] As Devora walked down the corridor toward her classroom, she spotted Rivkeh, her friend. Rivkeh stopped in her tracks and waited for Devora to catch up. The bell rang and the two girls hurried to their class. Moreh Hartman was just beginning the session as the girls headed for their seats. Moreh Hartman waited for the two to settle down before she began. The girls took their *chumashim*[4] out of their briefcases and turned the pages to the story of Joseph and his brothers.

"Are there any questions on yesterday's lesson, before we go on?" Moreh Hartman asked. Rivkeh Landau raised her hand.

"Yes, Rivkeh. You have a question?"

Rivkeh Landau stood up with her open *chumash*.

"I just wanted to know if the following *posuk*[5] in the *chumash* is talking about making mummies."

The class broke into muffled giggles. Rivkeh herself also smiled and restrained herself from joining her friends. Moreh Hartman bit her lip to prevent herself from laughing, too.

"Now, let's give Rivkeh a chance to ask her ques-

---

3. Teacher.
4. Plural for *chumash*, the Five Books of Moses (or the Torah).
5. Verse.

tion, girls, please stop this silly behavior. Go ahead, Rivkeh. Which *posuk* are you referring to?"

Rivkeh swallowed her laugh and strained to keep a serious face.

"'And Joseph commanded his servants, the physicians to embalm his father'."[6]

Moreh Hartman cleared her throat.

"If you must know, Rivkeh, yes, it was a process similar to what we know as Egyptian mummies. Our sages teach us that Joseph followed the Egyptian custom in this case because only the greatest people of Egypt were so embalmed, and if he would not have done this to his own father, Jacob, the Egyptians would have misunderstood and seen it as disrespect to his father. In fact, Joseph himself was embalmed in the same manner when he died, as you will see at the end of the chapter."[7]

Rivkeh sat down.

"I might as well inform you," Moreh Hartman continued, "that there is a special exhibit in the museum, which includes a mummy from around the same period in which Joseph lived. I think it will be on display one more day before they fly it back to Egypt. It's a pity our class didn't have a chance to see it together."

Devora's eyes lit up. She would have wanted to visit the museum and see the exhibition. By recess time, she had already decided to approach Rivkeh with the idea.

6. Genesis, 50:2.
7. Genesis, 50:26.

"Go see a mummy?" Rivkeh asked, surprised. "I don't want to see any mummy. I'm not *that* interested, I just wanted to know if the Torah was referring to the same thing, that's all."

"Come on, Rivkeh," Devora coaxed her. "Please come with me. I really want to see what it looks like, but I can't go alone. Moreh Hartman doesn't let us go to public places alone. Neither do my parents. Come on, Rivkeh, please?"

"Well, okay, Devora. But when do you want to go?"

"When? Right after school."

"What? Today? So fast?"

"Rivkeh, first of all, we have a half day today because of Washington's birthday. And second of all, Moreh Hartman said that she was not sure whether the exhibit would be around more than another day or two days."

"I sure was looking forward to a nice long afternoon at home today, Devora, not looking at some mummy."

"Rivkeh. Please. It will be a real special treat for me if you go with me."

"Well, okay. After school, we'll go home and ask our parents for their permission. Then I have to do a few things around the house. So about three or half past three, I should be ready."

"But Rivkeh, that's cutting it close! The museum closes at four-thirty, I think. We'll only have enough time to *look* for the mummy. Can't you be ready earlier?"

"I can't promise anything, but I'll try."

The bell rang and the girls returned to the class for the next session. The girls put away their *chumashim* and took out their *nachs*[8] to resume their study of the Book of Kings.

"Okay, class," Moreh Hartman began. "Yesterday, we talked about the two ways a person could do good deeds. Leah Silber, please tell us about these two ways."

Leah Silber put down her pencil and stood up, her eyes fixed on the ceiling.

"Um . . . the . . . um . . . uh . . . one way is when the person does something good because Hashem[9] wants him to. He does it to do the will of Hashem. And the other way a person can do a good deed is if he just does it because he's in the mood, or it's his personality or something."

"Very good, Leah. Devora, can you tell us what sometimes goes wrong with the second way of doing good?"

"There is a danger. If a person does good only because he feels like it and not because it is Hashem's will, then he'll end up doing good only *when* he feels like it, when it is convenient. And sometimes his idea of good gets mixed up with what is really bad."

---

8. Books of the Prophets and later biblical writings.
9. G-d.

"Good," Moreh Hartman said, nodding her head. "And our example for this important lesson, is the ancient king of Israel, Achav. Our sages teach us that Achav seemed like a very good-hearted person. He was far from being a miser and always gave away his money freely. The only problem was, though, that his 'kindness' was not based on the Torah, on Hashem's will, but on his own wishy-washy moods. As a result, while he gave lots of money freely to the Torah sages of his time, he also gave away his money freely to his wife, Jezebel, for the purpose of idol-worship. So you see how his idea of what was 'good' was all mixed up, because his so-called kindness was not based on the Torah but only on himself. While it is certainly a good trait to give of one's money freely and not be a miser, at the same time, it depends what you give the money for, right?"

The session went on excitedly, with all the girls becoming involved in the discussion. There were many questions asked, and Moreh Hartman was forced to bring more and more examples, from the Torah as well as from modern-day situations. Before everyone realized it, it was time to go home. The bell rang, but the interest aroused by Moreh Hartman captivated the girls so, that Moreh Hartman had to practically chase them out of the classroom so she could make her dentist appointment.

Devora, too, had forgotten the excitement of visiting the museum and had been overtaken by the excitement of Moreh Hartman's lesson. As much as she longed to go to the museum, or do a little detective work, she preferred to stay another hour in the yeshiva listening to Moreh Hartman.

Devora walked Rivkeh part of the way home and then turned down her own street toward the Doresh home. Chaim also had a half-day because of the national holiday, and his yeshiva bus was just pulling away as Devora approached her house. Chaim greeted his sister and the two entered the house, heading straight for the kitchen to eat lunch.

Mrs. Doresh had their lunch ready on the table and took out a container of orange juice and began to pour.

"Does Abba also have only a half day today?" Chaim wanted to know. Mrs. Doresh smiled and filled his glass.

"No, Chaim, Abba teaches older boys and they remain in the yeshiva all day, studying Torah. Torah never takes a holiday. Abba will be home regular time, around dinner."

Devora washed her hands for the bread and recited the proper blessing before biting into her tuna fish sandwich. After several bites and a couple of swallows of juice, Devora decided it was a good time to ask her mother the big question.

"You know," she said, "Moreh Hartman told us a little bit about mummies today."

"Abbas, too?" Chaim exclaimed, chewing on a sardine. He always preferred sardines to any other fish.

"No, Chaim," Devora explained while Mrs. Doresh chuckled. "Not that kind of mommy . . . I mean, not mommies, like mommy. I said 'mummy.' You know what a mummy is?"

Chaim shook his head from side to side.

"Well, you see, in the old days, in Egypt, when someone very important died, they would smear him with special ointments and wrap him up completely in very long strips of cloth, like bandages."

"Yech!" said Chaim. "Why would they do that?"

"In order to keep him fresh, I guess. But what's the difference? That's what they used to do. We Jews believe that after you die, the *neshamah*[10] lives on, and the Egyptians of that time believed that the body lived on, so they wanted to keep it from spoiling. And that's also why they put the mummy inside those big pyramid structures, together with the dead person's belongings."

Mrs. Doresh fixed herself a cup of coffee and sat down with her children.

"What made Moreh Hartman discuss mummies, Devora?" She asked.

"Oh, because someone asked whether Joseph had Jacob embalmed also, in the same manner as a mummy. And then Moreh Hartman mentioned that there is a real Egyptian mummy in the museum. They're having a special exhibition and it's only going to be for another day."

Mrs. Doresh swallowed some more coffee and

10. Soul.

cleared her throat. She then looked at Devora out of the corner of her eyes and sighed.

"You want to go, don't you?" She guessed.

"Go? Me? Oh. Um . . . yeah, well, yes, I guess I do want to go. Can I, Mother?"

"Well, if you could find one of your friends to go along with you, I don't see why not. But I can't go with you. I'm expecting Aunt Baila in a few hours. She's in the city doing some shopping."

"Well, I already asked Rivkeh Landau and she's willing to come with me. I just have to call her to double check."

"Sure, go ahead, then."

Devora was in the corridor talking to Rivkeh on the phone. Completing the conversation, she hung up and returned to the kitchen, a slight frown on her face.

"What's wrong, Devora?" her mother asked.

"Nothing much. Rivkeh can't make it before three-thirty. By the time we get there it will be four o'clock and the museum closes a half-hour later."

"Well, how much time does one need to look at a mummy, anyhow?" Asked Mrs. Doresh.

At 3:15, the doorbell rang. It was Rivkeh. She greeted Mrs. Doresh through the screen door and waited for Devora to put on her jacket and join her.

"Enjoy yourselves, girls!" her mother called as Devora left the house with Rivkeh. The girls walked quickly toward the bus stop. The bus arrived shortly and the girls waited for some of the passengers to step off before they got on. Once in their seats, the bus moved quickly through the streets, spending very little time at each stop and within twenty minutes they were near the museum. By the time they arrived at the museum door, it was nearly four o'clock and the two ran up the huge steps leading to the magnificent, majestic entrance to the museum. Once inside, they slowed down and tried to catch their breath. Devora was at a loss of where to go first, but Rivkeh spotted the sign about the Egyptian exhibition. It was on the second floor.

Arriving on the second floor, the girls walked quietly through the wide, marble corridor toward the hall in which the mummy and its relics were on display. There were only a few visitors left since the hour was late and most of the people there were walking casually toward the nearest "Exit" signs. Even the museum guards were preparing the doors of the various rooms for the final closing.

"Wow, Devora, look!" Rivkeh exclaimed, covering her mouth with her hands. "The mummy. It's over there." She pointed in the direction of a very large casket made of heavy stone and marble. The lid, a thick slab of marble, was slightly suspended over the stone casket by several iron poles so that visitors could look inside and catch a little glimpse of the mummy.

"I remember reading somewhere that these things weigh several tons," Rivkeh whispered as they approached the display. "They must use special equipment to get the lid off like that," she said.

The girls marvelled at the ancient art engraved on the surface of the stone. Then, gathering courage, they bent over and peered into the encasement. It was pitch dark inside, and faintly visible in the dim light of the museum ceiling, was the form of a person, heavily wrapped in strips of cloth.

Rivkeh stood up and gasped.

"Yeeeeew," she said, shaking her head. "It's horrible. Devora, how can you stand looking at him."

Devora straightened up and smiled at her friend.

"What are you afraid of? It's only a mummy. All you see is the wrappings. What's so horrible about that?"

"I don't know," Rivkeh said. "I guess it's just the thought that there's a real dead person in there."

Devora bent over again and peered into the mummy case.

"It's pretty dark in there," she muttered. "It's not fair, you know. The lighting is real bad. They brought this thing all the way from Egypt, and you can barely make it out."

A guard walked into the room and bent down to undo the chain holding the doors open. Noticing the girls, he shouted to them.

"Closing time, girls. Better get moving, we're locking up."

The girls walked toward the guard and followed

him out. Then, as the guard entered another room, Rivkeh grabbed Devora by the arm.

"What's the matter, Rivkeh?" Asked Devora.

"I forgot something. My mother's pin. It's very valuable. It used to belong to my grandmother. It must have fallen off."

"Oh, no. Rivkeh. The place is closing up."

"The door to the mummy room is still open, can't we just run in real quick and see if we could find it?"

"Okay, but I think these doors lock automatically all at once as soon as the guard has completed all his rounds. Let's hurry."

The girls ran into the mummy room and began searching the shiny floor for the pin. Devora walked around the mummy case very slowly, her eyes fixed on the area around it. Rivkeh scanned the room in general, sliding her shoes across the floor in hopes of kicking the pin.

Suddenly the lights went out and the room was pitch dark. The girls began making their way toward the doors when suddenly the doors slid shut. Devora ran to the door and started pounding loudly on it.

"Help!" She shouted. "Let us out! We're locked in!" But it seemed the guards had already completed their rounds and were downstairs preparing to leave for home. Devora and Rivkeh pounded together, growing frightened at the silence that remained when they stopped pounding and yelling.

The girls sat down on the floor and leaned against
the heavy steel doors. Devora began feeling frightened.
It was dark and eery and the thought of a corpse lying
in the room made her shiver. Rivkeh was also trembling
and Devora felt bad she had talked her friend into coming with her to the museum.

"I feel so bad, Rivkeh. I shouldn't have talked you
into coming here with me. I think that deep down I was
also interested in snooping around the museum to find
out more about the jewel thefts. Maybe this is to teach
me a lesson that I have to be more humble and not to
look for mysteries to solve."

Rivkeh patted Devora on the shoulder.

"If this is happening to teach *you* a lesson, Devora,
then why am I here?" Rivkeh asked. "This lesson is for
me, too. So don't feel bad."

"What did *you* ever do to deserve this? You're such a
good friend," said Devora.

"Yeah. I'm real good alright. Remember that great
night in camp this past summer? Remember how I and a
few others sneaked into the dining hall late at night
when the counselors were having their midnight
snacks? I thought it was real fun then. We flicked off the
lights suddenly and bolted the doors so they couldn't
get out. Then we made a whole lot of scary noises and
banged on the walls. Some of us climbed up on the roof
and stomped our feet. They were scared. Real scared.
We jokers were laughing our heads off, though, as we

ran away. It was just a joke, we felt. A harmless trick on our counselors. But now I know what it's like to be helpless and scared. Nothing funny about it."

"Well," Devora said, "let's ask *Hashem* for forgiveness for what we did. Please, *Hashem,* we both realize where we went wrong and the message of this lesson. Now that we've learned what you wanted us to learn, please let us out of here!"

Devora, expecting a miracle, pulled at the door and then pushed, but it would not move in the slightest. The girls sat down on the cold floor and leaned against the wall.

"Well," Devora said. "Here we are, stuck ·in a museum, sharing a room with a mummy."

"How are we going to get out of here, Devora?" Asked Rivkeh.

"I don't know, Rivkeh. All I know is that our parents will soon be worrying about our delay. And maybe they'll have the police check out the museum tonight. And after that, well, we are going to have a lot of explaining to do."

"It's all my fault, Devora. If I wouldn't have worried so much about that pin of mine. I could have returned tomorrow to look for it."

"Maybe your pin fell into the mummy case," Devora mused. "The mummy is returning to Egypt tomorrow, they say. They'll find your pin inside the mummy case a few years from now and they'll probably add it to the ancient jewels on display in Cairo."

"Ha ha ha. Very funny, Devora. Big detective you are. But then again. Maybe you're right. I did bend over the casing to look in a lot. Maybe I rubbed the pin against it and it fell in."

Devora stood up.

"Hey, you know something?" she said. "This room is next to the room from where the jewels were stolen."

Rivkeh got up and followed her friend to the other side of the dark, eerie room.

"How do you know, Devora?" she asked.

"I remember hearing it on the radio. The news commentator said that these two rooms of ancient Egyptian art, were next to one another and carefully guarded by special security people. Yet, somehow, the thief or thieves were able to steal the jewels and make them disappear into thin air."

"They must have been Egyptian magicians," laughed Rivkeh. "Remember we learned in class that the ancient Egyptians were experts in magic?"

"Ha! You think an ancient Egyptian magician came back to life and took the jewels?"

Rivkeh smiled. "Maybe the mummy took the jewels."

Devora shook her head. "I doubt that the old mummy could get out of all those bandages. But the police are baffled, all kidding aside. None of the alarms went off during the robbery."

Devora looked around the big room. The silence was deafening.

"Of course," Devora said, "it's possible that the jewels were never taken out of the museum at all."

"Then they weren't stolen?" Rivkeh asked.

"That's not what I meant, Rivkeh. A thief could have removed them and hidden them some place else in the museum. Later, he would get them out of the building somehow. And if that was the case, the thief would have probably hidden them near the room from which he took them. Not in the same room, though, because that would be the first place the police would search. The thief would probably have hidden the jewels in the next room."

"But this is the next room, Devora!" Rivkeh exclaimed, trembling slightly. "And there's no place to hide anything in this room except maybe in the . . . in the mummy case!"

Devora pursed her lips.

"Hmmmm. The police did suspect an inside job. The thief could very well have dropped them into the mummy case. Then he can return at his leisure to get them out."

Rivkeh grabbed Devora by the arm.

"But Devora! You said the mummy is going back to Egypt tomorrow!"

"Oh my," Devora said. "That means the thief will be coming for the jewels early tomorrow morning, or possibly . . . possibly tonight!"

Suddenly, they heard footsteps in the hall outside the door. Devora and Rivkeh held each other tightly and stared at the door.

"This is our chance to get out of here, Devora," Rivkeh said. "Someone's coming! Maybe it's the police, looking for us. Or the janitor, or whoever. Let's scream, Devora."

Devora put her hand over her friend's mouth.

"Wait," she whispered. "We don't know who it is for sure."

Rivkeh clung to Devora's sweater.

"You mean it might be the jewel thieves? But that was only an idea. That was just our imagination."

The footsteps grew louder and louder. There were several of them. Then they heard voices and the jingling sound of keys. The girls looked at each other.

"Take your shoes off and hang on to them." Devora whispered.

The girls removed their shoes and ran across the room to a huge slab of stone with ancient Egyptian writing engraved on it. The girls crouched behind the stone on the floor and bit their lips, terrified. They heard a key being inserted into the door from outside and then a loud click.

The door slid open and several men entered, two of them holding flashlights. Devora leaned out a bit to catch a glimpse but the flashlights were of no help since they shone only in the direction of the mummy display.

"Okay, boys," a deep voice was heard saying. "Lift the lid just a bit more so we could get that thing out of the casket."

Devora watched as two tall, burly figures positioned

themselves at the front of the heavy lid and began to lift
it with the help of a special lever. A third man handed
his flashlight to the man with the deep voice. He then
reached into the mummy encasement.

"Hold on tight, now," he mumbled. "If this thing
falls shut, my arms are gonna end up in Egypt, see." He
lifted the mummy out of the casket and flung it across
the floor as if it were a doll. The mummy rolled across
the room to where Devora and Rivkeh were hiding.
Rivkeh almost let out a scream at the sight of the
mummy lying beside her. Devora quickly cupped her
right hand over her friend's mouth to keep her from
making any sounds. The mummy had become slightly
unwrapped in the fall, and Devora noticed a plastic
hand sticking out of the mummy's wrappings.

"Look, Rivkeh," she whispered very softly. "Look
at the mummy's hand. It's plastic. It's not a real
mummy." Rivkeh felt relieved.

Devora then peeked out again from behind the stone
and watched as the third man placed several heavy bags
into the mummy case. He then stood back and joined
the man with the deep voice.

"Okay, boys, let the lid down. Slowly," he said.

The burly men could be heard grunting and strain-
ing as they slowly lowered the lid and removed the
iron poles which had suspended it during the week of
its display.

"Jimmy," the man with the deep voice said. "I don't
know how to thank you and your boys."

"Don't mention it, Charlie, just give us our cash and we'll be even. Twenty grand keeps me quiet and ten grand each for my boys keeps their lips sealed more tight than this ton of concrete here."

Devora and Rivkeh watched as the deep-voiced man handed Jimmy a small suitcase.

"It's all in here, Jimmy. Unmarked bills, just like you asked."

"Good. Now, these boys here are going back with the stuff to Cairo and they'll take care of everything there. They'll remove the jewels in the Cairo museum and put the real mummy back in."

"How do I know they're not going to then take off with the jewels?"

"Abdul Alrui will be there when the flight comes in, remember? These two work for him, they take care of the real mummy, follow it around on world tours and so on. And you can trust Abdul Alrui. Especially since he is well aware that if he double-crosses us, we expose him. And if he's exposed, there's no place he could possibly hide and his family will be in danger. He won't double-cross us, don't worry."

"You're a genius, Jimmy. But I'll still be a nervous wreck until I fly to Cairo on vacation next month. Those Jewels mean a lot to me. I've been watching them for years here, just sitting in their glass encasements. Millions of dollars worth."

The men turned their backs to where the girls were hiding, and counted the money. Seeing her chance,

Devora whispered to Rivkeh and the girls dashed from their hiding place, across the room to the open doors.

The girls ran out of the room into the wide corridor, whose walls were dimly lit by small light bulbs, and they kept running until they saw the red light of the "Exit" sign. They pushed open the door leading to the stairwell and ran down to the first floor. At the ground level there were two doors, one leading into the main lobby and the other leading out to the alley. Devora shoved at the fire exit door leading out to the alley. The door swung open and the girls ran outside, and kept running until they came to the main avenue. Out of breath, they sat down on the stoop of a storefront and put their shoes on.

"Phew," Rivkeh sighed. "We made it. I don't believe it. We really made it. We're free. Let's go home, the clock on the bank across the street says seven-thirty. Our parents are probably worried sick."

"*Baruch Hashem*,[11] we're safe," Devora said. "But we've got to get hold of the police immediately."

Devora opened her purse and took out a dime. The girls crossed the intersection from the museum and found a row of phone booths.

"Oh, no, Rivkeh," Devora sighed. "Look. The phone has been vandalized. Isn't that sick? How can anyone do this? Now we can't call the police."

"Maybe there's a police car riding around here,

11. "Thank G-d."

somewhere," suggested Rivkeh. The girls walked half way up the block, looking for a police car. Then Devora had an idea. She flagged down a taxi. The cab pulled up at the curb and the driver leaned over to the passenger side of the car and rolled down the window.

"Where do you want to go?" he asked.

"We must contact the police right away, sir," Devora said. "There's a robbery going on inside the museum right now."

The cab driver chewed on some gum and turned his head to look at the dark, quiet museum building across the street. He then turned back to the girls.

"Oh yeah? What else is new? Listen, you want a ride or not? I haven't got time for games."

"Honestly!" Rivkeh exclaimed. "We were just in there. We got locked in and these jewel thieves are in there right now in the mummy room. The jewels are in the mummy case."

The cab driver continued chewing his gum and then blew a large bubble which popped.

"Yeah," he said, looking at the two. "Yeah, right. Okay, girls, I'll go get Doctor Frankenstein right away, or maybe I'll radio Sherlock Holms, okay? Now play nicely, girls."

The taxi sped off leaving a long trail of smoke behind.

"Well, looks like we'll have to wait until we get home," said Devora.

"Think our parents will even believe us?" Rivkeh

asked. "That cab driver was right. I wouldn't have believed us either if I were him."

"Well, do we have a choice?" Said Devora. "Let's catch the bus and go home. It's late."

The girls walked over to the bus stop. The bus arrived within a few minutes. On the way home, they both laughed together about how scared they had been, and they took turns imitating the men they had heard in the museum. When the bus arrived in their neighborhood, Devora walked Rivkeh home and then walked the extra block to her own house by herself.

"Devora!" Mrs. Doresh shouted as she entered. "Where were you all this time? I was getting worried. Another few minutes and I was getting ready to call Sergeant O'Malley. It's eight o'clock, did you know that? Your supper's been ready since six!"

Rebbe Doresh came down the stairs, holding onto a *gemara.*[12]

"Devora!" he exclaimed. "*Baruch Hashem* you're home and safe! What happened?"

"We got locked in the museum," Devora explained. "It was so scary."

"Locked in the museum?" Mrs. Doresh asked. "How did you two manage that?"

"Well, Rivkeh lost her pin, a very valuable one her mother had given her. We were about to go home at closing time when she noticed the pin missing. We ran

12. Tractate of the Talmud.

back into the room and spent only a few minutes looking for it when suddenly the lights went out and the
doors slid shut and locked. It's on an automatic system."

"How did you get out, then?" Asked Rebbe
Doresh.

"The Jewel thieves, Abba. They came."

"What?" Rebbe Doresh exclaimed. "The ones who
stole the jewels? The ones mentioned on the radio?"

"Yes, Abba. It turns out they were hiding the jewels
in the mummy case so they could smuggle them out of
the country without being detected. Rivkeh and I hid
from them and then we ran out of the room when we
saw our opportunity. The fire exits leading to the street
can be opened from the inside even though they are
locked from the outside. So we got out."

"And they didn't see you running out of the room?"
Mrs. Doresh asked.

"No, mother. The room was dark, they were busy
counting money and they only had flashlights. So
we took off our shoes and ran out of the room."

"Call O'Malley, Devora, right away," Rebbe
Doresh said.

Devora was about to lift the phone off the hook to
dial, when it rang. Mrs. Doresh rose and answered the
phone.

"Hello? . . . Oh, Rabbi Landau, how are you? . . .
Yes, hold on."

Mrs. Doresh turned to her husband and covered the
mouthpiece of the telephone with the palm of her hand.

"It's for you. Rabbi Landau."

Rebbe Doresh rose and took the phone.

"Yes, my friend," he said, "how are things? . . . Yes, Devora just got back . . . Rivkeh told you what? . . . Yes . . . Yes . . . Yes, I got the same story from my Devora. . . . If it's true? I wouldn't believe it if anyone else would have told me. But I believe my daughter. . . . I know it sounds crazy. But I'm sure they're telling the truth. Look, don't worry. They're safely home now and that's all that really counts. . . . Yes, yes. I'll keep you posted. Good-bye."

Devora picked the phone off the receiver and dialed the precinct again.

"Hello, is Sergeant O'Malley there?" There was a pause.

"Hello, Officer O'Malley? This is Devora. Boy am I glad you're in. Listen! We know where the jewels are! . . . What? Oh. Me and my friend Rivkeh Landau. We were both locked in at the museum tonight and we saw everything! . . . Okay, good-bye."

"What's happening?" Mrs. Doresh asked.

"O'Malley's on his way," Devora replied.

Devora sat down to have her dinner. When she finished it, she heard the doorbell ring. It was O'Malley. He tipped his cap at Mrs. Doresh and shook Rebbe Doresh's hand as he walked in.

"Boy, am I tired," he said, walking into the kitchen with Rebbe Doresh. "What a night. Two shifts, day and night. Wow. I'm not so young any more, you know. Like a half-hour ago, for example, I had this weird day-dream while I was awake. I dreamt Devora called me about her being locked up in the museum and about how she knew where those stolen Jewels were."

"You weren't dreaming, Sergeant," Rebbe Doresh remarked, smiling. "Sit down and let Devora tell you what happened."

The officer sat down and listened to Devora tell everything. When she had completed her story, he asked her to phone Rivkeh. Devora dialed Rivkeh's number and handed the phone to O'Malley.

"Hello? Rabbi Landau? . . . How are you? This is Sergeant O'Malley. Yes, I'm at the Doresh house. Listen, I think it would be a good idea if your Rivkeh joins us at the police station so we can get down all the information about their . . . hello? Rabbi Landau? Why are you laughing? . . . Yes, yes, I know. I know it all sounds crazy. But I've known Devora long enough to know otherwise. . . . Yes, I really think it's necessary. . . . Great. Thanks for your cooperation."

"Well," Sergeant O'Malley said. "If Devora's story is correct, those jewels will be skipping the country tomorrow morning. The mummy display is supposed to be flown back to Egypt then."

Devora grabbed her jacket and followed O'Malley out to his squad car. O'Malley put on his siren and sped up the street to where Rivkeh lived. Rivkeh was waiting on her front lawn when the car pulled up in front of her home. She jumped into the back seat and sat next to Devora.

"This is exciting," Rivkeh remarked. "I've never been in a police car before."

The squad car sped to the precinct and screeched to a halt. O'Malley led the girls into the station, past the desk sergeant and up the stairs to the Captain's office. The sergeant knocked once and entered, startling the chief who was sipping coffee.

"O'Malley!" the captain shouted, nearly spilling his black coffee over his newspaper. "What's going on here? Who are these girls?"

"This is Devora Doresh, sir. And this is her friend, Rivkeh Landau."

"Hello, girls," the captain said, smiling. He then turned angrily to O'Malley. "O'Malley, this is no time for introducing your friends. You must have been on duty too long. Why don't you take them outside and play jump-rope, or something?"

"Captain, sir," O'Malley continued, smiling. "These girls are here on serious business. About the missing jewels, sir."

"Sergeant, I think you're missing several jewels from your head. Now cut it out! I have enough on my mind."

"Devora," O'Malley said, turning to the girls. "Tell our interested chief everything you told me."

Devora began telling the story for the third time.

Rivkeh joined her every now and then, filling in bits and pieces of information which Devora had left out. The captain tried to ignore them and continued reading his newspaper while drinking his coffee.

"Okay, okay," the captain said after the girls had completed their story. "You both have great imagination. You should be writers."

"Captain, you have to take these girls seriously," O'Malley interceded. "Devora has helped me crack cases before. You know that as well as I do."

"Well, all right, all right." The captain rose and paced the floor. "Who do you think did it, Devora?" He suddenly asked, staring Devora in the eye.

"I don't know. But I have a feeling maybe the curator was involved."

"Why do you say that?"

"Well, the ringleader said he's been watching those jewels for years."

"Means nothing. Next."

"Uh . . . the thieves had the keys to the room where the display was. Only someone very high up would have had the keys to such a well-protected room, sir."

"Makes sense," the captain said, "go on."

Devora scratched her forehead and concentrated.

"Um. They called one of them 'Charlie.' What's the curator's name?"

"Charles Zopes. But that means nothing. There are lots of Charlies around. He had a high pitched voice, right?"

"No, sir. A very deep voice."

The captain looked startled and pulled out a note pad.

"Oh? Hmmmm. Go on."

"He said he was going to Egypt on a vacation next month."

"He did?"

The chief picked up his telephone.

"Hello, Gabe? Captain Greer here. Listen, you know Charles Zopes, the curator of the museum, don't you? Didn't you handle the contributions to the police fund? Right. Yeah, him. Know anything about him? He's a what? An Egyptologist? Goes to Egypt every year, huh? Interesting. Go on. Oh, I see, so he is the one who arranged for the mummy to come here, then. I see. He has lots of contacts in Cairo? I see. Hmmmmmmm. Okay, Gabe, thanks a lot. No, nothing. Just curious."

The chief got up and lit a cigarette.

"Nah," he said, looking at Devora. "Can't be him. Do you know who you're accusing? Charles Zopes has given thousands of dollars to our special fund for families of slain policemen. How could a contributor like that be a criminal?"

Devora remembered Moreh Hartman's lesson about Achav the king. She looked at Rivkeh and whispered, "Achav."

"Huh?" the captain asked. "What did you whisper?"

"Achav, sir," Rivkeh said.

"What? What's that mean?"

"He was one of the ancient kings of Israel, sir," Devora began. "Our sages taught us that he appeared very kind on the outside. He gave freely of his money to the sages. But at the same time, he also supported freely the institution of idolatry, the exact opposite of what the sages stood for. His standards, in other words, were based on himself only, on whatever *he* wanted and on whatever *he* felt was good, rather than what was really good and proper."

"Yeah," the captain mumbled. "I guess that's possible. That's what they teach you in the Jewish school?"

"Yes, sir," Rivkeh said.

"Another thing, Captain," Devora continued. "I was thinking that the curator of a museum would certainly examine a display carefully, before exhibiting it, wouldn't he? Especially a display specially flown in from Egypt."

"Yeah, so what?"

"Well, how would he have overlooked the fact that the mummy wasn't real? Even I realized it was only plastic."

"Yeah. Good point. You're getting me interested. Let's hear the story once more, slowly. O'Malley, take notes."

For the fourth time, Devora and Rivkeh repeated their adventures in the museum that night and everything they had heard and seen. When they finished, Captain Greer spoke into the intercom speaker on his desk and summoned his secretary. The door opened within moments and a tall woman entered.

"Annie," the captain said. "Get me the FBI on line 3 and the Egyptian embassy on line 4. No other calls. I don't want to be disturbed."

Several minutes later, the secretary buzzed the captain. Captain Greer lifted the telephone to his ear.

"Hi, Sam. It's me. Listen. Don't ask me for details and don't ask me where I got the information right now, okay? The jewels are in the mummy case that's headed back for Egypt today. There are two burly Egyptians going with it. They're involved. There's an American named Jimmy who's involved and so is Charles Zopes, the curator. We think. We're not sure. So don't do anything yet. . . . No, no, no. There's no mummy in there. There was only a *dummy* in there during the exhibition. Then they removed the dummy and put the stolen jewels inside instead. This way, it gets smuggled out neat and clean, no questions asked."

Another buzz sounded on Captain Greer's desk and he lifted a second phone to his other ear.

"Yes, this is Captain Greer of the police. Is Musa Latif there? . . . Oh, hi, Musa. Glad I got you right away. Listen carefully. You know those stolen Jewels that have been in the papers all week. . . . Well, they'll be on their way to Cairo inside the mummy case on flight K33 of your airlines. . . . Don't ask questions now. Just have somebody on that plane follow these guys around. Also, have your police inspect the casket only after it reaches Cairo and all the criminals gather

together. They'll be at the museum there. We have
information that the ringleader on your end is Abdul
Alrui. . . . Yeah? You guys know of him? . . . Gangster,
eh? Okay. Nail him. And get all the information you
can out of them when you catch them in Cairo. And
don't forget to call me right away when you find out
the names of those involved on our end. Okay?"

Captain Greer hung up line 4 and continued talking
on line 3 with the FBI officer. He told the FBI official
what he had told the Egyptian official and then he hung
up.

"Well," Captain Greer said, turning to the two girls
and a beaming O'Malley. "They ain't getting away.
We'll let them leave peacefully and arrive in Cairo
peacefully. Then, when they all meet at the Cairo
museum to get the jewels out and put back the real
mummy, whammo!"

"What about the American crooks?" Rivkeh asked.

"My FBI friend will keep an eye on your Charlie.
Then, once we get final evidence, that is, the confes-
sions of the Egyptian crooks, the case is closed. We
move in and arrest them."

"Who's Jimmy, though?" O'Malley asked.

"I don't know, Sergeant. Those two strongmen will
tell our friends in Egypt who he is. He paid them off,
didn't he? Now, I suggest that until we hear from
Cairo, you two girls get back to school before I have
you arrested for playing hooky."

Everyone laughed.

II

An entire day passed without any news. Then, on the third day, Sergeant O'Malley pulled up in front of the Doresh home. His eyes were very red and baggy. The break in the museum case had kept him through many shifts and now he was on his way home for a good day's rest. Rebbe Doresh saw him from the living-room window coming up the walk. He rose from the sofa and opened the door for the weary officer.

"Sergeant O'Malley! Welcome. What's the good word?"

"It's over, Rabbi Doresh. It's all over. The chief got the call from Cairo about five in the morning. The jewels arrived in the mummy case just like Devora said it would. This guy Abdul whats-his-name was there to greet it and the trap was sprung. Those burly guys put up a big fight as I understand it, but the Cairo police took good care of them. They confessed everything. Jimmy, they found out, was this New York gangster. We picked him up this morning while he was asleep in his suburban home. We also picked up the museum curator, Charles Zopes. It was him, alright. The jewels have been recovered and will be sent back by the Egyptians on their next flight to the states, under heavy guard. That's all."

"That's all?" Rebbe Doresh asked. Devora came into the livingroom. She had just finished *davening*.[13]

13. Praying.

"Well, not exactly," O'Malley continued. He unsnapped his jacket pocket and took out two envelopes.

"I have a couple of letters here for a Devora Doresh. One from the FBI office in New York. The other from the Egyptian Ambassador to the United States. Here."

Devora took the envelopes and opened the one from the Egyptian embassy.

"Dear Devora and Rivkeh:

I wish to thank you on behalf of my country for solving more than a New York mystery, but also a Cairo mystery. For two years, we have been unsuccessful at cracking a well-organized smuggling ring operating out of our capital city. Many lives have been lost and much money has been stolen because of these smugglers and their horrible ways. Your solving the mystery of the missing jewels in New York, has at the same time solved the mystery of the untouchable smuggling ring here in Cairo, of which Abdul Alrui was the leader.

May you be blessed with fulfillment of all your wishes and succeed in solving future mysteries.

Shalom."

The Counterfeiters

The Counterfeiters

ery few late-comers ever succeeded in sneaking into Yocheved High without being detected by Mrs. Hirsch, the principal's secretary. Seated in the office behind a large glass window which overlooked the hallway, Mrs. Hirsch, or "Radar", as she was known, seemed always to be automatically attracted to anything moving in the hallway outside her window. It was almost impossible to sneak in late without getting caught.

Mrs. Hirsch looked up from her typing and noticed Devora entering the office.

"Good morning, Devora," she said, "can I help you?"

"Is Rabbi Goodman in? I'd like to speak to him."

"Well, he's very busy right now. He's in his office with someone. Don't you have class now?"

"I'm in between classes now. I have a break now."

Mrs. Hirsch's eyes opened wide. She had sensed an unauthorized movement in the hall outside her glass window. She rose slightly from her chair and peered through the glass. There was no one there. Satisfied, she sat down again and resumed her typing.

"Is there anything I could help you with, Devora?" she asked.

"Well, I don't know," Devora replied. "I wanted to ask Rabbi Goodman if we could have some money to buy supplies for the school play. It's only a few weeks away."

"Money!" Mrs. Hirsch exclaimed. "Oh, that poor man. Rabbi Goodman is struggling terribly to keep this school open, Devora. Finances lately have been pretty low. We're in a great deal of debt right now."

"I know that, Mrs. Hirsch," Devora said. "But then again, the school play usually brings in a lot of money. And that's why the play is so important. We have to have certain supplies and a place to perform the play."

"What's wrong with our auditorium?" Mrs. Hirsch questioned, her eyes periodically throwing a quick glance out at the hallway.

"The auditorium, Mrs. Hirsch, is in bad need of repairs. Remember the leaking ceiling last year? Well, it's gotten worse and nothing has been done about it."

"You're not going to ask Rabbi Goodman to have it fixed, Devora, are you? I mean, the man is plagued by enough bills he can't pay, as it is already."

Devora was about to reply to Mrs. Hirsch when the door to the principal's office opened and Rabbi Goodman stepped out. An elderly gentleman accompanied him and the two walked into the main office together, Rabbi Goodman holding his hand on the man's shoulders.

"Mr. Raskin," he was saying, "I don't know how to

thank you properly for this. It couldn't have come to us at a better time."

As the two approached Devora's seat, she rose and the elderly man smiled at her.

"When I see this," he remarked to Rabbi Goodman, "my faith is renewed and strengthened. It makes me want to contribute more funds to the school, if only I had it. It gives me great pride when I see young Jewish children growing up with proper values and respect, in a world which is bankrupt of both."

Mrs. Hirsch ripped an envelope out of the typewriter and tore it up. Rabbi Goodman escorted the man to the door and shook his hands, bidding him farewell. Turning back toward the office, he walked hurriedly past Mrs. Hirsch's desk. Devora raised her hand to attract his attention.

"Yes, Devora, what is it?"

"Rabbi Goodman, I have some very important things to discuss with you. Uh . . . about the play."

"Oh, yes, yes, yes, about the play. Yes, probably about the auditorium, right? Well, let's see. I have to run to the bank right now to deposit some money before the yeshiva's checks begin bouncing. Tell you what. Why don't you come along with me to the bank and you can talk as we walk, okay?"

"Fine," Devora said.

Rabbi Goodman disappeared into his office and returned shortly with his hat and jacket on.

"Mrs. Hirsch," he said, "if anyone calls, tell them I'll be returning in ten minutes."

"Yes, Rabbi Goodman. Got a nice donation, eh?"

"Oh, the donation? Yes. Yes, indeed, Mrs. Hirsch. Mr. Raskin *davens*[1] in my *shul.*[2] He lost his wife recently and before she died, she told him to sell a very valuable candelabra she had inherited and donate the money to our school. Three thousand dollars, he just gave us. In cash. It is a miracle and nothing short of it. I needed at least $1500 to cover salaries for last month and I had no idea from where it would come. Thank G-d!"

The principal buttoned his jacket and motioned to Devora to follow. The two left the school building and walked briskly toward the main avenue where the bank was. As they walked, Devora gently reminded Rabbi Goodman about the unusable auditorium.

"Aaaah, yes, the auditorium," he sighed. "You don't have to remind me, Devora. I knew that's probably what you wanted to discuss with me, didn't I? The auditorium, that's right. Okay, now, here's what we'll do. The play is in less than four weeks from now, right? And it should bring in a couple of thousand dollars for the school. So the play is an investment, right?"

"You mean, you're going to use some of the donated money to repair the auditorium, Rabbi Goodman?" Devora asked excitedly.

---

1. Prays.
2. Synagogue.

"Yes," he said, smiling. "I certainly will."

The two entered the bank and headed toward one of the bank officers. The officer rose from his desk and extended his hand to Rabbi Goodman.

"Well, hello, Rabbi," he said. "I haven't seen you in a long while."

"I haven't had any funds in a long while, Mr. Bainbridge."

"I know. We've been covering your checks as best as we could, but we need a payment, you know."

"I know, and that's why I came over right away."

Mr. Bainbridge brought over another chair so Devora could sit down. Everyone took their seats and Rabbi Goodman reached into his jacket pocket and withdrew the bulky envelope.

"This is one of your daughters, Rabbi Goodman?" the officer asked, looking at Devora.

"No. This is Devora Doresh, one of my students. Uh . . . or I should say one of my creditors. She wants money to fix an auditorium."

Mr. Bainbridge chuckled and watched nervously as Rabbi Goodman emptied the envelope of its contents.

"Cash!" he exclaimed. "How much do you have here, Rabbi?"

"There should be three thousand dollars."

Mr. Bainbridge's eyebrows flew up.

"What happened? The school's never deposited so much at any one time before."

"This is a donation, Mr. Bainbridge. Now would

you mind counting it again to make sure we have the right amount."

"Sure." Mr. Bainbridge said. He took the bills into his hands and licked his fingers. He then flipped through them as if they were a stack of cards and returned them to the envelope.

"Yes," he said, smiling. "Three thousand on the button. Crisp, too." He picked up one of the bills and placed it underneath a small lamp. His smile suddenly turned into a frown and his face grew pale.

"Something wrong, Mr. Bainbridge?" Rabbi Goodman asked.

"Where did you get these bills?" the officer asked. He took another bill and held it beneath the lamp's light. Again he frowned. Rabbi Goodman and Devora watched him, astonished, as he took all the bills, one by one and held it beneath the light of the lamp.

"I don't understand," Rabbi Goodman exclaimed. "This is cash, you know. Our checks may not always be so good, but cash? I got it from an old friend, an elderly gentleman. His wife died recently and he sold a candelabra for two thousand dollars. With the two thousand he added his own thousand and gave the three to the school as a donation. That's how I got it, now will you mind telling me what is the matter with the money?"

Mr. Bainbridge looked at Rabbi Goodman solemnly.

"What you say checks out, Rabbi," he said. "There's a thousand dollars of good money here, from the old man's own funds."

"What do you mean?" Exclaimed Rabbi Goodman, leaning over the desk. "What about the other two thousand?"

"That's probably the two thousand he got from the sale of the candelabra."

"And?"

"And they are counterfeit."

"Counterfeit?"

"Counterfeit. Fake. False. No good."

Rabbi Goodman leaned back in the chair and shut his eyes.

"Oh, no," he sighed. "Oh, nononononononono. Poor Mr. Raskin."

"And poor Yocheved High School," Mr. Bainbridge added, stuffing the cash back into the envelope. "If you wish, Rabbi, I'll deposit the good thousand right now. And as for the other two thousand, I'm afraid I'll have to turn it over to the police. You understand, don't you?"

"Sure I do. Maybe the police will catch those counterfeiters fast and get Mr. Raskin's candelabra back."

"That would take a miracle, Rabbi. Counterfeit rings are difficult to track down. And as for the candelabra, they probably sold it by now."

"Well, can you please call the proper authorities immediately."

"Yes, of course, Rabbi." Mr. Bainbridge began dialing the police. "You don't have to wait around, Rabbi. It will probably be a while before they send a man down here to investigate, since there is no emergency.

I'll have them call your office when they get here."

"Thank you, Mr. Bainbridge." Rabbi Goodman said, rising. Devora got up and followed Rabbi Goodman out of the bank. The two walked silently up the street toward the school. As they approached the building, Rabbi Goodman broke the silence.

"The most distressing part of all this, Devora, is breaking the news to Mr. Raskin. He is a very respectful, sensitive man. You should have seen the proud look in his eyes when he gave me the cash. And on top of that, now his candelabra is lost."

"Did he tell you at all about how he sold the candelabra? And where?" Asked Devora.

"No, he didn't. But the police are going to want to know. They're going to want to ask Mr. Raskin a lot of questions. I wish there were some way we could keep Mr. Raskin out of this and spare him the agony of what has happened."

"I have an idea," Devora volunteered. The two walked into the school office and straight into Rabbi Goodman's private chamber. Mrs. Hirsch ripped an envelope out of the typewriter and tore it up.

"Sit down, Devora," Rabbi Goodman said. "What's your idea? I almost forgot you're supposed to be a big detective. Talk."

"Well, Rabbi Goodman, you said before that Mr. Raskin *davens* in your *shul,* right?"

"That's right. I see him practically every morning and evening."

"Well, tonight, ask him about the sale. He won't be

suspicious that you're asking him. After all, he sold it for two thousand dollars. So, you could remark to him how you can't get over that he was able to sell it for so much. I'm sure he'll come out and tell you how it happened, don't you think?"

Rabbi Goodman sat back in his swivel chair and thought.

"You're right, Devora. I know Mr. Raskin. He's the kind of man who would grab any opportunity to tell a story. I'll confront him tonight after *maariv*.[3] But then what?"

"Then call me right away. I'll get in touch with Sergeant O'Malley, a friend of mine at the police station. I'll tell him all the details so the police wouldn't have to call Mr. Raskin. I'll also explain to him how we're trying to keep Mr. Raskin out of the case so as not to hurt his feelings."

"Sounds good, Devora. After that, we can only pray that *Hashem*[4] help solve this crime and get Mr. Raskin's money back or at least his candelabra. Then it wouldn't hurt for him to know what happened. And if they don't solve the case at all, Mr. Raskin at least will go on thinking he made a good sale and a nice donation to the yeshiva."

Devora looked down at the floor.

"Yes, yes, I know, Devora," Rabbi Goodman said.

---

3. Evening prayer.
4. G-d.

"The auditorium. We almost had the money to repair it. I'll try my best to have it fixed as much as possible within the next few weeks. Maybe I'll borrow some money for it. But, no promises. If worse comes to worse, people will just have to sit in that leaky auditorium and watch the play. Maybe we'll tell everyone to bring their own umbrellas. Ha! Maybe we'll raise some money for the school by selling umbrellas at the door. Either way, people will realize then that the yeshiva needs funding badly. Now get back to your class, Devora and let me worry about this mystery."

That night, Devora told her parents about her day at school and her experience at the bank. Mrs. Doresh kept shaking her head in disbelief, and Rebbe Doresh stroked his beard in contemplation.

"It sounds to me like Mr. Raskin probably sold the candelabra to someone from the street," Rebbe Doresh remarked when Devora had finished the story. "There are a lot of wicked characters roaming the city looking for an unsuspecting victim like Mr. Raskin."

"Well, we'll find out soon," Devora said. "Rabbi Goodman is supposed to call any minute now with the story."

"But aren't the police going to get to Mr. Raskin first?" Devora's mother asked. "Didn't they contact Rabbi Goodman today, after you returned from the bank?"

"Probably, mother, but Rabbi Goodman is going to stall them. He probably told them he'd get his lawyer first before making any statements, you know, something like that. We'll keep stalling them till we can get O'Malley involved."

The phone rang. Mrs. Doresh reached for the phone, but Devora had already grabbed it.

"Hello? Yes, this is Devora. Rabbi Goodman! Yes. Oh? . . . Go on . . . Oh, my goodness. That's what my father thought. . . . Okay . . . Where?" Rebbe Doresh handed Devora a pen and a small notebook. Devora began writing notes, including the place where the sale of the candelabra took place. She then thanked Rabbi Goodman and hung up. Immediately, she dialed the local precinct.

"Hello? Is Sergeant O'Malley there, please? This is Devora Doresh. I must speak to him. Thank you."

"He's still there?" Rebbe Doresh asked.

"I hope so. He was about to leave. They're going to try and catch him." There was a long pause. "Hello? Yes. Sergeant O'Malley? Hi. This is Devora. Sure, I'm okay. Listen, I need your help. Our principal, Rabbi Goodman, got a donation earlier today . . . oh? You heard about that, too? Well, that's why I'm calling you. We want to spare the donor the agony of what happened. Rabbi Goodman doesn't want him to be told anything yet, he's an elderly man, you understand. Tonight, at the synagogue, Rabbi Goodman asked Mr. Raskin where he sold the candelabra. He explained that it was in a large jewelry exchange, called Midtown Shine. Know where it is? . . . Good. . . . No, he didn't sell it to the dealers. It seems Mr. Raskin was asking for two thousand dollars for it and none of the dealers wanted to pay that much. Then this stranger walked over to him as he was about to leave the exchange and offered to buy it from him for two thousand. I know that doesn't help much, but that's about all the donor could have told you himself, so why should the police bother him?"

There was another long pause as O'Malley spoke on the other end of the line. Rebbe and Mrs. Doresh sat motionless, trying to make out the faint sound coming from the other end of the line.

"So the police have to have a statement from the donor?" Devora said. "Otherwise what? Even Rabbi Goodman would be suspected? That seems odd. I don't understand. . . . Oh. Oh, I see. . . . Yes, I understand. Well, can you try just one thing, before getting the donor involved? It might work. Can you arrange for a decoy? . . . Right. Have some cop dress up like an unassuming elderly person trying to sell an expensive piece of silver. . . . Exactly. Have him go to the same place and ask for a price the dealers will certainly refuse to pay. You never know. The counterfeiter might show up, Sergeant. It might work. Please try it. . . . Thanks. . . . Okay, I will. Good-bye."

Devora hung up and sat down with her parents again.

"The decoy idea," Mrs. Doresh remarked, "was a good idea. I sure hope it works, for Mr. Raskin's sake

and for the yeshiva's sake. But what made you think of
that idea so quickly?"

"I think it came automatically to my mind because
of the play we're practicing for. Part of the play is based
on the story told in the Talmud about the wicked
emperor, Herod, and the blind sage, Babba Ben Butta.

"One day, Herod heard rumors that Ben Butta and
his followers were planning against him. The king
wanted to test Ben Butta's allegiance to him after hearing these rumors. So he dressed himself in the garb of a
very poor man and walked around Ben Butta's neighborhood in his rags, making believe he was an old,
angry man. When he approached Ben Butta, he muttered angry statements against the king and cursed him.
But Ben Butta admonished him, saying, 'You must not
speak that way about the king.' The disguised emperor
balked at Ben Butta and said, 'But look at what he's
done to *you!*' Ben Butta stood his ground. 'Regardless,'
he said, 'he is still our king and we must bear him no ill
will.' From then on, the king was satisfied that the
rumors were false and that Ben Butta and his followers
were not conspiring against him at all.

"Since the play, based on this story, is very clear in
my mind because of all the rehearsals, I thought right
away, why not apply the same idea to the case of the
counterfeiters? Use a decoy, just like in the story. I only
hope it works."

"Somehow," Rebbe Doresh mused, "I have a feeling it's going to work out. Mr. Raskin was doing a

mitzvah[5] by carrying out the last wishes of his wife and, in addition, donating an extra thousand of his own savings. And Rabbi Goodman and Devora are doing a great *mitzvah* trying to solve the mystery without alarming Mr. Raskin and hurting his feelings. With only *mitzvos* involved from all sides, the conclusion has to be good."

Chaim was in the dining room doing his homework. He came into the kitchen for a glass of orange juice and heard his father talking.

"Abba," he exclaimed. "We learned that yesterday in yeshiva."

Rebbe Doresh smiled at Chaim.

"What did you learn yesterday at the yeshiva?"

"What you said, Abba. Rebbi Akiva said that everything that happens to a person is for the good."

"That's right. We don't always see the good in everything right away. But in the long run, everything can work out for the best, depending on the individual's intentions."

The Doresh's completed their dinner and went about their evening routine of homework, household chores, schmoozing, and Torah study. Nothing more was mentioned about the counterfeit money case until the following evening.

The doorbell rang.

Rebbe Doresh opened the door and greeted Ser-

5. Good deed.

geant O'Malley and Rabbi Goodman. The two were invited into the livingroom and offered seats. Mrs. Doresh brought in a bowl of fruit and called Devora down from her room where she was doing her home-work. Devora entered the livingroom and greeted everyone. She felt right away that O'Malley had brought good news. Standing beside where he sat was a box and stretched across both his face and that of Rabbi Goodman, were only smiles.

"Well, Devora," O'Malley began. "You did it again. We had a decoy down at the silver exchange this afternoon. After a half an hour of being rejected by the dealers, he was approached by a short guy with a little mustache. He offered him just what he asked for and paid in cash. Our man looked for counterfeit signs on the bills, so we wouldn't grab the wrong guy, you know. He then signalled to us. We were outside wait-ing in an unmarked car. The bills were fake alright. So we cruised along the street, following the guy. He got into a fancy car on Fifth Avenue and about 38th Street. We had him followed by other unmarked cars so he wouldn't suspect he was being watched. As a result, we uncovered an entire ring of these characters who had been plaguing Manhattan for six months now."

Rabbi Goodman cleared his throat.

"And the police recovered Mr. Raskin's candelabra, Devora, look." He reached over to the box standing beside O'Malley and pulled out of it a large, graceful silver candelabra. But Devora was not as excited as the others appeared.

"I'm glad you broke up the counterfeit ring," she said, "but the only sad thing is that we are going to have to return the candelabra to Mr. Raskin and tell him everything. He's going to feel very bad that the school really got only one thousand of his three-thousand-dollar donation."

Rabbi Goodman kept smiling and so did O'Malley. Devora remembered her father's words. Everything will turn out for the best.

"Devora," Rabbi Goodman began. "Since this ring of counterfeiters have been plaguing the city for several months, the government had prepared a reward fund for the capture of these criminals. A reward of $5,000!"

Devora stood up and put her hands to her head in disbelief.

"Have them give it all to my school," she said, her eyes wide open with excitement. "Remember, Rabbi Goodman? Remember when Mr. Raskin said he felt bad he couldn't contribute more to the yeshiva? Well, his three thousand has now turned into five thousand!"

"And the candelabra!" Rebbe Doresh exclaimed. "It's still not sold yet. So you can add at least another thousand or two."

"So you see, Devora," Rabbi Goodman said. "It's not going to be painful now for Mr. Raskin to hear what actually happened. In fact, I can picture him beaming five thousand times brighter than he did in my office yesterday. And I can picture him repeating what he said yesterday while looking at you: 'When I see this, my faith is renewed and strengthened.'"

The Tattered Tallis

The Tattered Tallis

he airport terminal was extremely busy and noisy as the Doresh family edged their way in through the revolving doors. Chaim wanted to go around through the revolving door again, but Devora caught him by his jacket just in time.

Rebbe Doresh led the family through the tumultuous sea of people who had come to greet disembarking passengers from the El Al flight from London. Among the passengers would be their uncle, Rebbe Doresh's brother, Pesach. Uncle Pesach was a *Rosh Yeshiva*[1] in Jerusalem and was engaged in his annual fund raising tour through Europe and the United States. Now he was coming in from a two-week stay in London and the Doresh family craned their necks in their attempt to locate him in the terminal.

"See him?" Mrs. Doresh asked, following closely behind Rebbe Doresh. She held on tightly to Chaim's hand.

"No," Rebbe Doresh replied, scanning the terminal slowly with squinted eyes. "I thought *we* were late, but

1. Jewish seminary chancellor.

it seems that he hasn't come in through customs yet. It usually takes a while."

Devora was also searching the huge terminal for her uncle, who was slightly shorter than her father and had a little red tint in his beard. He also wore a long black frock and a black hat. On an El Al flight, however, that did not necessarily make him easier to spot, since there were many from Israel wearing such garb.

Then Devora saw him. He was walking slowly alongside a tall, thin man with a dark complexion. The man did not appear Jewish but was talking with Uncle Pesach very excitedly. Uncle Pesach was smiling as he listened to the man.

"There he is!" Mrs. Doresh exclaimed. Everyone walked hurriedly through the crowd to where the two were talking. Uncle Pesach saw his brother approaching with his family and excused himself from the stranger. Rebbe Doresh embraced his brother and welcomed him to the United States.

"*Sholom Aleichem,*[2] Pesach, how was the trip? How was it in London, were you successful?"

Chaim ran into Uncle Pesach's arms before he could answer Rebbe Doresh. Uncle Pesach hugged the eight-year-old tight and lifted him.

"*Baruch Hashem,*"[3] Uncle Pesach replied, "the trip was smooth and on schedule. London was a nice experi-

2. "Peace to you." A traditional Jewish greeting.
3. "Thank G-d."

ence, but times are hard there, too, and I hope I will be
more successful on my visit here. The yeshiva has a
tremendous debt to pay off for its new building, not to
mention our past debts and the annual budget for the
coming year. Oy! But, look, the *Ribono Shel Olam*[4] has
seen us through our financial hardships until now, and
I'm sure He will continue to do so for the coming year
as well."

Uncle Pesach turned around to face the tall thin
stranger who remained standing nearby patiently.

"Oh, this is a friend I met on the plane, Herr Ernest
Held, from Berlin."

"How do you do?" Rebbe Doresh greeted him.
Herr Held shook his hand and smiled warmly. "Here
on business?"

"Uh . . . yes, yes, sort of, yes indeed," Herr Held
answered.

Devora noticed the man was becoming uneasy. He
kept looking behind him every now and then and his
warm smile was contrived.

"Listen," Herr Held went on, turning to Uncle
Pesach, "I . . . uh . . . I really enjoyed our conversation
on the plane. I learned a great deal and really would
like to continue our conversation. Perhaps you can give
me your phone number where you are staying, so that I
can contact you while I'm here."

"Certainly," Uncle Pesach replied. He took out a

4. Master of the universe.

small piece of paper and scribbled the phone number of the Doresh family on it and handed it to the stranger. The man took it, smiled at everyone and left hurriedly through the terminal.

"He sure looks like he's in a hurry," Mrs. Doresh remarked.

"Probably has some people waiting for him," Uncle Pesach said. "He's a very important businessman, it seems. Too bad I couldn't get a donation from him."

The group began to walk toward the terminal exit.

"Did you *try* to get a donation?" Rebbe Doresh asked.

"No. You probably think I'm joking about asking him for a donation, don't you? He's actually a Jew."

"Really?" Mrs. Doresh exclaimed. "I would never have guessed it. The way he looks, and his name, I wouldn't have known if you hadn't have told me."

"I wouldn't have guessed so myself," Uncle Pesach said. "I didn't know he was Jewish at first, but the more we spoke, the more he told me about himself. He was orphaned during the Second World War and adopted by a non-Jewish family in Berlin. They raised him as a Christian all his life."

"So how did he know he was Jewish?" Asked Devora.

"Well, he had memories, you know. He was about five or six when he was separated from his family. And then, he told me, he was reminded several times of his Jewish background whenever his foster parents would grow angry at him during his teen years. Whenever he would rebel they would mumble, 'once a Jew, always a Jew.'"

The Doresh family crossed the busy taxi stand to the airport parking lot and headed toward the area where their car was parked. Rebbe Doresh carried Uncle Pesach's large suitcase and Chaim carried his *tallis*[5] bag.

"Funny thing about that man," Uncle Pesach continued as they walked. "He was sitting beside me on the plane for an hour without saying a word. Then, I stood up and put on my *tallis* and *tefillin*[6] to *daven*,[7] because I took a predawn flight, as you know. As soon as I finished *davening* an hour later, he started opening up. He wanted to know what I was wearing. What were the black straps around my arm, on top of my forehead, and so on. After I had removed my *tallis,* he wanted to examine it. It fascinated him a great deal. I thought he was a fashion designer the way he looked at it. He didn't spend so much time looking at my *tefillin.* Strange."

"After all, Pesach," Rebbe Doresh remarked as they approached the car. That's what the *tzitzis*[8] are for. The Torah states 'You shall have it as a fringe, so that when you *look* at it you will remember to do all the com-

5. Prayer shawl.
6. Phylacteries.
7. Pray.
8. Fringes.

mandments of Hashem."[9] So the *tzitzis* are made for the purpose of looking, more so than are the *tefillin*. And sure enough, Herr Held's looking at them made him remember who he really was."

The family got into the car and Rebbe Doresh started it. The car coughed and sputtered. To everyone's relief, it finally began moving. The car pulled out of the lot and onto the road leading to the parkway.

"The car," Uncle Pesach remarked, "it's not working so well, I see."

"It has its moods, Pesach," replied Rebbe Doresh. "Sometimes it starts right away and other times you have to turn the key a few times."

"Nu, but at least it starts eventually."

The car pulled onto the parkway and the family relaxed. Uncle Pesach took his *tallis* bag from Chaim and unzipped it. He pulled out a long, narrow plastic bag with a gold-trimmed strip of cloth inside.

"My dear brother," he said, pulling the cloth out from the bag. "A silver *atara*[11] for your *tallis*."

"Pesach," Rebbe Doresh exclaimed, smiling, "you shouldn't have! It's not necessary. You should have used the money for the yeshiva."

"Well, look at it this way. From now on, whenever you'll be praying for my yeshiva, you'll look better with this beautiful *atara* on your *tallis*."

---

9. Numbers, 15:39.
11. Ornamented collar sewn onto prayer shawls.

Mrs. Doresh chuckled. "I'll sew it on your *Shabbos*[12] *tallis*," she said. "Tomorrow is Friday already. So please remember to bring home your other *tallis* after *shul* in the morning, and I'll sew it on."

Uncle Pesach looked at Chaim and smiled.

"When I was a young boy," he said, "I remember hearing a beautiful story about a *tallis* weaver from Baghdad. He would make the most glamorous *talleisim* for the men in the city. After a while, though, he began to take all the credit for his special skills. He stopped thanking Hashem for his abilities and talents, which he used to do when he first started his business.

"That week, a very wealthy merchant ordered a *tallis* made for him. The weaver again forgot to thank Hashem for the honor and instead praised himself for being such a great and famous *tallis* weaver. Since the merchant was very wealthy, the weaver took extra pains to be even more careful and meticulous in making this man's *tallis*. He spent a great deal of time on it, setting aside all other work orders.

"The following week, the weaver presented the rich man with his proud handiwork, but, alas, the merchant took one look at it and threw it back at him. 'There is nothing special about this *tallis*,' he said angrily, and he refused to pay the weaver for it. Worse yet, word spread of the rich man's disappointment with the weaver's work and the weaver began losing customers.

12. Sabbath.

"Well, naturally, the weaver was very sad and disturbed about what had happened to him and he decided to journey to the famous 'Jew of Pschischeh', a great Hassidic Rebbe in Europe. When he arrived at the Rebbe's home, he tearfully told the Rebbe everything that had happened to him.

"'Why has Hashem done this to me?' he cried. 'I used to do the most beautiful weaving, acceptable to all, and now whatever I make is rejected by my customers!' The Rebbe placed his hands on the weaver's shoulders and consoled him. 'Go home,' he said softly, 'and re-sew the merchant's *tallis* again. Start from scratch.'

"The *tallis* weaver looked surprised. Was that the Rebbe's 'advice'? Surely there must be more to it. But the Rebbe said no more and the sulken weaver returned home. He realized that the 'Jew of Pschischeh' was a very holy man and that he had to listen to his strange advice if he wished to succeed again. He began immediately to take apart the *tallis* which the merchant had rejected, and he weaved it all over again from scratch. Then he brought it to the rich man and presented it humbly to him. The man's eyes flew wide open and he gasped at the sight of it. 'This is beautiful!' he shouted. 'It's very different and special looking!'

"The weaver was astonished at the sudden turn of events and before he knew it, word of his skills spread throughout the city again and more customers flocked to him than ever before. As happy as he was, though, the weaver was desperate for an explanation of the sudden turn of events. So, again he journeyed to Pschischeh to see the Rebbe. The Rebbe smiled at the puzzled weaver and said, 'When you first sewed the *tallis* for that rich man, the threads were threads of too much self-pride. A *tallis* cannot contain such threads. But the second time, after you recognized how Hashem had always helped you in your work, and that He gifted you with your special skills—then the *tallis* which you made became beautiful, having been weaved with the proper threads. Threads of humility.' It was said that from then on, no one was ever able to weave a *tallis* as magnificently as the weaver of Baghdad."

Rebbe Doresh grinned.

"Pesach," he said, "I think you know how to weave a good tale, but the point is well taken. Hashem is always our partner in our accomplishments. But even though he is our *silent* partner, we must never forget to thank him, and recognize his assistance."

Uncle Pesach turned around to where Devora was sitting thinking quietly to herself.

"Nu, Devora, why are you so quiet?" he asked. "How has your detective work been going? I have a great mystery for you to solve."

"What is it?" Devora asked with interest.

"I want you to try and solve the mystery of how I can successfully raise the funds I need for my yeshiva. That is a mystery that has baffled me for years."

Devora laughed. "That's a real tough one, Uncle Pesach," she said. "I'll need a couple of days at least.

But right now I'm thinking about that man who was with you."

"Who? Herr Held?"

"Yes. I feel we should invite him for *Shabbos* or something. I mean, the man is beginning to grow curious about his own Jewishness and everything. It seems to me we should help him along."

"You're right," Uncle Pesach said. "Come to think of it, there were a few other interesting things he told me. He said he has been having these strange dreams lately. He dreams of an old man in a *tallis* calling him 'Benny.' He's had these dreams again and again during the last two months or so."

Mrs. Doresh reached over to Devora and patted her on the head. "Aha! There's a mystery for you to solve right there!"

The car pulled up in front of the Doresh home and everyone climbed out, stretching their limbs. Rebbe Doresh took the large suitcase again and led Uncle Pesach to the door. Mrs. Doresh entered the house first and rushed to the kitchen to fix Uncle Pesach a decent meal to refresh him from his flight.

Chaim urged Uncle Pesach to follow him to his room so he could show him a brochure he had designed for Uncle Pesach's yeshiva. Devora went along while her father continued down the hallway to the guest room where Uncle Pesach would be staying.

The following morning, Rebbe Doresh and Uncle Pesach went to *shul,* and when they returned, Rebbe

Doresh brought home his *Shabbos tallis.* After breakfast, Mrs. Doresh sat down to sew the new *atara* onto her husband's *tallis.* Uncle Pesach whispered something to Rebbe Doresh and then went to get his own *tallis.*

"I appreciate your sewing it on so I could have it for *Shabbos,*" Rebbe Doresh remarked to his wife. "If you have some time afterward, do you think you could also sew a few stitches on Pesach's *tallis?* This morning, in *shul,*[13] he noticed a little tear along the seam of *his atara.*"

Mrs. Doresh looked up from her work.

"Of course. Tell Pesach to bring me his *tallis* right now and I'll do his next."

Uncle Pesach came in with the *tallis* bag and removed his *tallis.*

"It's very strange," he said. "I didn't notice the tear until this morning in *shul.* I wonder how it happened?"

"Don't worry. It happens with time," Mrs. Doresh said, placing a pin with some thread between her lips. "I'll fix it in a jiffy, it's very minor."

Devora sat across the room studying her *chumash,*[14] looking up at her distinguished looking uncle every now and then. Here was a man, she thought to herself, who is responsible for several hundred students, some of them married, and an entire institution of Torah study so many miles away. She marvelled at the greatness of

13. Synagogue.
14. Five Books of Moses (Torah).

her uncle and his undertaking and felt helpless in her wish that he would succeed in his fundraising.

Devora was about to continue reviewing the portion of the Torah which would be read on that *Shabbos,* when the doorbell rang. Rebbe Doresh walked over to the door and opened it.

"Officer O'Malley!"

Rebbe Doresh stepped back to let the sergeant into the house. He then mentioned to Uncle Pesach to join them in the corridor.

"Sergeant, I'd like you to meet my older brother, Pesach, who just arrived from Israel via London."

Sergeant O'Malley and Uncle Pesach shook hands and exchanged greetings. O'Malley kept looking at Uncle Pesach while he took out a small photograph from his shirt pocket.

"You're just the man I want to see," O'Malley said.

Rebbe Doresh and his brother exchanged looks of puzzlement and then waited for the officer to explain himself.

"You were on Flight K22 from London, right?" O'Malley asked.

"That's correct," replied Uncle Pesach. "How did you know?"

"Well, when you come into the country, they give you these cards to fill out, remember? You know, about where you'll be staying and so on. Well, the information about the whereabouts of each passenger on that flight was filtered down to all the precincts in the city so we could locate the passengers."

"What in the world for?" Asked Rebbe Doresh.

"Questioning. See, one of the passengers happened to be a defecting East German intelligence agent. And he was carrying with him a microfilm with top-secret information on communist defense weapons. I guess, he figured that since he was escaping to the United States, he would warn our government of the latest communist progress in weapons and missile production. Something like that. It's not clear to us. We're just local cops. This stuff is top-secret."

"Well, what is the problem, though?" Uncle Pesach questioned. "The man missed the flight? He never made it to the states? What happened?"

"He made it here okay," O'Malley replied. "But not long after he landed, he was kidnapped, probably by East German or Soviet agents here in the states. They probably found out his plans and were afraid he would be smuggling some secret information to America in the course of his escape. Now they got him. We think. Here's his picture."

O'Malley handed Uncle Pesach the photograph and watched Uncle Pesach's mouth fly open and his eyebrows raise high.

"That's Herr Held!" he exclaimed. "That's Ernest Held. I sat with him throughout the entire trip from London. We had a long conversation! I didn't know!"

Rebbe Doresh took the photograph from his startled brother and his eyebrows raised, too, as he nodded in confirmation.

"Yes, that's him. We met him when we went to pick up my brother from the airport."

Mrs. Doresh came in, followed by Devora.

"What's the commotion?" she asked. "What do I hear about Mr. Held?"

Rebbe Doresh gave her the photograph.

"That's him. Herr Ernest Held, right? What's wrong?"

"Well," O'Malley explained to the surprise of everyone. "His name is not really 'Ernest Held.' He's an East German intelligence agent who decided to escape to the United States, along with some very important secret information that would help our government. But now he's been kidnapped."

"What's his real name?" Asked Devora.

"His real name is Erick Schmidt. He is reported to have first gone to London on official business and then to have left in the middle of the night from his hotel, without telling anyone where he went."

"How did they kidnap him, then?" Rebbe Doresh wanted to know. Devora answered her father's question before O'Malley could open his mouth. "They probably alerted their agents of his disappearance," she said. "First place they would look would be the airport and for incoming flights from London. In fact, I remember seeing him act kind of nervous in the terminal."

"Yes," Mrs. Doresh added. "He seemed to be in a very big hurry."

"Well," O'Malley said, taking the photograph back from Rebbe Doresh. "We just wanted to confirm whether he really was on that flight."

"How did the United States know he was going to defect?" Asked Devora.

"He probably let them know secretly. But he didn't want to risk his escape by letting American agents know when and how he was going to do it. Now, we don't know where to begin looking for him."

"I sure hope you find him," Uncle Pesach said, shaking his head from side to side. O'Malley questioned Uncle Pesach on the nature of their conversation and Uncle Pesach recounted everything he had told the Doresh's. Sergeant O'Malley took notes as Uncle Pesach spoke and then closed his notebook.

"Well, I better be getting back with this report. It's a break compared to most of the information we received so far. Most of the passengers questioned couldn't remember him. Well, have a great day, people." He left the house in a hurry.

"Devora," Chaim remarked, chomping on an apple. "You've got so many mysteries to do and it's soon *Shabbos!* What are you going to do?"

Devora looked at her brother and smiled.

"I'm going to help mommy with the *Shabbos* pre-parations. That's what. And so are you. Come on."

II

On Sunday morning, Devora rose earlier than usual and *davened*. Today, her class was going to meet for a trip to Brownsville in Brooklyn, where they would visit elderly Jews in a senior citizen center. Since her mother and Chaim were still asleep, Devora moved quietly through the house, fixing her own breakfast and even preparing breakfast for Rebbe Doresh and Uncle Pesach who were in *shul*.

After breakfast, she left the house quietly, closing the front door behind her softly, and headed to her friend's house down the block. Shaindy was sitting on her stoop and yawning, her eyes baggy underneath the lower eyelids. Shaindy stood up and took her lunch bag off the stoop.

"Good morning, Devora. I'm glad to see you. I thought maybe you had to go take care of some mystery."

Devora smiled at her friend and the two walked quickly in the direction of Yocheved High School for Girls. From a distance, they saw that most of the class had already gathered around the front door of the yeshiva, waiting for Rabbi Landau to arrive with the bus.

The two friends crossed the intersection to the school building and were about to greet the others when everyone's attention was distracted by the yeshiva bus pulling up in front of the building.

A loud cheer was heard for Rabbi Landau as he opened the folding-door of the bus and twenty-eight girls boarded. Moreh Hartman and her husband joined the girls and came up to the bus. Mr. Hartman sat up front with his wife and spoke with Rabbi Landau as the bus pulled into the avenue on its way to Brownsville.

Rabbi Landau was a widower with five children. His oldest daughter, Rivkeh, was one of Devora's classmates and closest friends. Mrs. Landau had passed away two years earlier following a prolonged illness, leaving Rabbi Landau with the responsibility of raising all the children, from age 5 up to age 12.

The trip to Brownsville was part of the school's "Torah Action" program. Each month, the girls would volunteer their Sundays to a different institution or center for the elderly in order to cheer up the men and women who were there. Brownsville was especially visited because there were still several Jewish senior citizens who lived there in dilapidated houses, confined to their apartments because of the very high crime rate. Many of these people refused to move elsewhere since they had been living in the community for such a long time. Recognizing this, the Jewish community established a center for them in which they could socialize with one another and receive assistance when needed. These people eagerly anticipated the Sunday visits of girls from different yeshivos.

After an hour's ride through the streets of Brooklyn, the bus pulled into a neighborhood which reminded Rabbi Landau of the "war years."

"I was only a boy then," he said, throwing a quick glance at Mr. Hartman through the rear-view mirror. "But the condition of this place reminds me of the war years, after the bombings. Look at it. And to think that our own fellow Jews are still stuck here."

The bus pulled up in front of the Center, which had a few smashed windows and whose front door was smeared with grafitti. The door of the bus opened and the girls streamed into the Center, Moreh Hartman and her husband following behind. Rabbi Landau moved the bus further down the street to park it near an open drugstore.

Parking the bus, he shut all its windows and locked the front door. He then walked down the block to the Center to participate in the *mitzvah*[15] of cheering those in need of it.

Walking into the day room, where most of the girls were chatting with patrons of the Center, he spotted Mr. Alkili sitting in the corner. Devora was seated beside him, reading to him from a book with commentaries on the Torah. Mr. Alkili enjoyed Rabbi Landau's

---

15. Good deed.

presence whenever he came and Rabbi Landau headed
straight toward him. Since Mr. Alkili was blind, Rabbi
Landau took his hand gently and announced himself.
Immediately, the elderly man's face lit up and he blessed
him in Hebrew. Devora stopped reading and waited for
the two to exchange their usual words of greeting.

"This the first time you're reading to Mr. Alkili,
Devora?" Asked Rabbi Landau. Devora nodded.
"Well, then, I think you should hear Mr. Alkili's excit-
ing story. You should know what he went through.
You will then feel that much more privileged to be
reading for him."

Devora waited attentively for Mr. Alkili to begin
his story. He had told it so many times before to so
many others, and each time he told it, it seemed as if it
were the first time. At certain points of the story, tears
would well up in eyes that once witnessed terror until
they had been blinded by it.

Mr. Alkili had been born in Spain and raised there.
He grew up in a Torah observant home and aspired to a
career as a land surveyor after spending several years of
full-day study in a French yeshiva. His secular studies
led him to Germany where he enrolled in the top land-
surveyance institute.

"I met my wife in Frankfort," Mr. Alkili said, a tear
oozing from his left eye. "The Jews there were very
hospitable to me. Some of them were descendants of
Jews who were expelled from Spain all the way back in
1492. She was a member of one of those families. I was

invited often to her home for *Shabbos* while I was in the university there."

The Alkilis had two children, twins, a boy and a girl. But the new family lasted only six years. Soon, a mad paperhanger named Adolph Hitler took over the country and World War Two began. Even though Spain was then a neutral country and Mr. Alkili carried his Spanish passport with him, the Nazis ignored his status. He was Jewish and that was all that mattered.

"I took our two little children to a fellow student, a friend I had become close with in the university. He promised to care for them. Then my wife and I went into hiding, hoping to arrange means of escape and fetch our children once all the arrangements were made."

Mr. Alkili stopped speaking. Devora watched his face. It told a story on its own about the hardships which the man had experienced in his youth. It mirrored the anger and frustration he must have felt when his wife was arrested by the Gestapo and taken away. He told of how he ran after them as they dragged her away. The German soldiers turned on him and beat him unconscious. When he awoke, he was lying on his back in an overcrowded freight train on its way to Auschwitz Concentration Camp.

"Did you ever see your family again?" Asked Devora in a near whisper.

"Only my daughter. She is all I have left. My wife was never heard of again. And my son probably met his fate when the family who hid him were arrested and sent away. But I never stop hoping that perhaps he's still alive, somewhere. I pray for him every night. I pray that he still be alive."

"How did you find your daughter?" Devora wanted to know.

The old man smiled.

"I didn't. She found me. After they liberated the camps, we were sent to a Displaced Persons camp. Everyone was overjoyed there when they would find their loved ones and be reunited with them again. As for me, the Nazi animals had blinded me while I was in their hands, and I was unable to look for my family. But my daughter, Tova, she was in the same DP camp as I was, and she found me."

A smartly dressed woman walked over to where Devora was sitting with Mr. Alkili and Rabbi Landau. The woman took the elderly man's hand in hers and bent over to kiss his forehead. The old man smiled.

"Tova," he said softly. "I was just speaking about you."

"I know, papa, I heard. Who are your friends?" She asked.

Mr. Alkili groped for Rabbi Landau's hand and held it up. "This is Rabbi Landau, a friend of whom I've spoken about to you many times, Tova."

"Rabbi Landau," Tova said, smiling warmly, "my father has indeed told me a great deal about you, and I really appreciate your frequent visits to him. He's not impressed by too many people. But he likes you a great deal."

"Well," Rabbi Landau said, clearing his throat. "Your father is an extremely interesting person. He has a lot to share of his experiences, and is very alert for a man his age, having gone through what he went through."

Mr. Alkili groped around for the book Devora was reading to him.

"This is my reader for today, Devora. I can tell she really believes what she is reading from the words of our sages. She is a good young lady."

Tova took Devora's hand and shook it. "Pleased to meet you, Devora. Thanks for volunteering your time to my father. What's your family name?"

"Doresh," replied Devora.

"Papa," Tova said, turning to her father. "Since you're telling stories, did you tell Devora about the tattered *tallis?*"

The tattered *tallis.* It had saved him from death. He remembered the old man, with the uneven white beard that had been ripped piecemeal from his chin by the Nazis. They were in the same barracks in the concentration camp. The old man was very ill and each day he grew worse. Then one night, he shook Alkili awake and whispered weakly to him that he was about to die.

"Please. You were a great help to me," he said, "you gave me of your food and water. I want you to have my *tallis.*"

"Your *what?*" Alkili had asked in puzzlement. He knew well that no one was able to bring any of his belongings into the camp, especially religious articles.

"That's right," the old man stammered with his last ounce of strength. "A *tallis*. I made it. It took me many months while confined to this camp. But I have finally finished it. I made it out of torn blankets and strips of wool which I have been pulling out in little bits and pieces from my clothes. I even had to use the metal springs from inside our matress, to reinforce it."

The old man broke into tears and pulled a neatly folded grey cloth from beneath his head. Alkili noticed fringes hanging from its corners.

"Please. You must take it and wear it," the old man went on. "I worked very hard making it, risking my life each day. And now that it's finished, it seems that I am also finished. I will not be able to wear it. You must wear it. Let not my work have been in vain. *Hashem*[16] will bless you through the merit of your fulfilling a dying man's wish. Please."

Alkili took the tattered, patched-up *tallis* which the old man had made. The man smiled at him and he closed his eyes. The very next morning, Alkili wasted no time in putting on the *tallis* and recited his prayers. He knew the guards would be coming around any moment and that he would surely suffer at their hands for donning the *tallis*. But the stubborn spirit of the old

16. G-d.

tallis-maker seemed to fill his heart as he enwrapped himself boldly in the makeshift shawl.

"Then it happened," Mr. Alkili said, swallowing hard. It was as if he were back in time to the moment it actually happened. Devora watched his facial expression carefully. She, too, wanted to be a part of his history. Moreh Hartman had told the girls often of the importance of remembering that all Jews at any time in history are bound up as one. All of Jewish history was interconnected.

"The guards came in to get us up for work. They spotted me immediately, standing in my new *tallis*. A *tallis* in a concentration camp? They couldn't believe their eyes. It was the greatest act of defiance possible under such circumstances," said Mr. Alkili, smiling.

The sergeant of the guard came over and shoved Alkili against the wall of the barracks.

"Dog!" He shouted. "What is the meaning of this?"

Alkili remained calm and confident. He lifted the fringes in front of the sergeant's face and said, "These? These are to remind the Jew of his responsibilities to G-d, whenever he looks at them."

The officer beat Alkili fiercely on his eyes with a short whip. Alkili was blinded.

"There," the officer said, triumphantly. "Now you cannot *look* anymore at these, and never again be reminded of your responsibilities to your G-d. Instead, Jew, you will always remember your responsibilities to the German race! Now remove that rag and get rid of it, or we will do just that to you!"

Alkili was blinded. He saw nothing but the image of the old man in the darkness of the previous night, his frail form leaning out of his bunk, holding the tattered *tallis* out for Alkili to take. But Alkili was not through with the Germans yet.

"Understand this, Mr. German," He said. "The more you beat the Jew, the more you remind him that he *is* a Jew, and that he has responsibilities to G-d. Perhaps because some of us were not reminded of G-d by these fringes, that animals like you have become our reminder instead. But in the end, as throughout our history, you and your 'race' will be reduced to museum exhibitions, and we will again flourish as a proud and strong nation."

The officer swallowed hard several times, restraining himself from losing his mind in frustration over the unrelenting Jew.

"Turn around," he said, slowly, his teeth gritting behind his curled lips. "Turn around, Jew. And we will teach you a lesson you will unfortunately not live to learn. We shall see who will survive this war."

Alkili turned around slowly. He heard the cocking of a pistol. The officer was aiming a gun at his back. Alkili knew he would soon join the old *tallis* maker, but at least he had worn the old man's handiwork. Loudly and clearly, he recited the verse in the Torah which

Jewish martyrs before him had pronounced when they gave their lives for G-d and Torah: "Sh'ma Yisroel, Hashem Elokenu, Hashem Echad" (Hear O Israel, the L-rd is our G-d, the L-rd is one).

A single shot rang out and Alkili dropped to the floor.

Mr. Alkili smiled at Devora. He could not see her, but he envisioned the excited look on her face, the suspenseful expression in her eyes.

"Don't worry, Devora, I was alive," he said. "I felt a sharp pain in my back. But no bullet had penetrated me. The other inmates helped me to my bunk and brought me some water. They, too, were shocked to discover that I was not only alive, but that I was also unharmed by the gunshot. I still couldn't believe it. So I removed the *tallis* and ran my fingers along the back of it. Sure enough, I felt a fresh bullet hole in it. The *tallis* had saved my life. One of the metal threads had actually deflected the bullet. It was a miracle. The old man had used his remaining strength and had risked everything to make this *tallis*. Because of this, the *tallis* became very holy, very special. It became more than a shawl for prayer. It became a shield of armor."

"Do you still have this *tallis?*" Asked Devora.

"Yes, my dear girl. I do. I refuse to *daven* in any other *tallis* in the world. It is very special to me. It cost me my sight, but I was repaid with my life."

"Is the hole still there?" Devora wanted to know.

"Of course it is. It is a memory of a miracle."

Tova sat down beside Devora and chuckled to herself.

"Pappa's always felt funny about that," she said. "He's been a tailor all these years. Even without his sight. And people always used to remark how he was so good at mending other people's holes but his own."

"Never," Mr. Alkili said, smiling. "I will never mend the hole no matter what people think."

Rabbi Landau looked at his watch. It was time to go. He had promised his children he would be back by four and take them to the Jewish Youth Library in Boro Park. Time had passed very quickly as the listeners had been so involved in Mr. Alkili's story.

Moreh Hartman gathered the students in the front lobby and took attendance to make sure everyone was there. Rabbi Landau bid Mr. Alkili farewell and then stood up to go, when he noticed Tova did not have a wedding ring on her finger, although her head was covered. Perhaps she was a widow, too, he thought. She was pretty and very pleasant.

"Listen," he offered, "if you need a ride to get your father home, I'll be glad to give you both a lift in my bus."

Tova smiled and helped her father slowly to his feet.

"My father still lives here in Brownsville. I have my own apartment in Flatbush. But I'll certainly take you up on your offer. I hate walking these streets with pappa. The neighborhood is horrible. It used to be such a safe, thriving Jewish community when I was growing up. Now it's not even safe in broad daylight."

"Why don't you move your father out of this neighborhood?" Rabbi Landau asked her. Devora reached for Mr. Alkili's cane and placed it in his hand.

"Well, you see he was about to move last week," Tova answered, frowning. "But the famous *tallis* he was telling you about got lost."

"No!" Mr. Alkili exclaimed suddenly. "It's not lost. It must be somewhere in the apartment. But I refuse to leave without it. I must have that *tallis*. I will move as soon as it is found."

"How did it suddenly get lost?" Devora asked. "Did you lose it in the *shul* perhaps?"

"No," Tova answered. "Pappa hasn't been to *shul* in months. It's too dangerous to walk the streets around here and the *shul* has been vandalized almost on a weekly basis. Always something else, a smashed window, stones being thrown, swastikas painted, and so on."

"So the *tallis* must be in the apartment," said Devora.

"I guess so," Tova remarked as they walked into the front lobby. "I hired a cleaning lady to tidy up pappa's place last week. Seems like she may have misplaced it, but she claims she never saw it."

"It's in the apartment," Mr. Alkili said stubbornly, "and we shall find it. Otherwise, I don't move. Period."

Rabbi Landau left the building quickly to get the

bus. He drove the bus around to the front of the Center and opened the door. The girls waited until Mr. Alkili had climbed aboard with his daughter's help. Then everyone else boarded.

The bus pulled out and drove through the garbage-strewn streets to where Mr. Alkili lived. Rabbi Landau sighed as he studied the broken windows of the building and the cracked front door. Garbage was lying alongside fallen trash cans and several people were sitting at their windows staring down at the street.

Rabbi Landau helped Mr. Alkili down from the bus and escorted him and his daughter to the old man's apartment on the third floor.

"Would you like a ride to Flatbush?" Rabbi Landau offered Tova.

"No, thank you," Tova replied. "I'm very nervous about my father, his being alone and all. I must find that *tallis* of his. I can't tolerate another day of his living here. I worry at night, I worry at my job during the day, it's too much."

"I wish I could help you," said Rabbi Landau. "I'm in a peculiar position. I have a busload of kids waiting downstairs and a house full of kids of my own waiting at home. Listen. It's not safe for you to be here, unless you intend on staying overnight in your father's apartment?"

"I guess that's what I'll do. I appreciate your concern. Thank you for everything."

Rabbi Landau called his farewell to Mr. Alkili and

left. Downstairs, he jumped aboard the bus and drove off toward Yocheved High School.

III

Devora placed her lunch into her briefcase and was preparing to leave for the yeshiva. She kissed her mother and walked briskly to the door. It was Monday morning and time for school again. As she opened the door to leave, she found Officer O'Malley standing by the door with his finger on the doorbell.

"Well, good morning, young lady," he said, removing his finger from the bell. "You just saved your parents a millionth of a penny on their electric bill by making it unnecessary for me to ring the bell."

"Good morning, Sergeant O'Malley," Devora returned. "I'm off to school. Any word on Herr Held, yet?"

"That's why I'm here, Devora. I have some interesting information."

Devora looked at her watch. It was another half hour before yeshiva started. If she walked fast enough, she could make it there in ten minutes. Devora turned back and followed O'Malley into the house. Rebbe Doresh and Uncle Pesach greeted him and shook his hand. Mrs. Doresh disappeared into the kitchen. There was still some schtrudel left over from Shabbos, O'Malley's favorite snack. She took it out of the freezer, wrapped a piece in tin foil and threw it into the oven to thaw. She then joined the others in the living-room where Chaim was busy showing the officer the brochure he had made in his arts and crafts class for his uncle's yeshiva.

"See?" Chaim said excitedly, flipping the crooked pages of stapled construction paper before the officer's eyes.

"What are those?" O'Malley asked, pointing to the pictures Chaim had painted. "A bunch of lollipops?"

"No! They're the students in the yeshiva, can't you see? That's their heads and this is their bodies."

"Look pretty skinny," O'Malley remarked.

"Well," Chaim suggested, "maybe you want to give my uncle a donation to help feed them better?"

Everyone laughed. Mrs. Doresh smelled something burning in the oven and went quickly to fetch the schtrudel for Sergeant O'Malley. She came back shortly and placed it in front of the officer on a small tea dish.

"Okay," O'Malley started. "Now that I've got my schtrudel, I can talk."

He bit into the schtrudel and watched everyone waiting eagerly for his report on Herr Schmidt.

"The latest we've heard from the New York office of the Central Intelligence Agency (CIA) is that he was probably kidnapped for more than just microfilm of secret Soviet weapons reports which he was going to give our government. It's very likely, they say, that on the same microfilm are photographs of East German spies assigned to spy in the United States. It has the pictures of a few key spies and their whereabouts. So the CIA claims he was kidnapped to prevent him from leaking this information so these spies wouldn't get caught."

O'Malley took another bite of the schtrudel before continuing.

"The CIA people also believe that whoever kidnapped him is going to get rid of him whether they find the microfilm on him or not because he could always identify them now that he's seen them. Unless they blindfolded him. But even if they did, the CIA doubts whether they'll let him free."

Uncle Pesach nodded his head from side to side.

"What a shame. What a shame. Such a nice fellow. Is that all that's been found out until now?"

"Not really. Some officials at the CIA have studied this guy Schmidt for some time now while he was still working for the communists. They say he's a top agent and would never be caught with any information on his person. They claim he probably left it off somewhere, maybe on the plane, maybe in a flower pot at the airport, maybe who knows where. He's known to have done that before when he suspected he was being followed."

"How do they know he was being followed?" Uncle Pesach asked.

Officer O'Malley smiled.

"From my report. That is, from my report of what Devora and Mrs. Doresh remarked, you know, about him being a little nervous at the airport, looking over his shoulder all the time, being in a hurry to go, and so forth. So when these characters at the CIA read my report of your report, they figured that if he knew he was being followed, he would have made sure not to have that microfilm on him."

"Where could he possibly have put it?" Rebbe Doresh asked.

"We don't know. The airport has been turned inside out. That's why I'm here this morning, really. It seems that your brother here had the most contact with Herr Schmidt, on the plane and in the airport, before the kidnapping took place. There's a chance he may have slipped the microfilm on him somehow."

Uncle Pesach's eyebrows raised.

"On me?"

"That's right, sir. We're not sure, of course, but you seem to be our only clue. If we could locate that microfilm, we could then identify those enemy agents who kidnapped Schmidt. Their pictures and whereabouts may be on that microfilm."

Uncle Pesach nearly jumped out of his seat.

"What are we waiting for?" he exclaimed excitedly. "A man's life is in danger. Who knows how long they'll hold their patience?"

He walked quickly to the guest room, Sergeant O'Malley following behind with Rebbe Doresh. Devora remained in the livingroom, thinking, while the men busied themselves searching through Uncle Pesach's clothes.

The phone rang. Mrs. Doresh got up from the sofa to go and answer it in the kitchen. As she walked by the coffee table, she absently picked up Uncle Pesach's *tallis* bag to place it in the den where it belonged. Devora watched her take it and her eyes lit up.

"Mommy! Please give me Uncle Pesach's *tallis* bag." She called. Her mother had no time. to question her because the phone was ringing. She gave Devora the bag and continued toward the kitchen.

Chaim ran up to where Devora was seated with the bag. He watched his sister undo the zipper and pull the *tallis* out of it, gently.

"What are you doing, Devora?" Chaim asked.

"I'm not sure. But I have a hunch that the microfilm might be in here."

"What's a 'hunch?'"

"A hunch is an 'inkling.'"

Chaim stopped questioning. He watched as Devora unfolded the *tallis* until the *atara* was completely visible.

"Chaim," she called. "Please bring the scissors from the drawer of the telephone table, okay?"

"What are you going to do, Devora?"

"Just bring me the scissors, Chaim, and you'll see."

Chaim ran to the telephone table in the corridor and returned shortly with a pair of scissors. Devora took the scissors and began cutting gently along the seam of the *atara* in the area where her mother had only recently sewn it. Then she screamed.

"I found it!"

Everyone came running back into the living room except Mrs. Doresh, who was still on the phone.

O'Malley took the tiny strip of film and held it to the sunlight coming in through the livingroom window. Rebbe Doresh held his daughter close to him, beaming with pride while Uncle Pesach was clapping his hands with joy. Mrs. Doresh came in and joined the celebration.

"Where in the world did you find it?" O'Malley asked, still looking at the microfilm.

"I found it in my uncle's *atara*. Uh . . . his prayer shawl."

"Devora!" Uncle Pesach exclaimed excitedly. "Of all places, what made you look beneath my *atara?*"

"I remembered the morning when mommy was sewing my father's new *atara* on his *tallis* and you brought her your own *tallis* because the *atara* on your *tallis* had a little tear at the seam which wasn't there before. Then I recalled what you said on the way from the airport about Mr. Schmidt examining your *tallis* on the plane and spending more time with the *tallis* than with your *tefillin*. It would have been a good opportunity for him to slip it into your *atara* with a simple slit along its seam. And that's probably also why he asked for our phone number, so he could contact you for the return of the microfilm after he got settled safely in this country."

"Fascinating!" O'Malley said. "Devora, you did it again. Where's the phone? I must call this in right away. Then I have to bring this film into the station so we could alert the CIA of where to look for Schmidt. Maybe there's still time to rescue him!"

Mrs. Doresh bit her lower lip.

"Oh, uh . . . the phone, yes, well, I'll have him call back."

"Who's on the phone?" Rebbe Doresh asked.

"It's Rabbi Landau. He wants to speak to Devora about something very important, but he can call back."

O'Malley put his cap on and headed for the door.

"Forget the phone, folks. I'm going to head straight into the city and get this search started for Schmidt. You'll be hearing from me!"

He ran through the door and jumped into his squad car, taking off with the siren on. Devora went to the phone.

"Rabbi Landau? . . . Yes, this is Devora . . . No . . . I'm getting ready to leave for school. Okay . . . Yes . . . I'll ask my parents, hold on . . . what? Oh. You've already asked my mother? . . . Okay. So you'll pick me up? . . . Okay. Good-bye."

"What's wrong?" Rebbe Doresh asked. Mrs. Doresh began to explain before Devora could answer.

"Rabbi Landau just called. He just received a phone

call from the daughter of an elderly man who knows Devora from the Center."

"Mr. Alkili," Devora said.

"Right, Mr. Alkili. He's blind and lives alone in Brownsville. His daughter was about to move him to a better neighborhood, where she lives, but he refuses to move because he can't find his *tallis*. It's very dear to him; Rabbi Landau didn't have time to explain everything."

"Last night," Devora explained, taking over from her mother, "his daughter spent the night with him because she's really afraid to let him live there alone. She tried looking for the *tallis,* unsuccessfully."

"Granted," Rebbe Doresh said, "so they probably want you to look for the *tallis,* but what's the emergency? Why does it have to be now? Why not after yeshiva?"

"Well, last night, some teenagers broke into several apartments in Mr. Alkili's building and beat up the elderly occupants and robbed them. Tova, his daughter, is scared to stay there much longer and her father refuses to leave until he's found his *tallis.*"

"Well," Rebbe Doresh contemplated. "In that case, you better rush."

Devora put on her windjacket and left the house. As she stepped down from the front porch, Rabbi Landau drove up in his stationwagon. Devora got into the back seat and put down her school books. The car sped off in the direction of Brownsville.

Twenty minutes later, they arrived in front of the old apartment building. The two got out and locked the car doors. They ran upstairs to Mr. Alkili's apartment and Rabbi Landau knocked gently on the door.

"How did they get to call *you?*" Devora asked while they waited for a response.

"Mr. Alkili has had my number for some time now, ever since my visits with him on other Sunday trips. I told him he could call me if he ever needed anything."

Someone approached the door from the inside. It was Tova. She asked who it was. When she heard Rabbi Landau's voice, she opened the door immediately and let them in.

"I'm at my wit's end," she said. Devora noticed rings around her eyes. She had been up a good part of the night, it appeared. "I can't find it," she said, defeatedly. "My father insists it is here and I don't know what to do. I can't spend another night in this neighborhood, nor am I going to leave my father alone in this place, especially after what happened last night. It's in today's paper. A lady down the hall said robberies are in the papers every week and happens often in this neighborhood."

"Tova" Devora asked, "what did the cleaning lady do when she was here?"

"She did all kinds of work. She dusted, cleaned all the floors, did the laundry, the woodwork, some of the windows, and just general tidying up, I guess. The place looked a lot neater after she put in her day's work than it did before, that's all I can tell you. I used to come here myself to clean up once a week, but my job is taking more of my time now and I can't come here as often as I'd like, and when I do, I lack the energy after a whole day's work. So I hired the woman to come last week. She's good. I'd hire her again in the future."

Devora walked into the dining room and began looking around while Rabbi Landau sat in the kitchen talking with Mr. Alkili and Tova. She walked into Mr. Alkili's room and looked all around, in the closets, his drawers, his bed and the crowded top of his bookshelf. Nothing.

Then it struck her. The tattered *tallis* was originally constructed from blankets. Maybe Mr. Alkili had left it lying around after his prayers the morning the cleaning lady had come. She may have mistaken it for a blanket of some sort. Devora walked briskly to the linen closet in the bathroom. She went through the layers of sheets and blankets carefully. Sure enough, there it lay, sandwiched between a quilt and a pile of mattress covers.

"I found it!" she shouted excitedly.

Rabbi Landau and Tova came running to where Devora stood. Tova grabbed her instantly and hugged her tightly while Rabbi Landau hurried with the tattered *tallis* to where Mr. Alkili sat.

Mr. Alkili's face remained expressionless as he took the *tallis* from Rabbi Landau's hand. Slowly, he felt the cloth with his bony fingers, running them up and down along the *tallis*. His fingers reached the bullet hole and stopped. A broad smile appeared on his face and he held the *tallis* close to his chest.

Tova and Devora came into the kitchen. When Tova saw her father's face beaming with joy again, she began to cry. Rabbi Landau reached into his deep jacket pocket and took out a bunch of tissues which he gave to her.

"Listen to me," Rabbi Landau said. "Let's take your father to Flatbush right now."

"What about his belongings?" Tova asked, wiping her cheeks.

"I have an idea," Rabbi Landau said, walking over to a telephone book which lay on the window sill. He began leafing through the phone book. "Here it is. Call this company. It's a nice Jewish moving company. They'll come and move everything out of here. For an extra fee they'll package everything, too. These are Torah observant Jews and you can trust them with everything and to do an expert, careful job. You better speak to them because I don't know where you're moving your father. But meanwhile, your father can stay at my house. Let him rest there while you take care of other necessary arrangements. Later, you can call for him or pick him up. You have my number."

Rabbi Landau helped Mr. Alkili to his feet and led him to his roon to fetch some immediate belongings which he would need until he was settled. Meanwhile, Tova made the call to the moving and storage company.

When she had finished the call, she joined Devora and the others in her father's room and helped Rabbi Landau pack a few small suitcases and shopping bags.

When everything was packed for Mr. Alkili's temporary move, Tova went into the kitchen to prepare some snacks for Devora and Rabbi Landau. It would be at least an hour, they agreed, before the movers would arrive. Rabbi Landau and Tova spoke about the changing neighborhood and other subjects, while Devora decided to browse around the apartment with Mr. Alkili as his guide. Walking through the living room, Mr. Alkili pointed to his library collection with his silver cane, as if he could see exactly what books were on which shelf. Then Mr. Alkili stopped guiding the tour and stood motionless, listening to the conversation in the kitchen. Devora saw a faint smile make its way across his face.

"How do they look, Devora?" he asked. "Would they make a nice couple?"

Devora thought for a moment and then said, "They look as good to me as they sound to you, Mr. Alkili."

The old man smiled broadly. "Good," he said.

After an hour and a half, the movers arrived. They greeted Mr. Alkili warmly and spoke with Rabbi Landau and Tova at length, concerning what had to be moved and what required storage.

"Leave it to us," a heavyset man with curly *payyos*[1]

---

1. Earlocks.

said. "You can go on your way and we'll do exactly as you said. When we're through, we'll lock up the apartment and leave the keys with the superintendent."

"Thank you very much," Tova said. "I hope nobody gives you trouble while you're in the neighborhood."

The man smiled.

"If anyone gives us trouble, lady, they're going to find themselves in worse shape than these buildings here."

Rabbi Landau led Mr. Alkili slowly from the apartment, Devora and Tova following behind. Mr. Alkili still clutched his *tallis* tightly as they walked down the aged staircase. Once everyone was seated in the car, Rabbi Landau pulled out of the neighborhood and headed home. As they rode, Tova explained to her father what was going to happen. He would stay with the Landau family until she comes for him later in the afternoon. Meanwhile, she would complete the necessary arrangements so he could move into a nice, small apartment around the corner from her one-bedroom apartment. They would be near one another now, no more lengthy travels by subway.

The car entered the neighborhood where Devora lived.

"Well, Devora," Rabbi Landau remarked, "should I drop you off at the yeshiva? We're only a few blocks away?"

"Um. Well, it's lunch time about now. Do you

mind just stopping for a real short while at my house? I really want my father to meet Mr. Alkili, and see his miraculous *tallis.*"

"Okay with me," Rabbi Landau replied. "Mr. Alkili is it okay with you, too?"

"Sure. It would be a pleasure," Mr. Alkili said. "I'd like very much to meet the family of this smart young lady."

Rabbi Landau turned the corner and pulled up in front of the Doresh home. As Rabbi Landau helped Mr. Alkili from the car, Mr. Alkili remarked that he had not *davened* yet.

"Is there still time to *daven?*" he asked Rabbi Landau.

"Certainly. You have about twenty more minutes at the most." Rabbi Landau answered. "I guess you'll be real happy to *daven* in your *tallis* again."

Mr. Alkili smiled and nodded his head. Rebbe Doresh greeted everyone at the door and Rabbi Landau introduced Tova and Mr. Alkili to the Doresh family as they walked into the livingroom. Mr. Alkili whispered to his daughter, requesting that she get his *tefillin* out of the suitcase immediately. When she brought him his *tefillin,* he was already enwrapped in his unusual, tattered *tallis,* weeping joyfully.

Devora pointed to the bullet hole on the back of the *tallis* and whispered to her father about how it got there. Mrs. Doresh invited everyone out of the livingroom to the dinette, and offered lunch. As she served Rabbi

Landau and Tova, she looked at them dreamingly. Devora noticed the look in her eyes. Perhaps, she thought, her mother was thinking the same thing Mr. Alkili was hoping for. Soon Rebbe Doresh joined them.

As they ate lunch and spoke, the doorbell rang. Rebbe Doresh excused himself and hurried to the door so that the bell would not ring again and disturb Mr. Alkili in his prayers. It was Sergeant O'Malley, accompanied by two neatly attired, official looking gentlemen, and Herr Schmidt, wearing a thick gauze taped to his forehead.

"Shhhhhh." Rebbe Doresh greeted them. "We have a man involved in prayer right now, so please follow me quietly into the kitchen." The group complied and followed Rebbe Doresh to the kitchen. There, he introduced everyone and unfolded several folding chairs which were stored in the closet. Uncle Pesach came in from his room and couldn't restrain himself from embracing Herr Schmidt upon seeing him.

"You're alive!" he shouted. "Thank G-d! You're alive."

"That's the gentleman who met Schmidt on the plane," O'Malley explained to the two CIA agents with him. "These gentlemen are agents from the Central Intelligence Agency."

Uncle Pesach shook their hands warmly.

"Are you responsible for rescuing my friend here?" He asked. The men nodded quietly. "I thank you. You've done a good job."

"Thanks to you," one of the men said.

"No, no, no," Uncle Pesach corrected. "Thanks to my niece here, Devora."

"That's the girl?" the other agent asked, turning to O'Malley.

"That's her. Devora Doresh herself. She found the microfilm."

Mrs. Doresh beamed proudly as Herr Schmidt heaped praises upon praises for Devora's rescuing him from certain death.

"They would have surely killed me," he said. "Another hour or so and I would have been a dead man. Good thinking, Devora, good thinking. I wish to reward you somehow. Really. I have a lot of money with me, my life's savings. In the bank, of course. Listen, I'm going to give you enough money to send you through the best universities in the United States! I mean you have a brain in that head of yours worth all the investment in the world!"

Everyone laughed. Devora blushed. She became even more embarrassed as everyone fixed their eyes on her, waiting for her response. She looked to her parents for help, but they wanted her to respond on her own. She was capable and they knew it.

"I'm very grateful to you, Mr. Schmidt, for what you want to do. But I can think of greater priorities if you really want to thank us so generously. You may not be able to understand our priorities since we have very different values, but . . ."

"Go on, young lady, go on," Herr Schmidt urged.

"My uncle here, your fellow passenger on the flight from London, he could really use your generosity. He has an entire institution he has to support on his own, an institution devoted to the furtherance of Torah knowledge and observance among the Jewish people. These are *our* goals, *our* ideals, *our* values. Those are *our* priorities."

There was silence for what seemed to be a long period of time. The two agents got up and whispered to O'Malley that they were going to wait outside.

Herr Schmidt looked around him. Now all eyes were on him. His eyes dropped and he stared at the colorful kitchen linoleum.

"You know something," he said, very softly, "these should be *my* values as well. Remember, I, too, am really a Jew. I know I was raised by my foster parents as a Christian, but somehow, everything seems to be directing me back to who I really am. A Jew can never escape his identity. Never."

He raised his eyes at everyone and swallowed hard before continuing.

"You see, that's how I came to defect from my country. I grew up in East Germany, which is communist-controlled territory. I was such a loyal communist that I became a spy for my country, as you know. But then Soviet Jews kept getting in the newspapers. Almost every month there would be a news item about a Soviet Jew resisting the communists stub-

bornly and giving up everything just to go to Israel.
Even those who were never allowed to leave for Israel
continued to stand their ground even as they were
shipped off to Siberian labor camps. This made me
think a great deal. It made me think of my own background. I was born a Jew. As Jews we were persecuted
and as Jews our families were separated. Hitler created a
supermachinery for destroying all of the world's Jews.
But today, the Jews are still here. Not only that, but
they have their own *land!* Every day they are in the
newspapers. Either concerning Soviet Jewry or the land
of Israel. The more the world tries to blot out the Jew,
the more the Jew seems to persevere. All this made me
think. And then came the dreams. Almost every night.
Sometimes I wouldn't have it for a few days and then it
would come again."

"What kind of dreams?" Rabbi Landau asked.

"Dreams of an elderly man in a Jewish prayer shawl
calling out to me. 'Benny!' he would call, 'Benny!' It
was as if my ancestors were calling me back, I guess. I
don't know. My name isn't Benny. you know."

"Erick," Uncle Pesach said softly. "When a man
makes the first move, when he starts the search for the
truth, G-d comes into the picture and helps him the rest
of the way. The Talmud teaches us this, 'In the way a
person wishes to go, he is led.'"

"Yes," Erick continued. "That's exactly the way it
has been with me. My thinking led me to decide that I
did not belong in East Germany, that I was not cut-out

to be a communist, and that I had to search out my own history. Once I adopted this attitude, I no longer saw the United States or the Western world as bad. Instead, I began to see the communist world as an obstacle in the way of human progress and freedom. I decided to leave. And I did."

"You see?" Uncle Pesach remarked, smiling, "you just happened to take my flight from London. G-d's direct guidance. He led you to where you are now."

"Tova," a voice said hoarsely. Everyone looked at the doorway which separated the kitchen from the livingroom. It was Mr. Alkili. "Tova," he said. "Could you please get me some water?"

Erick looked up, startled. He stared hard at the old man enwrapped in the tattered *tallis,* and his mouth slowly opened.

"Very unusual," Erick muttered, half to himself. "Very unusual indeed."

Mrs. Doresh noticed Erick's astonished look and heard him muttering to himself.

"Is there anything wrong?" she asked him. Everyone returned their attention to Erick.

"This gentleman," Erick said slowly, his eyes still fixed on Mr. Alkili. "He reminds me vividly of the old man I keep seeing in my dreams. And that shawl . . . that shawl he's wearing . . . gray and patched, exactly as in the strange dreams."

Mr. Alkili took the glass of water from Tova and smiled. He could not see Erick, but as he stood waiting for the water, he had heard what he said.

"I was in your dreams, young man?" Mr. Alkili asked, grinning. "What would I be doing in your dreams?" Mr. Alkili chuckled. He then recited a blessing over the water and sat down on a nearby chair to drink.

"Tova," he called, "who is this young man?"

"His name is Erick Schmidt, pappa," Tova replied.

"Your accent, Mr. Schmidt," Mr. Alkili continued, "it gives you away. Are you from Switzerland, or maybe Germany?"

"Germany, sir," Erick replied.

"Interesting. You have family there?"

"No, sir. I lost my family during the war. They were taken away, I believe, I'm not quite sure what happened, I was only about five years old at the time."

"Aah, yes," Mr. Alkili sighed. "Orphans of the war, yes, indeed. Your parents probably hid you, did they? How did you survive?"

"Well, they didn't exactly hide me, sir. I remember very vaguely being carried into a German home and left with the family. My sister was with me. I remember her being as little as I was."

Mr. Alkili's lips began to quiver and his face paled. Slowly he placed the empty glass on the broad arm of the chair and clasped his hands together tightly. Then, clearing his throat, Mr. Alkili continued.

"I . . . I assume the name of the family was Schmidt, then?" He asked. Erick smiled and nodded negatively.

"No, sir," he said. "That was the name of the second family with which I stayed. In fact I was raised by the second family. The first one didn't last too long."

"I don't understand, Mr. Schmidt, please explain," Mr. Alkili said.

"Well, the family I was left with first was later arrested for hiding us, that is myself and my sister. I assume that some of the neighbors reported them. My sister and I became separated during the raid. Then I remember them throwing me into a truck filled with luggage. Probably the belongings of those arrested during that day. There was a guard sitting in the truck and he reached over to grab me so I wouldn't jump off the truck. But I jumped. I was scared of him. I jumped off and ran. The guard shot at me. He missed and I kept running."

"Where did you run to?" Tova asked, caught up in the excitement of Mr. Schmidt's adventure.

"I ended up in an old bombed-out building. I slept there. I remember being very cold and hungry, but even more tired. So I slept. That's when the Schmidt family came into the picture. They were on civil duty filling sandbags, as I found out later, and when they found me half-starved, they took pity on me and brought me to their home. And . . . I grew up there."

Mr. Alkili sat motionless. A solitary tear oozed from his right eye. In his private world of darkness, he beheld the sight of a small boy running happily through an apartment he had once lived in with his young family, in Germany. Blinded only weeks after he had seen his two small children for the last time, they were all that remained of the images in his mind during the ensuing years.

"Is your father all right?" Mr. Schmidt asked, noticing the solemn look on Mr. Alkili's face and his tear-stained cheek.

Tova looked at her father and swallowed hard.

"I think pappa's remembering the war years again, Mr. Schmidt," she said.

"Oh, I'm sorry. I'm sorry for bringing it up. I was only . . ."

"It's okay, Mr. Schmidt. Pappa thinks often of those years. He thinks of his son a lot. My brother. We were twins, you see. Just like you, Mr. Schmidt, my brother and I were also left with a family."

Tova's eyes lowered and she stared at the floor. Her face began to pale as she continued.

"It's strange," she said. "Our stories. They're very much alike. I had a brother and you had a sister. The two of us was placed with German families. The family that cared for you was arrested. The family that cared for us was arrested, too. And I became separated from my brother during the raid, as you were from your sister."

There was silence.

"But how old was your brother at the time?" Erick asked.

"We were twins. We were both five." Tova replied.

"And . . . and how old are you now?"

"Forty."

There was a pause.

"So am I," he said softly.

"Is it possible?" Tova asked, trembling slightly. Rebbe Doresh shrugged his shoulders and remarked, "You do look alike somewhat." The others nodded in agreement.

"For years," Mr. Alkili broke in, "I have been praying that my little son still be alive, somewhere. For years, I have begged for the privilege of holding his hand again. Perhaps you are my son, Mr. Schmidt. Your story is too familiar. Perhaps I was indeed in your dreams. Each night, all these years, I prayed that I would meet my son again as I was blessed to meet Tova again."

"But the man in the dream called me 'Benny! Benny!'" Mr. Schmidt said.

Devora spoke up.

"Could I just say something?"

"Of course, Devora," Mr. Alkili said. "I've forgotten all about you."

"Mr. Schmidt, maybe he was calling you *'Be-nee'*, not 'Benny.' *'Be-nee'* means 'my son.'"

Tova stood up, her mouth wide open.

"Devora! You're right! Many times I have found my father crying in his sleep, muttering *'be-nee, be-nee.'*"

Mr. Alkili rose from the chair and walked toward

where Erick was sitting. Tears were streaming down his cheek and his right hand was outstretched.

"Be-nee! Be-nee!" he cried. Erick rose and tearfully embraced his father. Tova fell on the shoulders of the two of them and wept loudly.

Uncle Pesach nudged the joyful trio into the living-room and everyone followed. Rebbe Doresh and Mrs. Doresh went about getting a few bottles of liquor and some small glasses.

Mr. Alkili wrapped the tattered *tallis* around Erick and Tova and cried: *"Zeh ha-yom assah Hashem, na-gillah v'nismechah bow!* This is the day which G-d has made; let us be glad and rejoice in it!"[2]

Devora noticed how Mr. Alkili looked twenty years younger, at least! He held his son's arm tightly and held his weeping daughter's head close to his cheek.

"Hashem sure works in mysterious ways," Devora whispered hoarsely. Sergeant O'Malley got up and excused himself.

"Where are you going?" Rebbe Doresh asked him.

"Me? Oh, I . . . uh . . . I was going to join the CIA boys outside."

"What will happen with Erick?" Devora asked O'Malley.

"Well, the CIA wants a couple of days with him, you know, to question him, get as much information as they can about what's going on behind the Iron Cur-

2. Psalms, 118:24.

tain. But he could apply for immigrant status at any time and start making his new home here in America."

"Don't you think he should be left alone now?" Rebbe Doresh suggested. "Can you tell those boys from the CIA that he will be with them tomorrow? I'm sure they'll understand."

"I'm sure they will, Rabbi. Take care." He saluted and left. Rebbe Doresh and Devora returned to the celebrants in the livingroom.

"Your name is Alkili," Mr. Alkili was telling Erick, "not Schmidt. Your real full name is Reuven Alkili, don't you remember?"

"Pappa," Reuven said, "I remember very little. I was only five when we were separated. I was raised as Erick Schmidt. I remember only a few small things from childhood, pappa."

There was a period of silence. Everyone simply sat and enjoyed the happiness that had found its way into the tattered lives of the Alkilis. Mrs. Doresh could not keep her eyes off Rabbi Landau and Tova. Perhaps, she thought to herself, Mr. Alkili's joy was only beginning.

"Devora," Reuven called. "All this is your doing, you know. Your cunning saved my life, and as I hear from my father, it has changed his, too. We may not even have met each other at all if it wasn't for you."

Devora shook her head from side to side.

"It wasn't me," she said. "It is the pattern in which Hashem has woven your life."

Mr. Schmidt smiled and turned to Uncle Pesach.

"As for you, Rabbi Pesach Doresh, I am certainly going to help your institution."

Mr. Alkili drew Reuven close to him again and spread the tattered *tallis* around his children a second time.

"It used to be," he said, "that whenever I would wear my tattered *tallis,* I was reminded of the horrors of the past. From now on, I shall be reminded of the joys of the present and future. That is the life of a Jew, as an individual and as a nation. In all destruction, there is renewal. In all despair, there is hope, for Hashem is always with us."

The *Tallis*

The *Tallis*, or prayer shawl, is a large four-cornered garment with *tzitzis* (fringes) hanging from each corner. The commandment to have *tzitzis* on all four-cornered garments worn by Jewish males, is from the Torah, in Numbers (*Bamidbar*), 15:37–41. During the morning prayers, the Jew enwraps himself in a large *tallis*, and throughout the day, he wears a *tallis katan*, a small *tallis*.

The *tzitzis* are to remind the Jew of his Torah responsibilities every time he sees the fringes. Thus, the numerical value of the Hebrew word, *tzitzis*, is 600. Add the eight threads and five knots of each *tzitzis*, and you have 613, the number of commandments in the Torah. In the time of the *Beis HaMikdash* (Holy Temple), two threads of blue were included in each corner of the garment. The blue was extracted from a rare fish called *Chalaza*, and it resembled the hue of the ocean which, in turn, resembled the blue color of the heavens. The color of the heavens reminded the Jew of the presence of G-d. The *Chalaza* no longer exists. Today, Jews wear only white threads for the *tzitzis*.

Acknowledgements

I am grateful to many people without whose editorial assistance this third volume of the *Devora Doresh Mysteries* would still be on the planning board.

—Gershon Winkler for his many imaginative and insightful contributions, as well as for his constructive criticism and editing.

—Yochanan Jones, for his skillful illustrations.

—Ms. Bonnie Goldman, for her practical editorial contributions to the series.

Particularly, I wish to express my gratitude to Mr. Jack Goldman of Judaica Press whose faith, encouragement and invaluable guidance spurred the swift continuation of this series.

C.K.H.

About the Author

Carol Korb Hubner, daughter of the late Rabbi Moshe Korb and Mrs. Devora (Korb) Gartenberg, was born and raised in Chicago, Ill. until her early teens when she moved to Brooklyn with her family. She pursued her higher education at Stern College for Women where she received her B.A.

Mrs. Hubner has been a member of the presidium of the National Council of Bnos Agudath Israel and editor of its weekly newsletter. As counselor and head counselor of Camp Bnos her reputation as a story teller became legendary.

Wife to Rabbi Ehud Hubner, who is involved in scholarly talmudic research, mother of four children, and Bais Yaacov teacher, Mrs. Hubner's avocation is writing stories for young adults.

Temple Israel
Minneapolis, Minnesota

IN HONOR OF THE BIRTH OF
JONATHAN KENNEDY
FROM
RABBI STEPHEN H. PINSKY

Technology of
FLUOROPOLYMERS

MICHIGAN MOLECULAR INSTITUTE
1910 WEST ST. ANDREWS ROAD
MIDLAND, MICHIGAN 48640

Technology of
FLUOROPOLYMERS

Jiri George Drobny

CRC Press
Boca Raton London New York Washington, D.C.

Library of Congress Cataloging-in-Publication Data

Drobny, J. George (Jiri George)
    Technology of fluoropolymers / by J. George Drobny.
      p. cm.
    Includes bibliographical references (p.) and index.
    ISBN 0-8493-0246-3 (alk. paper)
    1. Fluoropolymers. I. Title.
TP1180.F6 D76 2000
668.4′238—dc21   00-009775
                                                                    CIP

© 2001 by CRC Press LLC

No claim to original U.S. Government works
International Standard Book Number 0-8493-0246-3
Library of Congress Card Number 00-009775
Printed in the United States of America 1 2 3 4 5 6 7 8 9 0
Printed on acid-free paper

About the Author

 **Jiri George Drobny,** native of the Czech Republic, was educated at the Technical University in Prague in chemical engineering, specializing in processing of plastics and elastomers, and at the Institute of Polymer Science of the University of Akron in physics and engineering of polymers. He also earned an M.B.A. in finance and management at Shippensburg State University in Shippensburg, PA. His career spans over 40 years in the polymer processing industry in Europe, the United States, and Canada, mainly in research and development with senior and executive responsibilities. Currently, he is President of Drobny Polymer Associates, an international consulting firm specializing in fluoropolymer science and technology, radiation processing, and elastomer technology. Mr. Drobny is also active as an educator, author, and a technical and scientific translator. He is member of the Association of Consulting Chemists and Chemical Engineers, Society of Plastic Engineers, American Chemical Society, and SAMPE and is listed in *Who's Who in America, Who's Who in Science and Engineering*, and *Who's Who in the East*. He resides in New Hampshire.

Preface

The first major endeavor to review the growing field of fluoropolymers was the book *Fluorocarbons* by M. A. Rudner published by Reinhold Publishing Corporation in 1958 (second printing, 1964), covering the state of the art of fluoropolymer technology. The next major publication, which focused on the chemistry and physics of these materials, was *Fluoropolymers,* edited by L. A Wall in 1972, published by Wiley Interscience. Without doubt, it has been and still is a valuable resource to scientists doing academic and basic research, but it placed relatively little emphasis on practical applications. Information applicable to the industrial practice, whether development or manufacture, has been available mostly in encyclopedias, such as *Kirk-Othmer Encyclopedia of Chemical Technology* or *Polymer Materials Encyclopedia,* and occasional magazine articles. The work *Modern Fluoropolymers: High Performance Fluoropolymers for Diverse Applications*, published in 1997 by John Wiley and Sons in Wiley Series in Polymer Science and edited by J. Scheirs, covers the significant advancements in the field over the past decade or so. It is a collection of chapters written by a number of experts in their respective fields with an emphasis on structure/property behavior and diverse applications of the individual fluoropolymers.

Technology of Fluoropolymers has the goal of providing systematic fundamental information to professionals working in industrial practice. The main intended audience is chemists or chemical engineers new to fluoropolymer technology, whether the synthesis of a monomer, polymerization, or a process leading to a product. Another reader of this book may be a product or process designer looking for specific properties in a polymeric material. It can also be a useful resource for recent college and university graduates. Because of the breadth of the field and the wide variety of the polymeric materials involved, it does not go into details; this is left to publications of a much larger size. Rather, it covers the essentials and points the reader toward sources of more specific and/or detailed information.

With this in mind, this book is divided into nine separate sections, covering the chemistry of fluoropolymers, their properties, processing, and applications. A distinction is made between fluoroplastics and fluoroelastomers because of the differences in processing and in the final properties, as well as in applications. Technology, i.e., processing and applications, is combined into one chapter. Other topics include effects of heat, radiation, and weathering. Because processing of water-based systems is a distinct technology, it is covered in a separate chapter. Materials that have become commercially available during the past decade or so and some of their applications are included in Chapter 8. Chapter 9 covers recycling.

This book began as lectures and seminars given at the Plastics Engineering Department of the University of Massachusetts at Lowell and to varied professional groups and companies. It draws on the author's more than 40 years of experience as a research and development professional and more recently as an independent international consultant.

My thanks are due to the team from CRC Publishers particularly to Carole Gustafson, Gerald Papke, and Helena Redshaw for bringing this work to fruition and to my family for continuing support. Special thanks go to my daughter, Jirina, for meticulous typing and help in finishing the manuscript, and to Ms. Kimberly Riendeau for expert help with illustrations. Helpful comments and recommendations by Dr. T. L. Miller from DeWAL Industries are highly appreciated.

Jiri George Drobny
Merrimack, New Hampshire, January 2000

Dedication

To MZV

Contents

Chapter 3

Chapter 6

Chapter 7

Chapter 8

1   Introduction

Fluoropolymers represent a rather specialized group of polymeric materials. Their chemistry is derived from the compounds used in the refrigeration industry, which has been in existence for more than 60 years. In the 1930s, efforts were made to develop nontoxic, inert, low boiling liquid refrigerants mainly for reasons of safety. The developed refrigerants based on compounds of carbon, fluorine, and chlorine, commonly known as freons, quickly became a commercial success. Eventually, they also became widely used as aerosol propellants.

The serendipitous discovery of polytetrafluoroethylene (PTFE) by Plunkett[1] in 1938 in the laboratories of the E. I. du Pont de Nemours & Company during the ongoing refrigerant research opened the field of perfluoropolymers and their commercialization. PTFE was commercialized by that company as Teflon® only in 1950; but the technology had been used exclusively in the Manhattan Project during World War II.[2] Since that time, a large number of new types of fluorine containing polymers have been developed and a relatively high proportion of those in the last two decades. Some of them are derivatives from the original PTFE; some contain other elements, such as chlorine, silicon, or nitrogen, and represent a sizable group of materials with a formidable industrial utility. The factors determining the unique properties of fluoropolymers are the strong bond between carbon and fluorine and shielding of the carbon backbone by fluorine atoms.

Monomers for commercially important large-volume fluoropolymers and their basic properties are shown in Table 1.1. These can be combined to yield homopolymers, copolymers, and terpolymers. The resulting resins range from rigid resins to elastomers with unique properties not achievable by any other polymeric materials. Details about the basic chemistry and polymerization methods are included in Chapter 2, fundamental properties of the resulting products are discussed in Chapter 3, and processing and applications in Chapter 4.

Several fluoropolymers have very high melting points, notably PTFE and PFA (perfluoroalkoxy resins), some are excellent dielectrics, and most of them exhibit a very high resistance to common solvents and aggressive chemicals. Commercial fluoropolymers with the exception of PTFE and polyvinylfluoride (PVF) are melt-processible into films, sheets, profiles, and moldings using conventional manufacturing methods. They are widely used in chemical, automotive, electrical, and electronic industries; in aircraft and aerospace; in communications, construction, medical devices, special packaging, protective garments, and a variety of other industrial and consumer products.

During the last two decades, many special fluoropolymers have been developed, such as fluorosilicones; fluorinated polyurethanes; fluorinated thermoplastic elas-

TABLE 1.1
Monomers Used in Commercial Fluoropolymers

Compound	Formula
Ethylene	$CH_2=CH_2$
Tetrafluoroethylene	$CF_2=CF_2$
Chlorotrifluoroethylene	$CF_2=CClF$
Vinylidene fluoride	$CH_2=CF_2$
Vinyl fluoride	$CFH=CH_2$
Propene	$CH_3CH=CH_2$
Hexafluoropropene	$CF_3CF=CF_2$
Perfluoromethylvinyl ether	$CF_3OCF=CF_2$
Perfluoropropylvinyl ether	$CF_3CF_2CF_2OCF=CF_2$

TABLE 1.2
Categories of Fluoropolymers

		Partially Fluorinated	Perfluorinated
Crystalline	Resin	ETFE	PTFE
		PVDF	PFA
		PVF	FEP
		PCTFE	
Amorphous	Resin	LUMIFLON®	CYTOP®
			TEFLON® AF
	Elastomer	FKM	KALREZ®
		AFLAS®	ZALAK®

Source: Sugiyama, N., in *Modern Fluoropolymers,* Scheirs, J., Ed., John Wiley & Sons, New York, 1997. With permission.

tomers; new, second-generation polymers and copolymers based on PTFE; amorphous PTFE; and a variety of polymers used for specialty coatings and sealants. Categories of commercial fluoropolymers are in Table 1.2.

The worldwide annual production capacity for fluoropolymers is estimated to be 135,000 metric tons, with the market demand being about 85,000 metric tons in 1997. From that, the USA accounts for 45,000 tons, Europe 24,000 tons, and Japan 13,000 tons. PTFE represents 60% or slightly more of the total.[3] In general, overall annual growth of production of fluoropolymers is 6 to 7% (in some cases even over 10%).[4] Current manufacturers of fluoropolymer resins are listed in Table 1.3.

Because of their special properties and relatively low production volumes when compared with typical engineering resins, their prices are relatively high, ranging typically from $7 to $22 per pound for the more common types and may be $50 or more per pound for the specialty products. Examples of current published prices of some fluoropolymers are in Table 1.4.

TABLE 1.3
Current Manufacturers of Fluoropolymers

Manufacturer	Products
AG Fluoropolymers	ETFE, PFEVE, PTFE, Amorphous PTFE
Ausimont	ECTFE, FEP, MFA, PFA, PFPE, PTFE, PVDF
	Fluorocarbon elastomers (VDF-HFP, VDF-HFP-TFE, VDF-HPFP, VDF-HPFP-TFE)
Daikin	ETFE, FEP, PCTFE, PFA, PFPE, PTFE, PVDF
	Fluorocarbon elastomers (VDF-HFP, VDF-HFP-TFE)
DuPont	ETFE, FEP, PFA, PTFE, Amorphous PTFE, PVF
DuPont Dow Elastomers	Fluorocarbon elastomers (VDF-HFP, VDF-HFP-TFE, TFE-PMVE-CSM, VDF-HFP-TFE-CSM, VDF-TFE-CSM)
Dyneon	PCTFE, THV Fluoroplastic (THV-HFP-VDF)
	Fluorocarbon elastomers (TFE-PP, VDF-CTFE, VDF-HFP-TFE-CSM)
Elf Atochem	PCTFE, PVDF
Honeywell	PCTFE
Kureha	PVDF
Solvay	PVDF

TABLE 1.4
Current Prices of Selected Fluoropolymers

Resin	Price $/pound[a]
PCTFE	45.00
ECTFE	11.00
ETFE	12.30–16.00
FEP	10.00–15.00
PFA	18.50–24.00
PTFE	5.00–9.00
PVDF	6.50–7.00

[a] Unfilled, natural color, in truckload quantities..

Source: Plastics Technology, 46(7), 67 (July 2000).

The continuing research and development, truly of global nature, provides new interesting products that will help advance other technological fields, health care, and consumer products, to name a few, and will greatly contribute to the improvement of the quality of life.

REFERENCES

1. Plunkett, R. J., U.S. Patent 2,230,654 (February 4, 1941).
2. Miller, T. L., personal coomunication.
3. Nieratschker, J., *Kunststoffe Plast. Eur.,* 89(10), 41(October 1999).
4. Nieratschker, J., *Kunststoffe Plast. Eur.,* 86(10), 36 (October 1996).

2 Basic Chemistry of Fluoropolymers

The first major work in the field of fluoroolefin chemistry was that of Swarts done near the end of the 19th century,[1-3] which included the reaction

$$C_nCl_{2n+2} \xrightarrow[SbCl_5]{SbF_3} C_nCl_{2n+2-a}F_a$$

where a is the number of chlorine atoms converted to fluorine atoms by the reaction. This reaction gave the early fluorine chemists a tool to prepare many fluoroalkanes. Thus they were able to prepare a variety of chlorofluoroethanes from hexachloroethane. Investigators working on refrigerants used this method for the synthesis of compounds later known commercially as Freons®, produced by E. I. du Pont de Nemours & Co. These materials have subsequently become precursors of most of the fluoroolefins, which represent the most important group for the manufacture of commercial fluoropolymers.

Chlorotrifluoroethylene (CTFE) was the first fluoroolefin that became of industrial importance. The most common method of preparing it involves the dechlorination of 1,1,2-trichloro-1,2,2-trifluoroethane (commercial name Freon 113).[4] Tetrafluoroethylene (TFE), which is currently the most widely used monomer in the fluoropolymer technology was first synthesized by Ruff and Brettschneider in 1933 by pyrolysis of tetrafluoromethane in an electric furnace.[5] Other methods to prepare TFE are from 1,2-dichlorotetrafluoroethane or 1,2-dibromotetrafluoroethane by simple dehalogenation.[4] However, the preferred commercial synthesis involves pyrolysis of dichlorodifluoromethane as described in the section on PTFE. Hexafluoropropylene, another commercially important monomer, can by prepared by several methods, including conversion of TFE (monomer) under reduced pressure at 1400°C (2552°F) by passing it over a platinum wire[6] or by thermal cracking of PTFE under special conditions.[7] Fluoroolefins containing hydrogen are generally prepared by conventional organic processes.[8] The processes involved will be discussed in detail in the sections of this chapter that follow.

2.1 POLYTETRAFLUOROETHYLENE (PTFE)

2.1.1 INDUSTRIAL SYNTHESIS OF TETRAFLUOROETHYLENE (TFE)

The manufacturing process of TFE consists of the following four steps:

$$CaF_2 + H_2SO_4 \rightarrow CaSO_4 + 2HF$$

$$CH_4 + 3Cl_2 \rightarrow CHCl_3 + 3HCl$$

$$CHCl_3 + 2HF \rightarrow CHClF_2 + 2HCl$$

$$2CHClF_2 \leftrightarrow CF_2 = CF_2$$

The first step is set up to produce hydrogen fluoride and the second yields trichloromethane (chloroform). Chloroform is then partially fluorinated with hydrogen fluoride to chlorodifluoromethane using antimony fluoride as catalyst in the third step. Finally, in the fourth step, chlorodifluoromethane is subjected to pyrolysis in which it is converted to tetrafluoroethylene. The pyrolysis is a noncatalytic gas-phase process carried out in a flow reactor at atmospheric or subatmospheric pressure and at temperatures 590 to 900°C (1094 to 1652°F) with yields as high as 95%. This last step is often conducted at the manufacturing site for PTFE because of the difficulty of handling the monomer.[9]

The major by-product in this synthesis is HCl, although a large number of halogenated products are formed, the most significant being hexafluoropropylene, perfluorocyclobutane, 1-chloro-1,1,2,2-tetrafluoroethane with trace amounts of others. Perfluoroisobutylene, $CF_2=CF_2(CF_3)_2$, one of the by-products occurring in a small amount, is very toxic. Because of the presence of a large amount of corrosive acids (HCl and HF), the reactor has to be made from highly corrosion-resistant materials (e.g., platinum-lined nickel reactors). The use of superheated steam as diluent in certain proportions improves the process efficiency.[10] After pyrolysis, the cooled gas stream is scrubbed by water and alkali to remove the acids and then it is dried by calcium chloride or sulfuric acid. Subsequently, it is compressed and subjected to refrigerated distillation to recover the unreacted chlorodifluoromethane and to obtain highly purified TFE.

2.1.2 PROPERTIES OF TETRAFLUOROETHYLENE

TFE (molecular weight 100.02) is a colorless, tasteless, odorless nontoxic gas.[11] It is stored as a liquid (its vapor pressure at −20°C is 1 MPa) and polymerized usually above its critical temperature of 33.3°C (91.9°F) and below its critical pressure 3.94 MPa (571 psi). The polymerization reaction is exothermic. In the absence of air it disproportionates violently to yield carbon and carbon tetrafluoride. This reaction generates the same amount of energy as an explosion of black powder. The decomposition is initiated thermally; therefore, the equipment used in handling and polymerization of TFE has to be without hot spots. The flammability limits are 14 to 43%; TFE burns when mixed with air and forms explosive mixtures with air and oxygen. The ignition temperature is 600 to 800°C (1112 to 1472°F).[12] When stored in steel cylinder it has to be under controlled conditions and with a suitable inhibitor.

2.1.3 USES OF TETRAFLUOROETHYLENE

The largest proportion of TFE is used for the polymerization into a variety of PTFE homopolymers. It is also used as comonomer in the copolymerization with hexafluoropropylene, ethylene, perfluorinated ether, and other monomers and also as a comonomer in a variety of terpolymers. Other uses of TFE are to prepare low-molecular-weight polyfluorocarbons, carbonyl fluoride oils, as well as to form PTFE *in situ* on metal surfaces,[13] and in the synthesis of hexafluoropropylene, perfluorinated ethers, and other oligomers.[14]

2.1.4 POLYMERIZATION OF TETRAFLUOROETHYLENE

Essentially, TFE in gaseous state is polymerized via a free radical addition mechanism in aqueous medium with water-soluble free radical initiators, such as peroxydisulfates, organic peroxides, or reduction–activation systems.[15] The additives have to be selected very carefully since they may interfere with the polymerization. They may either inhibit the process or cause chain transfer that leads to inferior products. When producing aqueous dispersions, highly halogenated emulsifiers, such as fully fluorinated acids,[16] are used. If the process requires normal emulsifiers, these have to be injected only after the polymerization has started.[17] TFE polymerizes readily at moderate temperatures (40 to 80°C) (104 to 176°F) and moderate pressures (0.7 to 2.8 MPa) (102 to 406 psi). The reaction is extremely exothermic (the heat of polymerization is 41 kcal/mol).

In principle, there are two distinct methods of polymerization of tetrafluoroethylene. When little or no dispersing agent is used and the reaction mixture is agitated vigorously, a precipitated polymer is produced, commonly referred to as granular resin. If proper type and sufficient amount of dispersant is used and mild agitation is maintained, the resulting product consists of small negatively charged oval-shaped colloidal particles (longer dimension less than 0.5 µm). The two products are distinctly different, even though both are high-molecular-weight PTFE polymers.

The aqueous dispersion can be either used for the production of fine powders or further concentrated into products used for direct dipping, coating, etc. (see Chapter 6). A flowchart describing the processes involved is shown in Figure 2.1, and the details pertaining to these three different products are discussed below.

2.1.4.1 Granular Resins

Granular PTFE resins are produced by polymerizing tetrafluoroethylene alone or with a trace of comonomers[18,19] with initiator and sometimes in the presence of an alkaline buffer. In the very early stages, an unstable dispersion is formed, which coagulates at very low solids content, approximately 0.2% by weight. The product from the autoclave can consist of a mixture of water with particles of polymer of variable size and irregular shape. After the water is removed from the mixture, the polymer is dried, and to obtain usable product it is disintegrated before or after drying. The powder flow is improved by presintering the dried disintegrated powder. The presintered powder is then redisintigrated. Such presintered products are par-

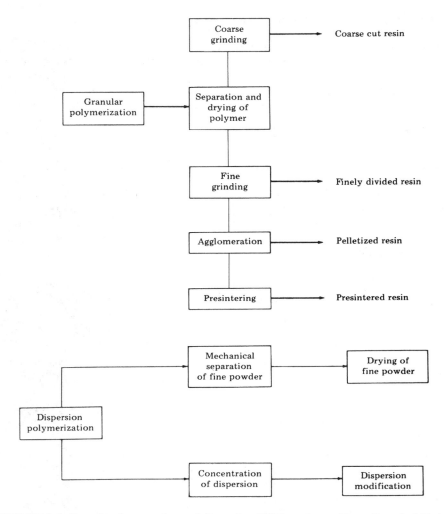

FIGURE 2.1 Granular, fine powder, and dispersion PTFE products. (From Gangal, S.V., in *Kirk-Othmer Encyclopedia of Chemical Technology,* Vol. 11, 3rd ed., John Wiley & Sons, New York, 1980, 2. With permission.)

ticularly suitable for extrusion. Finished powders usually have mean particle size 10 to 700 μm and apparent density 200 to 700 g/l, depending on grade.[20]

2.1.4.2 Fine Powder Resins

The first step in the manufacture of fine powder resins is to prepare an aqueous colloidal dispersion by polymerization with initiator and emulsifier present.[21] Although the polymerization mechanism is not a typical emulsion type, some of the principles of emulsion polymerization apply here. Both the process and the ingredients have significant effects on the product.[22] The solids contents of such dispersions can be as high as 40% by weight (approximately 20% by volume, because of the high density of PTFE). The dispersion has to be sufficiently stable through the polymerization not to coagulate in the autoclave yet unstable enough to allow subsequent controlled coagulation into fine powders. Gentle stirring ensures the stability of the dispersion. The finished dispersion is then diluted to a solids content of about 10% by weight and coagulated by controlled stirring and the addition of an electrolyte. The thin dispersion first thickens to give a gelatinous mass; then the viscosity decreases again and the coagulum changes to air-containing, water-repellent agglomerates that float on the aqueous medium.[23] The agglomerate is dried gently; shearing must be avoided. The finished powder consists of agglomerates of colloidal particles with the mean size of 300 to 700 µm and has an apparent density in the range between 350 and 600 g/l.

2.1.4.3 Aqueous Dispersions

PTFE aqueous dispersions are made by the polymerization process used to make fine powders. Raw dispersions are polymerized to different particle sizes.[24] The optimum particle size for most applications is about 0.2 µm. The dispersion from the autoclave is stabilized by the addition of nonionic or anionic surfactants, followed by concentration to a solids content of 60 to 65% by electrodecantation, evaporation, or thermal concentration.[25] After further modification with chemical additives, the commercial product is sold with a polymer content of about 60% by weight, viscosity of several centipoise, and specific gravity around 1.5. The processing characteristics of the dispersion depends on the conditions for the polymerization and the type and amounts of the chemical additives contained in it.

2.1.4.4 Filled Resins

To improve the properties of the raw polymer (wear resistance, creep resistance, thermal and electrical conductivity), various fillers, such as glass fibers, powdered metals, and graphite, are combined with all three types of PTFE polymers mostly by intimate mixing. Filled fine powders are produced mostly by adding fillers into a dispersion and then coagulating the mixture.

2.2 FLUORINATED ETHYLENE PROPYLENE (FEP)

Fluorinated ethylene-propylene (FEP) is a copolymer of tetrafluoroethylene (TFE) and hexafluoropropylene (HFP). It has a branched structure containing units of $-CF_2-CF_2-$ and $-CF_2-CF(CF_3)-$. It retains most of the favorable properties of PTFE but its melt viscosity is low enough for conventional melt-processing. The introduction of HFP reduces the melting point of polytetrafluoroethylene from 325°C (617°F) to about 260°C (500°F).[26]

2.2.1 INDUSTRIAL SYNTHESIS OF HEXAFLUOROPROPYLENE (HFP)

There are several methods to produce HFP. For example, thermal cracking of TFE at reduced pressure and temperatures 700 to 800°C (1292 to 1472°F) produces HFP in high yield.[27,28] Another process is pyrolysis of polytetrafluoroethylene under vacuum at 860°C (1580°F) with a 58% yield.[29] Additional routes to HFP are described in Reference 30.

2.2.2 PROPERTIES OF HEXAFLUOROPROPYLENE

Hexafluoropropylene does not polymerize into a homopolymer easily; therefore, it can be stored as a liquid. However, it forms industrially useful copolymers and terpolymers with other fluorinated monomers. Oxidation of HFP yields an intermediate for a number of perfluoroalkyl perfluorovinyl ethers.[30]

2.2.3 INDUSTRIAL PROCESS FOR THE PRODUCTION OF FEP

There are several methods of copolymerization of hexafluoropropylene and tetrafluoroethylene using different catalysts at different temperatures.[31-33] Aqueous and nonaqueous dispersion polymerizations appear to be the most convenient commercial routes. The conditions for this type of process are similar to those for the dispersion homopolymerization of TFE. FEP is a random copolymer; that is, HFP units add to the growing chain at random intervals. The optimal composition of the copolymer is such that the mechanical properties are retained in the usable range and that it has low enough melt viscosity for an easy melt-processing.[34] Commercial FEP is available as low melt viscosity grades for injection molding, grades for extrusion, medium viscosity grades, high viscosity grades, and as aqueous dispersions with 55% solids by weight.[34,35]

2.3 PERFLUOROALKOXY RESIN (PFA)

2.3.1 INDUSTRIAL SYNTHESIS OF PERFLUOROALKOXY MONOMERS

The classic process involves the chemistry of fluorocarbon epoxides. Its initial step is a catalytic oxidation of HFP into a fluoroepoxide. The fluoroepoxide is then reacted with a metal fluoride to obtain an acid fluoride, which is then pyrolyzed over calcium carbonate at 250°C (482°F) to obtain propylvinyl ether (PVE).[36,37]

The hypofluorite process, known since the 1970s, has been developed only recently for commercial application. The starting material is carbonyl fluoride, which is fluorinated in the presence of a catalyst to produce methyl hypofluorite:

$$FCOF + F \xrightarrow{CsF} CF_3OF$$

Subsequent addition of methyl hypofluorite to 1,2-dichlorofluoroethylene followed by dehalogenation yields methylvinyl ether (MVE), another fluoroalkoxy monomer[38]:

$$CF_3OF + CFCl = CFCl \rightarrow CF_3OFCl-CF_2Cl \xrightarrow{Zn} CF_3OCF=CF$$

2.3.2 INDUSTRIAL PROCESS FOR THE PRODUCTION OF PERFLUOROALKOXY RESINS

Perfluoroalkoxy resins are prepared by copolymerization of TFE and perfluoroalkyl monomers in either aqueous or nonaqueous media.[39-41]

In aqueous copolymerization, which has similar reaction conditions to emulsion polymerization of PTFE, inorganic peroxy compounds, such as ammonium persulfate, are used as initiators, and also a perfluorinated emulsifying agent, such as ammonium perfluorooctanoate, is added.[42]

In a nonaqueous copolymerization, fluorinated acyl peroxides are added that are soluble in the medium.[43] A chain transfer agent may be added to control the molecular weight of the resin. The polymer is separated from the medium and converted into useful forms such as melt-extruded cubes for processes working with melt (e.g., extrusion, injection molding). The resins are also available as aqueous dispersions, molding powders, and fine powders for powder coating.[44,45]

2.4 POLYCHLOROTRIFLUOROETHYLENE (PCTFE)

2.4.1 INDUSTRIAL SYNTHESIS OF CHLOROTRIFLUOROETHYLENE MONOMER

The commercial process for the synthesis of chlorotrifluoroethylene has two steps. The first step is hydrofluorination of perchloroethane:

$$CCl_3\text{–}CCl_3 + HF \rightarrow CCl_2F\text{–}CClF_2$$

The product, 1,1,2-trichloro-1,2,2-trifluoroethane (CFC113) is then in the second step dechlorinated by zinc to give CTFE:[46]

$$CCl_2F\text{–}CCl\,F_2 + Zn \rightarrow CF_2\text{=}CFClF + ZnCl_2$$

The monomer will not autopolymerize at ambient temperatures; therefore, it can be transported without an inhibitor. Like all fully or partially fluorinated ethylenes, CTFE can undergo a disproportionation reaction and thus must be handled properly. It forms high-molecular peroxides in reaction with oxygen and these can precipitate from solution. Thus, oxygen concentration of commercial CTFE is maintained below 50 ppm.[47]

2.4.2 INDUSTRIAL PROCESS FOR THE PRODUCTION OF PCTFE

Commercial process for the production of PCTFE is essentially free radical-initiated polymerization at moderate temperatures and pressures in an aqueous system at low temperatures and moderate pressures. It is reported that it is possible to polymerize CTFE in bulk, solution, suspension, and emulsion. According to some reports the emulsion system produces the most stable polymer.[46] The tendency of PCTFE to become brittle during use can be reduced by incorporating a small amount (less than 5%) of vinylidene fluoride during the polymerization process.[48]

2.5   POLYVINYLIDENE FLUORIDE (PVDF)

2.5.1   INDUSTRIAL SYNTHESIS OF VINYLIDENE FLUORIDE (VDF) MONOMER

One process to produce VDF starts with acetylene, which reacts with 2 mol of hydrogen fluoride using a Lewis acid (BF_3) as catalyst giving 1,1-difluoroethane (CFC152)[49]:

$$CH \equiv CH + 2HF \xrightarrow{\quad BF_3 \quad} CH_3CHF_2$$

CFC152 is then chlorinated to 1-chloro-1,1-difluoroethane (CFC142)[50]:

$$CH_3CHF_2 + Cl_2 \rightarrow CH_3CClF_2 + HCl$$

Subsequently, CFC142 is dehydrochlorinated yielding vinylidene fluoride[51]:

$$CH_3CClF_2 \rightarrow CH_2{=}CF_2 + HCl$$

Another, somewhat different process starts from 1,1,1-trichloroethane which after dehydrochlorination gives CFC142. The second step, dehydrochlorination of CFC142, is the same as above. The dehydrochlorination may be done either thermally or catalytically. At any rate, the production equipment has to be made from a highly corrosion-resistant material.[52]

Catalytic pyrolysis, which is described in References 53 and 54, starts from 1,1,1-trifluoroethane and yields VDF at high conversion and purity.

VDF is used either for the production of homopolymer or as a comonomer for a number of fluorinated monomers (HFP, TFE, CTFE) for the production of fluoroplastics and fluoroelastomers.

2.5.2   INDUSTRIAL PROCESS FOR THE PRODUCTION OF PVDF

The most common methods of producing homopolymers and copolymers of vinylidene fluoride are emulsion and suspension polymerizations, although other methods are also used.[55]

Emulsion polymerization requires the use of free radical initiators, fluorinated surfactants, and often chain transfer agents. The polymer isolated from the reaction vessel consists of agglomerated spherical particles ranging in diameter from 0.2 to 0.5 μm.[56] It is then dried and supplied as a free-flowing powder or as pellets, depending on the intended use. If very pure PVDF is required, the polymer is rinsed before the final drying to eliminate any impurities such as residual initiator and surfactants.[57]

Aqueous suspension polymerization requires the usual additives, such as free radical initiators, colloidal dispersants (not always), and chain transfer agents to control molecular weight. After the process is completed, the suspension contains spherical particles approximately 100 μm in diameter. Suspension polymers are available as free-flowing powder or in pellet form for extrusion or injection molding.[58]

The powdered polymers from emulsion or suspension polymerizations intended to be used for solvent-based coatings are often milled into finer particle size with higher surface area for easier dissolution when used as coatings for metal and other substrates.[58]

Small amounts of comonomers (typically less than 6%) are often added to improve specific performance characteristics in cases where homopolymer is deficient. A higher level of comonomer than that (for example, HFP) would yield a product with elastomeric characteristics.[58]

Commercial products based on PVDF contain various amounts of comonomers such as HFP, CTFE, and TFE that are added at the start of the polymerization to obtain products with different degrees of crystallinity. Products based on such copolymers exhibit higher flexibility, chemical resistance, elongation, solubility, impact resistance, optical clarity, and thermal stability during processing. However, they often have lower melting points, higher permeation, lower tensile strength, and higher creep than the PVDF homopolymer.[58]

Barium and strontium salts have been added to PVDF to improve its thermal stability.[59]

2.6 POLYVINYL FLUORIDE

2.6.1 INDUSTRIAL SYNTHESIS OF VINYL FLUORIDE MONOMER

There are several methods to prepare vinyl fluoride (VF) monomer. One of the methods described in patent literature is a two-step method.[60] The first step is the reaction of hydrogen fluoride with acetylene in the presence of a suitable catalyst to yield ethylidene fluoride, which is subsequently pyrolyzed:

$$CH{\equiv}CH + HF \rightarrow CH_3CHF_2 \xrightarrow{\text{pyrolysis}} CH_2{=}CHF$$

Other methods are described in Reference 61, however, the commercial process for the synthesis of vinyl fluoride is not described in the literature for proprietary reasons.[61] Addition of HF to acetylene and fluorination of vinyl chloride are the most likely industrial routes to the production of VF.[62]

As with TFE, it is essential that the VF monomer be purified prior to polymerization.[61]

2.6.2 INDUSTRIAL PROCESS FOR THE PRODUCTION OF PVF

Vinyl fluoride is polymerized by free radical processes as most common commercial fluororopolymers, but it is more difficult to polymerize than TFE or VDF and requires higher pressures.[62] The temperature range for the polymerization in aqueous media is reported as being from 50 to 150°C (122 to 302°F) and pressures range from 3.4 to 34.4 MPa (500 to 5000 psi). Catalysts for the polymerization are peroxides and azo-compounds.[63] A continuous process, also in aqueous media, is carried out at a temperature of 100°C (212°F) and pressure of 27.5 MPa (4000 psi).[64] The use of perfluoroalkylpropylamine salts as emulsifiers in the aqueous polymerization enhances the polymerization rate and yield and produces a polymer with an excellent color.[65] The polymerization temperature has influence on the crystallinity and the melting point of the resulting polymer. Higher temperatures increase branching.[63]

2.7   ETHYLENE-CHLOROTRIFLUOROETHYLENE COPOLYMER (ECTFE)

2.7.1   INDUSTRIAL PROCESS FOR THE PRODUCTION OF ECTFE

The copolymerization of ethylene and chlorotrifluoroethylene is performed as a free radical suspension process in aqueous media at low temperatures. Lowering the temperature reduces the number of ethylene blocks in the polymer backbone that are susceptible to thermal degradation. A commercial polymer with an overall CTFE to ethylene ratio of 1:1 contains ethylene blocks and CTFE blocks in the proportion lower than 10 mol% each.[66] Reaction pressure is adjusted to give the desired copolymer ratio.[67] Typical pressures during the process are on the order of 3.5 MPa (508 psi). In some cases modifying monomers are added to reduce high-temperature stress cracking of the pure ECTFE copolymer. The modified products typically have a lower degree of crystallinity and lower melting points.[66]

During the copolymerization the product precipitates as a fine powder, with particles typically less than 20 µm in major dimension. These particles eventually agglomerate into roughly spherical beads and the reactor product is a mixture of beads and powder. The product is then dewatered and dried. It is further processed into extruded pellets for melt-processing (extrusion, injection molding, blowmolding, etc.) or ground and screened into powder coating grades.[68]

2.8   ETHYLENE-TETRAFLUOROETHYLENE COPOLYMER (ETFE)

2.8.1   INDUSTRIAL PROCESS FOR THE PRODUCTION OF ETFE

Commercial products based on copolymers of ethylene and TFE are made by free radical–initiated addition copolymerization.[69] Small amounts (1 to 10 mol%) of modifying comonomers are added to eliminate a rapid embrittlement of the product at exposure to elevated temperatures. Examples of the modifying comonomers are perfluorobutyl ethylene, hexafluoropropylene, perfluorovinyl ether, and hexafluoroisobutylene.[70] ETFE copolymers are basically alternating copolymers,[70] and in the molecular formula, they are isomeric with polyvinylidene fluoride (PVDF) with a head-to-head, tail-to-tail structure. However, in many important physical properties, the modified ETFE copolymers are superior to PVDF with the exception of the latter's remarkable piezoelectric and pyroelectric characteristics.

2.9 TERPOLYMERS OF TFE, HFP AND VDF (THV FLUOROPLASTIC)

THV Fluoroplastic is prepared by an emulsion copolymerization. The resulting dispersion may be used directly or may be concentrated with the addition of an emulsifier. If it is coagulated, washed, and dried, the final products are either powders (after grinding) or pellets (after extrusion and pelletizing). Currently, Dyneon Company is producing four commercial grades of THV Fluoroplastic (three dry and one aqueous dispersion) differing in monomer ratio, which affects the melting points, chemical resistance, and flexibility.[71]

2.10 FLUOROELASTOMERS

The first commercial fluoroelastomer, Kel-F, was developed by the M. W. Kellog Company in the early to mid-1950s and is a copolymer of vinylidene fluoride (VDF) and chlorotrifluoroethylene (CTFE). Another fluorocarbon elastomer, Viton® A, is a copolymer of VDF and hexafluoropropylene (HFP) developed by du Pont was made available commercially in 1955. The products developed thereafter can be divided into two classes: VDF-based fluoroelastomers and tetrafluoroethylene (TFE)-based fluoroelastomers (perfluoroelastomers).[72] The current products are mostly based on copolymers of VDF and HFP, VDF and MVE, or terpolymers of VDF with HFP and TFE. In the combination of VDF and HFP, the proportion of HFP has to be 19 to 20 mol% or higher to obtain amorphous elastomeric product.[73] The ratio of VDF/HFP/TFE has also to be within a certain region to yield elastomers as shown in a triangular diagram (Figure 2.2).[74]

2.10.1 INDUSTRIAL PROCESS FOR THE PRODUCTION OF FLUOROELASTOMERS

Fluoroelastomers are generally prepared by high-pressure, free radical emulsion polymerization.[75] Organic or inorganic peroxy compounds, such as ammonium persulfate, are used as initiators. Inorganic initiators generally produce ionic chain ends, such as $-CH_2OH$ and $-CF_2COOH$, which contribute to the colloidal stability of the latex formed during the polymerization.[76] In this case, suitable emulsifiers, such as ammonium perfluorooctoate, are not strictly required.[77] The ionic chains derived from the polymerization initiators also have important effects on the properties of the resulting polymer, such as rheology, mechanical properties, and even sealing properties.[76] Chain transfer agents, such as carbon tetrachloride, methanol, and acetone dodecylmercaptane, are used to control the molecular weight of the polymer. The polymerization may be either a batch or a continuous process.[78] The resulting latex is most frequently coagulated into a crumb by adding salt or acid, or a combination of both, or by a freeze–thaw process. The crumb is filtered and washed to remove coagulant and water-soluble residues, washed, and dried. The finished product is supplied as pellets, lumps, or milled sheets.[78] Some fluoroelastomers are also available in latex form.

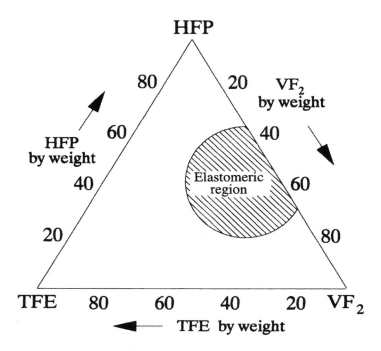

FIGURE 2.2 Compositions of VDF/HFP/TFE. (Arcella, V. and Ferro, R., in *Modern Fluoropolymers,* Scheirs, J., Ed., John Wiley & Sons, New York, 1997, 77. With permission.)

2.11 FLUOROSILICONES

There are a variety of compounds containing the combination of silicon and fluorine. However, only fluorinated polymers with a siloxane backbone are currently available commercially.

The original and by far the most widely available fluorosilicone since its introduction in the 1950s is polymethyltrifluoropropylsiloxane (PMTFPS), more rigorously known as poly[methyl(3,3,3-trifluoropropyl)siloxane] or poly[methyl(1H,1H, 2H,2H-trifluoropropyl)siloxane]. Unless specifically mentioned, the unfluorinated carbons are those nearest to silicon, i.e., poly(methylnonafluorohexyl)siloxane (PMNFHS) is poly[methyl(1H,1H,2H,2H-nonafluorohexyl)siloxane]. Currently, only copolymers of PMTFPS and PMNFHS with polysiloxane (PDMS) are available commercially.[79]

2.11.1 INDUSTRIAL PROCESS FOR THE PRODUCTION OF
FLUOROSILICONES

Hydrosilylation is by far the most important route for obtaining monomers and other precursors to fluorinated polysiloxanes. Hydrosylilation[80] is the addition of silicon hydride moiety across an unsaturated linkage using transition metal complexes of platinum or rhodium such as Speier's catalyst, hexachloroplatinic acid in isopropanol.[79] The preparation of methyl(3,3,3-trifluoropropyl)dichlorosilane, which is the precursor of the industrially most important polymethyltrifluoropropylsilane (PMTFPS), is described in patent literature.[81]

The most common route for the preparation of PMTFS is through the base-catalyzed ring-opening polymerization of the cyclic trimer, which is obtained through hydrolysis of the corresponding dichlorosilane. Copolymers are prepared by the same polymerization technique.[82]

Details about chemistry and processes pertaining to the manufacture of fluoro-silicones are found in Maxson, Norris, and Owen.[83]

REFERENCES

1. Swarts, F., *Bull. Acad. R. Bel.* 24 (3), 474 (1892).
2. Swarts, F., *Bull. Acad. R. Bel.* 29 (3), 874 (1895).
3. Swarts, F., *Centralblat* 1, 3 (1903).
4. Fearn, J. E., in *Fluoropolymers* (Wall, L. A., Ed.), Wiley-Interscience, New York, p. 3 (1972).
5. Ruff, O. and Brettschneider, O., *Z. Anorg. Allg. Chem.* 210, 173 (1933).
6. Benning, A. F. et al., U.S. Patent 2,394,582 (February 12, 1946).
7. Downing, E. B. et al., U.S. Patent 2,480,560 (August 30, 1949).
8. Fearn, J. E., in *Fluoropolymers* (Wall, L. A., Ed.), Wiley-Interscience, New York, p. 4 (1972).
9. Gangal, S. V., in *Kirk-Othmer: Encyclopedia of Chemical Technology,* Vol. 11, 3rd ed., John Wiley & Sons, New York, p. 2 (1980).
10. Sheratt, S., in *Encyclopedia of Chemical Technology,* Vol. 9, John Wiley & Sons, New York, p. 811 (1966).
11. Gangal, S. V., in *Kirk-Othmer Encyclopedia of Polymer Science and Technology,* Vol. 16 (Mark, H. F. and Kroschwitz, J. I., Eds.), John Wiley & Sons, New York, p. 579 (1989).
12. Sheratt, S., in *Kirk-Othmer Encyclopedia of Chemical Technology,* Vol. 9, John Wiley & Sons, New York, p. 809 (1966).
13. Toy, M. S. and Tiner, N.A., U.S. Patent 3,567,521 (March 2, 1971).
14. Gangal, S. V., in *Encyclopedia of Polymer Science and Technology,* Vol. 16 (Mark, H. F. and Kroschwitz, J. I., Eds.), John Wiley & Sons, New York, p. 579 (1989).
15. Sheratt, S., in *Kirk-Othmer Encyclopedia of Chemical Technology,* Vol. 9, John Wiley & Sons, New York, p. 812 (1966).
16. Berry, K. L., U.S. Patent 2,559,752 (July 10, 1951).
17. Duddington, J. E. and Sheratt, S., U.S. Patent 3,009,892 (November 21, 1961).
18. Doughty, T. R., Sperati, C. A., and Un, H., U.S. Patent 3,855,191 (December 17, 1974).
19. Mueller, M. B., Salatiello, P. P., and Kaufman, H. S., U.S. Patent 3,655,611 (April 11, 1972).
20. Sheratt, S., in *Kirk-Othmer Encyclopedia of Chemical Technology,* Vol. 9, John Wiley & Sons, New York, p. 813 (1966).
21. Bankoff, S. G., U.S. Patent 2,612,484 (September 30, 1952).
22. Gangal, S. V., in *Encyclopedia of Polymer Science and Technology,* Vol. 16 (Mark, H. F. and Kroschwitz, J. I., Eds.), John Wiley & Sons, New York, p. 581 (1989).
23. Sheratt, S., in *Kirk-Othmer Encyclopedia of Chemical Technology,* Vol. 9, John Wiley & Sons, New York, p. 814 (1966).

24. Gangal, S. V., U.S. Patent 4,342,675 (August 3, 1982).
25. Berry, K. L., U.S. Patent 2,478,229 (August 9, 1949).
26. Gangal, S. V., in *Encyclopedia of Polymer Science and Technology,* Vol. 16 (Mark, H. F. and Kroschwitz, J. I., Eds.), John Wiley & Sons, New York, p. 601 (1966).
27. Nelson, D.A., U.S. Patent 3,758,138 (August 7, 1956).
28. Atkinson, B. and Trenwith, A. B., *J. Chem. Soc.,* Pt. II, 2082 (1953).
29. Wadell, J. S., U.S. Patent 2,759,783 (August 21, 1956).
30. Gangal, S. V., in *Encyclopedia of Polymer Science and Technology,* Vol. 16 (Mark, H. F. and Kroschwitz, J. I., Eds.), John Wiley & Sons, New York, p. 602 (1966).
31. Miller, W. T., U.S. Patent 2,598,283 (May 27, 1952).
32. Naberezhnykh, R. A. et al., *Dokl. Akad. Nauk SSSR* 214, 149 (1974).
33. Kabankin, A. S., Balabanova, S. A., and Markevich, A.M., *Vysokomol. Soed. Ser.* A 12, 267 (1970).
34. Gangal, S. V., in *Encyclopedia of Polymer Science and Technology,* Vol. 16 (Mark, H. F. and Kroschwitz, J. I., Eds.), John Wiley & Sons, New York, p. 603 (1989).
35. Gangal, S.V., in *Encyclopedia of Chemical Technology,* 3rd ed., Vol. 11 (Grayson, M. Ed.), John Wiley and Sons, New York, p. 24 (1978).
36. Fritz, C. G., Moore, E. P., and Selman, S., U.S. Patent 3,114,778 (1963).
37. Moore, E. P., U.S. Patent 3,322,826 (1967).
38. Pozzoli, M., Vitta, G., and Arcella, V., in *Modern Fluoropolymers* (Scheirs, J., Ed.), John Wiley & Sons, New York, p. 378 (1997).
39. Harris, J. F. and McCane, D. I., U.S. Patent 3,132,123 (May 5, 1964).
40. Carlson, D. P., U.S. Patent 3,642,142 (February 15, 1972).
41. Gresham, W. F. and Vogelpohl, A. F., U.S. Patent 3,635,926 (January 18, 1972).
42. Hartwimmer, R. and Kuhls, J., U.S. Patent 4,262,101 (April 14, 1981).
43. Hintzer, K. and Löhr, G., in *Modern Fluoropolymers* (Scheirs, J., Ed.), John Wiley & Sons, New York, p. 224 (1997).
44. Sperati, C. A., in *Handbook of Plastics Materials and Technology* (Rubin, I. I., Ed.) John Wiley & Sons, New York, p. 112 (1990).
45. Gangal, S. V., in *Encyclopedia of Polymer Science and Technology,* Vol. 16 (Mark, H.F. and Kroschwitz, J. I., Eds.), John Wiley & Sons, New York, p. 616 (1989).
46. Booth, H. S. and Burchfield, P. E., *J. Am. Chem. Soc.* 55, 2231 (1933).
47. Stanitis, G., in *Modern Fluoropolymers* (Scheirs, J., Ed.), John Wiley & Sons, New York, p. 526 (1997).
48. Carlson, D. P. and Schmiegel, W., in *Ullmann's Encyclopedia of Industrial Chemistry* (Gerhartz, W., Ed.), Vol. A11, VCH Publishers, Weinheim, West Germany, p. 411 (1988).
49. Burk, R. E., Coffman, D. D., and Kalb, G. H., U.S. Patent 2,425,991 (1947).
50. Calfee, J. D. and Florio, P. A., U.S. Patent 2,499,129 (1950).
51. Feasley, C. F. and Storer, W. H., U.S. Patent 2,627,529 (1953).
52. Arcella, V. and Ferro, R., in *Modern Fluoropolymers* (Scheirs, J., Ed.), John Wiley & Sons, New York, p. 76 (1997).
53. Japanese Patent, Open, 130,507 (1979).
54. Japanese Patent, Open, 235,409 (1986).
55. Seiler, D. A., in *Modern Fluoropolymers* (Scheirs, J., Ed.), John Wiley & Sons, New York, p. 489 (1997).
56. Dohany, J. E. and Humphrey, J. S., in *Encyclopedia of Polymer Science and Engineering,* Vol. 17 (Mark, H. F. and Kroschwitz, J. I., Eds.), John Wiley & Sons, New York, p. 534 (1989).
57. Locheed, T., *Chemical Processing,* 37–38 (January 1993).

58. Seiler, D. A., in *Modern Fluoropolymers* (Scheirs, J., Ed.), John Wiley & Sons, New York, p. 490 (1997).
59. Carlson, D. P. and Schmiegel, W., in *Ullmann's Encyclopedia of Industrial Chemistry,* Vol. A11, VCH Publishers, Weinheim, West Germany, p. 414 (1988).
60. Skiles, B. F., U.S. Patent 2,674,632 (April 1, 1954).
61. Brasure, D. and Ebnesajjad, S., in *Encyclopedia of Polymer Science and Engineering,* Vol. 17 (Mark, H. F. and Kroschwitz, J. I., Eds.), John Wiley & Sons, New York, p. 471 (1989).
62. Haszeldine, R. N. et al., *Polymer* 14, 221 (1973).
63. Carlson, D. P. and Schmiegel, W., in *Ullmann's Encyclopedia of Industrial Chemistry,* Vol. A11, VCH Publishers, Weinheim, West Germany, p. 416 (1988).
64. Hecht, J. L., U.S. Patent 3, 265,678 (1966).
65. Uschold, R. E., U.S. Patent 5,229,480 (July 20, 1993).
66. Reimschuessel, H. K., Marti, J., and Murthy, N.S., *J. Polym. Sci., Pt. A, Polym. Chem.* 26, 43 (1988).
67. Schulze, S., U.S. Patent 4,053,445 (October 11, 1977).
68. Stanitis, G., in *Modern Fluoropolymers* (Scheirs, J., Ed.), John Wiley & Sons, New York, p. 528 (1997).
69. Sperati, C. A., in *Handbook of Plastics Materials and Technology* (Rubin, I. I., Ed.) John Wiley & Sons, New York, p. 87 (1990).
70. Kerbow, D. L., in *Modern Fluoropolymers* (Scheirs, J., Ed.), John Wiley & Sons, New York, p. 302 (1997).
71. Hull, D. E., Johnson, B. V., Rodricks, J. P., and Staley, J. B., in *Modern Fluoropolymers* (Scheirs, J., Ed.), John Wiley & Sons, New York, p. 257 (1997).
72. Arcella, V. and Ferro, R., in *Modern Fluoropolymers* (Scheirs, J., Ed.), John Wiley & Sons, New York, p. 71 (1997).
73. Ajroldi, G., Pianca, M., Fumagalli, M., and Moggi, G., *Polymer* 30, 2180 (1989).
74. Arcella, V. and Ferro, R., in *Modern Fluoropolymers* (Scheirs, J., Ed.), John Wiley & Sons, New York, p. 73 (1997).
75. Grootaert, W. M., Millet, C. H., and Worm, A. T., in *Kirk-Othmer Encyclopedia of Chemical Technology,* 4th ed., Vol. 8, John Wiley & Sons, New York, p. 990 (1995).
76. Arcella, V. and Ferro, R., in *Modern Fluoropolymers* (Scheirs, J., Ed.), John Wiley & Sons, New York, p. 77 (1997).
77. Logothetis, A. L., *Progr. Polym. Sci.* 14, 257 (1989).
78. Carlson, D. P. and Schmiegel, W., in *Ullmann's Encyclopedia of Industrial Chemistry* (Gerhartz, W., Ed.), Vol. A11, VCH Publishers, Weinheim, West Germany, p. 419 (1988).
79. Maxson, M. T., Norris, A. W., and Owen, M. J., in *Modern Fluoropolymers* (Scheirs, J., Ed.), John Wiley & Sons, New York, p. 360 (1997).
80. Speier, J. L., *Adv. Organomet. Chem.* 17, 409 (1979).
81. Bajzer, W. X., Bixler, Jr., R. L., Meddaugh, M. D., and Wright, A. P., U.S. Patent 4,798,818 (January 17, 1989).
82. Maxson, M. T., Norris, A. W., and Owen, M. J., in *Modern Fluoropolymers* (Scheirs, J. Ed.), John Wiley & Sons, New York, p. 362 (1997).
83. Chapter 20 in *Modern Fluoropolymers* (Scheirs, J., Ed.), John Wiley & Sons, New York, (1997).

3 Properties of Commercial Fluoropolymers

3.1 PROPERTIES AS RELATED TO THE STRUCTURE OF THE POLYMERS

Fluoropolymers represent a group of macromolecules offering a variety of unique properties, in particular, a good-to-outstanding chemical resistance and stability at elevated temperatures. Because of these, they have been used increasingly in applications where most hydrocarbon-based polymers would fail, such as chemical processing, oil wells, motor vehicle engines, nuclear reactors, and space applications. On the other hand, they exhibit some deficiencies when compared with most engineering polymers. They typically have poorer mechanical properties, higher permeabilities, and often considerably higher cost. Some of the specific shortcomings of fluoropolymers are listed in Table 3.1.[1] Knowing the advantages and disadvantages and understanding how properties, performance, and structure are correlated is very important for a proper selection of processing technology and suitability for specific practical applications. In general, the unique properties of fluoropolymers are the result of the very strong bond between carbon and fluorine[2] and shielding the carbon backbone by fluorine atoms and of the fact that they are fully saturated macromolecules.

3.1.1 FLUOROPLASTICS

PTFE has a conformation of a twisting helix comprising 13 CF_2 groups every 180° turn. This configuration is thermodynamically favored over planar zigzag (typical for polyethylene), because of the mutual repulsion of the adjacent fluorine atoms. The helix forms an almost perfect cylinder comprising an outer sheath of fluorine atoms enveloping a carbon-based core (Figure 3.1).[3] This morphology is conducive for PTFE molecules to pack like parallel rods. However, individual cylinders can slip past one another. This contributes to a relatively strong tendency of PTFE to cold-flow. The mutual repulsion of fluorine atoms tends to inhibit the bending of the chain backbone. Therefore, the PTFE chain is very stiff. The outer sheath of fluorine atoms protects the carbon backbone, thus providing the chemical inertness and stability. It also lowers the surface energy giving PTFE a low coefficient of friction and nonstick properties.[2]

TABLE 3.1
List of Achilles Heels of Common Fluoropolymers

Fluoropolymer	Achilles Heel
PTFE	Ionizing radiation, creep
PVDF	Ketones, strongly alkaline solutions
PCTFE	High processing temperatures
FEP	Fatigue, poor high-temperature properties
ETFE	Elevated temperatures + oxygen
VDF-HFP	Amines, cryogenic temperatures
PFA	Low heat deflection temperature
PVF	Aluminum + sunlight

Source: Scheirs, J., in *Modern Fluoropolymers*, Scheirs, J., ed., John Wiley & Sons, New York, 1997. With permission.

The extremely high molecular weight of the PTFE polymer results in a melt viscosity, which is about six orders of magnitude higher than that of most common thermoplastic polymers (10^{10} to 10^{12} Pa·s or Poise). Such an extremely high viscosity even suppresses a normal crystal growth. Thus, the virgin polymer has a degree of crystallinity in excess of 90% and a melting point of approximately 340°C (644°F). After being melted, even after slow cooling of the melt, the degree of crystallinity rarely reaches 70% and the melting point is reduced to about 328°C (622°F).

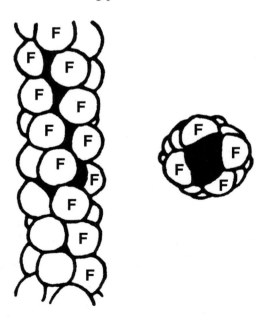

FIGURE 3.1 Schematic representation of the polytetrafluoroethylene helix. (Adapted from Bunn, C. W. and Howels, E. R., in *Nature* 174 (1954). With permission from Macmillan Magazines, Ltd.)

The exceptional chemical resistance, resistance to ultraviolet (UV) radiation, and thermal stability can be further explained by the fact that the C–F and C–C bonds in fluorocarbons are among the strongest known in organic compounds.[4]

FEP, a copolymer of tetrafluoroethylene (TFE) and hexafluoropropylene (HFP), is essentially PTFE with an occasional methyl side group attached. The methyl groups have effect as defects in crystallites and therefore reduce the melting point. These side groups also impede the slipping of the polymer chains past each other, thus reducing the cold flow.

PFA is a copolymer of TFE and perfluoro(propylvinyl ether) (PPVE) in a mole ratio approximately 100:1. Even such a small amount of comonomer is sufficient to produce a copolymer with a greatly reduced crystallinity. The relatively long side chains also markedly reduce the cold flow. **MFA**, a copolymer of TFE and perfluoro(methylvinyl ether) (PMVE) has similar properties with a somewhat lower melting point.

ETFE, a copolymer of TFE and ethylene, has a higher tensile strength than PTFE, FEP, and PFA because its molecular chains adopt a planar zigzag configuration.[5] A strong electronic interaction between the bulky CF_2 groups of one chain and the smaller CH_2 groups of an adjacent chain causes an extremely low creep.[6]

PVDF comprises alternating CH_2 and CF_2 groups. These alternating units can crystallize with larger CF_2 groups adjacent to smaller CH_2 units on an adjacent chain.[5] This interpenetration gives rise to high modulus. In fact, PVDF has the highest flexural modulus of all fluoropolymers (see below). The above alternating groups create a dipole that renders the polymer soluble in highly polar solvents, such as dimethylformamide, tetrahydrofurane, acetone, and esters. Other consequences of this structure are a high dielectric constant and high dielectric loss factor and piezoelectric behavior under certain conditions. The shielding effect of the fluorine atoms adjacent to the CH_2 groups provides the polymer with a good chemical resistance and thermal stability.

PCTFE has better mechanical properties than PTFE because the presence of the chlorine atom in the molecule promotes the attractive forces between molecular chains. It also exhibits greater hardness, tensile strength, and considerably higher resistance to cold flow than PTFE. Since the chlorine atom has a greater atomic radius than fluorine, it hinders the close packing possible in PTFE, which results in a lower melting point and reduced propensity of the polymer to crystallize.[7] The chlorine atom present in **ECTFE**, a copolymer of ethylene and CTFE, has a similar effect on the properties of the polymer.

3.1.1.1 Mechanical Properties

Mechanical properties of fluoroplastics can be ranked into two categories based on whether the polymers are fully fluorinated or contain hydrogen atoms in their structures. Generally, the fluoroplastics with hydrogen in their structure have about 1.5 times the strength of fully fluorinated polymers and are about twice as stiff. Fully fluorinated polymers, on the other hand, exhibit higher maximum service temperature and greater elongation (see Figures 3.2 and 3.3).[8,9]

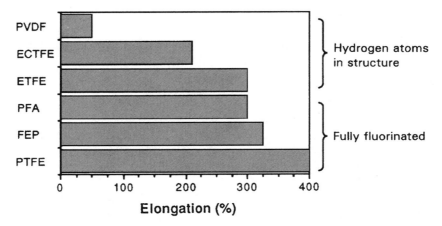

FIGURE 3.2 Elongation values from commercial fluoropolymers (ASTM D638). (From Scheirs, J., in *Modern Fluoropolymers,* Scheirs, J., Ed., John Wiley & Sons, New York, 1997. With permission.)

PVDF has one of the highest flexural moduli among the fluoropolymers (Figure 3.4).[9] Its high modulus can be intentionally reduced by copolymerization with HFP (typically less than 15%). Such lower-modulus copolymers have increased impact strength and elongation. **ECTFE** and **ETFE** also possess relatively high moduli due to interchain attractive forces. **PTFE, FEP,** and **PFA** display low stiffness (despite the rigidity of their molecular chains) because of their very low intermolecular attractive forces.[9]

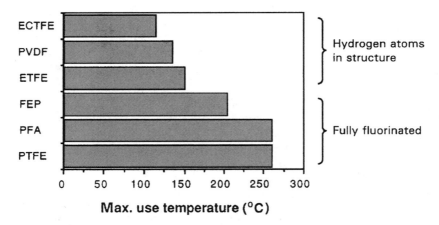

FIGURE 3.3 Maximum service temperatures for commercial fluoropolymers (UL-746B). (From Scheirs, J., in *Modern Fluoropolymers,* Scheirs, J., Ed., John Wiley & Sons, New York, 1997. With permission.)

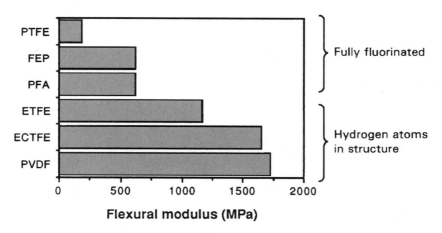

FIGURE 3.4 Flexural modulus values (ASTM D790). (From Scheirs, J., in *Modern Fluoropolymers,* Scheirs, J., Ed., John Wiley & Sons, New York, 1997. With permission.)

3.1.1.2 Optical Properties

FEP and **PFA** despite being melt-processible are crystalline (between 50 and 70%). The crystallinity results in poor optical properties (low clarity) and a very poor solubility in organic solvents. The latter makes the preparation of thin optical coatings exceedingly difficult.[10] **TEFLON AF**, an amorphous fluoropolymer, contains in its molecule a bulky dioxole ring, which hinders crystallization. As a result, the polymer has an exceptionally high clarity and excellent optical properties. Its refractive index is the lowest of any plastic.[11]

3.1.2 FLUOROELASTOMERS

Fluoroelastomers are for the most part based on the combination of vinylidene fluoride (VDF) with other monomers, which disrupt the high crystallinity typical for the PVDF homopolymer. The properties of the resulting elastomeric materials are determined by the short VDF sequences and low or negligible crystallinity.

Elastomers based on VDF and TFE–VDF–HFP consist of fine particles 16 to 30 nm in diameter in contrast to PTFE which has a rodlike microstructure in which the elementary fibrils are approximately 6 nm wide and the molecular chains are all extended.[12] For example, the properties of a VDF–HFP elastomers such as their resilience and flexibility can be related to spherical domains with diameter approximately 25 nm that are interconnected.[10] The diameter of these particles was found to be proportional to the molecular weight of the elastomer.[12]

3.2 PROPERTIES OF INDIVIDUAL COMMERCIAL FLUOROPOLYMERS

As shown in the previous section, many of the fundamental properties of the polymers depend on their structure, mainly on the nature of monomeric units composing them. This section will concentrate on the specific properties of individual fluoropolymers, more specifically fluoroplastics, and how they relate to their utility in practical applications. The properties of fluoroelastomers are discussed in Chapter 5.

3.2.1 POLYTETRAFLUOROETHYLENE (PTFE)

3.2.1.1 Molecular Weight

Molecular weight of standard PTFE is rather high, in the range 1 to 5×10^6.[13] Such a high value is the main reason for the extremely high melt viscosity, which is about 1 million times higher than that of most polymers (see Section 3.1.1) and consequently too high for melt-processing methods used in the fabrication of common polymers. However, this high melt viscosity is also a reason why PTFE has an exceptionally high continuous service temperature of 260°C (500°F). Molecular weight also affects the crystallization rate (decreases with increasing molecular weight)[14] and specific gravity. So-called standard specific gravity (SSG) is calculated from the number–average molecular weight (M_n) using the mathematical expression below[15]:

$$SSG = 2.612 - 0.058 \log_{10} M_n$$

3.2.1.2 Molecular Conformation

The molecules of PTFE are very long and unbranched. Consequently, the virgin polymer, i.e., the powder produced by polymerization, is highly crystalline with values of degree of crystallinity of 92 to 98%.[16] The CF_2 groups are along the polymer chain and the whole chain twists into a helix as in a length of a rope; the fluorine atoms are simply too large to allow a planar zigzag conformation, so the carbon chain twists to accommodate them.[17]

3.2.1.3 Crystallinity and Melting Behavior

The initial high degree of crystallinity, reported to be well over 90%, can never be completely recovered after melting (i.e., sintering), presumably because of entanglements and other impediments caused by the extremely high molecular weight.[18] However, it has been established that rapidly cooled PTFE, although lower in the degree of crystallinity, has the same molecular conformation and basic crystalline structure as slowly cooled PTFE.[19]

As pointed out earlier, the fluorine atoms are too large to allow planar zigzag structure, which confers rigidity on the polymer.[20] The PTFE molecule has a regular folded structure, which produces a laminar crystal.[16]

The true densities of crystalline and amorphous PTFE differ considerably, and 100% crystalline PTFE densities of 2.347 at 0°C (32°F) and 2.302 at 25°C (77°F) were calculated from X-ray crystallographic data.[21] The density decrease of about 2% between these temperatures includes the decrease of approximately 1% due to the transition at 19°C (66°F), which results from a slight uncoiling of the helical conformation of molecules on heating through the transition. By contrast, the density of amorphous PTFE is not affected by the transition at 19°C and values

TABLE 3.2
Transitions in Polytetrafluoroethylene

Type of Transition	Temperature, °C	Region Affected	Technique Used
First order	19	Crystalline, angular displacement causing disorder	Thermal methods, X-ray, NMR*
	30	Crystalline, crystal disordering	Thermal methods, X-ray, NMR
	90 (80 to 110)	Crystalline	Stress relaxation, Young's modulus, dynamic methods
Second order	−90 (−110 to −73)	Amorphous, onset of rotational motion around C–C bond	Thermal methods, dynamic methods
	−30 (−40 to −15)	Amorphous	Stress relaxation, thermal expansion, dynamic methods
	130 (120 to 140)	Amorphous	Stress relaxation, Young's modulus, dynamic methods

* Nuclear Magnetic Resonance.

Source: Gangal, S. V., in *Kirk-Othmer Encyclopedia of Chemical Technology,* Vol. 11, 3rd ed., 1980. John Wiley & Sons, New York, With permission.

around 2.00 have been reported from extrapolations of specific volume measurements to zero crystallinity.[15]

The density of PTFE undergoes complicated changes during processing and can be monitored by the values of true specific volume. Discontinuity in such data show the transitions at 19 and 30°C (66 and 86°F) and also the very pronounced transition at the crystalline melting point of 327°C (621°F), the latter of which is due to the destruction of crystallinity.[22] The melting of the polymer is accompanied by a volume increase of approximately 30%.[23] The coefficient of linear expansion of PTFE has been determined at temperatures ranging from −190 to 300°C (−310 to 572°F).[24]

Effects of structural changes on properties, such as specific heat, specific volume, and/or dynamic mechanical and electrical properties, are observed at various temperatures. A number of transitions were observed by various investigators; their interpretation and the modes of identification are listed in Table 3.2.

Besides the transition at the melting point, the transition at 19°C is of great consequence because it occurs around ambient temperature and significantly affects the product behavior. Above 19°C, the triclinic pattern changes to a hexagonal unit cell. Around 19°C, slight untwisting of the molecule from a 180° twist per 13 CF_2 groups to a 180° per 15 CF_2 groups occurs. At the first-order transition at 30°C, the hexagonal unit disappears and the rodlike hexagonal packing of the chains in the lateral direction is retained.[25] Below 19°C, there is almost a perfect three-dimensional order, between 19 and 30°C the chain segments are disordered, and above 30°C, the preferred crystallographic direction is lost and the molecular segments oscillate above their long axes with a random angular orientation of the lattice.[26,27] PTFE transitions occur at specific combinations of temperatures and mechanical or electrical vibrations. As dielectric relaxations, they can cause wide fluctuations in the values of dissipation factor (see Section 3.2.1.7).

3.2.1.4 Mechanical Properties

The mechanical properties of PTFE at room temperature are similar to those of medium-density polyethylene, i.e., relatively soft with high elongation, and remaining useful over a wide range of temperatures, from cryogenic (just above absolute zero) to 260°C (500°F) its recommended upper use temperature.[28] Stress–strain curves are strongly affected by the temperature; however, even at 260°C (500°F) the tensile strength is about 6.5 MPa (942 psi).[29]

Under a sustained load, PTFE will creep (exhibit cold flow), which imposes limitations on PTFE in such applications as gasket material between bolted flange faces.[29] This tendency can be greatly reduced by the addition of mineral fillers, such as chopped glass fibers or bronze or graphite particles. These fillers also improve its wear resistance, but do not have any significant effect on its tensile strength.[29] Fillers can improve impact strength of the polymer significantly, but reduce its elongation.[31]

In general, mechanical properties of PTFE depend on processing variables, for example, preforming pressure, sintering temperature and time, cooling rate, and the degree of crystallinity. Some properties, such as flexibility at low temperatures, coefficient of friction, and stability at high temperature, are relatively independent of the conditions during fabrication. Flex life, stiffness, impact strength, resilience, and permeability depend greatly on molding and sintering conditions.[32] A summary of mechanical properties is given in Table 3.3.

3.2.1.5 Surface Properties

The surface of PTFE material is smooth and slippery. It is considered to be very low energy surface with γ_c = 18.5 dyne/cm (mN/m)[33] and can be, therefore, completely wetted by liquids with surface tensions below 18 mN/m, for example, solutions of perfluorocarbon acids in water.[34] The PTFE surface can be treated by alkali metals to improve this wettability and consequently the adhesion to other substrates,[35] but this increases its coefficient of friction.[36]

3.2.1.6 Absorption and Permeation

Because of the high chemical inertness of PTFE to the majority of industrial chemicals and solvents and its low wettability, it absorbs only small amounts of liquids at ambient temperatures and atmospheric pressure.[37]

Gases and vapors diffuse through PTFE much more slowly than through most other polymers. The higher the degree of crystallinity, the lower the rate of permeation. Voids greater than molecular size increase the permeability. Thus, it can be controlled by molding PTFE articles to low porosity and high density. Optimum density for that is 2.16 to 2.195.[37] Permeability increases with temperature due to an increase in activity of the solvent molecules and the increase in vapor pressure of the liquids. Swelling of PTFE resin and films in any liquid is very low.

3.2.1.7 Electrical Properties

The *dielectric constant* of polytetrafluoroethylene is 2.1 and remains constant within the temperature range from –40 to 250°C (–40 to 482°F) within the frequency range

TABLE 3.3
Typical Mechanical Properties of PTFE Resins

Property	Granular Resin	Fine Powder	ASTM Method
Tensile strength at 23°C, MPa[a]	7–28	17.5–24.5	D 638
Elongation at 23°C, %	100–200	300–600	D 638
Flexural strength at 23°C, MPa[a]	Does not break		D 790
Flexural modulus at 23°C, MPa[a]	350–630	280–630	D 747
Impact strength, J/m,[b] at 21°C	106.7		D 256
24°C	160		
77°C	>320		
Hardness, Durometer, D	50–65	50–65	D 1706
Compressive stress, MPa[b]			
At 1% deformation at 23°C	4.2		D 695
At 1% offset at 23°C	7.0		D 695
Coefficient of linear thermal expansion per °C, 23-60°C	12×10^{-5}		D 696
Thermal conductivity, 4.6 mm, W/(m · K)	0.24		Cenco-Fitch
Deformation under load, %			
26°C, 6.86 MPa,[a] 24 h			
26°C, 13.72 MPa,[a] 24 h	15	2.4	D 621
Water absorption	<0.01	<0.01	D 570
Flammability	Nonflammable		D 635
Static coefficient of friction against polished steel	0.05–0.08		

[a] To convert MPa to psi, multiply by 145
[b] To convert J/m to lbf.ft/in., divide by 53.38.

Source: Mechanical Design Data Bulletin (DuPont).

from 5 Hz to 10 GHz. It changes somewhat, however, with density and factors that affect density. The dielectric constant was found not to change over 2 to 3 years of measurements.[38]

The *dissipation factor* is affected by the frequency, temperature, crystallinity, and void content of the fabricated structure. At certain temperatures the crystalline and amorphous regions become resonant. Because of the molecular vibrations, the applied electrical energy is lost by internal friction within the polymer and this leads to an increase in dissipation factor. The dissipation factor peaks for these resins correspond to well-defined transitions.[38]

The *volume resistivity* of polytetrafluoroethylene remains unchanged even after a prolonged soaking in water, because it does not absorb water.

The *surface arc-resistance* of PTFE resins is high and is not affected by heat aging. They do not track or form a carbonized path when subjected to a surface arc in air.[39]

The electrical properties of PTFE are summarized in Table 3.4.

TABLE 3.4
Electrical Properties of Polytetrafluoroethylene

Property	Granular	Fine Powder	ASTM Method
Dielectric strength, short time, 2 mm, V/mm	23,600	23,600	D 149
Surface arc-resistance, s	>300	>300	D 495
Volume resistivity, ohm-cm	>10^{18}	>10^{18}	D 257
Surface resistivity, ohm/sq	>10^{16}		D 257
Dielectric constant, at 60 to 2×10^9 Hz	2.1	2.1	D 150
Dissipation factor, at 60 to 2×10^9 Hz	0.0003		D 150

Source: Mechanical Design Data Bulletin (DuPont).

3.2.2   COPOLYMERS OF TETRAFLUOROETHYLENE AND HEXAFLUOROPROPYLENE (FEP)

The copolymerization of tetrafluoroethylene (TFE) with hexafluoropropylene (HFP) introduces a branched structure and results in the reduction of the melting point from the original 325°C (617°F) to about 260°C (500°F). Another consequence of that is a significant reduction of crystallinity, which may vary between 70% for virgin polymer and 30 to 50% for molded parts,[40] depending on processing conditions, mainly the cooling rate after melting. The melting point is the only first-order transition observed in FEP. Melting increases the volume by 8%.[41]

3.2.2.1   Mechanical Properties

Mechanical properties of FEP are in general similar to those of PTFE with the exception of the continuous service temperature, 204°C (400°F) as compared with that of PTFE (260°C or 500°F). Unlike PTFE, FEP does not exhibit a marked volume change at room temperature because it is lacking the first-order transition at 19°C. FEP resins are useful above −267°C (−449°F) and are highly flexible above −79°C (−110°F).[42]

The static *friction* decreases with increasing load and the static coefficient of friction is lower than the dynamic coefficient.[43] The coefficients of friction are independent of fabrication conditions.

Perfluorinated ethylene-propylene tends to *creep* and this has to be considered when designing parts for service under continuous stress. Creep can be reduced significantly by the use of suitable fillers, such as glass fibers or graphite. Graphite, bronze, and glass fibers also improve wear resistance and stiffness of the resin. The choice of fillers improving properties of FEP and their amounts are limited, however, because of processing difficulties of such mixtures.[44]

FEP resins have a very *low energy surface* and are, therefore, very difficult to wet. Surface preparation for improved wetting and bonding of FEP can be done by a solution of sodium in liquid ammonia or naphthalenylsodium in tetrahydrofurane,[44]

TABLE 3.5
Electrical Properties of FEP Copolymer, Typical Values

Property	Value	ASTM Method
Dielectric strength short time, 0.2 cm thickness, V/m	23.6	D 149
Surface arc-resistance, s	>300	D 495
Volume resistivity, ohm-cm	>10^{18}	D 257
Dielectric constant, 60 Hz to 2 GHz	2.1	D 150
Dissipation factor, 60 Hz to 2 GHz	$(2-12) \times 10^{-4}$	D 150
Surface resistivity, ohm /sq	10^{16}	D 257

Source: Teflon Fluorocarbon Resins, Mechanical Design Data, 2nd ed. DuPont (1965).

by the exposure to corona discharge[45] or to amines at elevated temperatures in an oxidizing atmosphere.[46]

FEP resins exhibit a very good *vibration damping* at sonic and ultrasonic frequencies. However, to use this property for welding of parts, the thickness of the resin must be sufficient to absorb the energy produced.[44]

3.2.2.2   Electrical Properties

Perfluorinated ethylene-propylene has outstanding electrical properties, practically identical to those of PTFE within its recommended service temperature. Its volume resistivity remains unchanged even after prolonged soaking in water.

The dielectric constant of FEP is constant at lower frequencies, but at frequencies 100 MHz and higher, it drops slightly with increasing frequency. Its dissipation factor has several peaks as a function of temperature and frequency. The magnitude of the dissipation peak is greater for FEP than for PTFE because the FEP structure is less symmetrical. The dielectric strength is high and unaffected by heat aging at 200°C (392°F).[47] The electrical properties of FEP are listed in Table 3.5.

3.2.2.3   Chemical Properties

FEP resists most chemicals and solvents, even at elevated temperatures and pressures. Acid and bases are not absorbed at 200°C (392°F) and exposures of 1 year. Organic solvents are absorbed only a little, typically 1% or less, even at elevated temperatures and long exposure times. The absorption does not affect the resin and its properties and is completely reversible. The only chemicals reacting with FEP resins are fluorine, molten alkali metal, and molten sodium hydroxide.[48]

Gases and vapors permeate FEP at a rate that is lower than for most plastics. It occurs only by molecular diffusion, because the polymer was melt-processed. Because of the low permeability and chemical inertness, FEP is widely used in the chemical industry. Its permeation characteristics are similar to those of PTFE with some advantage because of the absence of microporosity often present in PTFE. For the permeation through FEP films an inverse relationship between permeability and film thickness applies.[49]

3.2.2.4 Optical Properties

FEP films transmit more UV, visible, and infrared radiation than ordinary window glass. They are considerably more transparent to the infrared and UV spectra than glass. The refractive index of FEP films is in the range 1.341 to 1.347.[50]

3.2.2.5 Other Properties

Products made from FEP resins resist the effects of weather, extreme heat, and UV radiation. This subject is covered in more detail in Chapter 7.

3.2.3 COPOLYMERS OF TETRAFLUOROETHYLENE AND PERFLUOROALKYLETHERS (PFA AND MFA)

Because of the high bond strength between carbon, fluorine, and oxygen atoms, PFA and MFA exhibit nearly the same unique properties as PTFE at temperatures ranging from extremely low to extremely high. Since they can be relatively easily processed by conventional methods for thermoplastics into film and sheets without microporosity, they have distinct advantage over PTFE in certain applications, such as corrosion protection and antistick coatings.[51] These polymers are semicrystalline and the degree of crystallinity depends on the fabrication conditions, particularly on the cooling rate. General properties of PFA and MFA are listed and compared with FEP in Table 3.6.

3.2.3.1 Physical and Mechanical Properties

Commercial grades of PFA have a melting point in the range from 300 to 315°C (572 to 599°F) depending on the content of PPVE. The degree of crystallinity is typically 60%.[52]

There is only one first-order transition at –5°C (23°F) and two second-order transitions, one at 85°C (185°F) and one at –90°C (–130°F).[52]

TABLE 3.6
General Properties of Perfluorinated Melt Processable Polymers

General Properties	Method (ASTM)	Unit	PFA	MFA	FEP
Specific gravity	D 792	g/cm³	2.12–2.17	2.12–2.17	2.12–2.17
Melting temperature	D 2116	°C	300–310	280–290	260–270
Coefficient of linear thermal expansion	E 831	1/K 10⁻⁵	12–20	12–20	12–20
Specific heat	—	kJ/kg K	1.0	1.1	1.2
Thermal conductivity	D 696	W/K · m	0.19	0.19	0.19
Flammablility	(UL 94)		V–O	V–O	V–O
Oxygen index	D 2863	%	>95	>95	>95
Hardness Shore D	D 2240		55–60	55–60	55–60
Friction coefficient (on steel)	—		0.2	0.2	0.3
Water absorption	D570	%	<0.03	<0.03	<0.01

Source: Pozzoli, M., Vita, G., and Arcella, V., in *Modern Fluoropolymers,* Scheirs, J., Ed., John Wiley & Sons, New York, 1997. With permission.

In general, mechanical properties of PFA are very similar to those of PTFE within the range from −200 to +250°C (−328 to +482°F). The mechanical properties of PFA and MFA at room temperature are practically identical; differences become obvious only at elevated temperatures, because of the lower melting point of MFA.

In contrast to PTFE with measurable void content, the melt-processed PFA is intrinsically void free. As a result, lower permeation coefficients should result because permeation occurs by molecular diffusion. This is indeed the case, but the effect levels off at higher temperatures.[53]

The most remarkable difference between PTFE and PFA is the considerably lower resistance to deformation under load (cold flow) of the latter. In fact, addition of even minute amounts of PFA to PTFE improves its resistance to cold flow[52] (see also Section 8.7).

3.2.3.2 Electrical Properties

PFA and MFA exhibit considerably better electrical properties than most traditional plastics. In comparison with the partially fluorinated polymers, they are only slightly affected by temperature up to their maximum service temperature.[54]

The dielectric constant remains at 2.04 over a wide range of temperature and frequencies (from 100 Hz to 1 GHz). The dissipation factor at low frequencies (from 10 Hz to 10 kHz) decreases with increasing frequency and decreasing temperature. In the range from 10 kHz to 1 MHz, temperature and frequency have little effect; while above 1 MHz the dissipation factor increases with the frequency.[55]

3.2.3.3 Optical Properties

Generally, fluorocarbon films exhibit high transmittance in the UV, visible, and infrared regions of the spectrum. This property depends on the degree of crystallinity and the crystal morphology in the polymer. For example, 0.025-mm (0.001-in.)-thick PFA film transmits more than 90% of visible light (wavelength 400 to 700 nm). A 0.2-mm (0.008-in.)-thick MFA film was found to have a high transmittance in the UV region (wavelength 200 to 400 nm). The refractive indexes of these films are close to 1.3.[56]

3.2.3.4 Chemical Properties

PFA and MFA have an outstanding chemical resistance even at elevated temperatures. They are resistant to strong mineral acids, inorganic bases, and inorganic oxidizing agents and to most of the organic compounds and their mixtures common in the chemical industry. However, they react with fluorine and molten alkali.[55]

Elemental sodium, as well as other alkali metals, reacts with perfluorocarbon polymers by removing fluorine from them. This reaction has a practical application for improving surface wettability and adhesive bonding of perfluorocarbon polymers to other substrates.[57]

The absorption of water and solvents by perfluoropolymers is in general very low.[57] Permeability is closely related to absorption and depends on temperature, pressure, and the degree of crystallinity. Since these resins are melt-processed, they are usually free of voids and, therefore, exhibit much lower permeability than PTFE. Permeation through PFA occurs via molecular diffusion.[58]

3.2.4 COPOLYMERS OF ETHYLENE AND TETRAFLUOROETHYLENE (ETFE)

Copolymers of ethylene and tetrafluoroethylene (ETFE) essentially comprise alternating ethylene and TFE units. They have an excellent balance of physical, chemical, mechanical, and electrical properties, are easily fabricated by melt-processing techniques, but have found little commercial utility, because they exhibit a poor resistance to cracking at elevated temperatures.[59] Incorporation of certain termonomers, so-called modifiers, in amounts 1 to 10 mol% markedly improves the cracking resistance, while maintaining the desirable properties of the copolymer.[60,61]

ETFE resins are manufactured by several companies under different tradenames: AG Fluoropolymers (Aflon®), Ausimont (Halon ET®), Daikin (Neoflon ET®), DuPont (Tefzel®), and Dyneon (Dyneon ETFE™).

3.2.4.1 Structure and Related Properties

The carbon chain is in a planar zigzag orientation and forms an orthorhombic lattice with interpenetration of adjacent chains.[61] As a result of this structure, ETFE has an exceptionally low creep, high tensile strength, and high modulus compared to other thermoplastic fluoropolymers. Interchain forces hold this matrix until the alpha transition occurs at about 110°C (230°F), where the physical properties of ETFE begin to decline and more closely resemble perfluoropolymers properties at the same temperature. Other transitions occur at –120°C (–184°F) (gamma) and about –25°C (–13°F) (beta).[62]

The monomer ratio in the copolymer has an effect on the polymer structure and properties, mainly on the degree of crystallinity and on the melting point. As normally produced, ETFE has about 88% of alternating sequences and a melting point of 270°C (518°F).[63]

3.2.4.2 Mechanical, Chemical, and Other Properties

ETFE exhibits exceptional toughness and abrasion resistance over a wide temperature range and a good combination of high tensile strength, high impact strength, flex and creep resistance, combining mechanical properties of hydrocarbon engineering polymers with the chemical and thermal resistance of perfluoropolymers. Friction and wear properties are good and can be improved by incorporating fillers such as fiberglass or bronze powders. Fillers also improve creep resistance and increase the softening temperature.[61]

Continuous upper service temperature of commercial ETFE is 150°C (302°F).[64] Physical strength can be maintained at even higher temperatures when the polymer is cross-linked by peroxide or ionizing radiation.[65] Highly cross-linked resins can be subjected to temperatures up to 240°C (464°F) for short periods of time.[64]

ETFE exhibits excellent *dielectric properties*. Its dielectric constant is low and essentially independent of frequency. The dissipation factor is low, but increases with frequency and can be also increased by cross-linking. Dielectric strength and resistivity are high and are unaffected by water. Irradiation and cross-linking increase dielectric loss.[64]

Modified ETFE has excellent resistance to most common solvents and chemicals.[66] It is not hydrolyzed by boiling water and weight gain is less than 0.03% in water at room temperature. Strong oxidizing acids, such as nitric acid, and some organic bases cause depolymerization at high concentrations and high temperatures.[64] ETFE is also an excellent barrier to hydrocarbons and oxygenated components of automotive fuels.[64]

ETFE resins have a good thermal stability; however, for high-temperature applications thermal stabilizers are often added.[67] A wide variety of compounds, mostly metal salts, such as copper oxides and halides, aluminum oxide, and calcium salts, will act as sacrificial sites for oxidation. Addition of certain salts can alter the decomposition from oligomer formation to dehydrofluorination. Iron and other transition metal salts accelerate the dehydrofluorination. Hydrofluoric acid itself destabilizes ETFE at elevated temperatures and the degradation becomes self-accelerating. For that reason, extrusion temperatures higher than 380°C (716°F) should be avoided.[68]

Ionizing radiation at lower levels affects ETFE polymers very little; therefore, they are being used for wire coatings and molded parts in the nuclear energy industry.[68] More details are in Chapter 7.

ETFE resins do not support combustion in air and have typical limiting oxygen index (LOI) about 30 to 31. LOI depends on monomer ratio in the polymer and it increases gradually as the fluorocarbon content is increased to the alternating composition and then increases more rapidly to the LOI values for PTFE.[68]

ETFE resins are very often compounded with varied ingredients, such as glass fibers and bronze powder, to attain certain mechanical properties. For example, glass fibers are added at 25 to 35 wt% levels to increase modulus and improve wear and friction characteristics. By adding 25% glass fibers, for example, the dynamic coefficient of friction is reduced from about 0.5 to about 0.3.[69]

3.2.5 POLYVINYLIDENE FLUORIDE (PVDF)

PVDF homopolymer is a semicrystalline polymer. Its degree of crystallinity can vary from 35 to more than 70%, depending on the method of preparation and thermomechanical history.[70] The degree of crystallinity greatly affects the toughness and mechanical strength as well as the impact resistance of the polymer. Other major factors influencing the properties of PVDF are molecular weight, molecular weight distribution, and extent of irregularities along the polymer chain and the crystalline form. Similar to other linear polyolefins, crystalline forms of polyvinylidene fluoride involve lamellar and spherulitic forms. The differences in the size and distribution of the domains as well as the kinetics of crystal growth are related to the method of polymerization.[70]

PVDF exhibits a complex crystalline polymorphism, which cannot be found in other known synthetic polymers. There are a total of four distinct crystalline forms: alpha, beta, gamma, and delta. These are present in different proportions in the material, depending on a variety of factors that affect the development of the crystalline structure, such as pressure, intensity of the electric field, controlled melt crystallization, precipitation from different solvents, or seeding crystallization (e.g., surfactants). The alpha and beta forms are most common in practical situations. Generally, the alpha form is generated in normal melt processing; the beta form develops under mechanical deformation of melt-fabricated specimens. The gamma form arises under special circumstances, and the delta form is obtained by distortion of one of the phases under high electrical fields.[70] The density of PVDF in the alpha crystal form is 1.98 g/cm^3; the density of amorphous PVDF is 1.68 g/cm^3. Thus, the typical density of commercial products in the range from 1.75 to 1.78 g/cm^3 reflects a degree of crystallinity around 40%.

The structure of polyvinylidene fluoride chain, namely, alternating CH$_2$ and CF$_2$ groups, has an effect on its properties which combine some of the best performance characteristics of both polyethylene (–CH$_2$–CH$_2$–)$_n$ and polytetrafluoroethylene (–CF$_2$–CF$_2$–)$_n$. Certain commercial grades of PVDF are copolymers of VDF with small amounts (typically less than 6%) of other fluorinated monomers, such as HFP, CTFE, and TFE. These exhibit somewhat different properties than the homopolymer.

3.2.5.1 Mechanical Properties

PVDF exhibits excellent mechanical properties (Table 3.7), and when compared with perfluorinated polymers, it has much higher resistance to elastic deformation under load (creep), much longer life in repeated flexing, and improved fatigue resistance.[71,72] Its mechanical strength can be greatly increased by orientation.[70] Some additives, such as glass spheres and carbon fibers,[73] increase the strength of the base polymer.

3.2.5.2 Electrical Properties

Typical values of electrical properties of the homopolymer without additives and treatments are in the Table 3.8. The values can be substantially changed by the type of cooling and post-treatments, which determine the morphological state of the polymer. Dielectric constants as high as 17 have been measured on oriented samples that have been subjected to high electrical fields (poled) under various conditions to orient polar crystalline form.[74]

The unique dielectric properties and polymorphism of PVDF are the source of its high piezoelectric and pyroelectric activity.[75] The relationship between ferroelectric behavior, which includes piezoelectric and pyroelectric phenomena and other electrical properties of the polymorphs of polyvinylidene fluoride, is discussed in Reference 76.

The structure yielding a high dielectric constant and a complex polymorphism also exhibits a high dielectric loss factor. This excludes PVDF from applications as an insulator for conductors of high frequency currents since the insulation could heat up and possibly even melt. On the other hand, because of that, PVDF can be readily melted by radio frequency or dielectric heating and this can be utilized for certain fabrication processes or joining.[77] High-energy radiation cross-links polyvinylidene fluoride and the result is the enhancement of mechanical properties (see

TABLE 3.7
Properties of Polyvinylidene Fluoride

Properties	Value or Description
Clarity	Transparent to translucent
Melting point, crystalline, °C	155–192
Specific gravity	1.75–1.80
Refractive index n_D^{25}	1.42
Mold shrinkage, average, %	2–3
Color possibilities	Unlimited
Machining qualities	Excellent
Flammability	Self-extinguishing, nondripping
Tensile strength, MPa[a]	
At 25°C	42–58.5
At 100°C	34.5
Elongation, %	
At 25°C	50–300
At 100°C	200–500
Yield point, MPa[a]	
At 25°C	38–52
At 100°C	17
Creep, at 13.79 MPa[a] and 25°C for 10,000 h, %	2–4
Compressive strength, at 25°C, MPa[a]	55–90
Modulus of elasticity, at 25°C, GPa[b]	
In tension	1.0–2.3
In flexure	1.1–2.5
In compression	1.0–2.3
Izod impact, at 25°C, J/m[c]	
Notched	75–235
Unnotched	700–2300
Durometer hardness, Shore, D scale	77–80
Heat-distortion temperature, °C	
At 0.455 MPa[a]	140–168
At 1.82 MPa[a]	80–128
Abrasion resistance, Taber CS-17, 0.5 kg load, mg/1000 cycles	17.6
Coefficient of sliding friction to steel	0.14–0.17
Thermal coefficient of linear expansion, per °C	$0.7–1.5 \times 10^{-4}$
Thermal conductivity, at 25–160°C, W/(m · K)	0.17–0.19
Specific heat (J/(kg · K)[d]	1255–1425
Thermal degradation temperature, °C	390
Low temperature embrittlement, °C	–60
Water absorption, %	0.04
Moisture vapor permeability, for 1 mm thickness, g/(24 h) (m²)	2.5×10^{-2}
Radiation resistance (^{60}CO), MGy[e,f]	10–12

[a] To convert MPa to psi, multiply by 145.

[b] To convert GPa to psi, multiply by 145,000.

[c] To convert J/m to ftlbf/in., divide by 53.38.

[d] To convert J to cal, divide by 4.184.

[e] Retains tensile strength of about 85% of its original value.

[f] To convert Gy to rad, multiply by 100.

Source: Dohany, J. E. and Humphrey, J. S., in *Encyclopedia of Polymer Science and Technology,* Vol. 17, Mark, H. F. and Kroschwitz, J. I., Eds., John Wiley & Sons, New York, 1989.

TABLE 3.8
Electrical Properties of Poly(vinylidene Fluoride) Homopolymer

Property	60 Hz	10^3 Hz	10^6 Hz	10^9 Hz
Dielectric constant at 25°C	9–10	8–9	8–9	3–4
Dissipation factor	0.03–0.05	0.005–0.02	0.03–0.05	0.09–0.11
Volume resistivity, ohm · m				2×10^{12}
Dielectric strength, short time, V/2.54 × 10^{-5} m				
0.003175 m thickness				260
0.000203 m thickness				1300

Source: Dohany, J. E. and Humphrey, J. S., in *Encyclopedia of Polymer Science and Technology,* Vol. 17, Mark, H. F. and Kroschwitz, J. I., Eds., John Wiley & Sons, New York, 1989.

Section 7.2.2). This feature makes it unique among vinylidene polymers, which typically are degraded by high-energy radiation.[74]

3.2.5.3 Chemical Properties

Polyvinylidene fluoride exhibits an excellent resistance to most inorganic acids, weak bases, and halogens, oxidizing agents even at elevated temperatures, and to aliphatic, aromatic, and chlorinated solvents. Strong bases, amines, esters, and ketones cause its swelling, softening, and dissolution, depending on conditions.[78] Certain esters and ketones can act as latent solvents for PVDF in dispersions. Such systems solvate the polymer as the temperature is raised during the fusion of the coating, resulting in a cohesive film.[79]

PVDF is among the few semicrystalline polymers that exhibit thermodynamic compatibility with other polymers,[80] in particular with acrylic or methacrylic resins.[81] The morphology, properties, and performance of these blends depend on the structure and composition of the additive polymer, as well as on the particular PVDF resin. These aspects have been studied and are reported in some detail in Reference 82. For example, polyethyl acrylate is miscible with polyvinylidene fluoride, but polyisopropyl acrylate and homologues are not. Strong dipolar interactions are important to achieve miscibility with PVDF, as suggested by the observation that polyvinyl fluoride is incompatible with polyvinylidene fluoride.[83]

3.2.6 POLYCHLOROTRIFLUOROETHYLENE (PCTFE)

The inclusion of the relatively large chlorine into the polymeric chain reduces the tendency to crystallize. Commercially available grades include a homopolymer, which is mainly used for special applications, and copolymers with small amounts (less than 5%) of vinylidene fluoride.[84] The products are supplied as powder, pellets, pellets containing 15% glass fiber, and dispersions. Low-molecular-weight polymer is available as oil or grease. The oil is used to plasticize PCTFE.[85]

3.2.6.1 Thermal Properties

PCTFE is highly suitable for applications at extremely low temperatures; however, at elevated temperatures it is inferior to other fluoropolymers with the exception of

PVDF. It has a relatively low melting point of 211°C (412°F), and it exhibits thermally induced crystallization at temperatures below its melting point, which results in brittleness.[84]

3.2.6.2 Mechanical, Chemical, and Other Properties

As long as thermally induced crystallization (see above) is avoided, PCTFE exhibits excellent mechanical properties. It also has an excellent resistance to creep.[83] The addition of glass fibers (typically 15%) improves high-temperature properties and increases hardness, but also increases brittleness.[86]

PCTFE has an excellent chemical resistance, especially the resistance to most very harsh environments, particularly to strong oxidizing agents, such as fuming oxidizing acids, liquid oxygen, and ozone, and to sunlight. PCTFE alone has a good resistance to ionizing radiation that is further improved by copolymerization with small amounts of VDF (see above).[86] The homopolymers and copolymers with VDF exhibit outstanding barrier properties.[87]

PCTFE does not absorb visible light, and it is possible to produce optically clear sheets and parts up to 3.2 mm (1/8 in.) thick by quenching from melt.[86,87]

The disadvantage of PCTFE is that it is attacked by many organic materials and has a low thermal stability in the molten state. The latter requires great care during processing to maintain high enough molecular weight necessary for good mechanical properties of the fabricated parts.[86]

3.2.7 COPOLYMER OF ETHYLENE AND CHLOROTRIFLUOROETHYLENE (ECTFE)

Commercial polymer with an overall CTFE-to-ethylene ratio of 1:1 contains ethylene blocks and CTFE blocks of less than 10 mol% each. The modified copolymers also produced commercially exhibit improved high-temperature stress cracking. Typically, the modified copolymers are less crystalline and have lower melting points.[88] Modifying monomers are hexafluoroisobutylene (HFIB), perfluorohexylethylene, and perfluoropropylvinyl ether (PFPVE).[89]

3.2.7.1 Properties of ECTFE

ECTFE resins are tough, moderately stiff, and creep resistant with service temperatures from −100 to +150°C (−148 to +302°F). The melt temperature depends on the monomer ratio in the polymer and is in the range of 235 to 245°C (455 to 473°F). Its chemical resistance is good and similar to PCTFE. ECTFE, as most fluoropolymers, has an outstanding weathering resistance. It also resists high-energy gamma and beta radiation up to 100 Mrad.

3.2.8 TERPOLYMER OF TETRAFLUOROETHYLENE, HEXAFLUOROPROPYLENE, AND VINYLIDENE FLUORIDE (THV FLUOROPLASTIC)

The driving force for the development of THV Fluoroplastic was the requirement for a fluoropolymer that could be used as a coating for polyester fabrics and provide protection similar to that of PTFE or ETFE in outdoor exposure. An additional requirement was that it could be used with PVC-coated polyester fabric without significantly compromising overall flexibility.[90]

Chemically, THV Fluoroplastic (hereafter referred to as THV) is a terpolymer of tetrafluoroethylene (TFE), hexafluoropropylene (HFP), and vinylidene fluoride (VDF) produced by emulsion polymerization. The resulting dispersion is either processed into powders and pellets or concentrated with emulsifier and supplied in that form to the market.[91] Currently, the manufacturer is Dyneon LLC and there are essentially nine commercial grades (five dry and four aqueous dispersions) available that differ in the monomer ratios and consequently in melting points, chemical resistance, and flexibility.

3.2.8.1   Properties

THV has a unique combination of properties that include relatively low processing temperatures, bondability (to itself and other substrates), high flexibility, excellent clarity, low refractive index, and efficient electron-beam cross-linking.[91] It also exhibits properties associated with fluoroplastics, namely, very good chemical resistance, weatherability, low friction, and low flammability. Typical properties of the dry grades are summarized in Table 3.9 and those of THV in aqueous dispersion form in Table 3.10.

The melting temperatures of the THV commercial products range from 120°C (248°F) for THV-200 to 185°C (365°F) for THV-x610. The lowest melting grade has the lowest chemical resistance and is easily soluble in ketones and ethyl acetate, is the most flexible, and is the easiest to cross-link by electron beam of all grades. The highest melting grade THV-500 has the highest chemical resistance and resistance to permeation.[91]

THV Fluoroplastic can be readily bonded to itself and to many plastics and elastomers and unlike other fluoroplastics does not require surface treatment, such as chemical etching or corona treatment. However, in some cases tie layers are required to achieve a good bonding to other materials.[92]

THV is transparent to a broad band of light (UV to infrared) with an extremely low haze. Its refraction index is very low and depends on the grade[93] (see Table 3.10).

3.2.9   POLYVINYL FLUORIDE

3.2.9.1   General Properties

PVF exhibits excellent resistance to weathering, outstanding mechanical properties, inertness toward a wide variety of chemicals, solvents, and staining agents, excellent hydrolytic stability, and high dielectric strength and dielectric constant.[94]

3.2.9.2   Chemical Properties

Films of polyvinyl fluoride retain their form and strength even when boiled in strong acids and bases. At ordinary temperatures, the film is not affected by many classes of common solvents, including hydrocarbon and chlorinated solvents. It is partially

TABLE 3.9
Typical THV Properties (Nominal Values, Not for Specification Purposes)

Property	ASTM Method	THV 220	THV X 310	THV 415	THV 500	THV X 610
Physical form (A = agglomerate, G = pellet)		A, G	A, G	A, G	A, G	A, G
Specific gravity, g/cm³	D792	1.95	1.97	1.97	1.98	2.04
Melting point, °C	D4591	120	140	155	165	185
Melt index, g/10 min (at 265°C/5kg)	D1238	20	10	15	10	10
Hardness, Shore D	D2240	44	50	53	54	58
Tensile strength (23°C), MPa	D638	20	24	28	28	28
psi		2,900	3,480	4,060	4,060	4,060
Elongation at break, (23°C), %	D638	600	500	500	500	500
Flexural modulus (23°C), MPa	D790	80	100	180	210	490
psi		12,000	14,500	26,000	30,000	71,000
Izod impact strength (23°C, notched), J/m	D256	no break	no break	no break	no break	no break
(−40°C, notched)		no break	no break	no break	no break	no break
(−40°C, unnotched)		no break	no break	no break	no break	no break
Dielectric constant (23°C) @ 1MHz	D150	5.72	5.23	5.02	4.82	4.66
Dissipation factor (23°C) @ 1 MHz	D150	0.14	0.11	0.10	0.10	0.09
Dielectric breakdown strength, 0.25 mm film, kV/mm	D149	62	52	56	48	56
Limiting oxygen index, %	D2863	>65	>65	>65	>75	>75
Thermal glass transition (Tg), °C (DSC)	D3418	5	16	21	26	34
Refractive index, n_D, 100 micron film	—	1.363	1.357	1.357	1.355	1.353
UV-Vis light transmission, %T,	—					
100 micron film, 300 nm		87	92	89	85	82
600 nm		93	93	93	93	93

Source: Dyneon LLC from Dyneon™ Fluorothermoplastics, Product Comparison Guide, Publ. 98-0504-1025-1 (CPI), Issued 4/00. With permission.

TABLE 3.10
Typical THV Properties in Aqueous Dispersion Form (Nominal Values, Not for Specification Purposes)

Property	Test Method	THV 220D	THV 340D	THV 340C	THV 510D
Solids content, %	ISO 12086/ASTMD4441	31	34	50	32
pH	ISO 1148/ASTM E70	2.5	7	9.5	2
Melting point, °C	DIN ISO 3146/ASTM D4591	120	145	145	165
Melt index (at 265°C/5kg)	DIN 53735/ASTM D1238	20	40	40	10
Average particle size, nm	ISO 13321	95	90	90	90
Density, g/cm^3	ASTM D1298	1.21	1.23	1.32	1.21
Viscosity (D = 210 cm^{-1}), mPa.s	DIN 54453	34	20	76	21
Surface active ingredients	—	ionic	ionic	ionic	ionic

Source: Dyneon LLC from *Dyneon™ Fluorothermoplastics, Product Comparison Guide,* Publ. 98-0504-1025-1 (CPI), Issued 4/00. With permission.

soluble in a few highly polar solvents above 149°C (300°F). It is impermeable to greases and oils.[95]

3.2.9.3   Optical Properties

Transparent PVF films are essentially transparent to solar radiation in the near UV, visible, and near-infrared regions of the spectrum.[95]

3.2.9.4   Weathering Performance

Polyvinyl fluoride films exhibit an outstanding resistance to solar degradation. Unsupported transparent PVF films have retained at least 50% of their tensile strength after 10 years in Florida facing south at 45°. Pigmented films properly laminated to a variety of substrates impart a long service life. Most colors exhibit no more than five-NBS-unit (Modified Adams Color Coordinates) color change after 20 years vertical outdoor exposure. Additional protection of various substrates against UV attack can be achieved with UV-absorbing PVF films.[95]

3.2.9.5   Electrical Properties

PVF films exhibit high dielectric constant and a high dielectric strength.[96] Typical electrical properties for standard polyvinyl fluoride films are shown along with its physical properties in Table 3.11.

3.2.9.6   Thermal Stability

The polymer is processed into films routinely at temperatures near or above 204°C (400°F) and for short times as high as 232 to 249°C (450 to 480°F) using ordinary industrial ventilation. At temperatures above 204°C (400°F) or upon prolonged

TABLE 3.11
Typical Physical Properties of PVF Measured on Films

Melting point	185–190°C
Relative density	1.38–1.57
Tensile strength	40–120 MPa
Elongation	115–250%
Tensile modulus	1700–2600 MPa
Impact strength	10–22 kJ/m
Tear strength	174–239 kJ/m
Coefficient of thermal expansion	5×10^{-5} K^{-1}
Dielectric constant, 1 MHz	4.8
Dielectric strength, 0.1 mm film	120–140 kV/mm

Note: To convert MPa to psi, multiply by 145. To convert kJ/m to lb.ft/in, divide by 53380.

Source: Technical Information Bulletin TD-31, DuPont, 1979 and *Technical Information Bulletin TD-1A,* DuPont, 1974.

heating, film discoloration and evolution of small amounts of hydrogen fluoride vapor will occur. The presence of Lewis acids (such as BF_3 complexes) in contact with PVF is known to catalyze the decomposition of the polymer at lower-than-normal temperature. A thorough study of degradation of polyvinyl fluoride films is reported in Reference 97.

PVF films are available in large variety under the trade name TEDLAR® PVF from DuPont Fluoropolymers. Type 1 film has controlled shrinkage for surfacing fiberglass-surfaced polyester panels and truck trailer bodies; Type 2 clear film exhibits high tensile strength and high flex; Type 3, the standard film, is available in clear and pigmented forms. A clear film Type 4 has high elongation and high tear resistance. Type 5 TEDLAR film has been developed for applications where deep draw and texturing are required. Its ultimate elongation is almost twice of that of standard Type 3 film. The thickness of commercially available PVF films ranges from 0.5 to 2.0 mil (12.5 to 50 μm).

TEDLAR films are supplied with different surface characteristics. "A" (one side adherable) and "B" (both sides adherable) surfaces are used with adhesives for bonding to a wide variety of substrates. These surfaces can be bonded with a variety of adhesives, including acrylics, polyesters, epoxies, elastomeric adhesives, and pressure-sensitive mastics. The "S" surface has excellent antistick properties and is being used as a mold-release film for parts made from epoxies, phenolics, elastomers, and other polymeric materials.[94]

REFERENCES

1. Scheirs, J., in *Modern Fluoropolymers* (Scheirs, J., Ed.), John Wiley & Sons, New York, p. 2 (1997).

2. Pozzoli, M., Vita, G., and Arcella, V., in *Modern Fluoropolymers* (Scheirs, J., Ed.), John Wiley & Sons, New York, p. 374 (1997).

3. Koo, G. P., in *Fluoropolymers* (Wall. L. A., Ed.), Wiley-Interscience, New York, p. 508 (1972)

4. Sheratt, S., in *Kirk-Othmer Encyclopedia of Chemical Technology*, Vol.9, John Wiley & Sons, New York, p. 826 (1966).

5. Scheirs, J., in *Modern Fluoropolymers* (Scheirs, J., Ed.), John Wiley & Sons, New York, p. 3 (1997).

6. Kerbow, D. L., in *Modern Fluoropolymers* (Scheirs, J., Ed.), John Wiley & Sons, New York, p. 307 (1997).

7. Saunders, K. J., *Organic Polymer Chemistry*, Chapman & Hall, London, 2nd ed., Chapter 7, p. 149 (1988).

8. Scheirs, J., in *Modern Fluoropolymers* (Scheirs, J., Ed.), John Wiley & Sons, New York, p. 5 (1997).

9. Scheirs, J., in *Modern Fluoropolymers* (Scheirs, J., Ed.), John Wiley & Sons, New York, p. 6 and p. 33 (1997).

10. Scheirs, J., in *Modern Fluoropolymers* (Scheirs, J., Ed.), John Wiley & Sons, New York, p. 7 (1997).

11. Resnick, P. R. and Buck, W. H., Teflon® AF Amorphous Fluoropolymers, in *Modern Fluoropolymers* (Scheirs, J., Ed.) John Wiley & Sons, New York, Chapter 22 (1997).

12. Yamaguchi, S. and Tatemoto, M., Fine structure of fluorine elastomer emulsions, in *Sen'i Gakkaishi* 50, 414 (1994).

13. Sheratt, S., in *Kirk-Othmer Encyclopedia of Chemical Technology*, Vol. 9, John Wiley & Sons, New York, p. 817 (1966).

14. Gangal, S. V., in *Kirk-Othmer Encyclopedia of Chemical Technology*, Vol.11, 3rd ed., John Wiley & Sons, New York, p. 7 (1980).

15. Sperati, A. C. and Starkweather, H. W., *Fortschr. Hochpolym. Forsch.* 2, 465 (1961).

16. Gangal, S. V., in *Kirk-Othmer Encyclopedia of Chemical Technology*, Vol. 11, 3rd ed., John Wiley & Sons, New York, p. 8 (1980).

17. Bunn, C. W. and Howels, E. R., *Nature* 174, 549 (1954).

18. Sheratt, S., in *Kirk-Othmer Encyclopedia of Chemical Technology*, Vol. 9, John Wiley & Sons, New York, p. 819 (1966).

19. Clark, E. S. and Starkwater, H. W., *J. Appl. Polym. Sci.* 6, S41 (1962).

20. Bunn, C. W., *J. Polym. Sci.* 16, 332 (1955).

21. Clark, E. S. and Muus, L. T., *Z. Krystallogr.* 117, 119 (1962).

22. Sheratt, S., in *Kirk-Othmer Encyclopedia of Chemical Technology*, Vol. 9, John Wiley & Sons, New York, p. 820 (1966).

23. Gangal, S.V., in *Kirk-Othmer Encyclopedia of Chemical Technology*, Vol. 11, 3rd ed., John Wiley & Sons, New York, p. 8 (1980).

24. Kirby, R. K. Z., *J. Res. Natl. Bur. Std.* 57, 91 (1956).

25. Doban, R. C. et al., paper presented at the 130th Meeting of the American Chemical Society, Atlantic City, NJ, September 1956.

26. Clark, E. S. and Muus, L. T., paper presented at the 133rd Meeting of the American Chemical Society, New York, September 1957.

27. Clark, E. S., paper presented at the Symposium on Helics in Macromolecular Systems, Polytechnic Institute of Brooklyn, Brooklyn, NY, May 16, 1959.

28. Sperati, C. A., in *Handbook of Plastic Materials and Technology* (Rubin, I. I., Ed.), John Wiley & Sons, New York, p. 119 (1990).

29. Blanchet, T. A., in *Handbook of Thermoplastics* (Olabisi, O., Ed.), Marcel Dekker, New York, p. 988 (1997).

30. Blanchet, T. A., in *Handbook of Thermoplastics* (Olabisi, O., Ed.), Marcel Dekker, New York, p. 987 (1997).
31. TEFLON® Fluorocarbon Resin Mechanical Design Data, E. I. du Pont de Nemours & Co., Wilmington, DE.
32. Gangal, S. V., in *Encyclopedia of Polymer Science and Technology*, Vol. 16 (Mark, H. F. and Kroschwitz, J. I., Eds.), John Wiley & Sons, New York, p. 584 (1989).
33. Pittman, A., in *Fluoropolymers* (Wall, L. A., Ed.), Wiley-Interscience, New York, p. 426 (1972).
34. Bernett, M. K. and Zisman, W. A., *J. Phys. Chem.* 63, 1911 (1951).
35. Doban, R. C., U.S. Patent 2,871,144 (January 27, 1959).
36. Allan, A. J. G. and Roberts, R., *J. Polym. Sci.* 39, 1 (1959).
37. Gangal, S. V., in *Encyclopedia of Polymer Science and Technology*, Vol. 16 (Mark, H. F. and Kroschwitz, J. I., Eds.), John Wiley & Sons, New York, p. 587 (1989).
38. Gangal, S. V., in *Encyclopedia of Polymer Science and Technology*, Vol. 16 (Mark, H. F. and Kroschwitz, J. I., Eds.), John Wiley & Sons, New York, 589 (1989).
39. Gangal, S. V., in *Encyclopedia of Polymer Science and Technology*, Vol. 16 (Mark, H. F. and Kroschwitz, J. I., Eds.), John Wiley & Sons, New York, p. 590 (1989).
40. Carlson, D. P. and Schmiegel, W., in *Ullmann's Encyclopedia of Industrial Chemistry* (Gerhartz, W., Ed.) Vol. A11, VCH Publishers, Wesnhiem, West Germany, p. 403 (1988).
41. Gangal, S. V., in *Encyclopedia of Polymer Science and Technology*, Vol. 16 (Mark, H. F. and Kroschwitz, J. I., Eds.), John Wiley & Sons, New York, p. 604 (1989).
42. Benderly, A. A., *J. Appl. Polym. Sci.* 6, 221 (1962).
43. Gangal, S. V., in *Encyclopedia of Polymer Science and Technology*, Vol. 16 (Mark, H. F. and Kroschwitz, J. I., Eds.), John Wiley & Sons, New York, p. 605 (1989).
44. Gangal, S. V., in *Encyclopedia of Chemical Technology* (Grayson, M., Ed.), John Wiley & Sons, New York, p. 29 (1978).
45. Ryan, D. L., British Patent 897,466 (February 28, 1962).
46. Chesire, J. R., U.S. Patent 3,063,882 (November 13, 1962).
47. Gangal, S. V., in *Encyclopedia of Chemical Technology*, Vol. 11 (Grayson, M., Ed.), John Wiley & Sons, New York, p. 30 (1978).
48. Gangal, S. V., in *Encyclopedia of Polymer Science and Technology*, Vol. 16 (Mark, H. F. and Kroschwitz, J. I., Eds.), John Wiley & Sons, New York, p. 608 (1989).
49. Gangal, S. V., in *Encyclopedia of Polymer Science and Technology*, Vol. 16 (Mark, H. F. and Kroschwitz, J. I., Eds.), John Wiley & Sons, New York, p. 609 (1989).
50. TEFLON® FEP-Fluorocarbon Film, Bulletin 5A, Optical, E. I du Pont de Nemours & Co., Wilmington, DE.
51. Pozzoli, M., Vita, G., and Arcella, V., in *Modern Fluoropolymers* (Scheirs, J., Ed.), John Wiley & Sons, New York, p. 380 (1997).
52. Hintzer, K. and Löhr, G., in *Modern Fluoropolymers* (Scheirs, J., Ed.), John Wiley & Sons, New York, p. 230 (1997).
53. Hintzer, K. and Löhr, G., in *Modern Fluoropolymers* (Scheirs, J., Ed.), John Wiley & Sons, New York, p. 233 (1997).
54. Pozzoli, M., Vita, G., and Arcella, V., in *Modern Fluoropolymers* (Scheirs, J., Ed.), John Wiley & Sons, New York, p. 384 (1997).
55. Pozzoli, M., Vita, G., and Arcella, V., in *Modern Fluoropolymers* (Scheirs, J., Ed.), John Wiley & Sons, New York, p. 385 (1997).
56. Pozzoli, M., Vita, G., and Arcella, V., in *Modern Fluoropolymers* (Scheirs, J., Ed.), John Wiley & Sons, New York, p. 386 (1997).

57. Pozzoli, M., Vita, G., and Arcella, V., in *Modern Fluoropolymers* (Scheirs, J., Ed.), John Wiley & Sons, New York, p. 387 (1997).

58. Hintzer, K. and Löhr, G., in *Modern Fluoropolymers* (Scheirs, J., Ed.), John Wiley & Sons, New York, p. 233 (1997).

59. Kerbow, D. L., in *Modern Fluoropolymers* (Scheirs, J., Ed.), John Wiley & Sons, New York, p. 302 (1997).

60. Carlson, D. P., U.S. Patent 3,624,250 (November 30, 1971).

61. Kerbow, D. L., in *Modern Fluoropolymers* (Scheirs, J., Ed.), John Wiley & Sons, New York, p. 302 (1997).

62. Kerbow, D. L., in *Modern Fluoropolymers* (Scheirs, J., Ed.), John Wiley & Sons, New York, p. 303 (1997).

63. Kerbow, D. L., in *Modern Fluoropolymers* (Scheirs, J., Ed.), John Wiley & Sons, New York, p. 304 (1997).

64. Kerbow, D. L., in *Modern Fluoropolymers* (Scheirs, J., Ed.), John Wiley & Sons, New York, p. 305 (1997).

65. Gotcher, A. J. and Gameraad, P. B., U.S. Patent 4,155,823 (May 22, 1979).

66. TEFZEL® *Chemical Use Temperature Guide,* Bulletin E-18663-1, E. I. du Pont de Nemours & Co. Wilmington, DE (1990).

67. Anderson, J. C.. U.S. Patent 4,390,655 (June 28, 1983).

68. Kerbow, D. L., in *Modern Fluoropolymers* (Scheirs, J., Ed.), John Wiley & Sons, New York, p. 306 (1997)

69. Kerbow, D. L., in *Modern Fluoropolymers* (Scheirs, J., Ed.), John Wiley & Sons, New York, p. 307 (1997)

70. Dohany, J. E. and Humphrey, J. S., in *Encyclopedia of Polymer Science and Technology*, Vol. 17 (Mark, H. F. and Kroschwitz, J. I., Eds.), John Wiley & Sons, New York, p. 536 (1989).

71. Hertzberg, R. W., Manson, J. A., and Wu, W. C., *ASTM Bull*, STP 536, p. 391 (1973).

72. Hertzberg, R. W. and Manson, J. A., *Fatigue of Engineering Plastics,* Academic Press, Orlando, FL, pp. 82, 85, 90, 109, 131, 150, 151 (1980).

73. Seiler, D. A., in *Modern Fluoropolymers* (Scheirs, J., Ed.), John Wiley & Sons, New York, p. 490 (1997).

74. Dohany, J. E. and Humphrey, J. S., in *Encyclopedia of Polymer Science and Technology*, Vol. 17 (Mark, H. F. and Kroschwitz, J. I., Eds.), John Wiley & Sons, New York, p. 539 (1989).

75. Bloomfield, P. E., Ferren, R. A., Radice, P. F., Stefanou, H., and Sprout, O. S., *U.S. Naval Res. Rev.* 31, 1 (1978); Robinson, A. L., *Science* 200, 1371 (1978).

76. Lovinger, A. J., *Science* 220, 1115 (1983).

77. Nakagava, K. and Amano, M., *Polym. Comm.* 27, 310.

78. Dohany, J. E. and Humphrey, J. S., in *Encyclopedia of Polymer Science and Technology*, Vol. 17 (Mark, H. F. and Kroschwitz, J. I., Eds.), John Wiley & Sons, New York, p. 540 (1989).

79. Dohany, J. E. and Stefanou, H., *Am. Chem. Soc. Div. Org. Coat. Plast. Chem. Pap.* 35(2), 83 (1975).

80. Paul, D. R. and Barlow, J. W., *J. Macromol. Sci. Rev. Macromol. Chem.* C18, 109 (1980).

81. Mijovic, J., Luo, H. L., and Han, C. D., *Polym. Eng. Sci.* 22(4), 234 (1982).

82. Wahrmund, D. C., Bernstein, R. E., Barlow, J. W., and Barlow, D. R., *Polym. Eng. Sci.* 18, 877 (1978).

83. Guerra, G., Karasz, F. E., and Mac Knight, W. J., *Macromolecules* 19, 1935 (1986).

84. Sperati, C. A., in *Handbook of Plastic Materials and Technology* (Rubin, I. I., Ed.), John Wiley & Sons, New York, p. 102 (1990).
85. Sperati, C. A., in *Handbook of Plastic Materials and Technology* (Rubin, I. I., Ed.), John Wiley & Sons, New York, p. 104 (1990).
86. Sperati, C. A., in *Handbook of Plastic Materials and Technology* (Rubin, I. I., Ed.), John Wiley & Sons, New York, p. 103 (1990)
87. Sperati, C. A., in *Handbook of Plastic Materials and Technology* (Rubin, I. I., Ed.), John Wiley & Sons, New York, p. 106 (1990).
88. Reimschuessel, H. K., Marti, J., and Murthy, N. S., *J. Polym. Sci., Part A, Polym. Chem.* 26, 43 (1988).
89. Stanitis, G., in *Modern Fluoropolymers* (Scheirs, J., Ed.), John Wiley & Sons, New York, p. 529 (1997).
90. Hull, D. E., Johnson, B. V., Rodricks, I. P., and Staley, J. B., in *Modern Fluoropolymers* (Scheirs, J., Ed.), John Wiley & Sons, New York, p. 257 (1997).
91. Hull, D. E., Johnson, B. V., Rodricks, I. P., and Staley, J. B., in *Modern Fluoropolymers* (Scheirs, J., Ed.), John Wiley & Sons, New York, p. 258 (1997).
92. Hull, D. E., Johnson, B. V., Rodricks, I. P., Staley, J. B., in *Modern Fluoropolymers* (Scheirs, J., Ed.), John Wiley & Sons, New York, p. 260 (1997).
93. Hull, D. E., Johnson, B. V., Rodricks, I. P., and Staley, J. B., in *Modern Fluoropolymers* (Scheirs, J., Ed.), John Wiley & Sons, New York, p. 261 (1997).
94. TEDLAR®, Technical Information, Publication H-49725 (6/93), E. I. du Pont de Nemours & Company, Wilmington, DE.
95. TEDLAR®, Technical Information, Publication H-49719 (6/93), E. I. du Pont de Nemours & Company, Wilmington, DE.
96. TEDLAR®, Technical Information, Publication H-09905 (6/93), E. I. du Pont de Nemours & Company, Wilmington, DE.
97. Farneth, W. F., Aronson, M. T., and Ushold, R. E., *Macromolecules* 26, 4765 (1993).

4 Processing and Applications of Commercial Fluoroplastics

4.1 PROCESSING OF POLYTETRAFLUOROETHYLENE

PTFE is manufactured and offered to the market in essentially three forms, namely, as granular resins, as fine powders, and as aqueous dispersions. Although they are all chemically high-molecular-weight PTFE with an extremely high melt viscosity, each of them requires a different processing technique. This chapter will deal with the fabrication methods being used for granular resins and fine powders. The technology specific to aqueous dispersions is discussed in Chapter 6.

4.1.1 PROCESSING OF GRANULAR RESINS

Granular PTFE resins are most frequently processed by compression molding using a technique similar to that common in powder metallurgy and by ram extrusion. Each of these processes requires a specific type of granular resins.

4.1.1.1 Compression Molding

The basic molding process for the PTFE consists of the following three important steps: preforming, sintering, and cooling. In the *preforming* step the PTFE molding powder is compressed in a mold at ambient temperature into compacted form, with sufficient mechanical integrity for handling and sintering, called *preform*. The preform is then removed from the mold and *sintered* (heated above the crystalline melting point of the resin). During sintering, the resin particles coalesce into a strong homogeneous structure. During the subsequent step, *cooling*, the product hardens while becoming highly crystalline. The degree of crystallinity depends mainly on the rate of cooling. The weight of the parts fabricated by compression molding may vary from less than 1 g to several hundred kilograms.

Preforming
The loose bed of the molding powder is compacted in a mold placed in a hydraulic press. The molds used for compression molding are similar to those for thermosets

FIGURE 4.1 Mold assembly for small to medium size billets. (Reprinted from *Compression Moulding,* Technical Information, with permission from DuPont Fluoropolymers)

or powdered metals. The most common shape of a preform is a cylinder, commonly called a *billet.* The assembly for smaller size billets consists of the main mold and upper and lower end plates or pistons (Figure 4.1). Molds for larger billets are more complex. Molds and mandrels are normally made from tool steel and are nickel or chrome plated for corrosion protection. End plates can be made from tool steel, brass, or plastics (e.g., polyacetal or nylon).[1] Presses used for compression molding must have good controls for a smooth pressure application, must be capable of applying specific pressures up to 100 N/mm^2 (14,500 psi), must have sufficient daylight, and must allow easy access to molds. Typically, virgin resins require specific pressures up to 60 N/mm^2 (8700 psi) and filled compounds up to 100 N/mm^2 (14,500 psi). A press for large preforms is shown in Figure 4.2.

PTFE resins exhibit a first-order transition at 19°C (66°F) due to a change of crystalline structure from triclinic to hexagonal unit cell (see Section 3.2.1.3). A volume change of approximately 1% is associated with this transition (Figure 4.3). Another consequence is that the resin has a better powder flow below 19°C but responds more poorly to preform pressure. Billets prepared below this transition are weaker and tend to crack during sintering. For this reason, the resin should be conditioned at about 21 to 25°C (70 to 77°F) overnight before preforming to prevent that. The preforming operation should be done at room temperature, preferably higher than 21°C (77°F). Preforming at higher temperatures is sometimes useful to overcome press capacity limitations. As the temperature is raised, the resin particles exhibit higher plastic flow and consequently can be more easily compacted and become more responsive to preform pressure. Mold filling is another key factor in the quality of the final product. It has to be uniform and this is achieved by breaking up lumps of resin with a scoop or screening. The full amount of the powder has to

FIGURE 4.2 Compression molding press for PTFE billets.

be charged into the mold before the pressure is applied; otherwise, contamination, layering, or cracking at the interfaces may occur on sintering.

During the compression of the PTFE powder both plastic and elastic deformations occur. At low pressures the particles slip, slide, and tumble in place to align themselves into the best possible array for packing. With increasing pressure, contact points between adjacent particles are established and further enlarged by plastic deformation. Plastic deformation also eliminates internal particle voids.

When the maximum pressure required for compression is reached, it is held for a certain time, which is referred to as *dwell time*. This time is required for the transmittal of pressure throughout the preform and for the removal of entrapped air. Too short a dwell time can cause density gradients in the preform, which may lead to "hour-glassing" and property variation in the sintered billet. Incomplete removal of trapped air can cause microfissures and/or worsened properties. Dwell time is dependent on the rate of pressure application and on the shape and mass of the billet. Generally, 2 to 5 min/10 mm or 0.5 in. finished height for small and 1 to 1.5 min/10 mm or 0.5 in. finished height for large billets give satisfactory results.[2]

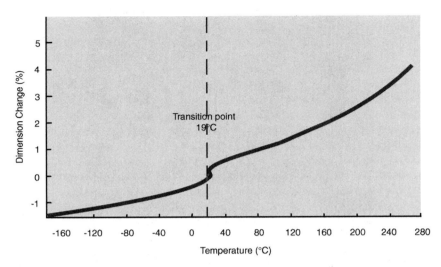

FIGURE 4.3 Transition point and linear thermal expansion of PTFE. (Courtesy of DuPont Fluoropolymers)

Pressure release after the dwell period should be very slow until the initial expansion and relaxation has taken place. Typically, this is done with a bleeder valve or a capillary. Sudden pressure decay can result in microcracks or visible cracks as the still entrapped air expands.

After preforming, there are still residual stresses and entrapped air in the preformed part, which invariably causes cracking mainly during the initial stage of sintering. The removal of entrapped air or "degassing" requires some time called *resting time*, which depends mainly on the wall thickness.

Sintering

The purpose of the sintering operation is to convert the preform into a product with increased strength and reduced fraction of voids. Massive billets are generally sintered in an air-circulating oven heated to 365 to 380°C (689 to 716°F). Both the sintering temperature and time have a critical effect on the degree of coalescence, which in turn affects the final properties of the product.

Sintering has two stages and consists of a variety of processes. During the first stage, the preform expands up to about 25% of its volume as its temperature is increased to and above the melting point of the virgin resin (about 342°C or 648°F). The next stage is coalescence of particles in which voids are eliminated. After that, the contacting surfaces of adjacent particles fuse and eventually melt. The latter process gives the part its strength. After reaching the melting point, the resin changes from a highly crystalline material to an almost transparent amorphous gel. When the first stage is completed, the billet becomes translucent, but it will require additional time to become fully sintered. This time depends not only on the sintering temperature, but also on conditions at which the part was preformed and on the type of resin. High pressures and small particle size facilitate fusion. As it is with preform pressure, sintering time eventually reaches a point beyond which there is no significant improvement in physical properties to justify longer sintering.

During sintering some degradation of the polymer takes place. Prolonging the process beyond the required time or using very high sintering temperature will invariably result in excessive degradation and considerable worsening of properties. To achieve a uniform heat distribution in the oven, turbulent airflow is required. Variability of heat distribution can cause billet distortion or even cracking. Massive billets should be loaded into the oven at maximum 100°C (182°F) to avoid thermal shock. A holding time of 1 to 2 hours before heat-up is usually required for the temperature to reach equilibrium.

The heating rate is very critical for the quality of the final product. Because of the very low thermal conductivity of PTFE resin, the billets have to be heated slowly to the sintering temperature or cracking may occur even before the resin is fully melted. The highest heating rate a given preform will tolerate depends on a complex interaction of many factors. Major parameters include thermal gradient (difference between the ambient temperature in the oven and the temperature in the midpoint of the preform wall) and the rate of internal stress relaxation. The thermal gradient, in turn, is related to the heating rate and the wall thickness. Internal stresses in the preform originate in the preforming process and are dependent mainly on the preform pressure, closure rate, and preform temperature. Normal heating rate for large billets is 28°C (50°F)/hour up to 300°C (572°F) at which point it is reduced to 6 to 10°C (11 to 18°F)/hour.

A proper rate for a given set of billet geometry and preforming conditions is usually determined experimentally. Another way to minimize thermal gradient is to introduce a series of hold periods. In this method a higher heating rate is used in the early phase of the heat-up cycle. Hold periods used between temperatures of 290°C and 350°C (554°F and 662°F) ensure a minimum temperature gradient through the melting transition and minimize any tendency to crack due to the about 10% volume change associated with melting.

At the point when the billet is in the gel state, the particles coalesce and the voids are eliminated. However, the rate of sintering near the melting point is very slow. To achieve more commercially acceptable sintering rates, the temperatures used for that purpose are in the range between 365°C and 380°C (689°F and 716°F). For massive billets, temperatures above 385°C (725°F) for virgin PTFE and 370°C (698°F) for filled compounds should be avoided since thermal degradation above these temperatures becomes significant. The time at the peak temperature depends on the wall thickness, type of resin used, and the method of sintering. Generally, prolonged sintering times have beneficial effects on properties, particularly on dielectric strength, provided that no significant degradation takes place. Typical sintering times for a complete sintering is fairly constant, about 2 hours after the resin has reached its optimum sintering temperature. Once the oven has reached the sintering temperature, it takes about 1 to 1½ hours to transmit the heat through each centimeter of thickness. As a rule of thumb, the time at sintering temperature should be 1.0 hour/cm or 0.4 in. of diameter for solid billets and 1.4 hour/cm or 0.4 in. of wall thickness for billets with a small hole in the middle. For small parts, sintering times

FIGURE 4.4 Typical production sintering oven.

of 0.8 hour/cm wall thickness are adequate. Production sintering ovens are in Figure 4.4 and sintered billets in Figure 4.5.

After sintering, the molten billet is cooled to the room temperature in a controlled fashion. As the freezing range of 320 to 325°C (608 to 617°F) is reached, crystallization starts to happen. The degree of crystallization in the cooled-down part depends on the cooling rate. Since a majority of properties depends on the degree of crystallinity, the cooling rate has to be closely controlled to achieve the desired results. The effect of cooling rate on crystallinity is shown in Table 4.1.[3] Melt strength and wall thickness are the key factors in determining the cooling rate. Typically, cooling rates between 8°C (14°F)/hour and 15°C (27°F)/hour are satisfactory for larger billets. Because of low thermal conductivity, slow cooling rates are necessary to avoid cracking due to excessive thermal gradients. This is particularly important during the transition in the freezing zone since stresses caused by a rapid volume change can tear the melt apart. Therefore, slower rates are maintained until the inside of the wall is below the freezing point and the center of the billet is crystallized. Then, faster cooling rates, about 50°C (90°F)/hour can be used since the sintered part can tolerate higher thermal gradients.[3]

Massive moldings often require *annealing* during the cooling period to minimize thermal gradients and to relieve any residual stresses. The temperature range for annealing is typically from 290 to 325°C (554 to 617°F). The temperature at which the annealing is carried out is very critical. If annealing is done in the temperature range 310 to 325°C (590 to 617°F), the molding exhibits a high degree of crystallinity, which may not always be desirable. The product is highly opaque and has low tensile strength, high stiffness, and high specific gravity. If a lower degree of crystallinity is desired, annealing should be done at 290°C (554°F).[3]

FIGURE 4.5 Medium size sintered billets.

Pressure sintering and cooling is more often used for compounds than for virgin resins. In this process the preform is either sintered and cooled in a confined mold or placed into a special self-supporting frame. The frame is placed into an oven with the pressure cylinder outside, actuating the piston to compress the preform in the mold. Different sinter/cooling/pressure cycles can minimize certain physical properties for each different compound. The disadvantage of this method is that the product has a decreased dimensional stability due to internal stresses. Stress relieving can offset this disadvantage, but it compromises the desired higher properties. Since melting point of PTFE increases with pressure (see Figure 4.6), the sintering temperature has to be adjusted accordingly.[3]

Billets are almost always subjected to some kind of finishing. The most frequent finishing is by machining. The machinery used for PTFE is the same as for other plastics. The achievable dimensional tolerances depend mainly on the quality of the cutting edge of the tools used, which controls the heat generation. At any rate,

TABLE 4.1
Effect of Cooling Rate on Crystallinity

Cooling Rate °C/min	% Crystallinity
Quenched in ice water	45
5	54
1	56
0.5	58
0.1	62

Reprinted from *Compression Moulding*, Technical Information. With permission from DuPont Fluoropolymers.

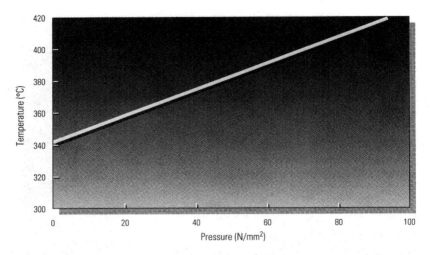

FIGURE 4.6 Dependence of PTFE melting point on pressure. (Courtesy of DuPont Fluoropolymers)

cooling is necessary to remove excess heat. To achieve very close tolerances, parts have to be stress-relieved prior to machining above the expected service temperature. The common practice is to use a holding time of 1 hour/25 mm (1 in.) of thickness, followed by slow cooling.

Compression molding method called *coining* is used for parts that are too complicated to be produced by machining. In coining, a sintered molding is heated to the melting point, then it is quickly pressed into a mold cavity and held under pressure until it solidifies.[4]

Other molding methods for granular PTFE resins are automatic molding and isostatic molding. *Automatic molding* is used to produce small parts, such as gaskets, bearings, seals, valve seats, etc. in automatic presses, with preform pressures and speeds higher than in compression molding. Molded parts made by this technique do not require additional finishing. High-flow resins are used in automatic molding.[4] *Isostatic molding* allows uniform compression from all directions. It uses a flexible mold, which is filled with a free-flowing granular powder then evacuated and tightly sealed. The mold is then placed into an autoclave containing a liquid that can be compressed to the pressure required for preforming. Isostatic molding is used to make complicated shapes that otherwise would require expensive machining, such as large tubes, valves, pumps, and thin-walled small tubes.[4] If close tolerances are required, the molded part must be finished to the required dimensions.

Films and sheets are produced by *skiving*, which is "peeling" of the billet in a similar fashion as wood veneer. A grooved mandrel is pressed into a billet and the assembly is mounted onto a lathe. A sharp cutting tool is used to skive a continuous tape of a constant thickness. The arrangement is shown in Figure 4.7. The range of thickness of films and sheets produced by skiving is typically from about 25 μm to 3 mm (0.001 to 0.125 in.). A modern, high-performance skiving machine capable of machining billets up to 1500 mm (60 in.) wide is shown in Figure 4.8.

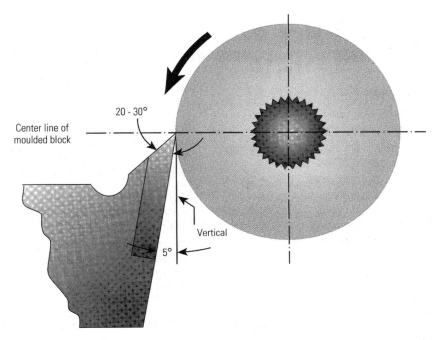

FIGURE 4.7 Typical arrangement of skiving knife. (Courtesy of DuPont Fluoropolymers)

FIGURE 4.8 Modern skiving machine. (Courtesy of Dalau, Inc.)

4.1.1.2   Ram Extrusion

Ram extrusion is a process to produce PTFE extrudates of continuous lengths. Granulated resins used in ram extrusion must have good flow characteristics so they can be fed readily to the extruder die tube. Presintered and agglomerated PTFE powders with bulk density ranging typically from 675 to 725 g/l are used for this process.[5]

The resin is fed into one end of a straight die tube of uniform diameter, where it is compacted by a ram and forced through the tube, which incorporates heated sintering zone. The ram is then withdrawn, the die tube refilled by the resin, and the cycle repeated. Thus, the compacted powder is forced stepwise through the die to its heated section where it is sintered and then through a cooler section where it is cooled and eventually emerges in a continuous length. A rise in temperature and excessive working, such as severe shearing or agitation, have an adverse effect on the flow of the powder. The temperature adjacent to the top of the die tube and in the feed system should be in the range of 21 to 30°C (70 to 85°F).[11] A vertical ram extruder is shown in Figure 4.9.

The powder is preformed to a void-free condition during the preforming stage and, as such, is moved through the die tube. The process maintains pressure on the molten PTFE in the sintering zone to coalesce the resin particles. The rate of compaction has to be slow enough to allow the air mixed with the resin to escape.

During the sintering, the powder is heated by conduction. Thus, the time needed to heat it to the sintering temperature depends on the size and shape of the extrudate as well as on its heat transfer properties. Temperature settings in the sintering zone are from 380 to 400°C (716 to 752°F), although for large-diameter rods where the center takes much longer time than the surface to reach sintering temperature, the setting can be as low as 370°C (700°F) to avoid degradation of the surface.[6]

The rate of cooling determines the degree of crystallinity of the extrudate and consequently its dimensions and properties. Very rapid cooling, especially of large-diameter rods, will produce a high internal stress in them. Such parts have to be annealed before they can be machined to close tolerances.

Granular PTFE resins are most frequently extruded as rods or tubes, but it is possible to produce extrudates of noncircular cross sections.

4.1.2   Processing of Fine Powders

Fine powder resins are extremely sensitive to shear and the sheared polymer cannot be processed. Because of that they have to be handled with a great care during transport and processing.

Most commonly, fine powder resins are processed in the form of a "paste." Such a paste is prepared by mixing the powder with 15 to 25% hydrocarbon lubricant, such as kerosene, white oil, or naphtha, with the resultant blend appearing much like the powder alone.[7]

Fine powder resins are shipped in specially constructed drums that typically hold 23 kg (50 lb) of resin. These shallow, cylindrical drums are designed to minimize compaction and shearing of the resin during shipment and storage. To assure further that the compaction is kept at an absolute minimum, the resin must

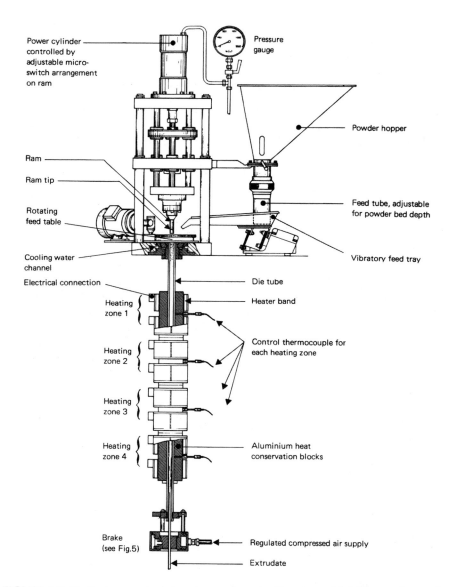

Power cylinder controlled by adjustable micro-switch arrangement on ram

Pressure gauge

Powder hopper

Ram

Ram tip

Rotating feed table

Feed tube, adjustable for powder bed depth

Cooling water channel

Vibratory feed tray

Electrical connection

Die tube

Heating zone 1

Heater band

Control thermocouple for each heating zone

Heating zone 2

Heating zone 3

Heating zone 4

Aluminium heat conservation blocks

Brake (see Fig.5)

Regulated compressed air supply

Extrudate

FIGURE 4.9 Vertical ram extruder, main components. (Courtesy of AG Fluoropolymers.)

be kept at a temperature below 19°C (66°F), its transition point during shipping and warehouse storage. Prior to blending with lubricants, the resin should be stored below its transition temperature for 24 hours. A safe storage temperature for most resins is 15°C (60°F). Generally, the particles form agglomerates, spherical in shape with an average size of 500 μm. If lumps have formed during shipping, the resin should be poured through a four-mesh screen immediately prior to blending. To prevent shearing, the screen should be vibrated gently up and down. Sharp objects, such as scoops, should not be used to remove the resin because they could shear and ruin the soft resin particles. It is best to avoid screening unlubricated powder unless it is absolutely necessary.

4.1.2.1   Blending with Lubricants and Pigments

Lubricants enable PTFE fine powders to be processed on commercial equipment. Liquids with a viscosity between 0.5 and 5 cP are preferred, although more viscous liquids are used occasionally. When selecting a lubricant, its ability to be incorporated easily into the blend and to vaporize completely and rapidly in a later processing step without leaving residues that would discolor the product or adversely affect its properties is important. The amounts of lubricant added are typically 16 to 19% of the total weight of the mix.

For colored products, pigments may be added during blending. These can be added dry directly to the powder prior to the addition of the lubricant, or as a wet blend in the lubricant. In the latter case, the pigment dispersion is added with the remaining lubricant.

All blending operations must be performed in an area in which the temperature is maintained below the PTFE transition temperature of 19°C (66°F) and the relative humidity should be kept at approximately 50%. A high level of cleanliness and an explosion-proof environment are additional requirements to assure high quality and safety.

Blending of small batches, up to about 4.5 kg (10 lb) is most frequently done in wide-mouth jars, placed on horizontal rollers, tumbling at approximately 15 rpm for about 20 min. Larger, commercial batches, sizes typically 10 to 136 kg (22 to 300 lb) are often prepared in twin-shell blenders (Figure 4.10) by tumbling 15 min at 24 rpm. The blend is screened again, transferred into a storage vessel, and allowed to age for at least 12 hours.[8]

4.1.2.2   Preforming

The properly aged lubricated powder is usually preformed at room temperature into a billet of the size required by the equipment in which it is to be later processed. Preforming removes air from the material and compacts is so that it has a sufficient integrity for handling during the manufacturing process. Preforming pressures are on the order of 0.7 MPa (100 psig) in the initial stage of the cycle and may increase up to 2 MPa (300 psig). Higher pressures do not increase compaction and may cause the lubricant to be squeezed out.[8] The compaction rate is initially up to 250 mm (10 in.)/min and is reduced toward its end. The finished preform is rather fragile and must be stored in a PVC or PMMA tube for protection against damage and contamination.

4.1.2.3   Extrusion

The extrusion step is performed at temperatures above 19°C (66°F), the first transition point of the resin, where it is highly deformable and can be extruded smoothly. The resin preform is placed in the extrusion cylinder, which is kept at a temperature of 38°C (100°F) for several minutes to heat up to the higher temperature.

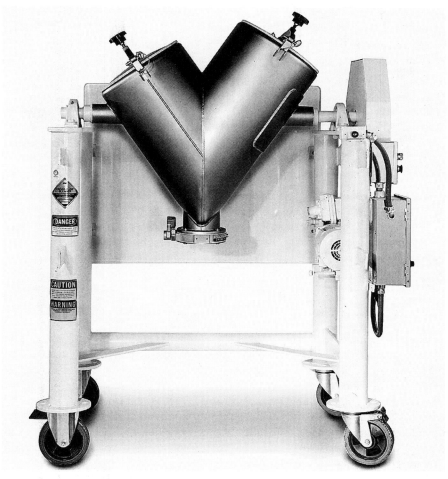

FIGURE 4.10 Twin shell blender. (Courtesy of Patterson-Kelley Co.)

Unsintered rod and tape for packing and unsintered tape for thread sealing and cable wrapping together represent one of the largest applications for this technology. Other applications are sintered thin-walled tubing and wire coating.

Extrusion of an unsintered rod is the simplest process for paste extrusion of PTFE fine powders. The extrusion is done by a simple hydraulic ram extruder with a total available thrust ranging from 10 to 20 tons. The ram speed is adjustable up to a maximum of 50 to 100 mm/min (2 to 4 in./min). The ram forces the lubricated powder through the orifice of the die. The head of the ram is usually fitted with a PTFE seal to prevent polymer from flowing back along the ram. The surfaces of the extrusion cylinder and die are made from corrosion-resistant steel and are highly polished. The pressures during the rod extrusion are normally in the range of 10 to 15 MN/m^2 (1500 to 2000 psi). The diameter of the extrusion cylinder is designed to accommodate the required size of the extrudate and the type of polymer used.

TABLE 4.2
Example of Extrusion Conditions for a Rod (diameter 10 mm)

Die tube

Diameter	10.6 mm
Unheated length at top of die tube	90 mm
Heated length	900 mm
Unheated length at bottom of die tube	400 mm
Total length	1550 mm
Heated length/diameter	85:1
Water cooling	Over top
	60 mm
Heating arrangements	Four separately controlled heated zones each with 2/1.5 kW heater bands.
Temperature profile (top) Zone 1	380°C
Zone 2	400°C
Zone 3	400°C
(bottom) Zone 4	350°C

Source: The extrusion of PTFE granular powders, Technical Note F2, 6th Ed. Reprinted with permission from AG Fluoropolymers.

The usual extrusion cylinder diameters are between 40 and 150 mm (1¹/₂ and 6 in.). The die consists of two parts, a conical and a parallel section. The conical part is more important, as the reduction in area between cone entry and exit determines the amount of work done on the polymer and, hence, to a high degree, the properties of the extrudate. The cone angle has also some effect on the extrudate and is most commonly 30°, although larger angles are used for large-diameter cylinders. The length/diameter ratio of the die parallel (die land), which also has some effect on the properties of the extrudate, may vary from 5 to 10 times the exit diameter. An example of conditions for rod extrusion is in Table 4.2.

Extruded rod can be used either for packing or converted into tape by calendering. Rod for packings is sometimes used with the lubricant still in it. If the lubricant is to be removed, this may be done in a simple in-line oven immediately after the extruder, or in a separate batch oven.

Manufacture of Unsintered Tape

The production of unsintered tape from extruded rod normally consists of the following sequence of operations:

1. Calendering
2. Removal of lubricant
3. Slitting
4. Reeling

The rod used in this method has a relatively large diameter, typically 10 to 15 mm (0.4 to 0.6 in.), and is calendered in a single pass to a tape about 100 to 200 mm

(4 to 8 in.) wide and 0.075 to 0.01 mm (0.003 to 0.004 in.) thick, which is subsequently slit to several tapes of desired width. No advantage has been found in using multiple-stage calendering.[9]

The rod is fed into the nip of the calender by means of a guide tube that prevents it from wandering and consequent variation in the width of the calendered tape. A tape with straight edges and controlled width is produced when a fishtail guide made from metals (e.g., aluminum) or plastics (e.g., acetal) is used successfully.[9]

The calender rolls are heated to temperatures up to 80°C (176°F) to produce a smooth, strong tape. They may be heated either electrically or by circulating hot water or oil.[9] Production speeds of 0.05 to 0.5 m/s (10 to 100 ft/min) are quite common.

The thickness of the calendered tape depends mainly on the calender nip setting. The tape width depends on several factors, such as lubricant type and content, reduction ratio and die geometry during the extrusion, and the speed and temperature of the calender rolls.[9]

Normally, the lubricant is removed by passing the calendered tape through a heated tunnel oven. If the lubricant used in the mixture has a very high boiling point, such as mineral oil, it may be removed by passing the calendered tape through a degreasing bath containing hot vapor of trichloroethylene or other suitable solvent. The slow output rate of this process and safety and health hazards associated with this method rarely offset the advantages of using heavy oils, such as virtually no loss of lubricant by evaporation between extrusion and calendering and the amount of work done on the polymer as a result of the much higher viscosity of the paste. Therefore, this technique is seldom used and only in cases where it is absolutely necessary.

After the lubricant is removed, the tape is slit to the desired width by leading it under a slight tension over stationary or rotating cutting blades. The slit tape is reeled onto small spools. An outline of the process is shown in Figure 4.11.

4.2 APPLICATIONS FOR PTFE

About one half of the PTFE resin produced is used in electrical and electronic applications[10] with major use for insulation of hookup wire for military and aerospace electronic equipment. PTFE is also used as insulation for airframe and computer wires, as "spaghetti" tubing, and in electronic components. PTFE tape is used for wrapping coaxial cables. An example of an application of PTFE wrap tape is shown in Figure 4.12.

Large quantities of PTFE are used in the chemical industry in fluid-conveying systems as gaskets, seals, molded packing, bellows, hose, and lined pipe[11] and as lining of large tanks or process vessels. PTFE is also used in laboratory apparatus. Compression-molded parts are made in many sizes and shapes (Figure 4.13). Examples of rods and slabs from PTFE are shown in Figure 4.14. Unsintered tape is used for sealing threads of pipes for water and other liquids. Pressure-sensitive tapes with silicone or acrylic adhesives are made from skived or cast PTFE films.

Because of its very low friction coefficient, PTFE is used for bearings, ball- and roller-bearing components, and sliding bearing pads in static and dynamic load supports.[11] Piston rings of filled PTFE in nonlubricated compressors permit operation at lower power consumption or at increased capacities.[12]

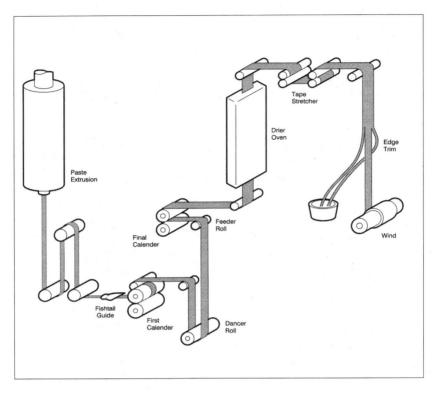

FIGURE 4.11 Schematic of the process for producing thread seal tape. (Courtesy of DuPont Fluoropolymers)

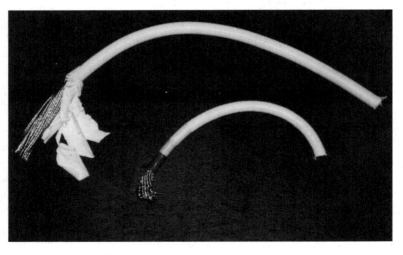

FIGURE 4.12 Cables with PTFE wrap. (Courtesy of DeWAL Industries.)

FIGURE 4.13 PTFE molded parts. (Courtesy of Dalau, Inc.)

The recently developed modified PTFE (e.g., Teflon® NXT), because of its improved processing, lower creep, improved permeation, less porosity and better insulation than standard PTFE, finds use in pipe and vessel linings, gaskets and seals, fluid-handling components, wafer processing, and electric and electronic industries. An example of a molded part from modified PTFE is shown in Figure 4.15.

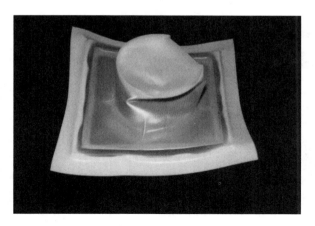

FIGURE 4.14 Molded part from modified PTFE. (Courtesy of DeWAL Industries.)

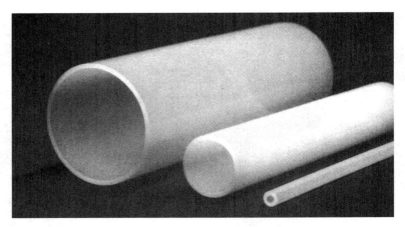

FIGURE 4.15 Extruded pipes from FEP. (Courtesy of DuPont Fluoropolymers.)

Since PTFE is highly inert and nontoxic, it finds use in medical applications for cardiovascular grafts, heart patches, ligaments for knees, and others.[12]

Highly porous membranes are prepared by a process based on the fibrillation of high-molecular-weight PTFE. Since they have a high permeability for water vapor and none for liquid water, it is combined with fabrics and used for breathable waterproof garments and camping gear. Other uses for these membranes are for special filters, analytical instruments, and in fuel cells.[13]

Micropowders, PTFE homopolymers with molecular weight significantly lower than normal PTFE, are commonly used as additives in a large number of applications where they provide nonstick and sliding properties. They are added to plastics, inks lubricants, and lacquers.[14]

4.3 PROCESSING OF MELT-PROCESSIBLE FLUOROPOLYMERS

4.3.1 MELT-PROCESSIBLE PERFLUOROPOLYMERS

The need for highly fluorinated thermoplastic polymers that, unlike PTFE, could be fabricated by conventional melt-processing methods led to the development of a group of resins that are copolymers of tetrafluoroethylene (TFE) with other perfluorinated monomers. Commercially, the copolymer of TFE and hexafluoropropylene (HFP) is commonly known as fluorinated ethylene propylene (FEP). Copolymerization of TFE with perfluoropropylvinyl ether (PPVE) leads to PFA resins, and copolymerization of TFE with perfluoromethylvinyl ether (PMVE) produces MFA resins.

4.3.1.1 Copolymers of Tetrafluoroethylene and Hexafluoropropylene (FEP)

FEP resins are available in low melt viscosity, as extrusion grade, in intermediate viscosity, in high melt viscosity, and as aqueous dispersions.[15]

They can be processed by techniques commonly used for thermoplastics, such as extrusion, injection molding, rotational molding, dip, slush molding, and powder and fluidized bed coating,[16] and can be expanded into foams.[17] Compression and transfer molding of FEP resins can be done, but with some difficulty. Extrusion of FEP is used for primary insulation or cable jackets and for tubing and films.

Processing temperatures used for FEP resins are usually up to 427°C (800°F), at which temperatures highly corrosive products are generated. Therefore, the parts of the processing equipment that are in contact with the melt must be made of special corrosion-resistant alloys to assure a trouble-free operation.

4.3.1.2 Copolymers of Tetrafluoroethylene and Perfluoropropylvinyl Ether (PFA)

PFA can be processed by standard techniques used for thermoplastics, such as extrusion and injection molding and transfer molding at temperatures up to 425°C (797°F). High processing temperatures are required because PFA has a high melt viscosity with activation energy lower than most thermoplastics, 50 kJ/mol.[18] Extrusion and injection molding are done at temperatures typically above 390°C (734°F) and relatively high shear rates. For these processing methods PFA grades with high melt flow indexes (MFI), i.e., with lower molecular weights, are used. Although PFA is thermally a very stable polymer, it still is subject to thermal degradation at processing temperatures, the extent of which depends on temperature, residence time, and the shear rate. Thermal degradation occurs mainly from the end groups; chain scission becomes evident at temperatures above 400°C (752°F) depending on the shear rate. Thermal degradation usually causes discoloration and bubbles.[18] PFA can be extruded into films, tubing, rods, and foams.[17]

Transfer molding of PFA is done at temperatures in the range of 350 to 380°C (662 to 716°F) and at lower shear rates. At these conditions chain scission does not occur. The gaseous products evolving from the thermal degradation of the end groups are practically completely dissolved in the melt since the molded parts are cooled under pressure. For transfer molding PFA resins with lower MFI, i.e., higher molecular weights, are preferred.[18] Because at the high processing temperatures large amounts of highly corrosive products are generated, the parts of the equipment have to be made from corrosion-resistant alloys to assure a trouble-free operation. PFA can also be processed as an aqueous dispersion (see Chapter 6).

4.4 PROCESSING OF OTHER MELT-PROCESSIBLE FLUOROPOLYMERS

4.4.1 COPOLYMERS OF ETHYLENE AND TETRAFLUOROETHYLENE (ETFE)

ETFE copolymers can be readily fabricated by a variety of melt-processing techniques.[19] They have a wide processing window, in the range 280 to 340°C (536 to 644°F) and can be extruded into films, tubing, and rods or as thin coating on wire and cables. Injection molding of ETFE into thin sections is considerably easier than injection molding of melt-processible perfluoropolymers because the former has critical shear rate at least two orders of magnitude greater than perfluoropolymers. When molding thick sections (thickness greater than 5 mm, i.e., approximately 0.2 in.), it is important to consider melt shrinkage occurring during freezing, which can be as great as 6%.[20]

Coatings can be prepared by hot flocking, by dipping the heated part into a fluidized bed of ETFE powder and removing it to cool. ETFE coatings can also be applied by other powder coating methods (e.g., electrostatically) or by spraying of water- or solvent-based suspensions followed by drying and baking.[20]

Welding of ETFE parts can be done easily by spin welding, ultrasonic welding, and conventional butt-welding using flame and ETFE rod. The resins bond readily to untreated metals, but chemical etch corona and flame treatment can be used to increase adhesion further.[21]

ETFE resins are very often compounded with varied ingredients (such as fiberglass or bronze powder) or modified during their processing. The most significant modification is cross-linking by peroxides or ionizing radiation. The cross-linking results in improved mechanical properties, higher upper-use temperatures, and a better cut-through resistance without significant sacrifice of electrical properties or chemical resistance.[20] The addition of fillers improves creep resistance, improves friction and wear properties, and increases softening temperature.[22] ETFE can also be processed as an aqueous dispersion.

4.4.2 POLYVINYLIDENE FLUORIDE (PVDF)

PVDF resins for melt processing are supplied as powders or pellets with a rather wide range of melt viscosities. Lower viscosity grades are used for injection molding of complex parts, while the low viscosity grades have high enough melt strength for the extrusion of profiles, rods, tubing, pipe, film, wire insulation, and monofilament. PVDF extrudes very well and there is no need to use lubricants or heat stabilizers.[23] The equipment for the melt processing of PVDF is the same as that for PVC or polyolefins, as during normal processing of PVDF no corrosive products are formed. Extrusion temperatures vary between 230 to 290°C (446 to 554°F), depending on the equipment and the profile being extruded. Water quenching is used for wire insulation, tubing, and pipe, whereas sheet and cast film from slit dies are cooled on polished steel rolls kept at temperatures between 65 and 140°C (149 and 284°F). Monofilament is extrusion-spun into a water bath and then oriented and heat-set at elevated temperatures.[24] PVDF films can be monoaxially and biaxially oriented.

PVDF resins can be molded by compression, transfer, and injection molding in conventional molding equipment. The mold shrinkage can be as high as 3% due to the semicrystalline nature of PVDF. Molded parts often require annealing at temperatures between 135 and 150°C (275 and 302°F) to increase dimensional stability and release internal stresses.[24]

Parts from PVDF can be machined, sawed, coined, metallized, and fusion bonded more easily than most other thermoplastics. Fusion bonding usually yields a weld line that is as strong as the part. Adhesive bonding of PVDF parts can be done; epoxy resins produce good bonds.[24] Because of a high dielectric constant and loss factor, PVDF can be readily melted by radio frequency and dielectric heating. This is the basis for some fabrication and joining techniques.[25]

PVDF can be coextruded and laminated, but the process has its technical challenges in matching the coefficients of thermal expansion, melt viscosities, and layer adhesion. Special tie-layers, often from blends of polymers compatible with PVDF, are used to achieve bonding.[26,27]

4.4.3 POLYCHLOROTRIFLUOROETHYLENE (PCTFE)

PCTFE can be processed by most of the techniques used for thermoplastics. Processing temperatures can be as high as 350°C (662°F) for injection molding with melt temperatures leaving the nozzle in the range of 280 to 305°C (536 to 579°F). In compression molding process temperatures up to 315°C (599°F) and pressures up to 69 MPa (10,000 psi) are required. Since relatively high molecular weight resins are required for adequate mechanical properties, the melt viscosities are somewhat higher than those usual in the processing of thermoplastics. The reason is a borderline thermal stability of the melt, which does not tolerate sufficiently high processing temperatures.[28]

4.4.4 COPOLYMER OF ETHYLENE AND CHLOROTRIFLUOROETHYLENE (ECTFE)

The most common form of ECTFE is hot-cut pellets, which can be used in all melt-processing techniques, such as extrusion, injection molding, blow molding, compression molding, and fiber spinning.[29] ECTFE is corrosive in melt; the surfaces of machinery that come in contact with the polymer must be lined with a highly corrosion-resistant alloy, for example, Hastelloy C-276. Recently developed grades with improved thermal stability and acid scavenging can be processed on conventional equipment.[30]

Electrostatic powder coating using fine powders and rotomolding and lining using very fine pellets are other processing methods. Formulated primers are used to improve adhesion and moisture permeability for powder-coated metal substrates. For roto-lining, primers are usually not used.[31]

4.4.5 THV FLUOROPLASTIC

THV Fluoroplastic can be processed by virtually any method used generally for thermoplastics, including extrusion, coextrusion, tandem extrusion, blown film extrusion, blow molding, injection molding, vacuum forming, and as skived film and solvent casting (only THV-220).

Generally, processing temperatures for THV are comparable to those used for most thermoplastics. In extrusion, melt temperatures at the die are in the 230 to 250°C (446 to 482°F) range. These relatively low processing temperatures open new options for combinations of different melts (coextrusion, cross-head extrusion, co-blow molding) with thermoplastics as well as with various elastomers.[32] Another advantage of the low processing temperatures is that they are generally below the decomposition temperature of the polymer; thus, there is no need to protect equipment against corrosion. Yet, as with any fluoropolymer, it is necessary to prevent long residence times in equipment and to purge the equipment after the process is finished. Also, an appropriate ventilation is necessary. THV was found to be suitable for coextrusion with a variety of materials into multilayer structures.[33]

THV can be readily processed by blow molding alone or with polyolefins. The olefin layer provides a structural integrity while THV provides chemical resistance and considerably reduced permeation.[32]

In injection molding, THV is processed at lower temperatures than other fluoropolymers, typically at 200 to 300°C (392 to 572°F) with mold temperatures being 60 to 100°C (140 to 212°F). Generally, standard injection molding equipment is used.[34]

THV can be readily bonded to itself and other plastics and elastomers. It does not require surface treatment, such as chemical etch or corona treatment, to attain good adhesion to other polymers, although in some cases tie-layers are necessary. For bonding THV to elastomers an adhesion promoter is compounded to the elastomer substrate.[35]

4.5   APPLICATIONS FOR MELT-PROCESSIBLE FLUOROPOLYMERS

4.5.1   Applications for FEP

The largest proportion of FEP is used in electrical applications, such as hookup wire, interconnecting wire, thermocouple wire, computer wire, and molded parts for electrical and electronic components. Chemical applications include lined tanks, lined pipes and fittings, heat exchangers, overbraided hose, gaskets, component parts of valves, and laboratory ware.[36] Mechanical uses include antistick applications such as conveyor belts and roll covers. FEP film is used in solar-collector windows because of its light weight, excellent weather resistance, high transparency, and easy installation.[36] FEP film is also used for heat-sealing of PTFE-coated fabrics, for example, architectural fabric. An example of extruded-pipes is shown in Figure 4.15.

4.5.2   Applications for PFA and MFA

Perfluoroalkoxy resins are fabricated into high-temperature electrical insulation and into components and parts requiring long flex life.[37] Certain grades are used in chemical industry for process equipment, liners, specialty tubing, and molded articles. Other uses are bellows and expansion joints, liners for valves, pipes, pumps, and fittings. Examples are shown in Figure 4.16. Extruded PFA films can be oriented and used as such for specialized applications.[38] PFA resins can be processed into injection-molded, blow-molded, and compression-molded components. High-purity grades are used in the semiconductor industry for demanding chemical applications.[38] Coated metal parts can be made by powder coating.

4.5.3   Applications for Copolymers of Ethylene and Tetrafluoroethylene

ETFE is used in electrical applications for heat-resistant insulations and jackets of low voltage power wiring for mass transport systems, for wiring in chemical plants,

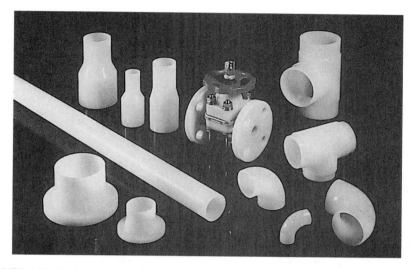

FIGURE 4.16 Variety of parts for chemical industry from MFA. (Courtesy of Ausimont USA.)

and for control and instrumentation wiring for utilities.[39] Because ETFE exhibits an excellent cut-through and abrasion resistance, it is used in airframe wire and computer hookup wire. Electrical and electronic components, such as sockets, connectors, and switch components, are made by injection molding.[40] ETFE has excellent mechanical properties; therefore, it is used successfully in seal glands, pipe plugs, corrugated tubing, fasteners, and pump vanes.[39] Its radiation resistance is a reason for its use in nuclear industry wiring.[41] The lower density of ETFE provides advantage over perfluoropolymers in aerospace wiring.[41]

Because of its excellent chemical resistance, ETFE is used in the chemical industry for valve components, packings, pump impellers, laboratory ware, and battery and instrument components and for oil well, down-hole cables.[41] Examples of such applications are shown in Figures 4.17 and 4.18.

Heat-resistant grades are used for insulation and jackets for heater cables and automotive wiring and for other heavy-wall applications where operating temperatures up to 200°C (392°F) are experienced for short periods of time or where repeated mechanical stress at 150°C (302°F) is encountered.[39] Another use is wiring for high-rise building and skyscraper fire alarm systems. Thin ETFE films are used in greenhouse applications because of their good light transmission, toughness, and resistance to UV radiation.[42] Biaxially oriented films have excellent physical properties and toughness equivalent to polyester films.[43]

Injection-molded parts such as electrical connectors and sockets, distillation column plates and packings, valve bodies pipe and fitting linings are easily made because ETFE exhibits a low shear sensitivity and wide processing window.[42]

ETFE can be extruded continuously into tubing, piping, and rod stock. An example of application of extruded tubing is automotive tubing, which takes advantage of its chemical resistance, mechanical strength, and resistance to permeation

FIGURE 4.17 Molded parts from ETFE. (Courtesy of DuPont Fluoropolymers.)

of hydrocarbons. A high weld factor (more than 90%) is utilized in butt welding of piping and sheet lining of large vessels.[42]

ETFE resins in the powder and bead form are rotationally molded into varied structures, such as pump bodies, tanks, and fittings and linings, mostly for the chemical process industries. Inserts can be incorporated to provide attachment points or reinforcement.[41] Adhesion to steel, copper, and aluminum can be up to 3 kN/m (5.7 pli) peel force.[44]

Carbon-filled ETFE resins (about 20% carbon) exhibit antistatic dissipation and are used in self-limiting heater cables and other antistatic or semiconductive applications.[42]

FIGURE 4.18 ETFE lined part for the chemical process industry. (Courtesy of DuPont Fluoropolymers.)

FIGURE 4.19 Parts from PVDF. (Courtesy of Elf Atochem.)

Certain grades of ETFE are used for extruded foams with void contents from 20 to 50%. The closed foam cells are 0.001 to 0.003 in. (0.02 to 0.08 mm) in diameter. Special grades of ETFE processed in gas-injection foaming process may have void contents up to 70%. Foamed ETFE is used in electrical applications, mainly in cables, because it exhibits lower apparent dielectric constant and dissipation factor and reduces cable weight.

4.5.4 APPLICATIONS FOR PVDF

PVDF is widely used in the chemical industry in fluid-handling systems for solid and lined pipes, fittings, valves, pumps, tower packing, tank liners (see Figure 4.19), and woven filter cloth. Because it is approved by the Federal Drug Administration for food contact, it can be used for fluid-handling equipment and filters in the food, pharmaceutical, and biochemical industries. It also meets high standards for purity, required in the manufacture of semiconductors and, therefore, is used for fluid-handling systems in the semiconductor industry.[45] Examples of rods made from PVDF are shown in Figure 4.20. PVDF is also used for the manufacture of microporous and ultrafiltration membranes.[46,47]

In electrical and electronic industries PVDF is used as a primary insulator on computer hookup wire. Irradiated (cross-linked) PVDF jackets are used for industrial control wiring[48] and self-limiting heat-tracing tapes used for controlling the temperature of process equipment as well as ordnance.[49,50] Extruded and irradiated heat-shrinkable tubing is used to produce termination devices for aircraft and electronic equipment.[51] Because of its very high dielectric constant and dielectric loss factor, the use of PVDF insulation is limited to only low-frequency conductors. Under certain conditions PVDF films become piezoelectric and pyroelectric. The piezoelectric properties are utilized in soundproof telephone headset, infrared sensing, a respiration monitor, a high-fidelity electric violin, hydrophones, keyboards, and printers.[52]

4.5.5 APPLICATIONS FOR POLYCHLOROTRIFLUOROETHYLENE

Major application for PCTFE is in specialty films for packaging in applications where there are high moisture barrier demands, such as pharmaceutical blister

FIGURE 4.20 High purity water lines made from PVDF. (Courtesy of Elf Atochem.)

packaging and health care markets. In electroluminescent (EL) lamps PCTFE film is used to encapsulate phosphor coatings, which provide an area light when electrically excited. The film acts as a water vapor barrier protecting the moisture-sensitive phosphor chemicals. EL lamps are used in aircraft, military, aerospace, automotive, business equipment applications, and in buildings (Figure 4.21). Another use for PCTFE films is for packaging of corrosion-sensitive military and electronic components. Because of excellent electrical insulation properties, these films can be used to protect sensitive electronic components, which may be exposed to humid or harsh environment. They can be thermoformed to conform to any shape and detail. PCTFE

FIGURE 4.21 Electroluminescent lamp with PCTFE film. (Courtesy of Honeywell.

FIGURE 4.22 Packaging of an electronic component with barrier films from PCTFE. (Courtesy Honeywell.)

films are also used to protect the moisture-sensitive liquid crystal display (LCD) panels of portable computers.[53]

PCTFE films can be laminated to a variety of substrates, such as PVC, polyethylene-terephtalate glycol (PETG), amorphous polyethylene terephtalate (APET), or polypropylene (PP). Metallized films are used for electronic dissipative and moisture barrier bags for sensitive electronic components (Figure 4.22), for packaging of drugs (Figure 4.23), and for medical devices (Figure 4.24).

Other applications for PCTFE are in pump parts, transparent sight glasses, flowmeters, tubes, and linings in the chemical industry and for laboratory ware.[54]

4.5.6 APPLICATIONS FOR ECTFE

The single largest application for ECTFE has been as primary insulation and jacketing[55] for voice and copper cables used in building plenums.[56] In automotive

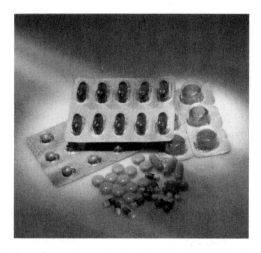

FIGURE 4.23 Packaging of drugs from barrier films from PCTFE. (Courtesy of Honeywell.)

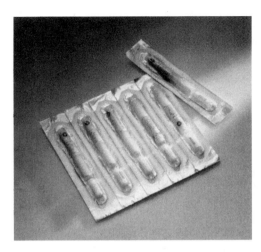

FIGURE 4.24 Packaging of medical devices from barrier films from PCTFE. (Courtesy Honeywell.)

applications, ECTFE is used for jackets of cables inside fuel tanks for level sensors, for hookup wires, and in heating cables for car seats. Chemically foamed ECTFE is used in some cable constructions.[57]

In the chemical process industry it is often used in chlorine/caustic environment in cell covers, outlet boxes, lined pipes (see Figure 4.25), and tanks. In the pulp and paper industries pipes and scrubbers for bleaching agents are lined with ECTFE. Powder-coated tanks, ducts, and other components find use in semiconductor and chemical process industries (see Figure 4.26). Monofilament made from ECTFE is used for chemical-resistant filters and screens.[58]

Other applications include rotomolded tanks and containers for the storage of corrosive chemicals, such as nitric or hydrochloric acid. Extruded sheets can be thermoformed into various parts, such as battery cases for heart pacemakers.[58] ECTFE film is used as release sheet in the fabrication of high-temperature composites for aerospace applications. Braided cable jackets made from monofilament strands are used in military and commercial aircraft as a protective sleeve for cables.[59]

4.5.7 APPLICATIONS FOR THV FLUOROPLASTIC

Because THV Fluoroplastic is highly flexible, resistant to chemicals and automotive fuels, and has good barrier properties, it is used as a permeation barrier in various types of flexible hose in automotive applications and in the chemical process industry. Liners and tubing can be made from an electrostatic dissipative grade of THV, which is sometimes required for certain automotive applications.[60]

THV is used for wire and cable jacketing, which is often cross-linked by electron beam to improve its strength and increase its softening temperature. It is also used as primary insulation in less demanding applications, where high flexibility is required.[61]

The low refractive index of THV (1.355) is utilized in light tubes and communication optical fiber applications where high flexibility is required. Its optical clarity

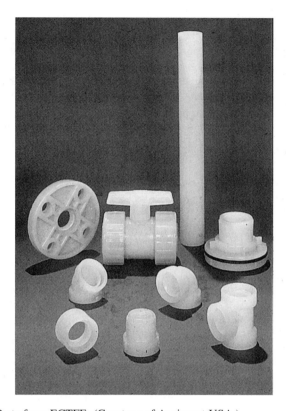

FIGURE 4.25 Parts from ECTFE. (Courtesy of Ausimont USA.)

FIGURE 4.26 Reactor coated inside by ECTFE applied by powder coating process. (Courtesy of Fisher Co. and Moore.)

and impact resistance make it suitable for laminated safety glass for vehicles and for windows and doors in psychiatric and correctional institutions. An additional advantage is that the film does not burn or support combustion, which may be a major concern in some applications.[62]

Other applications for THV are flexible liners (drop-in liners or bag liners), used in chemical process industries and other industries, and blow-molded containers, where it enhances the resistance to permeation when combined with a less expensive plastic (e.g., high-density polyethylene–HDPE), which provides the structural integrity.[61] Optical clarity, excellent weatherability, and flexibility make THV suitable as a protection of solar cell surface in solar modules.[63]

4.6   PROCESSING AND APPLICATIONS OF POLYVINYL FLUORIDE

4.6.1   PROCESSING OF POLYVINYL FLUORIDE

PVF is considered a thermoplastic, but it cannot be processed by conventional thermoplastic techniques because it is unstable above its melting point. However, it can be fabricated into self-supporting films and coatings by using latent solvents (see below).[64] It can be compression molded but this method is not commonly used.[65] Because of a large number of hydrogen bonds and a high degree of crystallinity, PVF is insoluble at room temperature. However, some highly polar latent solvents, such as propylene carbonate, dimethylformamide, dimethyl acetamide, butyrolactone, and dimethyl sulfoxide, dissolve it above 100°C (212°F).[64] The use of latent solvents is the basis of processes to manufacture films and coatings. A latent solvent suitable for that has to have the appropriate volatility to allow the polymer particles to coalesce before complete evaporation.

Structurally modified PVF has been extruded.[66] Thin films are manufactured by extrusion of a dispersion of PVF in a latent solvent.[67] Such dispersion contains usually pigments, stabilizers, plasticizers, and flame retardants as well as deglossing agents if needed. The solvent is removed by evaporation. The extruded film can be biaxially oriented and the solvent is removed by evaporation only after the orientation is completed.

Homopolymers and copolymers of vinyl fluoride can be applied to substrates as dispersion in a latent solvent or water or by powder coating. Usually, the substrate does not need to be primed.[68] The dispersions may be applied by spraying, reverse roll coating, dip coating, or centrifugal casting. Another method is dipping a hot article into the dispersion below 100°C (212°F). PVF films are most frequently produced by casting on a continuous moving belt.

PVF films often require a surface treatment to improve bonding to other materials. Among these are flame treatment,[69] electric discharge,[70] chemical etching, and plasma treatment.[71]

4.6.2   APPLICATIONS FOR POLYVINYL FLUORIDE

PVF is almost exclusively used as film for lamination with a large variety of substrates. Its main function is as a protective and decorative coating. PVF films can be made transparent or pigmented to a variety of colors and can be laminated to hardboard, paper, flexible PVC, polystyrene, rubber, polyurethane, and other substrates.[72] These laminates are used for wall coverings, aircraft cabin interiors, pipe covering, duct liners, etc. For covering metal and rigid PVC, the film is first laminated to flat, continuous metal or vinyl sheets using special adhesives, and then the laminate is formed into the desired shapes. The laminates are used for exterior sidings of industrial and residential buildings. Other applications are highway sound barriers,[73] automobile truck and trailer siding,[74] vinyl awnings, and backlit signs.[75] On metal or plastic, PVF surfaces serve as a primer coat for painting or adhesive joints.[76] PVF films are used as a release sheet for bag molding of composites from epoxide, polyester, and phenolic resins and in the manufacture of circuit boards.[77] Other uses of PVF films are in greenhouses, flat-plate solar collectors, and in photovoltaic cells. Dispersions of PVF are used for coating the exterior of steel hydraulic brake tubing for corrosion protection.[76]

REFERENCES

1. *Compression Moulding, Technical Information*, Publication H-59487, 05/95, E. I. Du Pont de Nemours & Co, Wilmington, DE, p. 3 (1995).

2. *Compression Moulding, Technical Information*, Publication H-59487, 05/95, E. I. Du Pont de Nemours & Co, Wilmington, DE, p. 9 (1995).

3. *Compression Moulding, Technical Information*, Publication H-59487, 05/95, E. I. Du Pont de Nemours & Co, Wilmington, DE, p. 17 (1995).

4. Carlson, D. P. and Schmiegel, N., in *Ulmann's Encyclopedia of Industrial Chemistry* (Gerhartz, W., Ed.), Vol. A 11, VCH Publishers, Weinheim, West Germany, p. 400 (1988).

5. *The Extrusion of PTFE Granular Powders*, Technical Service Note F2, 6th ed., Imperial Chemical Industries PLC, Blackpool, Lancs, U.K., p. 3 (1989).

6. *The Extrusion of PTFE Granular Powders*, Technical Service Note F2, 6th ed., Imperial Chemical Industries PLC, Blackpool, Lancs, U.K., p. 4 (1989).

7. Blanchet, T. A., in *Handbook of Thermoplastics* (Olabisi, O., Ed.), Marcel Dekker, New York, p. 990 (1997).

8. *Processing Guide for Fine Powder Resins*, Publication H-21211-2, E.I. Du Pont de Nemours & Co., Inc., Wilmington, DE, p. 4. (1994).

9. *The Processing of PTFE Coagulated Dispersion Powders*, Technical Service Note F3/4/5, 4th ed., ICI Fluoropolymers, Imperial Chemical Industries PLC, Blackpool, Lancs, U.K., p. 18 (1992).

10. McCane, D. I., in *Encyclopedia of Polymer Science and Technology,* Vol. 13 (Bikales, N. M., Ed.), John Wiley & Sons, New York, p. 623 (1970).

11. Carlson, D. P. and Schmiegel, W., in *Ullmann's Encyclopedia of Industrial Chemistry* (Gerhartz, W., Ed.), Vol. A11, VCH Publishers, Weinheim, West Germany, p. 401 (1988).

12. Sperati, C. A., in *Handbook of Plastic Materials and Technology* (Rubin, I. I., Ed.),. John Wiley & Sons, New York, p. 121 (1990).

13. 13. Hishinuma, Y., Chikahisa, T., and Yoshikawa, H., in *1998 Fuel Cell Seminar*, Nov. 16–19, 1998, Palm Springs Convention Center, Palm Springs, CA, p. 655 (1998).

14. Gangal, S. V., in *Encyclopedia of Polymer Science and Technology,* Vol. 16 (Mark, H. F. and Kroschwitz, J. I., Eds.), John Wiley & Sons, New York, p. 597 (1989).

15. Gangal, S. V., in *Encyclopedia of Polymer Science and Technology,* Vol. 16 (Mark, H. F. and Kroschwitz, J. I., Eds.), John Wiley & Sons, New York, p. 603 (1989).

16. Sperati, C. A., in *Handbook of Plastics Materials and Technology* (Rubin, I. I., Ed.), John Wiley & Sons, New York, p. 96 (1990).

17. Gupta, C. V., in *Polymeric Foams* (Frisch, K. C. and Klempner, D, Eds.), Chapter 15, Hanser Publishers, Munich, p. 349 (1991).

18. Hintzer, K. and Löhr, G., in *Modern Fluoropolymers* (Scheirs, J., Ed.), John Wiley & Sons, New York, p. 234 (1997).

19. *Extrusion Guide for Melt Processible Fluoropolymers,* Bulletin E-85783, E. I. Du Pont de Nemours & Co., Wilmington, DE.

20. Kerbow, D. L., in *Modern Fluoropolymers* (Scheirs, J., Ed.), John Wiley & Sons, New York, p. 307 (1997).

21. TEFZEL® *Fluoropolymer Design Handbook,* E-31302-1, 7/90, E. I. Du Pont de Nemours & Co., Wilmington, DE (1970).

22. Kerbow, D. L., in *Modern Fluoropolymers* (Scheirs, J., Ed.), John Wiley & Sons, New York, p. 304 (1997).

23. Dohany, J. E. and Humphrey, J. S., in *Encyclopedia of Polymer Science and Engineering*, Vol. 17 (Mark, H. F. and Kroschwitz, J. I., Eds.), John Wiley & Sons, New York, p. 540 (1989).

24. Dohany, J. E. and Humphrey, J. S., in *Encyclopedia of Polymer Science and Engineering*, Vol. 17 (Mark, H. F. and Kroschwitz, J. I., Eds.), John Wiley & Sons, New York, p. 541 (1989).

25. Nakagawa, K. and Amano, M., *Polym. Comm.* 27, 310, 1986.

26. Strassel, A., U.S. Patent 4,317,860 (March 2, 1982).

27. Kitigawa, Y., Nishioka, A., Higuchi, Y., Tsutsumi, T., Yamaguchi, T., and Kato, T., U.S. Patent 4,563,393 (1986).

28. Sperati, C. A., in *Handbook of Plastic Materials and Technology* (Rubin, I. I., Ed.), John Wiley & Sons, New York, p. 103 (1990).

29. Stanitis, G., in *Modern Fluoropolymers* (Scheirs, J., Ed.), John Wiley & Sons, New York, p. 528 (1997).

30. Stanitis, G., in *Modern Fluoropolymers* (Scheirs, J., Ed.), John Wiley & Sons, New York, p. 529 (1997).

31. Stanitis, G., in *Modern Fluoropolymers* (Scheirs, J., Ed.), John Wiley & Sons, New York, p. 530 (1997).

32. Hull, D. E., Johnson, B. V., Rodricks, I. P., and Staley, J. B., in *Modern Fluoropolymers* (Scheirs, J., Ed.), John Wiley & Sons, New York, p. 262 (1997).

33. Lavallée, C., The 2nd International Fluoropolymers Symposium, SPI, Expanding Fluoropolymer Processing Options (1995).

34. Hull, D. E., Johnson, B. V., Rodricks, I. P., and Staley, J. B., in *Modern Fluoropolymers* (Scheirs, J., Ed.), John Wiley & Sons, New York, p. 263 (1997).

35. Hull, D. E., Johnson, B. V., Rodricks, I. P., and Staley, J. B., in *Modern Fluoropolymers* (Scheirs, J., Ed.), John Wiley & Sons, New York, p. 260 (1997).

36. Gangal, S. V., in *Encyclopedia of Polymer Science and Technology,* Vol. 16 (Mark, H. F. and Kroschwitz, J. I., Eds.), John Wiley & Sons, New York, p. 611 (1989).

37. Gangal, S. V., in *Encyclopedia of Polymer Science and Technology,* Vol. 16 (Mark, H. F. and Kroschwitz, J. I., Eds.), John Wiley & Sons, New York, p. 625 (1989).

38. Carlson, D. P. and Schmiegel, W., in *Ullmann's Encyclopedia of Industrial Chemistry* (Gerhartz, W., Ed.), Vol. A11, VCH Publishers, Weinheim, West Germany, p. 408 (1988).

39. Gangal, S. V., in *Encyclopedia of Polymer Science and Technology,* Vol. 16 (Mark, H. F. and Kroschwitz, J. I., Eds.), John Wiley & Sons, New York, p. 641 (1989).
40. *Tefzel® Fluoropolymers, Product Information*, Du Pont Materials for Wire and Cable, Bulletin E-81467, E. I. Du Pont de Nemours & Co., Wilmington, DE, May 1986.
41. Kerbow, D. L., in *Modern Fluoropolymers* (Scheirs, J., Ed.), John Wiley & Sons, New York, p. 307 (1997).
42. Kerbow, D. L., in *Modern Fluoropolymers* (Scheirs, J., Ed.), John Wiley & Sons, New York, p. 308 (1997).
43. Levy, S. B., U.S. Patent 4,510,310 (April 9, 1985).
44. *Tefzel® Properties Handbook,* Publication No. E-31301-4, E. I. Du Pont de Nemours, Wilmington, DE (1993).
45. Humphrey, J. S., Dohany, J. E., and Ziu, C., *Ultrapure Water,* First Annual High Purity Water Conference & Exposition, April 12–15, p. 136 (1987).
46. Benzinger W. D. and Robinson, D. N., U.S. Patent 4,384,047 (May 17, 1983).
47. Sternberg, S., U.S. Patent 4,340,482 (July 20, 1982).
48. Lanza, V. L. and Stivers, E. C., U.S. Patent 3,269,862 (August 30, 1966).
49. Sopory, U. K., U.S. Patent 4,318,881 (March 9, 1982); U.S. Patent 4,591,700 (May 27, 1986).
50. Heaven, M. D., *Progr. Rubb. Plast. Tech.* 2, 16 (1986).
51. Bartell, F. E., U.S. Patent 3,582,457 (June 1, 1971).
52. Eyrund, L., Eyrund, P., and Bauer, F., *Adv. Ceram. Mater.* 1, 233 (1986).
53. Aclar® Barrier Films, Allied Signal Plastics, Morristown, NJ.
54. Carlson, D. P. and Schmiegel, W., in *Ullmann's Encyclopedia of Industrial Chemistry* (Gerhartz, W., Ed.), Vol. A11, VCH Publishers, Weinheim, West Germany, p. 412 (1988).
55. Robertson, A. B., *Appl. Polym. Symp.* 21, 89 (1973).
56. Stanitis, G., in *Modern Fluoropolymers* (Scheirs, J., Ed.), John Wiley & Sons, New York, p. 533 (1997).
57. Stanitis, G., in *Modern Fluoropolymers* (Scheirs, J., Ed.), John Wiley & Sons, New York, p. 534 (1997).
58. Carlson, D. P. and Schmiegel, W., in *Ullmann's Encyclopedia of Industrial Chemistry* (Gerhartz, W., Ed.), Vol. A11, VCH Publishers, Weinheim, West Germany, p. 413 (1988).
59. Stanitis, G., in *Modern Fluoropolymers* (Scheirs, J., Ed.), John Wiley & Sons, New York, p. 538 (1997).
60. Hull, D. E., Johnson, B. V., Rodricks, I. P., and Staley, J. B., in *Modern Fluoropolymers* (Scheirs, J., Ed.), John Wiley & Sons, New York, p. 265 (1997).
61. Hull, D. E., Johnson, B. V., Rodricks, I. P., and Staley, J. B., in *Modern Fluoropolymers* (Scheirs, J., Ed.), John Wiley & Sons, New York, p. 266 (1997).
62. Hull, D. E., Johnson, B. V., Rodricks, I. P., and Staley, J. B., in *Modern Fluoropolymers* (Scheirs, J., Ed.), John Wiley & Sons, New York, p. 267 (1997).
63. Hull, D. E., Johnson, B. V., Rodricks, I. P., and Staley, J. B., in *Modern Fluoropolymers* (Scheirs, J., Ed.), John Wiley & Sons, New York, p. 269 (1997).
64. Brasure, D. and Ebnesajjad, S., in *Encyclopedia of Polymer Science and Engineering*, Vol. 17 (Mark, H. F. and Kroschwitz, J. I., Eds.), John Wiley & Sons, New York, p. 480 (1989).
65. Scoggins, L. E., U.S. Patent 3,627,854 (December 14, 1971).
66. Stalings, J. P. and Paradis, R. A., *J. Appl. Polym. Sci.* 14, 461 (1970).
67. Barton, L. R., U.S. Patent 2,953,818 (September 27, 1960).

68. Usmanov, K. U. et al., *Russ. Chem. Rev.* 46(5), 462 (1977).
69. Guerra, G., Karasz, F. E., and MacKnight, W. J., *Macromolecules* 19, 1935 (1986).
70. Wolinski, L. E., U.S. Patent 3,274,088 (September 20, 1966).
71. Brasure, D. and Ebnesajjad, S., in *Encyclopedia of Polymer Science and Engineering*, Vol. 17 (Mark, H. F. and Kroschwitz, J. I., Eds.), John Wiley & Sons, New York, p. 486 (1989).
72. Carlson, D. P. and Schmiegel, W., in *Ullmann's Encyclopedia of Industrial Chemistry* (Gerhartz, W., Ed.), Vol. A11, VCH Publishers, Weinheim, West Germany, p. 416 (1988).
73. *Public Works* III, 78 (1980).
74. *Du Pont Magazine* 82, 8 (March–April 1988).
75. *Du Pont Magazine* 82, 13 (May–June 1988).
76. Brasure, D. and Ebnesajjad, S., in *Encyclopedia of Polymer Science and Engineering*, Vol. 17 (Mark, H. F. and Kroschwitz, J. I., Eds.), John Wiley & Sons, New York, p. 488 (1989).
77. Schmutz, G. L., *Circuits Manufacturing* 23, 51 (April 1983).

5 Properties and Processing of Fluoroelastomers

The introduction of fluorine into the elastomeric macromolecule generally produces materials exhibiting an improved retention of properties at high temperatures, an improved flexibility at low temperatures, and an improved resistance to solvents. Essentially, there are two groups of fluoroelastomers: fluoro-inorganic elastomers and fluorocarbon (or fluorohydrocarbon) elastomers.

Fluoro-inorganic elastomers, such as fluorosilicone[1] and fluorophosphazene[2] elastomers, comprise inorganic monomeric units having fluorinated organic pendant groups. This group of products exhibits a high retention of tensile properties and an exceptional low-temperature flexibility.[3] Fluorocarbon elastomers are the most common fluoroelastomers and comprise monomeric units with carbon–carbon linkages having fluorinated pending groups with varied amounts of fluorine. The latter group will be discussed in some detail in the following sections. A short section on fluorosilicone elastomers closes this chapter.

5.1 FLUOROCARBON ELASTOMERS

5.1.1 INTRODUCTION

Fluorocarbon elastomers representing the largest group of fluoroelastomers have, as pointed out earlier, carbon-to-carbon linkages in the polymer backbone and a varied amount of fluorine in the molecule. They can be based on several types of monomers: vinylidene fluoride (VDF), polytetrafluoroethylene (TFE), chlorotrifluoroethylene (CTFE), hexafluoropropylene (HFP), methyl vinyl ether (MVE), ethylene, and propylene. Proper combination of these monomers produces amorphous materials with elastomeric properties. A review of monomer combinations in commercially important fluorocarbon elastomers is given in Reference 4. VDF-based elastomers have been, and still are, commercially most successful among fluorocarbon elastomers. The first commercially available fluoroelastomer was Kel-F, developed by the M. W. Kellog Co. in the late 1950s. Since then, a variety of fluorocarbon elastomers have been developed and made available commercially.

Currently, there are four manufacturers producing fluorocarbon elastomers and these are listed in Table 5.1. In the ASTM D 1418, fluorocarbon elastomers have a designation FKM, and in ISO-R1629 their designation is FPM.

TABLE 5.1
Manufacturers of Fluorocarbon Elastomers

Company	Trademark
DuPont Dow Elastomers L.L.C.	VITON®
	KALREZ®
	ZALAK®
Dyneon L.L.C.	FLUOREL®
	KEL-F®
	AFLAS®
Ausimont USA	TECNOFLON®
Daikin Industries Ltd.	DAI-EL®

Perfluoroelastomers represent a special subgroup of fluorocarbon elastomers. They are essentially rubbery derivatives of PTFE and exhibit exceptional properties, such as unequaled chemical inertness and thermal stability. Currently, there are two types of known commercial perfluoroelastomers, KALREZ® and PERLAST®. These have ASTM designation FFKM.

5.1.2 PROPERTIES RELATED TO THE POLYMER STRUCTURE

Essentially, the high thermal and chemical stability of fluorocarbon elastomers, as of any fluoropolymers, is related to the high bond energy of the C–F bond, and also to the high bond energy of the C–C and C–H links, caused by the presence of fluorine.[5]

Copolymers of VDF and HFP, completely amorphous polymers, are obtained when the amount of HFP is higher than 19 to 20% on the molar base.[6] The elastomeric region of terpolymers based on VDF/HFP/TFE is defined by the monomer ratios. Commercially, VDF-based fluorocarbon elastomers have been, and still are, the most successful among fluoroelastomers.[7] The chemistry involved in the preparation of fluorocarbon elastomers is discussed in some detail in Chapter 2.

Swelling resistance of fluoroelastomers is directly related to the fluorine content in the molecule. This is demonstrated by data in Table 5.2.[8] For example, when the fluorine content is increased by mere 6% (from 65 to 71%), the volume swelling in benzene drops from 20 to 3%. Copolymers of VDF and HFP have excellent resistance to oils, fuels, and aliphatic and aromatic hydrocarbons, but they exhibit a relatively high swelling in low-molecular-weight esters, ketones, and amines, which is due to the presence of the VDF in their structure.[9] VDF-based fluoroelastomers (e.g., VITON®) have a very good resistance to strong acids. For example, they remain tough and elastic even after a prolonged exposure to anhydrous hydrofluoric acid or chlorosulfonic acid at 150°C (302°F).[9] General chemical resistance of fluorocarbon elastomers is shown in Table 5.3.[35]

Perfluoroelastomers, i.e., elastomers based on perfluoromethyl vinyl ether (PMVE) and TFE, exhibit a virtually unmatched resistance to a broad class of chemicals except fluorinated solvents. On the other hand, they are adversely affected by hydraulic fluid, diethyl amine, and fumed nitric acid resulting in swelling of the elastomer by 41, 61, and 90%, respectively.[10]

TABLE 5.2
Effect of Fluorine Content on Solvent Swell

FKM Polymer	% Fluorine	Percent Swell	
		Benzene/21°C	Skydrol D/21°C
VDF/HFP	65	20	171 (at 100°C)
VDF/HFP/TFE	67	15	127
VDF/HFP/TFE/CSM[a]	69	7–8	45
[b]TFE/PFMVE/CSM[a]	71	3	10

[a] Cure-site monomer.
[b] Perfluoroelastomer.

Source: Schroeder, H., in *Rubber Technology* (Morton, M., Ed.), 3rd ed., Van Nostrand Reinhold, New York, 1987. With permission from DuPont Fluoropolymers.

Fluoroelastomers based on TFE and propylene (e.g., AFLAS®) swell to a high extent in aromatic hydrocarbons because of the relatively low fluorine content (54%). However, because of the absence of VDF in their structure, they exhibit a high resistance to highly polar solvents such as ketones, which swell greatly, and fluoroelastomers containing VDF. In addition, elastomers based on copolymers of TFE and propylene exhibit a high resistance to dehydrofluorination and embrittlement by organic amines. This class of fluoroelastomers has a high resistance to steam and hot acids, but shows extensive swelling in chlorinated solvents such as carbon tetrachloride, trichloroethylene, and chloroform (86, 95, and 112%, respectively, after 7 days at 25°C, 77°F). Surprisingly, they have a high swelling (71%) in acetic acid.[11]

The low-temperature flexibility of fluoroelastomers depends on their glass transition temperature (T_g), which, in turn, depends on the freedom of motion of segments of the polymeric chain. If the chain segments are flexible and rotate easily, the

TABLE 5.3
General Chemical Resistance of Fluoroelastomers

Outstanding Resistance	Good to Excellent Resistance	Poor Resistance
Hydrocarbon solvents	Low-polarity solvents	Strong caustic
Automotive fuels[a]	Oxidative environments	(NaOH, KOH)
Engine oils[b]	Dilute alkaline solutions	Ammonia and amines
Apolar chlorinated solvents	Aqueous acids	Polar solvents
Hydraulic fuels	Highly aromatic solvents	(Ketones)
Aircraft fuels and oils	Water and salt solutions	(Methyl alcohol)

[a] Unleaded fuels give some problems due to the presence of methyl alcohol.
[b] Certain amine additives in engine oils can be detrimental.

Source: Arcella, V. and Ferro, R., in *Modern Fluoropolymers,* Scheirs, J., Ed., John Wiley & Sons, New York, 1997. With permission.

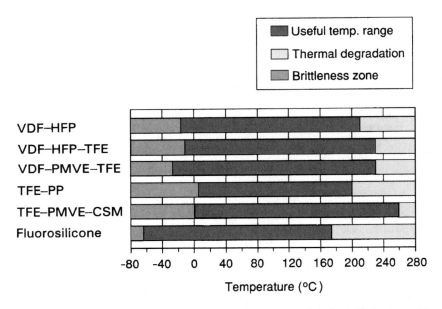

FIGURE 5.1 Useful service temperature ranges for commercial fluoroelastomers. (From Scheirs, J., in *Modern Fluoropolymers,* Scheirs, J., Ed., John Wiley & Sons, New York, 1997. With permission.)

elastomer will have a correspondingly low T_g and exhibit good low-temperature properties. Copolymers of VDF and HFP represent the largest segment of the fluorocarbon elastomer industry, but exhibit a T_g of only –20°C (–4°F), which results in very poor low-temperature properties of parts made from them. Terpolymers of VDF, TFE, and perfluoroalkoxy vinyl ethers (e.g., PMVE) have much better low-temperature properties, but are considerably more expensive. The importance of flexibility of vulcanizates from fluorocarbon elastomers at low temperatures is demonstrated by the well-known disaster of the space shuttle *Challenger*. The O-rings on its solid rocket boosters stiffened in the cold and consequently lost their ability to form an effective seal. Useful ranges of service temperature of some commercially available fluoroelastomers are shown in Figure 5.1.[12]

The thermal stability of fluorocarbon elastomers also depends on their molecular structure. Fully fluorinated copolymers, such as copolymer of TFE and PMVE (KALREZ®), are thermally stable up to temperatures exceeding 300°C (572°F). Moreover, with heat aging this perfluoroelastomer becomes more elastic rather than embrittled. Fluorocarbon elastomers containing hydrogen in their structures (e.g., VITON® and FLUOREL®) exhibit a considerably lower thermal stability than the perfluorinated elastomer. For example, the long-term maximum service temperature for VITON is 215°C (419°F) as compared with 315°C (599°F) for KALREZ. In addition, it was shown that heating VITON A at 150°C (302°F) results in unsaturation and that metal oxides promote this defluorination at even lower temperatures.[12] Copolymers of VDF and CTFE (e.g., Kel-F®) with upper long-term use temperature of about 200°C (392°F) are less heat resistant than copolymers of VDF and HFP.[13] Fluoroelastomers based on hydropentafluoropropylene (HPFP), such as Tecnoflon® SL (copolymer of HPFP and VDF) and TECHNOFLON® T (terpolymer of VDF–HPFP–TFE), because of a lower fluorine content than that of their analogues with HFP, also exhibit lower thermal stability when compared with them.[14,15]

Another factor affecting thermal stability of compounds based on flurocarbon elastomers is the curing (cross-linking) system used. This subject is discussed at some length in the section on compounding.

Raw-gum fluorocarbon elastomers are transparent to translucent with molecular weights from approximately 5000 (e.g., VITON LM with waxy consistency) to over 200,000. The most common range of molecular weights for commercial products is 100,000 to 200,000. Polymers with molecular weights over 200,000 (e.g., Kel-F products) are very tough and difficult to process. Elastomers prepared with vinylidene fluoride as comonomer are soluble in certain ketones and esters, copolymers of TFE and propylene in halogenated solvents; perfluorinated elastomers are practically insoluble.[16]

5.1.3 Cross-Linking Chemistry

Fluoroelastomers based on polyvinylidene fluoride (VDF) can be cross-linked by ionic mechanism. However, if the polymer has been prepared in the presence of a cure site monomer (CSM) it can be cross-linked (cured) by a free radical mechanism.

5.1.3.1 Cross-Linking by Ionic Mechanism

Fluorocarbon elastomers based on VDF/HFP and VDF/HFP/TFE can be cured by bis-nucleophiles, such as bisphenols and diamines. The mechanism, proposed in Reference 17, is outlined below:

1. Formation of $-C(CF_3)=CH-$ double bond by elimination of "tertiary" fluorine.
2. Double bond shift catalyzed by fluoride ion and formation of $-CH=CF-$ double bond.
3. Nucleophilic addition of the $-CH=CF-$ double bond with:
   a. Allylic displacement of fluoride affording the new $-C(CF_3)=CH-$ double bond;
   b. Addition/fluoride elimination from the same double bond.

The detailed description is in Figure 5.2,[18] where the bis-nucleophile Nu–R–Nu represents a bisphenol or diamine cross-linking agent.

The disadvantage of curing fluoroelastomers by ionic mechanism is that dehydrofluorination required for this reaction produces considerably more double bonds than required for the cross-linking itself. This excess of unsaturation represents weak points in the polymeric chain, which can be attacked by basic substances contained in a contact fluid. This has been actually found when parts cured by this method were exposed to new oil and fuels containing basic additives.[19,20]

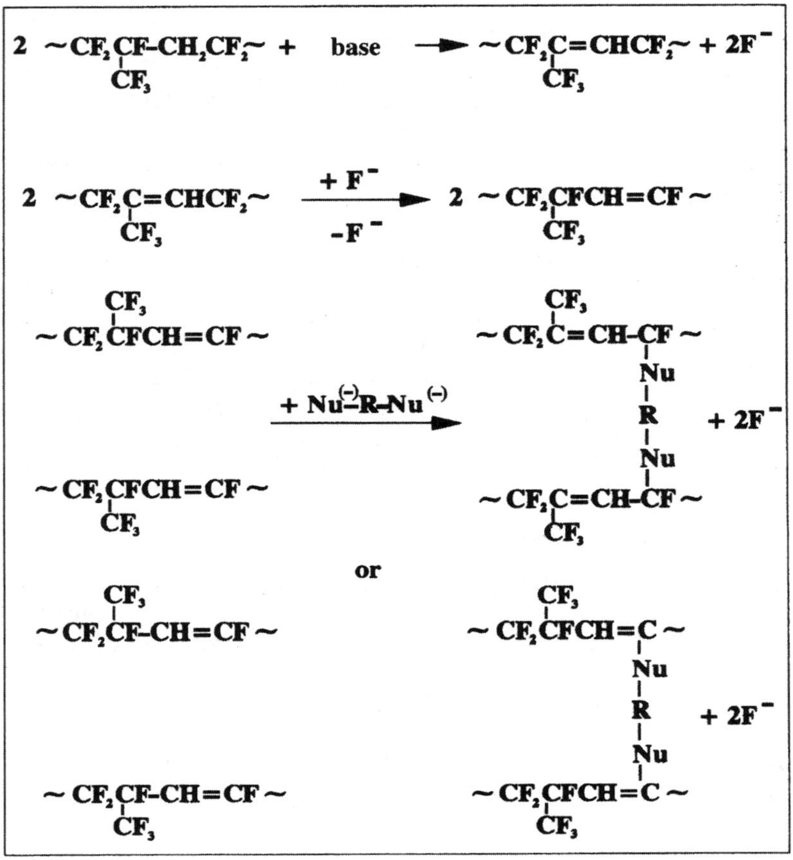

FIGURE 5.2 Reaction mechanism for ionic curing. (From Arcella, V. and Ferro, R., in *Modern Fluoropolymers,* Scheirs, J., Ed., John Wiley & Sons, New York, 1997. With permission.)

5.1.3.2 Cross-Linking by Free Radical Mechanism

The radical curing mechanism avoids the presence of unsaturation after the cross-linking reaction. The reaction is activated by an organic peroxide that decomposes thermally during the cure. The fluoroelastomer has to contain reaction sites to produce a sufficiently high cross-link density. Bromine-containing fluoroelastomers form a stable network in the presence of peroxide. However, bromine-based fluoroelastomers caused processing problems, mainly mold fouling. Iodine-based fluoroelastomers were found to be much better since they produce much less mold fouling and are suitable for more-sophisticated molding techniques, such as injection molding.[21] They also exhibit excellent sealing properties; however, their thermal stability is lower than that of bromine-based fluoroelastomers.[22] The use of peroxides for cross-linking requires the addition of a coagent, for example, triallyl isocyanurate (TAIC) or triallyl cyanurate (TAC).

5.1.4 Formulation of Compounds from Fluorocarbon Elastomers

When compounding fluorocarbon elastomers, the basic principles are the same as for other elastomers. The selection of the elastomer grade and of the remaining compounding ingredients depends on required physical and chemical properties of the vulcanizate (cured compound) as well as on the desired behavior of the compound during processing and curing.

A compound usually contains the following ingredients: one or more fillers, an acid scavenger (most commonly a metal oxide), an activator (hydroxide), a cure system (cross-linker and accelerator), and a processing aid. Inorganic or organic colorants are used for colored compounds. The development of a compound requires a great deal of experience and understanding of the chemistry involved and of the interactions among the individual ingredients. However, the compounding of fluorocarbon elastomers is relatively simpler than that of other types of elastomers.[23]

5.1.4.1 Fillers

The type and amount of filler affects not only the final properties of the vulcanizate but also the processing behavior of the compound. Since the compounds stiffen very soon after mixing, only relatively small amounts of fillers, typically 10 to 30 phr (parts per hundred parts of rubber), can be used.[24]

Various carbon blacks are used for black compounds. Medium thermal black (N990) is the most widely used grade, because it offers the best compromise between physical properties and cost. More-reinforcing grades of blacks, such as N774 or N750, produce a higher hardness and better physical properties at the expense of somewhat higher compression set and cost. Lowest compression set values are obtained with Austin Black.[24]

White (silica) fillers, often surface treated, are sometimes used to improve flow, moisture resistance, and tensile properties.[25-27]

Fillers commonly used in fluorocarbon elastomers are listed in Table 5.4.[33]

5.1.4.2 Acid Acceptor Systems

Acid acceptors serve the purpose of neutralizing the hydrogen fluoride generated during the cure or on prolonged aging at high temperatures. The compounds used for that purpose are listed in Table 5.5.[34] Low-activity magnesium oxide is used in diamine cures and *not* in bisphenol cures. High-activity magnesium oxide is used in bisphenol cures and *not* in diamine cures. PbO is recommended, where the vulcanizate is exposed to hot acids, dibasic Pb-phosphite together with ZnO if it is exposed to steam or hot water. Superior performance in dry heat is achieved with CaO and MgO.[28]

5.1.4.3 Curatives

Generally, as discussed previously, the mechanism involved in the cross-linking of fluoroelastomers is the removal of hydrogen fluoride to generate a cure site that then

TABLE 5.4
Fillers for Fluorocarbon Elastomers

Filler	Comments
MT Black (N908)	Best general-purpose filler; excellent compression set and heat aging
Austin Black (coal fines)	Better high-temperature compression-set resistance than MT, but less reinforcing and poorer in processing and tensile strength/elongation
SRF Black	High-strength, high-modulus compounds; aggravates mold sticking in peroxide cures
Blanc Fixe (BaSO$_4$)	Best compression set of nonblack fillers; neutral filler good for colors; poorer tensile strength than MT Black
Nyad 400 (fibrous CaSiO$_3$)	General-purpose mineral filler, neutral and good for control stocks; tensile comparable with MT
Ti-Pure R-960 (TiO$_2$)	Good for light-colored compounds; good tensile but poorer heat aging than other fillers
Red iron oxide	Used at 5 to 10 phr with other neutral mineral fillers for red-brown compounds
Graphite powder, or TEFLON® powder	Combined at 10 to 15 phr with other fillers to improve wear resistance
Celite 350	General-purpose neutral filler; good tensile strength

Source: Schroeder, H., in *Rubber Technology,* Morton, M., Ed., 3rd ed., Van Nostrand Reinhold, New York, 1987. With permission from DuPont Fluoropolymers.

reacts with diamine,[29] bisphenol,[30] or organic peroxides[31] that promote a radical cure by hydrogen or bromine extraction. Preferred amines are blocked diamines such as hexamethylene carbamate (Diak™ No. 1) or bis(cinnamylidene) hexamethylenediamine (Diak™ No. 3). Preferred phenols are hydroquinone and the bisphenols such as 4,4′-isopropylidene bisphenol or the corresponding hexafluoro-derivative bisphenol AF.

The nucleophilic curing system is most common and is used in about 80% of all applications. It is based on the cross-linker (bisphenol AF) and accelerator (phase

TABLE 5.5
Acid Acceptors

Acid Acceptor	Usage
Magnesium oxide (MgO) — low activity	General-purpose diamine cures
Magnesium oxide (MgO) — high activity	General-purpose bisphenol cures
Litharge (PbO)	Steam and acid resistance in all cure
Zinc oxide/basic lead phosphate (ZnO/Dyphos)	Low compound viscosity in bisphenol stocks
Calcium oxide (CaO)	Added to minimize fissuring; can aid metal adhesion
Calcium hydroxide (Ca(OH)$_2$)	General purpose with MgO

Source: Schroeder, H., in *Rubber Technology,* Morton, M., Ed., 3rd ed., Van Nostrand Reinhold, New York, 1987. With permission from DuPont Fluoropolymers.

TABLE 5.6
Cure Systems for Fluorocarbon Elastomers

Characteristics	Diamine	Bisphenol	Peroxide
Scorch safety	P–F[a]	G–E	G–E
Balance of fast cure and scorch safety	P	E	E
Mold release	G	E	F
Ability to single-pass Banbury mix	No or risky	Yes	Yes
Adhesion to metal	E	G	G
Tensile strength	G–E	F–E	G–E
Compression-set resistance	F	E	G
Steam acid resistance	F	G	E

[a] E = excellent; G = good; F = fair; P = poor

Source: Schroeder, H., in *Rubber Technology,* Morton, M., Ed., 3rd ed., Van Nostrand Reinhold, New York, 1987. With permission from DuPont Fluoropolymers.

transfer catalyst, such as phosphonium or amino-phosphonium salt). The diaminic cure is restricted to applications where compliance with the Food and Drug Administration regulations is required due to contact with food. This curing system is also used in some coating and extrusion applications.[32]

Peroxidic cure systems are applicable only to fluorocarbon elastomers with cure sites that can generate new stable bonds. Although peroxide-cured fluorocarbon elastomers have superior heat resistance, their difficult processing has been an obstacle to their wider use for years. Only recent improvements in chemistry and polymerization are offering more opportunities for this class of elastomers.[32]

Solid fluorocarbon elastomers are commercially available as pure gum polymers or precompounded grades usually with curing system included. Only a nucleophilic curing system is used in these compounds. Examples of commonly used curing systems are listed in Table 5.6.[34]

Precompounded grades are optimized by the supplier to provide the best combination of accelerator and cross-linker for a given application. Then, the final compounding consists of only the addition of fillers and/or other ingredients needed to achieve the required physical properties and processing characteristics.

Although development of a formulation for a specific product and process requires a great deal of knowledge and experience, there are some basic rules typical of FKM compounding. The levels of acid acceptor (MgO) and activator ($Ca(OH)_2$) in the bisphenol cure system strongly affect not only the cross-linked network as reflected by the physical properties of the material, but also the behavior of the compound during vulcanization. Therefore, the curing system must be optimized to achieve the best balance of properties.

5.1.4.4 Plasticizers and Processing Aids

Processing behavior of fluoroelastomers can be improved by the addition of plasticizers and processing aids. High-molecular-weight hydrocarbon esters, such as dioctyl phtalate (DOP) and pentaerythritol stearate, are effective plasticizers in fluoroelastomer compounds. Lower-molecular-weight esters also soften such compounds, but they reduce their high-temperature stability because they are less stable than fluorocarbons and highly volatile at the usual service temperatures. Carnauba wax, low-molecular-weight polyethylene (e.g., AC-617), and sulfones act as good processing aids. These additives ensure improved calendering, smoother extrusion, and an improved flow in molds. Low-molecular-weight polyethylene should not be used in compounds with peroxide-curing systems because it aggravates mold sticking. Other commercially available processing aids are low-viscosity fluorocarbon elastomers that improve processing without having an adverse effect on physical properties of the vulcanizate.[33]

5.1.4.5   Examples of Formulations

Compounds for Compression Molded Seals[34]

| | Amount (parts by weight) | |
	Compound I	Compound II
Ingredient		
FKM	100	100
N990 (Medium Thermal) Carbon Black	15	15
Magnesia	20	—
Calcium oxide	—	20
DIAK #3	3	—
HMDA-C[a]	—	1.2
Total	138.0	136.2

[a] Hexamethylene diamine carbamate (curing agent).

Scorch		
Mooney Scorch MS at 250°F (121°C)	25+	44
Minimum reading (units)	44	50

Physical Properties — Press-cured 30 min at 300°F (149°C), postcured in oven 24 h at 400°F (204°C)

Original Physical Properties		
Tensile strength, psi (MPa)	2640 (18.2)	1750 (12.0)
Elongation, %	305	195
Hardness, Durometer A	65	73
100% modulus, psi (MPa)	460 (3.2)	875 (6.0)

Aged in oven 16 h at 400°F (204°C)		
Tensile strength, psi (MPa)	1500 (10.3)	1460 (10.1)
Elongation, %	160	170
Hardness, Durometer A	79	80

Aged in oven 2 days at 600°F (316°C)

Tensile strength, psi (MPa)	Brittle	1160 (8.0)
Hardness, Durometer A	98	87

Compression set (ASTM D395 Method B), 22 h at 450°F (232°C)

% Set	47	38

Compounds for Extruded Goods[36]

	Amount (parts by weight)	
Ingredient	Compound I	Compound II
FKM	100	100
N990 (Medium Thermal) Carbon Black	35	15
N326 (High Abrasion Furnace) Carbon Black	—	5
N762 (Semi-Reinforcing Furnace) Carbon Black	—	7
Magnesium Oxide	3	9
Calcium Hydroxide	6	—
Carnauba Wax	1	1
Bisphenol AF	1.9	1.9
TPBPC (triphenyl benzyl phosphonium chloride)[a]	0.45	0.45
Total	147.35	139.35

[a] Accelerator.

Physical Properties (Press-cured 45 minutes at 160°C (320°F))

Tensile strength, MPa (psi)	7.6 (1102)	12.4 (1798)
Elongation at break, %	280	330
Hardness, Durometer A	75	75

Compound for Peroxide Cured Seal

Ingredient	Amount (parts by weight)
FKM (high fluorine, PMVE containing polymer)	100
Litharge	3
N990 (Medium Thermal) Carbon Black	30
Hard wax	1
Fatty acid amide	0.50
Stearic acid	0.25
TAIC (coagent)	3.00
50% DBPH (peroxide)[a]	3.00
Total	140.75

[a] 2,5-dimethyl-2,5 di (t-butylperoxy)hexane

Physical Properties (Fully cured)

Hardness, Durometer A	75–80

Compound for Closed Cell Sponge[35]

	Amount (parts by weight)
Ingredient	
FKM	100
Magnesia (low activity)	15
N990 (Medium Thermal) Carbon Black	25
Petrolatum	3
DIAK™ #1 (curing agent)	1.25
Cellogen AZ (blowing agent)	5
Diethylene glycol	2
Total	151.25

Cured in beveled compression mold 30 min at 325°F (163°C)

Properties:
Density: 22 lb/cu.ft (352 kg/m³).
Compression set (ASTM D395, Method B), 50% deflection, 22 h at 158°F (70°C).
Set value: 48%.

5.1.5 MIXING AND PROCESSING OF COMPOUNDS FROM FLUOROCARBON ELASTOMERS

5.1.5.1 Mixing

Compounds from solid fluorocarbon elastomers are mixed on the equipment common in the rubber industry. However, the mixing procedures typical for standard types of elastomers are often modified to be suitable for mixing fluorocarbon elastomers.

Open-mill mixing is used mainly for special compounds prepared in small volumes. The advantages of mill mixing are its simplicity, the fact that the operator can control the temperature of the material on the rolls, and an easy cleanup.

Mixing in internal mixers is considerably more productive; however, because of the high intensity of mixing in an enclosed chamber, there is relatively high risk of premature onset of cross-linking ("scorch"). Compounds tending to scorch are most commonly mixed in two steps ("passes"). In the first pass, the elastomer is mixed with processing aids, fillers, pigments, activators, and acid acceptors. The cross-linking agents are almost always added in the second pass.

5.1.5.2 Processing

Mixed compounds are almost always transformed into products with required shapes and dimensions. There are several methods to accomplish this. Tubes, solid round profiles and profiles with irregular, often complex shapes, are prepared by extrusion. Sheets, slabs, and rubber-coated fabrics are made by calendering.

5.1.5.2.1   Extrusion

Extrusion of tubes, hose, and profiles is done on standard extruders for rubber. The usual temperature pattern is a gradual increase of temperature from the feed zone to the die. The die temperature is typically 100°C (212°F) and the screw temperature is approximately the same as the temperature of the feed zone.[37] Processing aids are almost always required to improve the surface appearance and to increase the extrusion rate. Extrusion represents only a small proportion (about 10%) of the total consumption of fluorocarbon elastomers.[37]

5.1.5.2.2   Calendering

Calendering, as mentioned earlier, is used to produce sheets, slabs, and certain types of coated fabrics. The grades most suitable for calendering are those with low viscosity. Processing aids are necessary to improve surface smoothness and a good release of sheets from the rolls.

Mixed stocks should be used promptly or stored at temperatures below 18°C (65°F) to prevent scorching, and great care should be taken to exclude moisture. Typical roll temperatures for calendering recommended for VITON® E-60C or related FLUOREL types are[38]:

Top	85 ± 3.5°C (185 ± 5°F)
Middle roll	74 ± 3.5°C (165 ± 5°F)
Bottom roll	Cool
Speed	7 to 10 m/min or yd/min

5.1.6   SOLUTION AND LATEX COATING

Certain substrates (woven and nonwoven fabrics, foils, and films) are coated by dipping, spreading, or spraying with fluoroelastomers in liquid form. The older method using a solution of fluoroelastomers in volatile solvents (methyl ethyl ketone, toluene, etc.) is gradually being replaced by the use of water-based latexes (see Chapter 6).

5.1.7   CURING

Products made from fluorocarbon elastomers are cured (vulcanized) typically at temperatures from 170 to 220°C (338 to 428°F). However, to achieve optimum properties, postcure is required. Standard postcure conditions are 18 to 24 hours at 220 to 250°C (428 to 482°F).[39] Figure 5.3[39] illustrates the effects of postcure at different temperatures on tensile strength and compression set of a carbon black–filled fluorocarbon elastomer compound.[39]

The largest volume of fluoroelastomers (about 60% of total) is processed by compression molding. A blank (preform) is placed into a preheated mold, compressed, and cured at the appropriate temperature (see above) for a time established empirically. A good estimate for the curing time in the mold is the value of t_{90} from the measurements by oscillating disk rheometer. In the mold design, it is necessary

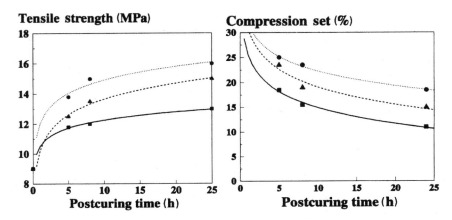

FIGURE 5.3 Effect of postcuring time and temperature on tensile strength and compression set. Postcuring temperature: ■ 200°C, ▲ 225°C, ● 250°C. (From Arcella, V. and Ferro, R., in *Modern Fluoropolymers,* Scheirs, J., Ed., John Wiley & Sons, New York, 1997. With permission.)

to take into consideration that fluoroelastomers shrink considerably more during cure than standard elastomers (3.0 to 3.5% vs. 1.5 to 2.0%).[40] The use of vacuum devices improves quality and reduces scrap.

Injection molding is another method to produce parts from fluoroelastomers. It is particularly suitable for small parts such as O-rings, seals, and gaskets produced in large series. The nozzle temperature is usually set at 70 to 100°C (158 to 212°F) and the mold temperature at 180 to 220°C (356 to 428°F). The best results are achieved by applying vacuum during the injection step to avoid air trapping, splitting, and porosity.

5.1.8 PHYSICAL AND MECHANICAL PROPERTIES OF CURED FLUOROCARBON ELASTOMERS

As discussed previously, fluorocarbon elastomers are chemically very stable. They exhibit a unique combination of properties, such as resistance to heat, aggressive chemicals, solvents, ozone, and light in which they excel over other elastomeric materials. Moreover, they have a very good high-temperature compression set and flexibility at low temperatures. A comparison of heat aging and oil resistance of typical FKM and several other elastomeric materials is in Table 5.7.[41]

5.1.8.1 Heat Resistance

Vulcanizates from fluorocarbon elastomers can be exposed continuously to temperatures up to 200°C (396°F) almost indefinitely without appreciable deterioration of their mechanical properties. With increasing temperature the time of service is reduced as illustrated in Table 5.8.[42] An example of heat resistance of two compounds is shown in Table 5.9.[43]

TABLE 5.7
Elastomer Comparison ASTM D2000-SAEJ200 Classification

Type	Heat Aging Temperature, °C (70 h)[a]	Volume Swell, % 10 h/130°C in ASTM No. 3 Oil
Nitrile[b]	100	10, 40 or 60
Polyacrylic[b]	130	0 or 60
Silicone	200 or 225	120 or 80
Fluorosilicone	200	10
Fluorocarbon (FKM)	250	10

[a] Tensile change ±30%, elongation change –50%, hardness change ±15 points.
[b] Varying acrylonitrile content or acrylate content.

Source: Schroeder, H., in *Rubber Technology,* Morton, M., Ed., 3rd ed., Van Nostrand Reinhold, New York, 1987. With permission from DuPont Fluoropolymers.

5.1.8.2   Compression Set Resistance

The largest volume of fluorocarbon elastomers is used for O-rings and seals. In these applications, compression set is the most important property affecting the performance of the seal. The lowest values of compression set are achieved when using phosphonium chloride accelerator system with bisphenol AF or other phenol cures with certain grades of FKM (e.g., VITON® E-60C or FLUOREL® 2170). Peroxide cures give generally poorer compression set than bisphenol cures. Coagents for the peroxide curing system have an effect on compression set: TAIC gives, for instance, a lower compression set than TAC.[44]

5.1.8.3   Low-Temperature Flexibility

Most commercial fluorocarbon elastomers have brittle points between –25°C (–13°F) and –40°C (–40°F). The low-temperature flexibility depends on the chem-

TABLE 5.8
Service Life vs. Temperature

Limit, h of service	Temperature, °C (°F)
>3000	230 (356)
1000	260 (410)
240	290 (464)
48	315 (509)

Source: Schroeder, H., in *Rubber Technology,* Morton, M., Ed., 3rd ed., Van Nostrand Reinhold, New York, 1987. With permission from DuPont Fluoropolymers..

TABLE 5.9
Heat Resistance of FKM Fluoroelastomers

	A-12	B-12
VITON® A	100	—
VITON® B	—	100
Magnesia	15	15
MT Carbon Black	20	20
Diak™ No. 3	2	3
Pressure: min/°C	30/163	30/163
Oven postcure: h/°C	24/204	24/204

	Original		100 days at 232°C (450°F)		20 days at 260°C (500°F)		2 days at 316°C (600°F)		1 day at 343°C (650°F)	
	A-12	B-12	A-12	B-12	A-12	B-12	A-12	B-12	A-12	B-12
Tensile strength										
MPa	15.0	15.5	6.90	4.31	8.62	3.79	7.24	3.45	Brittle	3.97
psi	2175	2250	1000	625	1250	550	1050	500		575
Elongation at break, %	470	410	160	480	100	400	60	240		15
Hardness, Duro A	68	74	87	75	94	83	91	83	99	91
Weight loss, %	—	—	—	—	—	—	18	11	36	22

Source: Schroeder, H., in *Rubber Technology,* Morton, M., Ed., 3rd ed., Van Nostrand Reinhold, New York, 1987. With permission from DuPont Fluoropolymers..

TABLE 5.10
Low-Temperature Properties

	VITON E-60C FLUOREL FC 2170	VITON B-910 FLUOREL FC 2350	VITON B-70	VITON GLT
Brittle point				
°C	−25 to −30	−35 to −40	−35 to −40	−51
(°F)[a]	(−13 to −22)	(−30 to −40)	(−30 to −40)	(−59)
Clash-Berg, °C (°F) at 69 MPa (1000 psi)	−16 (+2)	−13 (+9)	−19 (−3)	−31 (−24)

[a] These values are often difficult to reproduce.

Source: Schroeder, H., in *Rubber Technology,* Morton, M., Ed., 3rd ed., Van Nostrand Reinhold, New York, 1987. With permission from DuPont Fluoropolymers.

ical structure of the polymer and cannot be improved markedly by compounding. The use of plasticizers may help somewhat, but at a cost of reduced heat stability and worsened aging. Peroxide-curable polymers may be blended with fluorosilicones but such blends exhibit considerably lower high-temperature stability and solvent resistance and are considerably more expensive than the pure fluorocarbon polymer. VITON® GLT is a product with a low brittle point of −51°C (−59°F).[42] TECHNOFLON® FOR containing a stable fluorinated amide plasticizer reportedly exhibits improved low-temperature hardness, brittle point, and compression set without sacrificing physical properties.[45] Low-temperature characteristics of selected fluorocarbon elastomers are listed in Table 5.10.[8]

5.1.8.4   Resistance to Automotive Fuels

The use of aromatic compounds in automotive fuels, higher under-the-hood temperatures, combined with automotive regulations present a challenge for the rubber parts, such as hose, seals, and diaphragms, used in vehicles. Traditional elastomers do not have high enough resistance to meet all these requirements, but fluorocarbon elastomers do. They are being used successfully, for example, in automotive hoses for gasoline/alcohol mixtures and "sour" gasoline (containing peroxides), where epichlorohydrin copolymer depolymerizes and NBR materials embrittle.[46] Moreover, studies of permeation have shown that FKM hose has superior resistance to permeation in comparison with other fuel-resistant elastomeric materials, with permeation rates often over 100 times lower.[47] Swelling of selected fuel-resistant elastomeric materials is shown in Table 5.11.[48]

5.1.8.5   Resistance to Solvents and Chemicals

As pointed out earlier, fluorocarbon elastomers are highly resistant to hydrocarbons, chlorinated solvents, and mineral acids. Vulcanizates from them swell excessively in ketones and in some esters and ethers. They also are attacked by amines, alkali,

TABLE 5.11
Swelling of Different Elastomers in Fuel Blends

Fuels	Fuel Composition (volume %)				
Gasoline (42% aromatic)	100	85	75	85	75
Methanol	—	15	25	—	—
Ethanol	—	—	—	15	25

Rubber	Equilibrium Volume Increase % at 54°C				
VITON AHV	10.2	28.6	34.9	19.7	21.1
VITON B	10.2	22.9	25.6	17.3	18.3
VITON GF	7.5	13.6	14.6	12.6	13.1
Fluorosilicone (FK)	16.4	25.3	26.6	23.1	23.0
Nitrile rubber (NBR)	40.8	90.5	95.8	62.4	66.6
Epichlorohydrin (ECO)	42.4	92.6	98.1	75.6	78.5

Source: Schroeder, H., in *Rubber Technology,* Morton, M., Ed., 3rd ed., Van Nostrand Reinhold, New York, 1987. With permission from DuPont Fluoropolymers.

and some acids, such as hot anhydrous hydrofluoric acid and chlorosulfonic acid.[8] Generally, stability and solvent resistance increase with increasing fluorine contents, as shown earlier in Table 5.2.

Other than the type of fluorocarbon elastomer used, the main determinant of resistance to acids is the metal oxide used in the compound. Compounds containing litharge swell markedly less than those containing magnesium oxide or zinc oxide.[8] Compounds based on KALREZ® and AFLAS® are considerably more resistant to strong alkali and amines than are compounds based on FKM.[8]

FKM terpolymers cured with peroxides exhibit exceptional resistance to wet acidic exhaust gases in desulfurization systems in coal-fired plants.[47]

5.1.8.6 Steam Resistance

Resistance to steam of FKM-based vulcanizates increases with fluorine content. Peroxide cures are superior to diphenol and diamine cures. Compounds based on AFLAS and particularly on KALREZ surpass FKM in this respect.[48]

5.1.9 APPLICATIONS

In 1994, the total worldwide market for fluoroelastomers was estimated at about 9,000 to 10,000 tons, of which about 60% was automotive, 10% chemical and petrochemical, 10% aerospace, and 20% other markets. Annual growth is estimated at 5 to 8%, mainly for new applications or replacement of parts made previously from inferior elastomers.[49] O-rings and gaskets consume about 30 to 40%, shaft seals and oil seals about 30%, and hoses and profiles 10 to 15%.[50-54] Typical applications are listed in the following sections.

FIGURE 5.4 Valve stem and valve seals. (Courtesy of Daikin.)

5.1.9.1 Typical Automotive Applications

- Valve stem and valve seals (Figure 5.4)
- Shaft seals
- Transmission seals
- Engine head gaskets
- Water pump gaskets
- Seals for exhaust gas and pollution control equipment
- Bellows for turbo-charger lubricating circuits
- Fuel-handling systems (diaphragms for fuel pumps, see Figure 5.5, fuel hose or fuel hose liner, inject or nozzle seals, needle valves, filter casing gaskets, fuel shutoff valves, carburetor parts)
- Speedometer cable seals

5.1.9.2 Typical Aerospace and Military Applications

- Shaft seals
- O-ring seals in jet engines (Figure 5.6)
- Hydraulic hose
- O-ring seals in fuel, lubricant, and hydraulic systems
- Fuel tanks and fuel tank bladders
- Manifold gaskets
- Lubricating systems
- Electrical connectors
- Gaskets for firewalls
- Traps for hot engine lubricants

FIGURE 5.5 FKM diaphragms. (Courtesy of Diacom Corporation.)

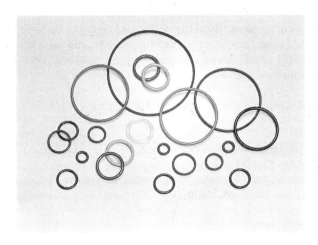

FIGURE 5.6 O-rings for different applications. (Courtesy of Daikin.)

- Heat-sealable tubing for wire insulation
- Tire valve stem seals
- Flares

5.1.9.3 Chemical and Petrochemical Applications

- O-rings (Figure 5.6)
- Expansion joints
- Diaphragms
- Blow-out preventers
- Valve seats
- Gaskets
- Hose
- Safety clothing and gloves
- Stack and duct coatings
- Tank linings
- Drill bit seals
- V-ring packers

5.1.9.4 Other Industrial Applications

- Valve seals
- Hose (rubber-lined or rubber-covered)
- Wire and cable covers (in steel mills and nuclear power plants)
- Diaphragms (Figure 5.5)
- Valve and pump linings
- Reed valves
- Rubber-covered rolls (100% fluorocarbon elastomer or laminated to other elastomers)
- Electrical connectors
- Pump lining and seals
- Seals in Food and Drug Administration–approved food-handling processes (Figure 5.6)

5.1.10 Applications of FFKM

Perfluoroelastomers (FFKM), such as KALREZ, are particularly suited for extreme service conditions. They are resistant to more than 1,500 chemical substances, including ethers, ketones, esters, aromatic and chlorinated solvents, oxidizers, oils, fuels, acids, and alkali and are capable of service at temperatures up to 316°C (600°F).[55] Because of the retention of resilience, low compression set, and good creep resistance, they perform extremely well as static or dynamic seals under conditions where other materials, such as metals, FKM, PTFE and other elastomers, fail. Parts from FFKM have very low outgassing characteristics and can be made from formulations, which comply with FDA regulations.[56] Primary areas of application of perfluoroelastomers are paint and coating operations, oil and gas recovery, semiconductor manufacture, pharmaceutical industry, chemical process industry, and aircraft and aerospace industry.[55] Examples of FFKM applications are[56]:

- O-ring agitator shaft seals in an oxidation reactor operating at temperatures above 220°C (428°F) and in contact with 70% acetic acid
- Mechanical seals of a process pump in a chemical plant pumping alternately acetone, dichloromethane, and methyl isocyanate at elevated temperatures
- Pipeline seal exposed to chloromethyl ether at elevated temperatures
- Pipeline seal exposed to dichlorophenyl isocyanate at elevated temperatures
- Seals for outlet valve exposed to a 50/50 mixture of methylene chloride/ethanol at ambient temperature
- Mechanical seal of a pump handling a mixture of ethylene oxide and strong acids at 200°C (390°F) and high pressures
- Static and dynamic seals in a pump for hot asphalt at 293 to 315°C (560 to 600°F)
- O-ring seals in a pump handling 99% propylene at –45°C (–50°F)
- O-ring seals in a pump pumping chromate inhibited water at 196°C (385°F)

Since perfluoroelastomer parts are primarily used in fluid sealing environments, it is essential to pay attention to seal design parameters, especially as they relate to the mechanical properties of the elastomeric material being used. The sealing performance depends on the stability of the material in the fluid, its mechanical properties, mechanical design, and installation of the seal.[57]

5.1.11   Applications of FKM in Coatings and Sealants

Coatings and sealants for varied industrial applications are made by dissolving compounds of low-viscosity FKM elastomers, such as VITON C-10, VITON A-35, or FLUOREL 2145, in methyl ethyl ketone, ethyl acetate, methyl isobutyl ketone, amyl acetate, or other related ketones.[47] Such products have typical useful storage life of 7 days at 24°C (75°F) and cure within 2 weeks.[58] The subject of coatings and sealants based on fluoroelastomers is covered in more detail in *Modern Fluoropolymers* (Scheirs, J., Ed.), Chapter 23 (Ross Jr., E. W. and Hoover, G. S.), John Wiley & Sons, New York (1997).

5.2   FLUOROSILICONE ELASTOMERS

5.2.1   INTRODUCTION

In this context, by the term *fluorosilicone* are meant polymers containing C–F bonds and Si–O bonds with hydrocarbon entities between them. Thus, the repeating structure may be generally written as $[R_f X (CH_2)_n]_x (CH_3)_y SiO_z$, where R_f is the fluorocarbon group.[56] Commercially available fluorosilicones are based on polymethyltrifluoropropylsiloxane (PMTFPS), or more accurately poly[methyl (3,3,3-trifluoropropyl)siloxane]. In some cases PMTFPS is copolymerized with polydimethyl siloxane (PMDS) for cost/benefit balance.[57] The manufacture of monomers for fluorosilicones is discussed in some detail in Reference 57. Fluorosilicone elastomers are sometimes referred to in literature as FMQ or FVMQ. The ASTM name is fluoro-vinyl polysiloxane. Currently, the three major suppliers are Dow Corning Corporation, General Electric Company, and Shinetsu Chemical Company.

5.2.2 POLYMERIZATION

The most common method of preparation of PMTFPS is through the base-catalyzed ring-opening polymerization of the corresponding cyclic trimer.[61,62] Details are in Section 2.11.1. A specific cure site for peroxide curing is developed by incorporating 0.2 mol% of methylvinyl siloxane.[63] Typically, fluorosilicone elastomers are copolymers of 90 mol% of trifluoropropylsiloxy and 10 mol% of dimethylsiloxy monomers, but the fluorosilicone content in commercial products ranges from 40 to 90 mol%.[63]

Fluorosilicone polymers are optically clear and are available in a broad range of viscosities, from very low viscosity fluids to very high viscosity gums. The physical properties of the raw polymers — such as viscosity, resistance to nonpolar fuels, oils, and solvents; specific gravity; refractive index; lubricity; solubility in polar solvents; the degree of crystallinity; and glass transition temperature (T_g) — depend on the structure, more specifically on the number of trifluoropropyl groups in the molecule. The mechical properties of the polymer depend on the molecular weight, dispersity, and mol % of vinyl groups.[64]

5.2.3 PROCESSING

Fluorosilicones can be compounded by the addition of mineral fillers and pigments. Fillers for such compounds are most commonly silicas (silicon dioxide), because they are compatible with the elastomeric silicon–oxygen backbone and thermally very stable. They range in surface areas from 0.54 to 400 m^2/g and average particle size from 100 to 6 nm. Because of these properties, they offer a great deal of flexibility in reinforcement. Thus, cured compounds can have Durometer A hardness from 40 to 80. Other fillers commonly used in fluorosilicones are calcium carbonate, titanium dioxide, and zinc oxide.

Mill and mold release is improved by the addition of a small percentage of dimetylsilicone oils or gums. Processing aids are mostly proprietary. Plasticizers are generally fluorosilicone oils of various viscosities. The lower the molecular weight, the more effective is the plasticizing action. On the other hand, the higher the molecular weight, the lower the volatility, which is critical when the service temperature is very high.

Fluorosilicone compounds can be processed by the same methods used for silicone elastomers based on PDMS. They can be milled, calendered, extruded, and molded. A large proportion of fluorosilicone compounds is used in compression molding. Molded parts produced in large series are made by injection molding, and parts with complex shapes are produced by transfer molding. Calendering is used to produce thin sheets and for coating of textiles and other substrates.

Cross-linking of fluorosilicones is done by essentially the same methods as conventional silicones. A comprehensive review of this subject is in Reference 65. Currently, there are three methods of cross-linking used in industrial practice:

- By peroxides (free radicals)
- Condensation reactions
- Hydrosilylation addition

For *peroxide cross-linking,* organic peroxides, such as dicumyl, di-*t*-butyl, and benzoyl peroxides, are used in amounts 1 to 3 phr (parts per hundred parts of rubber). Typical cure cycles are 5 to 10 min at temperatures 115 to 170°C (239 to 338°F), depending on the type of peroxide used. Each peroxide has a specific use. A postcure is recommended to complete the cross-linking reaction and to remove the residues from the decomposition of peroxide. This improves the long-term heat aging properties.[62]

Condensation reactions are used for cross-linking at ambient temperatures. The acetoxy-functional condensation system is widely used in fluorosilicone sealants. The cross-linking occurs after exposure to atmospheric moisture.[62] The limitation of this system is that it is effective for only relatively thin layers. Moreover, it often requires up to 14 days to cure and the acetic by-product may corrode certain substances.

Thicker sections can be cross-linked by *hydrosilylation addition.* This is the same chemistry used to produce fluorosilicone monomers with the vinyl functionality present on silicon. The catalyst reaction occurs between a vinyl group and silicone hydride.[66] The advantage of this system is that it does not produce volatile by-products. On the other hand, the disadvantage is that it is available only as a two-part system.[67] Recently, however, one-part, platinum-catalyzed products have been developed.[66] The reaction is very rapid and at room temperature it is completed in 10 to 30 minutes. It is accelerated with increasing temperature and at 150°C (302°F) it is completed within a few seconds. This makes the compounds ideal for fast automated injection molding operations.[68] One-part systems use the chemical complexing of the catalyst, which is activated at elevated temperatures, or its encapsulation into an impermeable shell, which is solid at room temperature and melts at elevated temperatures.[68]

Fluorosilicone polymers can be cross-linked by ultraviolet radiation or by electron beam, but these methods are not commonly used.[69]

5.2.4 PROPERTIES

5.2.4.1 Fluid and Chemical Resistance

In general, fluorosilicones exhibit a very good fuel and fluid resistance. The volume swelling in solvents decreases with increasing fluorine content. Cured fluorosilicone elastomers have good resistance to jet fuels, oils, hydrocarbons, and fuels (see Table 5.12).[67] However, higher swelling in ketones and esters are observed.[70] Relatively low swelling is found in alcohol/fuel blends; once the solvents are removed the physical properties return to nearly the original unswollen state.[71] Mechanical properties of PMTFPS elastomers are listed in Table 5.13.[77]

5.2.4.2 Heat Resistance

Fluorosilicone elastomers have an excellent heat resistance, although they have slightly lower high-temperature stability compared with PDMS.[72] The ultimate temperature stability depends on cure conditions and environment. A typical cured

TABLE 5.12
Fluid and Chemical Resistance of Fluorosilicone Elastomers (ASTM D 471)

Fluid	Immersion Conditions	Hardness Change (points)	Volume Change (%)
ASTM No. 1 oil	3 days/150°C	−5	0
Crude oil 7 API	14 days/135°C	−10	+5
JP-4 fuel	3 days/25°C	−5	+10
ASTM Ref. Fuel B	3 days/65°C	−5	+20
Benzene	7 days/25°C	−5	+25
Carbon tetrachloride	7 days 25°C	−5	+20
Methanol	14 days 25°C	−10	+4
Ethanol	7 days 25°C	0	+5
Hydrochloric acid (10%)	7 days 25°C	−5	0
Nitric acid (70%)	7 days 25°C	0	+5
Sodium hydroxide (50%)	7 days 25°C	−5	0

Source: Maxson, M. T. et al., in *Modern Fluoropolymers,* Scheirs, J., Ed., John Wiley & Sons, New York, 1997. With permission.

TABLE 5.13
Properties of Typical Commercial PMTFPS Elastomers

Property	Typical Range
Specific gravity (g/cm³)	1.35–1.65
Hardness (Shore A)	20–80
Tensile strength (MPa)	5.5–11.7 (22°C)
	2.4–4.1 (204°C)
Elongation (%)	100–600 (22°C)
	90–300 (204°C)
Modulus at 100% (MPa)	0.5–6.2
Compression set (%) (22 h/177°C)	10–40
Tear strength, die B[a] (kN/m)	10.5–46.6
Service temperature (°C)	−68–+232
Bashore resilience[b] (%)	10–40

[a] Die B refers to a particular specimen shape in ASTM D624.

[b] Bashore resilience is resilience measured by a falling metal plunger according to ASTM D2632.

Source: Maxson, M. T. et al., in *Modern Fluoropolymers,* Scheirs, J., Ed., John Wiley & Sons, New York, 1997. With permission.

fluorosilicone elastomer (PMTFPS) aged for 1350 hours at 200°C (392°F) will show a two-point reduction in durometer hardness, a 40% reduction in tensile strength, and a 15% reduction in elongation. There are essentially two mechanisms of degradation: reversion (occurs in confinement) or oxidative cross-linking. The latter occurs by radical abstraction of protons, which recombine to form additional cross-linking sites, and this ultimately leads to embrittlement of the vulcanizate.[73]

5.2.4.3 Low-Temperature Properties

The glass transition temperature of PMTFPS is −75°C (−103°F). Moreover, it does not exhibit low-temperature crystallization at −40°C (−40°F) as PMDS does. Because of this and the low T_g, fluorosilicone elastomers remain very flexible at very low temperatures. For example, the brittleness temperature by impact (ASTM D 746B) of a commercial fluorosilicone vulcanizate was found to be −59°C (−74°F).[62] This is considerably lower than the values typically measured on fluorocarbon elastomers. Fluorosilicones combine the superior fluid resistance of fluoropolymers with the very good low-temperature flexibility of silicones.

5.2.4.4 Electrical Properties

Electrical properties — dielectric constant (ε), representing polarization; dissipation factor (tan δ), representing relaxation phenomena; dielectric strength (E_B), representing breakdown phenomena; and resistivity (ρ_v), an inverse of conductivity — are compared with other polymers in Table 5.14.[74] The low dielectric loss and high electrical resistivity coupled with low water absorption and retention of these properties in harsh environments are major advantages of fluorosilicone elastomers over other polymeric materials.[74]

5.2.5 Applications

Commercial fluorosilicone elastomer compounds are made from high-molecular-weight PMTFPS (MW is typically 0.8 to 2.0 million) and are cross-linked by organic

TABLE 5.14
Electrical Properties of Selected Polymers

Polymer	E_b (60 Hz) V/mil	ε (100 Hz)	tan δ	ρ_v (ohm · cm)
Low-density polyethylene	742	2.2	0.0039	2.5×10^{15}
Natural rubber	665	2.4	0.0024	1.1×10^{15}
PDMS	552	2.9	0.00025	5.3×10^{14}
PMTFPS	350	7.0	0.20	1.0×10^{14}
Viton	351	8.6	0.040	4.1×10^{11}

Source: Maxson, M. T. et al., in *Modern Fluoropolymers,* Scheirs, J., Ed., John Wiley & Sons, New York, 1997. With permission.

peroxides. Such compounds contain some reinforcing filler (usually high-surface-area fuming silica), a small amount of low-molecular-weight fluorosilicone diol processing fluid, and a peroxide catalyst.[75] Other additives, such as extending fillers, pigments, and thermal stability enhancers, are often added to meet final product requirements.[76] Frequently, fluorosilicone elastomers are blended with PDMS silicones either to lower compound cost or to enhance properties of the silicone compound. Fluorosilicone elastomers can also be blended with fluoroelastomers to improve their low-temperature flexibility. Properties of cured fluorosilicone elastomers depend on the base polymer and compounding ingredients used.

Fluorosilicone elastomers are particularly suited for service where they come in contact with aircraft fuels, lubricants, hydraulic fuels, and solvents. Compared with other fuel-resistant elastomers fluorosilicones offer the widest hardness range and the widest operating service temperature range of any material.[71] The automotive and aerospace industries are the largest users of fluorinated elastomers. Typical automotive applications are fuel injector O-rings, fuel line pulsator seals, fuel line quick-connect seals, gas cap washers, vapor recovery system seals, electrical connector inserts, exhaust gas recirculating diaphragms, fuel tank access gaskets, and engine cover and oil pan gaskets. In the aerospace industry fluorosilicone O-rings, gaskets, washers, diaphragms, and seals are used in fuel line connections, fuel control devices, electrical connectors, hydraulic line connectors, and fuel system access panels.[77]

Medium-molecular-weight PMTFPS with vinyl or hydroxyl end blocks are used for adhesives and sealants. They are cured either at ambient temperature (RTV-room temperature vulcanization) or at elevated temperature. One-part moisture-activated RTV sealants have been available commercially for many years. Because of their very high resistance to jet engine fuels, excellent flexibility at very low temperatures, and high thermal stability, they have been used in both military and civilian aerospace applications.[78] Two-part, heat-cured fluorosilicone sealants have been used in military aircraft applications and for sealing automotive fuel systems.[79] Special class of fluorosilicone sealants are "channel sealants" or "groove injection sealants," sticky, puttylike compounds, which do not cure. They are used to seal fuel tanks of military aircraft and missiles.[75]

Adhesion of fluorosilicone compounds requires surface treatment. For particularly difficult surfaces plasma treatment is necessary. However, for most common applications, satisfactory bonding is achieved by using a specialized primer.[80]

5.2.6 Toxicity and Safety

Under normal conditions, PMTFPS is relatively inert. Skin tests performed on albino rabbits have shown no dermal irritation or toxicity. In over 40 years of industrial use of fluorosilicone compounds, no problems have been reported with respect to human dermal contact with these materials, uncured or cured.[74]

However, when PMTFPS is heated at elevated temperatures in air or burned, toxic fluorinated compounds are formed, which are harmful when inhaled. At temperatures above 150°C (302°F) 3,3,3-trifluoropropionaldehyde (TFPA) is formed and its amount depends upon temperature, percentage of fluorosilicone in the sample, sample surface area, and presence of oxygen.[74] In addition to TFPA, small amounts of formaldehyde are generated upon heating above 150°C (302°F). Although the amounts of these compounds are very small during the standard process (curing and postcuring) and application, it is prudent to minimize human exposure to these vapors.

REFERENCES

1. Pierce, O. R., Holbrook, G. W., Johannson, O. K., Saylor, J. C., and Brown, E. D., *Ind. Eng. Chem.* 52, 783 (1960).
2. Rose, S. H., *J. Polym. Sci. B*, 6, 873 (1968).
3. Kiker, G. S. and Antkowiak, T. A., *Rubber Chem. Technol.* 47, 32 (1974).
4. Logothetis, A. L., *Prog. Polym. Sci.* 14, 251 (1989).
5. Banks, R. E., *Fluorocarbons and Their Derivatives*, Macdonald, London, 17 (1970).
6. Ajroldi, G., Pianca, M., Fumagalli, M., and Moggi, G., *Polymer* 30, 2180 (1989).
7. Arcella, V. and Ferro, R., in *Modern Fluoropolymers* (Scheirs, J., Ed.), John Wiley & Sons, New York, p. 73 (1997).
8. Schroeder, H., in *Rubber Technology* (Morton, M., Ed.), 3rd ed., Van Nostrand Reinhold Co., New York, p. 430 (1987).
9. Scheirs, J., in *Modern Fluoropolymers* (Scheirs, J., Ed.), John Wiley & Sons, New York, p. 25 (1997).
10. Scheirs, J., in *Modern Fluoropolymers* (Scheirs, J., Ed.), John Wiley & Sons, New York, p. 29 (1997).
11. Scheirs, J., in *Modern Fluoropolymers* (Scheirs, J., Ed.), John Wiley & Sons, New York, p. 30 (1997).
12. Scheirs, J., in *Modern Fluoropolymers* (Scheirs, J., Ed.), John Wiley & Sons, New York, p. 35 (1997).
13. Novikov, A. S., Galil, F., Slovokhotova, N. A., and Dyumaeva, T. N., *Vysokomol. Soed.* 4, 423 (1962).
14. Scheirs, J., in *Modern Fluoropolymers* (Scheirs, J., Ed.), John Wiley & Sons, New York, p. 52 (1997).
15. Scheirs, J., in *Modern Fluoropolymers* (Scheirs, J., Ed.), John Wiley & Sons, New York, p. 53 (1997).
16. Schroeder, H., in *Rubber Technology* (Morton, M., Ed.), 3rd ed., Van Nostrand Reinhold Co., New York, p. 413 (1987).
17. Arcella, V., Chiodini, G., Del Fanti, N., and Pianca, M., paper 57 at the 140th ACS Rubber Division Meeting, Detroit, MI (1991).
18. Arcella V. and Ferro R., in *Modern Fluoropolymers* (Scheirs, J., Ed.), John Wiley & Sons, New York, p. 78 (1997).
19. Arcella, V., Geri, S., Tommasi, G., and Dardani, P., *Kautsch. Gummi Kunstst.* 39, 407 (1986).
20. Arcella, V., Ferro, R., and Albano, M., *Kautsch. Gummi Kunstst.* 44, 833 (1991).
21. Arcella V. and Ferro R., in *Modern Fluoropolymers* (Scheirs, J., Ed.), John Wiley & Sons, New York, p. 79 (1997).
22. Arcella V. and Ferro R., in *Modern Fluoropolymers* (Scheirs, J., Ed.), John Wiley & Sons, New York, p. 80 (1997).
23. Arcella V. and Ferro R., in *Modern Fluoropolymers* (Scheirs, J., Ed.), John Wiley & Sons, New York, p. 81 (1997).
24. Hoffmann, W., *Rubber Technology Handbook*, Carl Hanser Verlag, Munich, 122.
25. Skudelny, D., *Kunststoffe/German Plastics* 77 (11), 17 (1987).

26. Ferro, R., Giunchi, G., and Lagana, C., *Rubber Plastics News*, 19 Feb. (1990).
27. Struckmeyer, H., *Kautsch. Gummi Kunstst.* 43 (9), (1989).
28. Hoffmann, W., *Rubber Technology Handbook,* Carl Hanser Verlag, Munich, 123.
29. Smith, J. F. and Perkins, G. T., *Proc. Inst. Rubb. Conf.*, Preprint 575 (1959).
30. Moran, A. L. and Pattison, D.B., *Rubber World* 103, 37 (1971); Schmiegel, W. W., *Kautsch. Gummi Kunstst.* 31, 137 (1978).
31. Apotheker, D. and Krustic, P.J., U.S. Patent 4,214,060 (1980); Apotheker, D. et al., *Rubber Chem. Technol.* 55, 1004 (1982).
32. Arcella, V. and Ferro, R., in *Modern Fluoropolymers* (Scheirs, J., Ed.), John Wiley & Sons, New York, p. 81 (1997).
33. Schroeder, H., in *Rubber Technology* (Morton, M., Ed.), 3rd ed., Van Nostrand Reinhold Co., New York, p. 419 (1987).
34. Schroeder, H., in *Rubber Technology* (Morton, M., Ed.), 3rd ed., Van Nostrand Reinhold Co., New York, p. 418 (1987).
35. Stivers, D. A., in *The Vanderbilt Rubber Handbook* (Winspear, G. G., Ed.), R. T. Vanderbilt Co., New York, p. 201 (1968).
36. Lynn, M. L. and Worm, A. T., in *Encyclopedia of Polymer Science and Technology,* Vol. 7 (Mark, H. F. and Kroschwitz, J. I., Eds.), John Wiley & Sons, New York, p. 265 (1987).
37. Arcella, V. and Ferro, R., in *Modern Fluoropolymers* (Scheirs, J., Ed.), John Wiley & Sons, New York, p. 86 (1997).
38. Schroeder, H., in *Rubber Technology* (Morton, M., Ed.), 3rd ed., Van Nostrand Reinhold Co., New York, p. 421 (1987).
39. Arcella, V. and Ferro, R., in *Modern Fluoropolymers* (Scheirs, J., Ed.), John Wiley & Sons, New York, p. 87 (1997).
40. Arcella, V. and Ferro, R., in *Modern Fluoropolymers* (Scheirs, J., Ed.), John Wiley & Sons, New York, p. 85 (1997).
41. Schroeder, H., in *Rubber Technology* (Morton, M., Ed.), 3rd ed., Van Nostrand Reinhold Co., New York, p. 423 (1987).
42. Schroeder, H., in *Rubber Technology* (Morton, M., Ed.), 3rd ed., Van Nostrand Reinhold Co., New York, p. 427 (1987).
43. Schroeder, H., in *Rubber Technology* (Morton, M., Ed.), 3rd ed., Van Nostrand Reinhold Co., New York, p. 428 (1987).
44. Apotheker, D. et al., *Rubber Chem. Technol.* 55, 1004 (1982).
45. Geri, S., Lagana, C., and Grossman, R., New Easy Processing Fluoroelastomer, Montedison Paper #30.
46. Nersasian, A., Paper No. 790659 and MacLachlan, J. D., Paper No. 790657, SAE Passenger Car Meeting, Detroit (1979).
47. Schroeder, H., in *Rubber Technology* (Morton, M., Ed.), 3rd ed., Van Nostrand Reinhold Co., New York, p. 432 (1987).
48. Schroeder, H., in *Rubber Technology* (Morton, M., Ed.), 3rd ed., Van Nostrand Reinhold Co., New York, p. 431 (1987).
49. Arcella, V. and Ferro, R., in *Modern Fluoropolymers* (Scheirs, J., Ed.), John Wiley & Sons, New York, p. 88 (1997).
50. Streit, G., paper presented at the 3rd Brazilian Congress on Rubber Technology, San Paulo, September (1989).
51. Leblanc, J., Paper 900197, SAE Meeting, February 26–March 2, Detroit, MI (1990).
52. Aloisio, S., Paper 900956, SAE Meeting, February 28–March 2, Detroit, MI (1994).
53. Mastromateo, R., Paper 900195, SAE Meeting, February 26–March 2, Detroit, MI (1990).

54. Streit, G., *Kautsch. Gummi Kunstst.* 43 (11), 1990.
55. *Prolong the Life of Critical Seals and Rubber Components with KALREZ®,* Publication E86436-01 6/93, DuPont Co., Wilmington, DE.
56. *Seal in Savings with KALREZ® Parts,* Publication E-78267 3/88, DuPont Co., Wilmington, DE.
57. Schnell, R. W., *Seal Design Consideration Using KALREZ® Parts, Seal Design Guide,* Publication E-33808-3 7/92, DuPont Polymers, Wilmington, DE.
58. VITON® Technical Bulletin VT-240. C10, E. I. Du Pont de Nemours & Co.
59. Maxson, M. T., Norris, A. W., and Owen, M. J., in *Modern Fluoropolymers* (Scheirs, J., Ed.), John Wiley & Sons, New York, p. 359 (1997).
60. Maxson, M. T., Norris, A. W., and Owen, M. J., in *Modern Fluoropolymers* (Scheirs, J., Ed.), John Wiley & Sons, New York, p. 360 (1997).
61. Maxson, M. T., Norris, A. W., and Owen, M. J., in *Modern Fluoropolymers* (Scheirs, J., Ed.), John Wiley & Sons, New York, p. 361 (1997).
62. Maxson, M. T., Norris, A. W., and Owen, M. J., in *Modern Fluoropolymers* (Scheirs, J., Ed.), John Wiley & Sons, New York, p. 362 (1997).
63. Hertz, Jr., D. L., in *The Vanderbilt Rubber Handbook*, 13th ed. (Ohm, R. F., Ed.), R. T. Vanderbilt Co., New York, p. 239 (1990).
64. Waible, K. and Maxson, T., *"Silikonkautschuk, Eigenschaften und Verarbeitung,"* Würzburg, Germany, September 20, 1995, p. 2.
65. Thomas, D. R., in *Siloxane Polymers* (Clarkson, S. J. and Semlyen, J. A., Eds.), Prentice-Hall, Englewood Cliffs, NJ, 1993, p. 567.
66. Waible, K. and Maxson, T., *"Silikonkautschuk, Eigenschaften und Verarbeitung,"* Würzburg, Germany, September 20, 1995, p. 4.
67. Maxson, M. T., Norris, A. W., and Owen, M. J., in *Modern Fluoropolymers* (Scheirs, J., Ed.), John Wiley & Sons, New York, p. 363 (1997).
68. Waible, K. and Maxson, T., *"Silikonkautschuk, Eigenschaften und Verarbeitung,"* Würzburg, Germany, September 20, 1995, p. 5.
69. Waible, K. and Maxson, T., *"Silikonkautschuk, Eigenschaften und Verarbeitung,"* Würzburg, Germany, September 20, 1995, p. 3.
70. Gomez-Anton, M. R., Masegosa, R. M., and Horta, A., *Polymer* 28, 2116 (1987).
71. Norris, A. M., Fiedler, L. D., Knapp, T. L., and Virant, M. S., *Automotive Polym. Design* 19 (April), 12 (1990).
72. Knight, G. J. and Wright, W. W., *Br. Polym. J.* 21, 199 (1989).
73. Maxson, M. T., Norris, A. W., and Owen, M. J., in *Modern Fluoropolymers* (Scheirs, J., Ed.), John Wiley & Sons, New York, p. 364 (1997).
74. Maxson, M. T., Norris, A. W., and Owen, M. J., in *Modern Fluoropolymers* (Scheirs, J., Ed.), John Wiley & Sons, New York, p. 366 (1997).
75. Maxson, M. T., Norris, A. W., and Owen, M. J., in *Modern Fluoropolymers* (Scheirs, J., Ed.), John Wiley & Sons, New York, p. 370 (1997).
76. Maxson, M. T., *Gummi Fasern Kunstst.* 12, 873 (1995).
77. Maxson, M. T., Norris, A. W., and Owen, M. J., in *Modern Fluoropolymers* (Scheirs, J., Ed.), John Wiley & Sons, New York, p. 371 (1997).
78. Maxson, M. T., *Aerospace Engineering*, December, 15 (1990).
79. Maxson, M. T., Norris, A. W., and Owen, M. J., in *Modern Fluoropolymers* (Scheirs, J., Ed.), John Wiley & Sons, New York, p. 369 (1997).
80. Waible, K. and Maxson, T., *"Silikonkautschuk, Eigenschaften und Verarbeitung,"* Würzburg, Germany, September 20, 1995, p. 12.

6 Technology and Applications of Aqueous Fluoropolymer Systems

6.1 INTRODUCTION

The majority of fluoropolymers is produced by polymerization in aqueous systems, but in subsequent steps the dispersions obtained in the polymerization process are coagulated into a solid form and converted into powders or pellets. However, some operations, such as impregnation of fabrics or casting of films can be readily done using aqueous dispersions, suspensions, or latexes. Such systems have advantage over solutions in organic solvents in that they are safer to handle and do not require expensive solvent recovery systems to prevent environmental pollution. Moreover, preparing a solution of a polymer is an additional, often time-consuming operation, requiring specialized equipment and often explosion-proof environment. Finally, most of the perfluoropolymers would not dissolve at all or only in exotic and very expensive solvents, so aqueous systems are the only liquid form in which they are available. The disadvantage of waterborne systems is that they very often dry much slower than the usual solvents, such as ketones, esters, or chlorinated or fluorinated hydrocarbons, used for some of the fluoropolymers. Furthermore, some additives, such as surfactants, may not be removed completely from the dry film and may have adverse effects on the quality of the final product.

In general, waterborne fluoropolymer systems are handled and processed in a similar fashion as other organic coatings. They can be compounded by addition of fillers, pigments and colorants, resins, and other additives; they can be viscosified, blended with other waterborne polymeric systems, etc. Because of the nature of the base polymer, they differ in their processing behavior. For example, PTFE dispersions are very shear sensitive, whereas the others are not. Coating formulations from dispersions of perfluoropolymers are usually very simple, containing only the necessary surfactant. If fillers and pigments are used, the amounts, which can be added, are limited; otherwise poor-quality films would be obtained. Another aspect to consider is the processing temperature of the polymer; some pigments and colorants cannot tolerate the high processing temperatures required for perfluoropolymers. On the other hand, some fluoropolymers can be compounded into highly filled and pigmented coatings and paints.

The following fluoropolymers are commercially available in aqueous systems: PTFE, PFA, MFA, FEP, ETFE, PVDF, THV Fluoroplastic, fluorocarbon elastomers, fluoroacrylates, and fluorinated polyurethanes.

6.2 PTFE DISPERSIONS

Aqueous dispersions of PTFE resin are hydrophobic, negatively charged colloidal systems containing PTFE particles with diameters ranging from 0.05 to 0.5 μm suspended in water. Commercial products have a resin content of approximately 60% by weight.[1] Most PTFE dispersions typically contain 6 to 10% on the weight of the resin of nonionic wetting agent and stabilizer (essentially a surfactant). The specific gravity of such dispersion is about 1.50.

PTFE resin dispersions are milky-white liquids, with viscosity approximately 20 cP and pH about 10. The resin contained therein has the characteristics of fine powders, that is, a high sensitivity to shear.

Upon prolonged standing, the particles, which have specific gravity 2.2 to 2.3,[2] tend to settle with some classification of sizes. During storage, the particles settle gradually to the bottom of the container with gradually increasing clarification of the water phase on the top. Normally, the settled dispersion can be redispersed by gentle agitation completely. Essentially, stabilized dispersions have an indefinite shelf life as long as they are stirred occasionally[3] and kept from freezing.

Unstabilized PTFE dispersions are irreversibly coagulated by acids, electrolytes, and water-miscible solvents, such as alcohol and acetone, and by violent agitation, freezing, and boiling. A small addition of an ionic or nonionic surfactant stabilizes the dispersion so it tolerates some mechanical agitation and addition of water-miscible solvents. It also slows sedimentation. The lower limit for an adequate stabilization is about 1% of the surfactant on the weight of the polymer; however, for most coating and impregnating operations the amount is more like 10% to assure good wetting and penetration. Higher amounts than that may increase the viscosity of the dispersion to an undesirable level. Moreover, for cases where the dried coating is sintered, an increased amount of surfactant (12% or more) increases the amount of time necessary to remove the surfactant in the baking stage of the process (see below).

The pH of commercial PTFE dispersions as supplied is usually 10 and tends to drop during storage. Therefore, it is important to check the pH periodically and maintain it by adding ammonium hydroxide to prevent souring. This is particularly important during warm and humid weather when conditions can promote growth of bacteria. The bacteria feed on the surfactant present in the dispersion, causing a dark brown discoloration and a rancid odor. If souring occurs, the containers must be cleaned out and disinfected with sodium hypochlorite solution. The ammonium hydroxide used for maintaining pH is usually available as reagent grade of 29%. At this concentration about 5 g/gal of dispersion should be sufficient.[4]

The relationship between solids content and gravity is approximately linear and can be expressed by the equation[3]:

$$V = P(A - B/100\ AB) + 1/A \tag{6.1}$$

where V is the specific volume of the dispersion, P is the percent by weight of polymer solids; A is the specific gravity of water (0.9985) and B the specific gravity of polymer solids (2.25).

The viscosity of PTFE dispersions increases proportionally with increasing solids content up to about 30 to 35% solids, and beyond that the increase is much more rapid. Dispersions with surfactants exhibit the same pattern, but the rate of increase is faster and depends on the type and amount of surfactant.[5]

6.3 OTHER PERFLUOROPOLYMER DISPERSIONS

6.3.1 FEP DISPERSIONS

Commercial aqueous dispersions of FEP are supplied with 54 to 55% by weight of hydrophobic negatively charged particles with the addition of approximately 6% by weight of a mixture of nonionic and anionic surfactants based on polymer content. The particle size range is 0.1 to 0.26 μm. Nominal pH of the dispersion is 9.5 and the viscosity at room temperature is approximately 25 cP.[6]

6.3.2 PFA DISPERSIONS

Commercial aqueous dispersions of PFA contain 50% or more by weight of PFA particles and typically 5% of surfactants on the polymer content.[7]

6.3.3 ETFE DISPERSIONS

Comercial ETFE dispersion offered by Dyneon LLC under the designation Dyneon™ ET X 6425 has solids content of 20% and density 1.10 and contains non-ionic surface active ingredients (for details see Publication 98-0504-1025-1, 4/00 by Dyneon LLC).

6.4 PROCESSING OF PTFE DISPERSIONS

The major utility of PTFE dispersions is that they allow processing of PTFE resin, which cannot be processed as ordinary polymeric melt, because of its extraordinarily high melt viscosity, or as solution, because it is insoluble. Thus, PTFE dispersions can be used to coat fabrics and yarns, impregnate fibers, nonwoven fabrics, and other porous structures; to produce antistick and low-friction coatings on metals and other substrates; and to produce cast films.

Surfactants are an essential ingredient for sufficient wetting of various substrates including sintered PTFE and for the formation of continuous films by uniform spreading on substrates such as metals, glass, ceramics, and polytetrafluoroethylene. Generally, 6 to 10% of nonionic surfactant (e.g., alkylaryl polyether alcohol) based on polymer content is sufficient to impart wetting and film-forming properties. Sometimes a small amount of a fluorosurfactant (typically below 0.1% on the polymer content) can be added to increase the efficiency of the nonionic surfactant.

To convert a dispersion into a sintered PTFE film, four distinct steps are required: *casting* (dipping or flowing out) onto a supporting surface, *drying* to remove water, *baking* to remove the surfactant, and *sintering* to obtain a clear coherent film.

For a successful production of a cast film, the dispersion has to wet the supporting surface and spread uniformly. In drying, the thickness of the deposited layer is very important. If the deposit is too thick, it develops fissures and cracks, referred to as "mudcracking." These flaws cannot be eliminated in the sintering step. Thus, for each formulation there is a *critical cracking thickness*, which represents a limit below which cracking will not occur in a single application. It depends mainly on the particle size range, amount of surfactant used, and the solids content. Typical value under optimum conditions is 0.0015 in.[8] For thicker films multiple coats have to be applied. For a properly formulated dispersion, recoating over an unsintered or sintered coating is not a problem.

6.4.1 IMPREGNATION

Properly compounded PTFE dispersions are suitable for impregnation because of their low viscosity, very small particles, and ability to wet the surfaces. The surfactant aids the capillary action and wetting interstices in a porous material. After the substrate is dipped and dried, it may or may not be sintered. This depends on the intended application. In fact, the unsintered coating exhibits sufficiently high chemical resistance and antistick property. If required, the coated substrate may be heated to about 290°C (555°F) for several minutes to remove the surfactant. Lower temperatures and longer times are used if the substrate cannot tolerate such a high temperature. In some cases, the impregnated material is calendered or compressed in a mold to compact the PTFE resin and to hold it in place.

6.4.2 FABRIC COATING

6.4.2.1 Equipment

The largest proportion of PTFE dispersions is used for coating glass fabric. Equipment used for that purpose is a vertical coating tower consisting of three heated zones, namely, drying zone, baking zone, and sintering zone (see Figure 6.1). There are several systems for heating these zones and the choice of the heating system depends on the type of product to be made. The most common heating is by circulating hot air heated by gas burners. Air in drying and baking zones can be also heated by circulating hot oil. Infrared heating is another choice and its use has been growing over the past decade. Each method has its advantages and disadvantages. *Gas heating* is very effective, but requires a relatively long start-up time and is rather inflexible and difficult to control. *Hot oil heating* is very precise and effective, but requires very long start-up time and represents a very high investment cost and high operation costs. *Infrared heating systems* are very flexible and relatively inexpensive. They can be switched on and off very quickly and, if they burn out, replacement is very simple. Their disadvantage is nonuniform temperature across the width of the web and overall temperature control. In modern production coating towers the heating zones are heated independently.

A typical coating line consists of fabric pay-off, the tower, and a take-up for the coated goods. Some lines also include a festoon (accumulator) to avoid the need for stopping the line if the web is being spliced or if the take-up has to be stopped for roll change or a problem. The take-up may be arranged as a turret for a faster roll change.

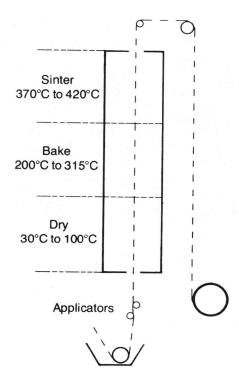

FIGURE 6.1 Schematic of a modern PTFE coating tower. (Courtesy of DuPont Fluoropolymers.)

A stainless-steel dip tank is on the bottom of the coating tower. Inside the tank is a submerged roll, sometimes called "dip bar," which may be made from stainless steel or PTFE.[9] The roll may be locked or rotated. A rotating bar most frequently has sleeve bearings, which are lubricated by the liquid in the tank. Some designs use multiple rolls (typically three, see Figure 6.2); this arrangement reduces differences in pickup between the two sides of the web.

If the process requires wiping of the excess liquid from the web, applicators of different design are used. The most wiping is achieved by sharp knives, the least with horizontally opposed, spring-loaded, fixed-gap metering rolls.[9] In actual industrial practice the most common wiping devices are round-edged knives, wire-wound rods ("Meyer rods") with varied wire diameter, and smooth bars (Figure 6.3). The larger the wire diameter, the greater thickness of the coating applied. Free dipping, i.e., without wiping, is another possibility. The amount of coating can be also controlled by the amount of solids and by viscosity and to a degree by the web speed.

Coating towers can be of straight-up design, or can be built in an up-and-down configuration. In the latter design, the drying and baking zones are in the first ("up") part of the tower and the sintering zone, including a section for web cooling, is in the "down" part. This design saves space, but has the disadvantages that sometimes the baked, unsintered coating is picked up by the rolls on the top of the tower, that

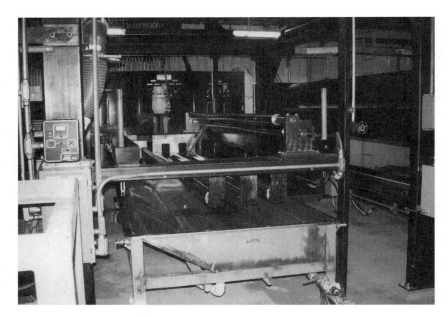

FIGURE 6.2 Dip tank with three dip bars.

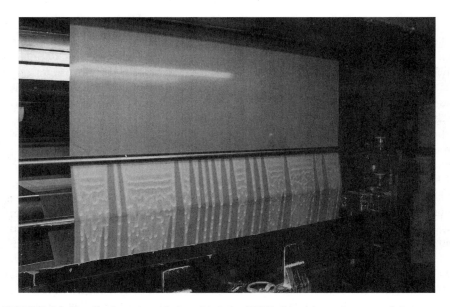

FIGURE 6.3 Detail of coating of glass fabric by PTFE dispersion using smooth bars.

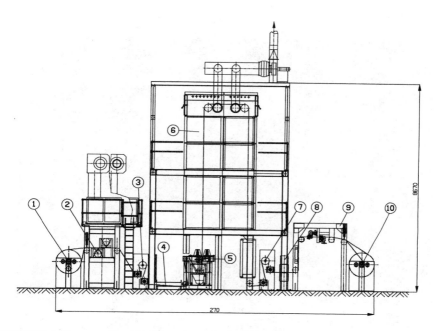

FIGURE 6.4 Up-and-down design of coating tower. 1 = unwinding unit; 2 = fabric cleaning unit; 3 = tensioning unit; 4 = operator platform; 5 = dip tank; 6 = oven (drying and baking zones); 7 = tensioning unit; 8 = beta gauge; 9 = inspection table, trimming device; 10 = wind-up unit. The sintering zone (on the right) is not numbered. (Courtesy of Gebrüder Menzel Maschinenfabrik GmbH & Co.)

the residual surfactant decomposes vigorously at the entry to the sintering zone, and that the products of decomposition condense on the top of the tower, mainly on the rolls. An example of this design is shown in Figure 6.4. Regardless of the design, each tower has an exhaust system on the top for the removal of the volatile decomposition products, which is often coupled with a combustion system to eliminate air pollution. Coating towers are built to process webs up to about 5 m (15 ft) wide, although the majority of them are in the 2 to 3 m (6 to 9 ft) range. A typical production coating tower is shown in Figure 6.5.

The coating speeds depend on the type of fabric and can vary between 0.3 and 14 m/min (1 to 45 ft/min). The speed is also limited by the process; it can be drying, or baking, or sintering. Too high a speed may cause blisters due to insufficient removal of water in the drying zone or insufficient removal of surfactant in the baking zone that may cause fire in the sintering zone or discoloration of the coating and impaired rewetting of the coating in the subsequent pass. Insufficient sintering (off-white, dull coating) is another possible consequence of too high a coating speed.

The temperatures in the individual zones may vary according to the type of fabric being coated. However, the goal is to remove water and other volatile components from the coating without boiling and before the web reaches the baking zone and then to remove surfactant in the baking zone. The sintering is almost

FIGURE 6.5 Production coating tower in operation.

instantaneous once the temperature is above the crystalline melting point of the PTFE resin. Typical air temperature ranges in the individual zones are:

Drying zone: 80 to 95°C (176 to 203°F)
Baking zone: 250 to 315°C (480 to 600°F)
Sintering zone: 360 to 400°C (680 to 750°F)

If any of the zones is heated by infrared systems, the surface temperature of the heating elements is set and controlled to attain the required temperature.

6.4.2.2 Formulations

As supplied, PTFE dispersions contain nonionic wetting agent (surfactant), which provides them with good wetting properties and a minimum tendency to foam. Generally, nonionic surfactants are preferred because they are less likely to induce abnormal viscosities due to thixotropic effects. Other acceptable surfactants are anionic types. Cationic wetting agents are not used because they tend to flocculate the dispersion.[4] The surfactants used in the formulation can be decomposed at the temperatures required for baking, minimizing residual contamination. Other additives, such as mineral fillers or colorants, may be added to achieve desired properties or appearance. Fillers and pigments must be added in the form of a paste, either purchased or prepared in house using ball mills or dispersion mills. Often the original PTFE dispersion is diluted by water to attain the required coat thickness.

The viscosity of a dispersion may be increased by adding a water-soluble viscosifier. There are several types, for example, HEC (hydroxyethyl cellulose) or acrylic viscosifiers, which are added in the form of an aqueous stock solution. To utilize their viscosifying effects fully, the pH of the formulation must be increased to a certain optimum value, typical for a given viscosifier.

When preparing formulations by blending or adding mineral fillers to PTFE dispersions, only mild agitation must be used. Propeller-type stirrers are best suited for that. High-speed, high-shear mixing is likely to result in coagulation.

6.4.2.3 Coating Process

Glass and aramid fabrics (e.g., Kevlar® or Nomex® (DuPont)) are currently the only fabrics that can withstand the high temperatures required for sintering of PTFE resin. Thus, they can be coated by it without being degraded greatly in the process. Glass fabrics come with a starch-based treatment (sizing) that is necessary in the weaving operation. However, this treatment interferes with the coating and has to be removed by "heat cleaning," which means that the fabric is heated to high temperatures to burn off the starch and other organic compounds used in the sizing. This operation is frequently the first pass of the coating process, in which the glass fabric passes through the tower without being coated. In some contemporary designs an infrared heater is placed between the let-off and the dipping tank. This way the treatment is removed in this heater and the fabric can be coated immediately. This heater also often contains a vacuum cleaner, which removes any loose contaminants from the surface of the fabric.

Depending on the fabric construction and required thickness, the number of passes can be as high as 12 or even more. In some cases undiluted dispersions (with typically 60% solids) are used for at least some of the passes. Each coat must be below the critical cracking thickness to avoid mud cracking. As an alternative, several unsintered coats are applied and the coated fabric is then calendered prior to sintering to seal the mud cracks. The calender rolls are heated to temperatures ranging from 148 to177°C (300 to 350°F) and operate at a pressure about 1 ton/linear in. to be effective. Wetting agents must be removed completely in the baking zone to prevent the coating from being picked off by the rolls. Calendering is also used to flatten the fabric and to bury filaments, which could be broken during coating.[7] Calenders used for this purpose consist either of one chrome-plated steel roll and a compressed paper backup roll or of two chrome-plated steel rolls. In the former design, only the steel roll can be heated. The result is that there is a difference in appearance between the two sides of the web, which, depending on the application, may or may not be a disadvantage. The advantage is that the roll combination exerts a gentler pressure. In the design with two steel rolls both rolls can be heated, and both sides of the calendered web are smooth. The disadvantage is that the nip may sometimes be too harsh on the glass fibers. However, in general, this design is more effective for the compaction of unsintered PTFE and consequently in sealing the mud cracks.

To obtain PTFE-coated fabrics that can be heat-sealed or laminated at lower temperatures, a thin coat of diluted aqueous dispersions of FEP or PFA is applied on top of the PTFE coating.

6.4.2.4 Lamination

PTFE-coated fabrics can be laminated in electrically heated presses at temperatures in the range 360 to 400°C (680 to 750°F) and pressures around 3.4 MPa (500 psi). If the fabric has a coat of FEP or PFA, the lamination temperatures are reduced to be above the melting points of the respective resins. Such fabrics can also be laminated on equipment operating continuously. Another lamination process is based on laminating two substrates having an unsintered baked layer of PTFE on the surface. The two adjacent unsintered layers act as a pressure-sensitive adhesive and as result of fibrillation under pressure[11] form a bond sufficiently strong mechanically to survive a free sintering (without pressure). After sintering, the bond will have the heat resistance of PTFE. This process is suitable for the lamination of coated fabrics as well as for lamination of PTFE cast films with PTFE-coated fabrics or a combination of PTFE with other materials in a continuous fashion.[11]

6.4.2.5 Applications for Coated Fabrics

The largest volume of PTFE-coated fabric is used in construction. The typical application is as roofing material for large structures, often with minimum support, such as sports buildings (Figure 6.6), shopping malls, airports (Figure 6.7), industrial warehousing, and cooling towers.[12,13] Recently, large tents for huge tent cities in the

FIGURE 6.6 PTFE stadium roof. (Courtesy of Chemfab Corporation.)

FIGURE 6.7 PTFE roofing elements at the Munich Airport Center. (Courtesy of Skyspan Europe GmbH.)

FIGURE 6.8 Arabian Tower Hotel in Dubai. (Courtesy of Skyspan Europe GmbH.)

Middle East were made from PTFE-coated glass fabric. A unique architecture using PTFE-coated glass fabric is shown in Figure 6.8. Other uses are in radomes, as belts in ceramic and food industries, as release sheets, as cooking sheets in fast-food establishments, as release sheets for baked goods, as industrial drying belts, in electrical and electronic industries, and as reinforcement for high-temperature pressure-sensitive tapes. PTFE-coated aramid fabrics laminated to PTFE cast films are used in protective clothing and specialty tents for protection against chemical warfare and as protective clothing in the chemical industry and in firefighting (Figure 6.9).

6.4.3 Cast Films

6.4.3.1 Cast Film Process

As pointed out earlier, PTFE homopolymer cannot be processed by melt extrusion because of its extremely high melt viscosity. Thus, other methods, such as skiving from compression molded and sintered billets (see Chapter 4) and by casting from dispersions, were found to prepare films. The original method for casting films from PTFE dispersions employs polished stainless-steel belts, which are dipped into a properly compounded dispersion. The thin coating of the liquid is then dried and the dry powdery layer is subjected to baking and sintering. To obtain a good-quality film, the thickness of the film has to be below the critical value to prevent mudcracking.

The equipment used is again a vertical coater with heated zones, very similar to the coating tower for fabric.[14] The speed of the belt is slow, about 0.3 to 1 m/min and there are no applicators used to remove excess dispersion. The amount of coating picked up by the belt is controlled mainly by the solids content of the dispersion and by the belt speed. A production machine is built with multiple stages. Thus, after a film is sintered, it is recoated in the next stage. At the end of the machine,

FIGURE 6.9 Protective clothing from fluoropolymeric laminates. (Courtesy of Chemfab Corporation.)

there is a device designed to strip the finished films from both sides of the belt and wind them up into rolls.

The advantage of this method is that each layer can be made from a different type of dispersion. For example, clear and pigmented layers can be made or the top layer can be prepared from an FEP or PFA dispersion to obtain films that can be heat-sealed or laminated. In fact, films with both surfaces heat-sealable can be produced by this method. In such an instance, PFA is applied as the first coat onto the belt and FEP as the last coat, because PFA can be stripped from the steel belt, whereas FEP would adhere to it and is impossible to strip. Another possibility is to make films with an unsintered last coat, which can be used for lamination with substrates coated with unsintered PTFE using the lamination method described earlier (see Section 6.4.2.4).

An improved process and equipment for cast PTFE films have been developed, which have considerably higher productivity than the method and equipment described above.[15] The process essentially uses a vertical coater with multiple stages. The carrier belt has to be made from a material of low thermal mass which can tolerate repeated exposure to the sintering temperature and has surface properties such that it can be wetted by the dispersion, yet the film can be stripped without being stretched. There are several possible belt materials, but KAPTON® H (DuPont) was found to be particularly suitable because of its heat resistance, dimensional stability, and surface characteristics.[15] The production speeds used in this process are 3 to 10 m/min (9 to 30 ft/min).

Unlike in the coater with steel belts, in this process equipment applicators such as wire-wound bars are used, which may be designed to rotate to assure a better, more uniform coating. The dip tanks are similar to those used in fabric coating, also using an immersed dip bar. To prevent coating defects due to shear, the dip tanks have double walls and are chilled by circulated chilled water to temperatures below 19°C (66°F), the first-order transition temperature.

The dispersions used in this process are formulated in such a way that they wet the carrier sufficiently and tolerate higher shear at the wire-wound bars due to a relatively high coating belt speed. This is accomplished by a combination of nonionic surfactants (e.g., octyl phenoxy polyethoxy ethanol) and fluorosurfactants. This subject is discussed in detail in Reference 15.

6.4.3.2   Applications for PTFE Cast Films

Because of the nature of the manufacturing process, there is no melt flow and consequently the cast films do not exhibit anisotropy typical for extruded films. PTFE cast films have higher tensile strength, elongation, and dielectric strength.[15] Another advantage is that they can be produced in layered form from different dispersions (e.g., two colors, with one layer clear, others pigmented, or with one layer having static-dissipative properties, or with one or both layers consisting of melt-processable perfluoropolymers, such as FEP or PFA). If suitable tie-layers are used, it is possible to produce a combination of PTFE film with a bonding layer based on a fluoroelastomer or other fluoropolymer, such as lower-melting THV Fluoroplastic or PVDF. Films with lower-melting bonding layers can be laminated with substrates, which normally would not tolerate the high PTFE sintering temperatures.

Cast PTFE films can be laminated with different substrates, most frequently with PTFE-coated glass and aramid fabrics. They also can be metallized, in particular with aluminum for use in electronics. Other applications include as release films for the manufacture of composite materials for aerospace vehicles, in electronics and electrical industries, as selective membranes, and in the chemical industry.

6.4.4   OTHER APPLICATIONS FOR PTFE AQUEOUS DISPERSIONS

PTFE aqueous dispersions are applied onto metal substrates by spraying, dipping, flow coating, electrodeposition, or coagulation to provide chemical resistance, nonstick, and low-friction surfaces. Nonstick cookware and bakeware are made from dispersion specifically formulated for that purpose with the use of a primer for the metal. After coating, the parts are dried and sintered.

PTFE fibers are made by spinning from aqueous dispersions, which are mixed with matrix-forming medium and forced through a spinneret into a coagulating bath. Then the matrix material is removed by heating and the fibers are sintered and oriented (drawn) in the molten state to develop their full strength.[15]

Another application of PTFE dispersions is the preparation of a variety of compositions with other materials, such as mineral fillers, other polymers in powdered form by co-coagulation. The dispersion of the other component is blended with the PTFE dispersion and the blend is then coagulated. The resulting composition can be processed by extrusion with lubricants (see processing of fine powders) or by compression molding.[16]

6.5 PROCESSING OF AQUEOUS DISPERSIONS OF FEP AND PFA

6.5.1 PROCESSING

Aqueous dispersions of these two melt-processible perfluoropolymers are processed in a way similar to PTFE dispersion. FEP dispersions can be used for coating fabrics, metals, and polyimide films. They are very well suited for bonding seals and bearings from PTFE to metallic and nonmetallic components and as nonstick and low-friction coatings for metals.[16] FEP can be fused completely into a continuous film in approximately 1 min at 400°C (752°F) or 40 min at 290°C (554°F).[17] PFA is used to coat various surfaces, including glass fabric, glass, and metals.

6.5.2 APPLICATIONS

Fabrics coated with FEP and PFA can be laminated and heat-sealed into protective garments, canopies, etc. FEP-coated polyimide films are used in electronics and as a wire tape. FEP-based anticorrosion coatings are used in the chemical industry and as chemical barriers.[18] A thin coating of FEP or PFA can be used as a hot melt adhesive for a variety of substrates, including PTFE-coated fabrics and laminates.

6.6 PROCESSING OF AQUEOUS DISPERSIONS OF POLYVINYLIDENE FLUORIDE

6.6.1 PROCESSING OF PVDF DISPERSIONS

Commercially available dispersions in latex form (e.g., KYNAR® Latex 32, Elf Atochem) contain approximately 19 to 20% by weight of homopolymer. They can be processed as coatings of fabrics or into thin cast films using equipment described in the section on the processing of PTFE dispersions. The fusing temperature for PVDF films is 230 to 250°C (446 to 482°F),[19] which is low enough for coating polyester fabrics and casting films on carriers that tolerate this temperature.

6.6.2 APPLICATIONS OF PVDF AQUEOUS DISPERSIONS

It is possible to cast thin films from PVDF aqueous dispersions. They can be pigmented and used for decorative surfaces.[20] PVDF aqueous dispersions alone or their blends with acrylic aqueous systems are used for coating fabrics or as decorative or protective coatings.

6.7 AQUEOUS DISPERSIONS OF THV FLUOROPLASTICS

6.7.1 PROCESSING OF THV DISPERSIONS

Aqueous dispersions of THV are available with solids content 31 to 34% (THV 220D, THV 340D, THV 510D) and 50% (THV 340C) with the addition of an ionic emulsifier. They can be processed in a similar fashion as dispersions of other melt-processible fluoropolymers, namely, for coating fabrics or cast thin films. Because of their low melting temperatures (140 to 150°C or 284 to 302°F),[21] they can be used to coat polyester fabrics and can be cast on carriers, tolerating the processing temperature (e.g., polyester film). THV aqueous dispersions when properly compounded can be foamed by whipping in a fashion similar to elastomeric latexes.[22]

6.7.2 Applications of THV Dispersions

Coated and laminated fabrics (the original application for THV resins) are used in many fabric applications where flexibility, weatherability, and/or low permeability are required.

Typical applications are protective covers, tarpaulins, awnings, and chemical-protective garments.[23] Thin THV films can be laminated onto temperature-sensitive substrates, such as plasticized PVC and polyester.[24]

6.8 FLUOROCARBON ELASTOMERS IN LATEX FORM, PROCESSING AND APPLICATIONS

A certain proportion of fluoroelastomers is used in latex form. The compounding techniques used are similar to those used for standard latexes; i.e., solid ingredients are first dispersed in water with the use of surface active agents and liquid ingredients are prepared as emulsions prior to their addition to the latex. The dispersions of solids are prepared in ball mills or high-speed mills (e.g., Kady).

Fluorocarbon elastomers in the form of highly concentrated latex (typically 70% solids by weight)[25] are used in the coating of fabrics to produce protective garments, expansion joints, etc. They can be blended with other compatible fluoropolymers and specialty polymers to attain specific properties. Coatings can be cross-linked chemically or by electron beam. Chemically cross-linked coatings can be two- or one-component systems curing at ambient or elevated temperatures. An example of a one-component water-based coating is that developed by Lauren International Co., which uses hydrolyzed and stabilized aminosilanes. Such system cures to optimum properties in about one hour at 100°C (212°F).[26,27] The consumption of fluoroelastomer latexes is growing since they are replacing solutions in volatile organic solvents used in coating applications to comply with lower solvent emission requirement.[25]

6.9 HEALTH AND SAFETY

Aqueous dispersions of fluoropolymers are in general neutral to moderately alkaline, with the exception of certain coatings for metals, which are strongly acidic. Some additives in the aqueous phase of the dispersion may irritate eyes and/or skin. Therefore, it is advisable to use protective garments, goggles, or facial shield. If the liquid comes in contact with skin, the affected spot must be flushed with water immediately. If the liquid comes in contact with the eyes, they must be flushed immediately and medical help provided as soon as possible.

When aqueous dispersions are processed at elevated temperatures, particularly above the melting point of the dispersed polymer, the same health and safety precautions must be taken as when corresponding resins in solid form are processed.

REFERENCES

1. *Teflon® PTFE, Dispersion Properties and Processing Techniques*, Bulletin No. X-50G, E. I. du Pont de Nemours & Co., Wilmington, DE, Publication E-55541-2, p. 2.
2. Renfrew, M. M. and Lewis, E. E., *Ind. Eng. Chem.* 38, 870 (1946).
3. Lontz, J. F. and Happoldt, Jr., W. B., *Ind. Eng. Chem.* 44, 1800 (1952).
4. *Teflon® PTFE, Dispersion Properties and Processing Techniques*, Bulletin No. X-50G, E. I. du Pont de Nemours & Co., Wilmington, DE, Publication E-55541-2, p. 3.
5. Lontz, J. F. and Happoldt Jr., W. B., *Ind. Eng. Chem.* 44, 1802 (1952).
6. *Teflon® FEP 120*, Product Information, E. I. du Pont de Nemours & Co., Wilmington, DE, Publication H-12035-1, p. 1.
7. Gangal, S. V., in *Encyclopedia of Polymer Science and Technology*, Vol. 16 (Mark, H. F. and Kroschwitz, J. I., Eds.), John Wiley & Sons, New York, p. 624 (1989).
8. *Teflon® PTFE, Dispersion Properties and Processing Techniques*, Bulletin No. X-50G, E. I. du Pont de Nemours & Co., Wilmington, DE, Publication E-55541-2, p. 4.
9. *Teflon® PTFE, Dispersion Properties and Processing Techniques*, Bulletin No. X-50G), E. I. du Pont de Nemours & Co., Wilmington, DE, Publication E-55541-2, p. 6.
10. Effenberger, J. A., Enzien, F. M., Keese, F. M., and Koerber, K. G., U.S. Patent 5,141,800 (August 25, 1992).
11. Forster, B., *J. Coated Fabrics* 15, July 25 (1985).
12. Fitz, H., *Tech. Rdsch. (Bern)* 75, No. 51/52, 20th December 10 (1983).
13. Petriello, J. V., U.S. Patent 2,852,811 (September 1958).
14. Effenberger, J. A., Koerber, K. G., Latorra, M. N., and Petriello, J. V., U.S. Patent 5,075,065 (December 24, 1991).
15. Steuber, W., U.S. Patent 3,051,545 (August 28, 1962).
16. Sperati, C. A., in *Handbook of Plastic Materials and Technology* (Rubin, I. I., Ed.), John Wiley & Sons, New York, p. 125 (1990).
17. Gangal, S. V., in *Encyclopedia of Polymer Science and Technology*, Vol. 16 (Mark, H. F. and Kroschwitz, J. I., Eds.), John Wiley & Sons, New York, p. 611 (1989).
18. Gangal, S. V., in *Encyclopedia of Polymer Science and Technology*, Vol. 16 (Mark, H. F. and Kroschwitz, J. I., Eds.), John Wiley & Sons, New York, p. 624 (1989).
19. Dohany, J. E. and Humphrey, J. S., in *Encyclopedia of Polymer Science and Technology*, Vol. 17 (Mark, H. F. and Kroschwitz, J. I., Eds.), John Wiley & Sons, New York, p. 542 (1989).
20. Dohany, J. E. and Humphrey, J. S., in *Encyclopedia of Polymer Science and Technology*, Vol. 17 (Mark, H. F. and Kroschwitz, J. I., Eds.), John Wiley & Sons, New York, p. 543 (1989).
21. 3M THV Fluoroplastics, Technical Information, Publication 98-0211-7012-5, 3M Specialty Fluoropolymers, St. Paul, MN.
22. THV Coating, Publication IPR/8-4-94, American Hoechst Corporation, Leominster, MA.

23. Hull, D. E., Johnson, B. V., Rodricks, I. P., and Staley, J. B., in *Modern Fluoropolymers* (Scheirs, J., Ed.), John Wiley & Sons, New York, p. 268 (1997).

24. Hull, D. E., Johnson, B. V., Rodricks, I. P., and Staley, J. B., in *Modern Fluoropolymers* (Scheirs, J., Ed.), John Wiley & Sons, New York, p. 269 (1997).

25. Arcella, V. and Ferro, R., in *Modern Fluoropolymers* (Scheirs, J., Ed.), John Wiley & Sons, New York, p. 86 (1997).

26. Kirochko, P. and Kreiner, J. G., *A New Waterborne Fluoroelastomer Coating,* Paper presented at the Conference Fluorine in Coatings III, Grenelefe, Orlando, FL, January 25–27 (1999).

27. Kirochko, P. and Kreiner, J. G., U.S. Patent 5,854,342 (Dec. 29, 1998).

7 Effects of Heat, Radiation, and Environment on Fluoropolymers

7.1 EFFECTS OF HEAT

Generally, fluoropolymers are among the organic materials with the highest resistance to thermal degradation; however, there are significant differences between them. Relative thermal stability of selected fluoropolymers was studied by thermogravimetry.[1] The findings indicated that ETFE has the lowest thermal stability, which can be explained by the presence of ethylene linkages in its molecule. FEP is next and in spite of being fully fluorinated, its lower-than-expected thermal stability is very likely due to a high degree of $-CF_3$ branching. PFA is more stable than FEP because of the presence of a stable, highly shielded ether group in its structure.[2] PTFE is the most stable of this group since its hydrocarbon backbone is protected by the large fluorine atoms attached by a very strong bond. There are two competing thermal degradation mechanisms, namely, unzipping (depolymerization) to form monomer and chain transfer reactions. The high-energy, very strong C–F bond makes depolymerization the dominant mechanism, whereas weaker C–H and C–Cl bonds promote thermal degradation by chain transfer reaction.[2]

7.1.1 Thermal Degradation of Perfluoropolymers

PTFE is extremely inert and stable up to temperatures of 250°C (482°F). When heated above that temperature, it begins to decompose very slowly, giving rise to small quantities of gaseous products. For example, the initial rate of weight loss for granular PTFE has been reported as 0.0001%/h at 260°C (500°F) and 0.004%/h at 371°C (700°F).[3] Thermal degradation of PTFE at different temperatures is illustrated by Table 7.1. Vacuum thermal degradation of PTFE results in monomer formation and studies established it to be a first-order reaction.[4] Mass spectroscopic analysis of PTFE indicates that degradation starts at about 440°C (824°F), peaks at 540°C (1004°F), and continues until 590°C (1094°F).[5] Because of that, processing PTFE at temperatures above 400°C (752°F) is not recommended. Inhalation of the fumes evolved during processing causes an influenza-like syndrome described as "polymer fume fever,"[6] which is further worsened by smoking tobacco. The signs and symp-

TABLE 7.1
Thermal Degradation of Polytetrafluoroethylene

Temperature, °C	Fine Powder	Granular Initial	Granular Steady State
232	0.0001–0.0002	0.00001–0.00005	1×10^{-11}
260	0.0006	0.0001–0.0002	100×10^{-11}
316	0.005	0.0005	0.000002
371	0.03	0.004	0.0009

Rate of Decomposition, % h

Source: Gangal, S. V., in *Kirk-Othner Encyclopedia of Chemical Technology,* Vol. 11, 3rd ed., John Wiley & Sons, New York, 1980. With permission.

toms, following a latent interval of a few hours, usually subside after 24 to 48 h without aftereffects.

FEP has a considerably lower thermal stability than PTFE and starts to degrade at temperatures above 200°C (392°F). There are essentially two stages in the degradation of FEP. The first involves preferential elimination of HFP from the backbone; in the second the remaining backbone undergoes decomposition at the same rate as that of PTFE.[7]

PFA is more stable thermally than FEP because of the presence of stable ether groups in the side chain (see above); however, it can degrade during processing or use at high temperatures due to the presence of reactive end groups (e.g., –COF or –CH$_2$OH). The result is cross-linking reactions and an increase in the molecular weight when the end groups decompose to form radicals, which then undergo radical recombination reactions.[8] PFA resins can be processed at temperatures up to 445°C (883°F). Aging below, but near the temperature of 285°C (545°F) increases the strength of PFA.[9]

7.1.2 THERMAL DEGRADATION OF OTHER FLUOROPOLYMERS

PVDF is considerably less thermally stable than PTFE but much more stable than PVF or PCTFE. Certain inorganic compounds (silica, titanium dioxide, and antimony oxide) can catalyze its decomposition at temperatures above 375°C (707°F).[10]

ETFE degradation is autocatalytic and similar to that of PVDF and is accompanied by the evolution of HF. Iron and transition metal salts can accelerate the degradation of ETFE by dehydrofluorination and oligomer formation.[10] Copper salts have been found to stabilize the polymer.[11] ETFE decomposes rapidly at temperatures above 380°C (716°F).[11]

PVF decomposes in air at temperatures above 350°C (682°F) by dehydrofluorination. At approximately 450°C (842°F), backbone cleavage occurs.[9] PVF films discolor at high temperatures, but retain considerable strength after heat-aging at 217°C (423°F).[12]

ECTFE has a thermal stability comparable to ETFE[13] and can be stabilized by the addition of an ionomer, which considerably reduces dehydrofluorination and dehydrochlorination reactions and suppresses the discoloration of the polymer.[14]

PCTFE can start to degrade at temperatures as low as 250°C (452°F). The mechanism of thermal degradation of PCTFE is a chain scission and leads to terminal unsaturation.[14] Since the processing temperature range from 230 to 290°C (446 to 554°F) approaches the decomposition temperature of the polymer, it is important to maintain tight temperature control during the processing of PCTFE. During thermal degradation, the polymer also tends to become brittle as a result of increasing crystallinity. The tendency to embrittle during high-temperature use can be offset by copolymerizing CTFE with a small amount of VDF (usually less than 5%).[13]

7.1.3 THERMAL DEGRADATION OF FLUOROELASTOMERS

Perfluoroelastomers, such as Kalrez (copolymer of TFE and PMVE), can maintain their thermal stability to temperatures as high as 300°C (572°F) or even higher, with a maximum continuous service temperature of 315°C (599°F). Moreover, instead of hardening, the elastomer becomes more elastic with aging.[13]

Fluorocarbon elastomers, such as copolymers of VDF and HFP, typically have a maximum continuous service temperature of 215°C (419°F). Some metal oxides may cause dehydrofluorination at a temperature of 150°C (302°F) or even lower.[16] Copolymers of VDF and CTFE (e.g., Kel-F®) have a maximum long-term service temperature of 200°C (392°F). Fluorocarbon elastomers based on copolymers of VDF/HPFP (hydropentafluoropropylene) and on terpolymers of VDF/HPFP/TFE have lower thermal stability than copolymers of VDF/HFP because they have a lower fluorine content than the latter.[17] A detailed study of thermal stability of fluoroelastomers was performed by Cox et al.[18]

7.1.4 THERMAL DEGRADATION OF FLUOROSILICONES

Thermal degradation of fluorosilicones can occur by a reversion mechanism and is accelerated by the presence of basic compounds. The maximum long-term service of fluorosilicone elastomers depends on cure conditions and environment and is typically 200°C (392°F).[19]

7.2 EFFECTS OF RADIATION

7.2.1 PERFLUOROPOLYMERS

PTFE is attacked by irradiation by γ-rays, high-energy electron beams, or X rays. The degradation of the polymer in air or oxygen occurs due to scission of the chain and is fairly rapid. Such scission results in molecular weight reduction.[20] When irradiated by an electron beam, the molecular weight is reduced up to six orders of magnitude to produce micropowders.[21]

FEP is degraded by radiation in a similar fashion to PTFE, namely, by chain scission and resulting reduction of molecular weight. The molecular weight reduction can be minimized by excluding oxygen. If FEP is lightly irradiated at elevated temperatures in the absence of oxygen, cross-linking offsets molecular breakdown.[22,23] The degree to which radiation exposure affects the polymer depends on the amount of energy absorbed, regardless of the type of radiation. Changes in mechanical properties depend on total dosage, but are independent of dose rate. The radiation tolerance of FEP in the presence or absence of oxygen is higher than that of PTFE by a factor of 10:1.[24]

PFA, like other perfluoropolymers, is not highly resistant to radiation.[25] Radiation resistance is improved in vacuum, and strength and elongation are increased more after low dosage (up to 3 Mrad) than with FEP or PTFE. At 3 to 10 Mrad it approaches the performance of PTFE and embrittles above 10 Mrad. After the exposure to the dosage of 50 Mrad, PTFE, FEP, and PFA are all degraded.[26]

7.2.2 OTHER FLUOROPOLYMERS

ETFE retains its tensile properties when exposed to low-level ionizing radiation, because the two competing processes, namely, chain scission and cross-linking, are occurring at an approximately equal rate so the net change in molecular weight is quite small. At higher levels of radiation, the tensile elongation of ETFE is severely affected and drops sharply when irradiated.[27] The change in mechanical properties is much pronounced in the presence of air.[28] The radiation resistance of ETFE is superior to both PTFE and FEP.

When exposed to low doses of ionizing radiation (either gamma or electron beam), ETFE becomes cross-linked. Cross-linking improves its high-temperature properties, such as cut-through by a hot soldering iron, and increases the continuous service temperature from 150°C (302°F) to 200°C (392°F).[29]

PVDF undergoes cross-linking when exposed to low-level radiation (up to 20 Mrad) as indicated by the increased gel fraction with increased dose.[30,31] Cross-linking in PVDF usually results in an increase in tensile strength of the polymer and in a reduction of both the degree of crystallinity and melting point. The overall radiation resistance to nuclear radiation is very good. Its tensile strength is virtually unaffected after 1000 Mrad of γ radiation in vacuum, and its impact strength and elongation are slightly reduced as a result of cross-linking. The only adverse effect observed on PVDF after radiation is discoloration, which has already occurred at relatively low doses.[32] It is attributed to the formation of double bonds due to dehydrofluorination.[33]

PVF becomes cross-linked as PVDF and forms a gel fraction when exposed to ionizing radiation. Irradiated PVF exhibits higher tensile strength, and resistance to etching increases with increasing dose but, as in PVDF, the degree of crystallinity and melting point decrease.[29]

PCTFE. Very little work was done on the effects of radiation on PCTFE but it is known that its resistance to radiation is superior to that of other fluoropolymers.[34]

Fluorocarbon elastomers, particularly copolymers of HFP and VDF, are cross-linked by low-level γ radiation (up to 20 Mrad) in the same fashion as PVDF. Radiation degradation of a VDF-HFP copolymer was studied by Zhong and Sun.[35] Their finding was that there is a linear relationship between the dose and the weight loss of the polymer. Fluorocarbon elastomers based on copolymers of TFE and propylene were found to be more resistant to γ radiation than Viton® elastomers.[36] Cross-linking of VDF-HFP, VDF-TFE, and tetrafluoroethylene-propylene (TFE/P) copolymers as well as of terpolymers VDF-HFP-TFE by ionizing radiation (gamma or electron beam) can be enhanced by prorads (cross-linking promoters), such as triallyl isocyanurate (TAIC) and trimethylolpropane trimethacrylate (TMPTM).[37]

7.3 EFFECTS OF UV RADIATION

Fluoropolymers as a group have intrinsically high resistance to degradation by UV radiation. The strength of the fluorine–carbon bond makes them resistant to pure photolysis. Moreover, they do not contain any light-absorbing chromophores either in their structure or as impurities. For example, no physical or chemical changes have been observed during 30 years of continuous exposure of PTFE in Florida.[38] The outdoor durability of a fluorinated coating is directly related to its fluorine content and is assessed by gloss retention.[39]

The degradation of some fluoropolymers outdoors occurs very slowly and can be detected only by very sensitive analytical methods, such as X-ray photoelectron spectroscopy (XPS)[40] or electron spin resonance spectroscopy (ESR).[41]

To assess the propensity of a polymer to UV degradation accurately, it is important to pay attention to the wavelength of the UV light employed. For example, FEP polymers absorb UV radiation only at wavelengths below 180 nm, which makes them susceptible to degradation only in the space.[42] Unlike FEP and other perfluoropolymers, UV degradation of PCTFE is greatly accelerated by UV light.[43] Copolymers of TFE and HFP have been reported to undergo scission and cross-linking when exposed to UV radiation.[44]

REFERENCES

1. Baker, B. B. and Kasporzak, D. J., *J. Polym. Degrad. Stab.,* 42, 181 (1993).
2. Scheirs, J., in *Modern Fluoropolymers* (Scheirs, J., Ed.), John Wiley & Sons, New York, p. 49 (1997).
3. Gangal, S. V., in *Kirk-Othmer Encyclopedia of Chemical Technology,* Vol. 11, 3rd ed., John Wiley & Sons, New York, p. 11 (1980).
4. Siegle, J. C. et al., *J. Polym. Sci.* A2, 391 (1964).
5. Shulman, G. P., *Polym. Lett.* 3, 911 (1965).
6. Harris, D. K., *Lancet* 2, 1000 (1951).
7. Carlson, D. P. and Schmiegel, W., Fluoropolymers, organic, in *Ullmann's Encyclopedia of Industrial Chemistry,* Vol. A11, VCH Publishers, Weinheim, West Germany, p. 39 (1988).
8. Gangal, S. V., in *Encyclopedia of Polymer Science and Engineering,* Vol. 16 (Mark, H. F. and Kroschwitz, J. I. Eds.), John Wiley & Sons, New York, p. 619 (1989).
9. Feiring, A. E., Imbalzano, J. F., and Kerbow, D. L., *Trends Polym. Sci.* 2, 26 (1994).
10. Scheirs, J., in *Modern Fluoropolymers* (Scheirs, J., Ed.), John Wiley & Sons, New York, p. 50 (1997).
11. Kerbow, D. L., in *Modern Fluoropolymers* (Scheirs, J., Ed.), John Wiley & Sons, New York, p. 306 (1997).
12. Nguyen, T., *Rev. Macromol. Chem. Phys.* C25, 227 (1985).
13. Scheirs, J., in *Modern Fluoropolymers* (Scheirs, J., Ed.), John Wiley & Sons, New York, p. 51 (1997).
14. Chen, C. S. and Chapoy, L. L., Eur. Patent Appl. 683 204 (1995), *Chem. Abstr.* 124.

15. Iwasaki, M. et al., *J. Polym. Sci.* 25, 377 (1957).
16. Novikov, A. S., Galil, F. A., Slovokhotova, N. A., and Dyumaeva, T. N., *Vysokomol. Soedin.*, 423 (1962).
17. Scheirs, J., in *Modern Fluoropolymers* (Scheirs, J., Ed.), John Wiley & Sons, New York, p. 53 (1997).
18. Cox, J. M., Wright, B. A., and Wright, W. W., *J. Appl. Polym. Sci.* 8, 2935 (1964).
19. Maxson, M. T., Norris, A. W., and Owen, M. J., in *Modern Fluoropolymers* (Scheirs, J., Ed.), John Wiley & Sons, New York, p. 364 (1997).
20. Blanchet, T. A., in *Handbook of Thermoplastics* (Olabisi, O., Ed.), Marcel Dekker, New York, p. 987 (1997).
21. Limkwitz, K., Brink, H. J., Handte, D., and Ferse, A., *Radiat Phys. Chem.* 33, 523 (1989).
22. Eby, R. K., *J. Appl. Phys.* 34, 2442 (1963).
23. Eby, R. K. and Wilson, F. C., *J. Appl. Phys.* 33, 2951 (1962).
24. Gangal, S. V., in *Encyclopedia of Polymer Science and Engineering,* Vol. 16 (Mark, H. F. and Kroschwitz, J. I. Eds.), John Wiley & Sons, New York, p. 605 (1989).
25. *Teflon® PFA Fluorocarbon Resins: Response to Radiation,* APD#3, Bulletin, E. I. du Pont de Nemours, & Co., Wilmington, DE (1973).
26. Gangal, S. V., in *Encyclopedia of Polymer Science and Engineering,* Vol. 16 (Mark, H. F. and Kroschwitz, J. I. Eds.), John Wiley & Sons, New York, p. 605 (1989).
27. Gangal, S. V., in *Kirk-Othmer Encyclopedia of Chemical Technology,* Vol. 11, John Wiley & Sons, New York, p. 671 (1980).
28. Clough, R. L., Gillen, K. T., and Dole, M., in *Irradiation Effects on Polymers* (Clegg, D. W. and Collyer, A., Eds.), Elsevier Applied Science, London, p. 95 (1991).
29. Scheirs, J., in *Modern Fluoropolymers* (Scheirs, J., Ed.), John Wiley & Sons, New York, p. 59 (1997).
30. Rosenberg, Y., Siegmann, A., Narkis, M., and Shkolnik, S., *J. Appl. Polym. Sci.* 45, 783 (1992).
31. Klier, I., Strachota, S., and Vokal, A., *Radiat. Phys. Chem.* 38, 457 (1991).
32. Kawano, Y. and Soares, S., *Polym. Degrad. Stab.* 35, 99 (1992).
33. Scheirs, J., in *Modern Fluoropolymers* (Scheirs, J., Ed.), John Wiley & Sons, New York, p. 60 (1997).
34. Scheirs, J., in *Modern Fluoropolymers* (Scheirs, J., Ed.), John Wiley & Sons, New York, p. 61 (1997).
35. Zhong, X. and Sun, J., *Polym. Degrad. Stab.* 35, 99 (1992).
36. Ito, M., *Radiat. Phys. Chem.* 47, 607 (1996).
37. Lyons, B. G., in *Modern Fluoropolymers* (Scheirs, J., Ed.), John Wiley & Sons, New York, p. 339 (1997).
38. Scheirs, J., in *Modern Fluoropolymers* (Scheirs, J., Ed.), John Wiley & Sons, New York, p. 61 (1997).
39. Scheirs, J., Fluoropolymer coatings; new developments, in *Polymeric Materials Encyclopedia* (Salamone, J., Ed.), CRC Press, Boca Raton, FL, pp. 2498–2507 (1996).
40. Sjostrom, C., Jernberg, P., and Lala, D., *Mater. Struct.* 24, 3 (1991).
41. Okamoto, S. and Ohya-Nishiguchi, H., *J. Jpn. Soc. Colour Mater.* 63, 392 (1990); *Chem. Abstr.* 114.
42. Scheirs, J., in *Modern Fluoropolymers* (Scheirs, J., Ed.), John Wiley & Sons, New York, p. 62 (1997).
43. Wall, L. A. and Straus, S., *J. Res. (Natl. Bur. Standards)* 65, 227 (1961).
44. Bowers, G. H. and Lovejoy, E. R., *Ind. Eng. Chem. Prod. Res. Dev.* 1, 89 (1962).

8 Recent Developments in Chemistry and Technology of Fluoropolymers

8.1 AMORPHOUS FLUOROPOLYMERS

A family of amorphous fluoropolymers based on copolymers of 2,2-bistrifluorom-ethyl-4,5-difluoro-1,3-dioxole (PDD) was developed by du Pont under the trade name Teflon® AF. They retain the outstanding chemical, thermal, and surface properties associated with perfluorinated polymers and exhibit unique electrical, optical, and solubility characteristics at the same time.[1] The structure of Teflon AF is shown in Figure 8.1. It is synthesized in four steps from hexafluoroacetone and ethylene oxide.[2] Hexafluoroacetone condenses with ethylene oxide to form a highly chemically stable dioxolane ring in quantitative yield. Exhaustive chlorination followed by chlorine–fluorine exchange yields 2,2-bistrifluoromethyl-4,5-dichloro-4,5-difluoro-1,3-dioxolane in greater than 90% yield. Dechlorination of this dioxolane with magnesium, zinc, or a mixture of titanium tetrachloride and lithium aluminum hydride gives PDD monomer. PDD is a clear, colorless liquid boiling at 33°C (91.4°F). It is highly reactive, and therefore it must be stored with trace amounts of radical inhibitor.[2]

PDD readily copolymerizes with tetrafluoroethylene and other monomers containing fluorine, such as VDF, CTFE, vinyl fluoride, and PVE via free radical copolymerization, which can be carried out in either aqueous or nonaqueous media. It also forms an amorphous homopolymer with a T_g of 335°C (635°F).[2]

The currently available commercial grades Teflon AF 1600 and Teflon AF 2400 produced by du Pont are copolymers of PDD and tetrafluoroethylene with respective glass transition temperatures of 160 and 240°C (320 and 464°F).[2] They are produced by aqueous copolymerization of PDD and TFE using fluorosurfactant and ammonium persulfate or other metal persulfate initiators.[3]

Teflon AF copolymers have a perfluorinated structure as do PTFE, PFA, and FEP, and therefore they exhibit similar high-temperature stability, chemical resistance, low surface energy, and low water absorption. Unlike PTFE, PFA, and FEP, which are semicrystalline, the completely amorphous Teflon AF copolymers differ considerably in that they are soluble in several perfluorinated solvents at room temperature and have high optical transmission across a broad wavelength region

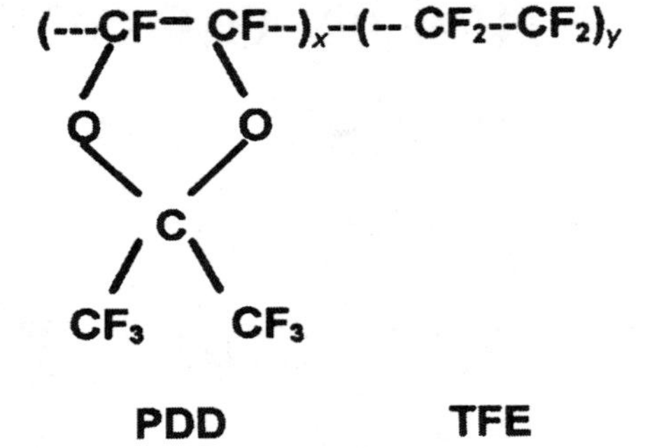

PDD   **TFE**

FIGURE 8.1 Structure of Teflon® AF. (Courtesy of CRC Press.)

from UV to near infrared.[4] Other differences are lower refractive indexes and dielectric constants and high gas permeability. The refractive index of Teflon copolymers is the lowest known for any solid organic polymer (the respective values for Teflon 1600 and 2400 are 1.31 and 1.29 at 20°C at the sodium line). The presence of the dioxole structure in the chain imparts a higher stiffness and high tensile modulus.[4] Table 8.1 illustrates some of the similarities of Teflon AF to commercial perfluoropolymers and some differences between them.

Teflon AF can be processed by a variety of methods. Melt processing includes extrusion, compression, and injection molding. Compression molding is usually done at temperatures 100°C above the glass transition temperatures. Extrusion and injection molding conditions depend on the type of part to be produced.[5] Solution-based methods are spin coating and dipping from solutions in perfluorocarbon solvents. Spin coating is used to obtain an ultrathin, uniform-thickness coating on flat surfaces. Nonplanar surfaces can be coated by dipping. Other solution-based methods are spraying with a paint used for more thickly coated layers. Ultrathin layers without the use of solvent are applied by laser ablation.[6]

Another pefluoropolymer of this type has been developed by Asahi Glass and is available on the market under the trade name CYTOP®. This polymer is prepared by cyclopolymerization of perfluorodiene. Its structure is shown in Figure 8.2.[7]

TABLE 8.1
Teflon AF Compared with the Other Teflon Polymers

Similarities	Differences
High-temperature stability	Non-crystalline, amorphous
Excellent chemical resistance	Soluble at ambient temperature in fluorinated solvents
Low surface energy	Transparent
Low water absorption	Lower refractive index
Limiting oxygen index (LOI) > 95	Stiffer
	High gas permeability

Source: Resnick, P. R. and Buck, W. H., in *Modern Fluoropolymers,* Scheirs, J., Ed., John Wiley & Sons, New York, 1997. With permission.

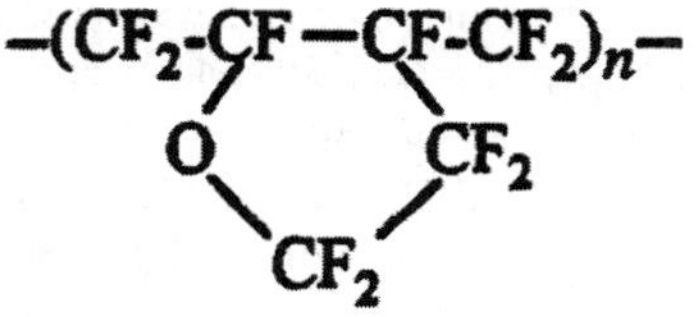

$$-(CF_2\text{-}CF\text{---}CF\text{-}CF_2)_n-$$

FIGURE 8.2 Structure of CYTOP®. (Courtesy of CRC Press.)

CYTOP has physical and chemical properties similar to PTFE and PFA. Its tensile strength and yield strength are higher than those of PTFE and PFA. It also has unique optical properties: its films are transparent in the range from 200 to 700 nm and its clarity is very high even in the UV region.[8] The properties of CYTOP are shown in Table 8.2.[9] CYTOP is soluble in selected fluorinated solvents. Such solutions have a very low surface tension, which allows them to be spread onto porous materials and to cover the entire surface. Films without pinholes and of uniform thickness can be prepared from solutions.[8]

8.1.1 APPLICATIONS

The main application of amorphous perfluoropolymers is as cladding of optical fibers, antireflective coatings, low dielectric coatings, and in the electronic industry (e.g., photoresists)[10-12] and as a low-dielectric-constant insulator for high-performance interconnects.[13]

TABLE 8.2
Physical and Mechanical Properties of CYTOP Compared with Competitive Polymers

Property	CYTOP	PTFE	PFA	PMMA	Remarks
Glass transition temperature (°C)	108	130	75	105 ~ 120	By DSC
Melting point (°C)	Not observed	327	310	160 (isotactic)	By DSC
Density (g cm⁻³)	2.03	2.14 ~ 2.20	2.12 ~ 2.17	1.20	At 25°C
Contact angle of water (°)	110	114	115	80	At 25°C
Critical surface tension (dyn cm⁻¹)	19	18	18	39	At 25°C
Water absorption (%)	<0.01	<0.01	<0.01	0.3	60°C, H₂O
Tensile strength (kg cm⁻²)	390	140 ~ 350	280 ~ 320	650 ~ 730	
Elongation at break (%)	150	200 ~ 400	280 ~ 300	3 ~ 5	
Yield strength (kg cm⁻²)	400	110 ~ 160	110 ~ 150	(650)	
Tensile modulus (kg cm⁻²)	12,000	4000	5800	30,000	

Source: Sugiyama, N., in *Modern Fluoropolymers,* Scheirs, J., Ed., John Wiley & Sons, New York, 1997. With permission.

The subject of amorphous perfluoropolymers is covered extensively by P. R. Resnick and W. R. Buck, Chapter 22 (pp. 397–419) and N. Sugiyama in Chapter 28 (pp. 541-555) in *Modern Fluoropolymers* (Schiers, J., Editor), John Wiley & Sons, New York (1997) and by M. H. Hung, P. R. Resnick, B. E. Smart, and W. H. Buck, in *Polymer Materials Encyclopedia* Vol. 4 (Salamone, J. C., Ed.), CRC Press, Boca Raton, FL (1995), pp. 2466–2475.

8.2　FLUORINATED ACRYLATES

Of a large number of possible fluorinated acrylates, the homopolymers and copolymers of fluoroalkyl acrylates and methacrylates are the most suitable for practical applications. They are used in the manufacture of plastic lightguides (optical fibers), resists, water-, oil-, and dirt-repellent coatings, and other advanced applications.[14] Several rather complex methods to prepare the α-fluoroalkyl monomers, such as α-phenyl fluoroacrylates, α-(trifluoromethyl) acrylic and its esters, and esters of perfluoromethacrylic acid, exist and they are discussed in some detail in Reference 14. Generally, α-fluoroacrylates polymerize more readily than corresponding nonfluorinated acrylates and methacrylates mostly by free radical mechanism.[15] Copolymerization of fluoroacrylates has been carried out in bulk, solution, or emulsion initiated with peroxides, azobisisobutyronitrile, or γ-irradiation.[16] Fluoroalkyl methacrylates and acrylates also polymerize by anionic mechanism, but the polymerization rates are considerably slower than those of radical polymerization.[17]

The homopolymers of poly(phenyl α-fluoroacrylate) (PPhFA) have a considerably higher glass transition temperature than usual acrylates. Its T_g is 180°C (356°F) and it resists to temperatures above 270°C (518°F). Its shortcoming is a rather low resistance to UV radiation. Other polymers, poly(fluoroalkyl methacrylates), exhibit exceptional optical properties. Poly(fluoroalkyl α-fluoroacrylates) (PFAFA) combine that with a greater resistance to elevated temperatures. Homopolymers and copolymers of perfluoroalkyl acrylates and methacrylates exhibit the lowest critical surface tension (γ_c) of all polymers, including PTFE. Values of γ_c for these polymers, depending mainly on the length, composition, branching, and terminal groups of fluoroalkyl side chains, may be as low as 10.6 dyn/cm as compared with 18.5 to 19 dyne/cm for PTFE.[18,19] Additional, rather comprehensive discussion of fluorinated acrylic esters is in Reference 20.

8.2.1　Applications

8.2.1.1　Textile Finishes

The low surface energy of fluoroacrylate polymers makes them suitable for the use as water- and oil-repellent coatings for fibers and textiles.[21] At present, the largest volume of fluoroacrylates and methacrylates produced in the world is used in this application. A large proportion are aqueous dispersions of copolymers of perfluoroalkyl acrylates and perfluoroalkyl methacrylates. These materials successfully compete with other fluorine-containing compounds for the same application.[21] To achieve the required water- and oil-repellent effect, it is necessary to use copolymers having a perfluoroalkyl pendant group with at least seven atoms. An acrylic polymer with such a structure has an ultimate surface tension value γ_c = 10.6 dyne/cm, almost half that of PTFE.[22,23]

Commercial products, used widely for the treatment of textiles, mainly apparel, soft furnishings, and carpets, are known under the trade names Scotchgard® (3M), Teflon (DuPont), Asahigard® (Asahi Glass), and Unidyne® (Daikin). This subject is reviewed in detail in Reference 24.

8.2.1.2 Optical Fibers

At present, fluorinated acrylic ester polymers are commercially used as cladding materials for polymeric optical fibers (POF), which have cores made of poly(methylmethacrylate), and in some cases for silica optical fibers (PCF: polymer-coated fibers). These applications, which are quite sizable, take advantage of the low refractive index, which is unique to fluoropolymers.[25] The cladding of POF is most frequently made from polymethacrylates or poly(2-fluoroacrylates) that have rather short fluoroalkyl side groups, such as CF_3CH_2-, HCF_2CH_2-, $CF_3CF_2CH_2-$, and $(CF_3)_2CH-$.[26] In addition, they are often copolymerized with other acrylic ester monomers to adjust the required properties. Although vinylidene fluoride (VDF)-based resins are also used in claddings, fluorinated acrylic ester polymers exhibit better transparency and lower attenuation loss.[27] Poly(fluoroalkyl α-fluoroacrylates) (PFAFA) exhibit significantly lower refractive indexes and higher thermal stability than similar poly(fluoroalkyl methacrylates) (PFAMA), but they are considerably higher in cost, which prohibits their wider use.[28]

8.2.1.3 Other Applications

In electronics, fluoroacrylates are used as resists in high-density electronic integrated circuits, and as protective coatings in printed circuit boards.[29] They are also often used in xerographic process for negative charge control.[30]

In optical applications, in addition to optical fiber claddings, special optical adhesives matching refractive indexes of optical glass components based on fluorinated epoxyacrylates and epoxymethacrylates are used.[29] Fluoroalkyl methacrylates are frequently incorporated as comonomers with siloxanyl methacrylates into contact lenses for the improvement of oxygen permeability.[31]

Fluorinated acrylic ester polymers are also used as *surface modifiers* to promote blending instead of coating, imparting functionality of the fluoroalkyl groups to the surfaces of other resins or paints. Since they tend to accumulate on the surface of the substrates facing the air, the surface is easily modified. The modifiers are usually added to paints to enhance leveling or dispersing pigments, and sometimes to improve moisture-proof qualities, and are blended to resins to give oil- and water-repellency, or low-friction properties. In addition, they are used as antiblocking agents.[32]

8.3 FLUORINATED POLYURETHANES

Introducing fluorine into polyurethane resins results in changes in properties similar to those seen with other polymers. Chemical, thermal, hydrolytic, and oxidative stability is improved. On the other hand, the polymer becomes more permeable to oxygen. Surfaces become more biocompatible and the capability to bond to other substances in contact with them is diminished.[33]

Fluorourethanes are used in products ranging from hard, heat-resistant electrical components to biocompatible surgical adhesives. The properties of a specific fluorourethane resin are determined by the raw materials and the manufacturing process used.

Raw materials used for the production of fluorinated polyurethanes are as follows:

- Fluorinated alcohols, typically straight-chain alcohols with all but α and β carbons fluorinated, which are most often used;
- Fluorinated diols;
- Fluorinated polyols with molecular weights between 500 and 10,000, which are preferred for most applications;
- Fluorinated acrylic polyols;
- Isocyanates and polyisocyanates, mostly nonfluorinated types, which are used because of their considerably lower cost in comparison with fluorinated ones;
- Miscellaneous fluorinated precursors, such as amines, anhydrides, oxiranes, alkenes, and carboxylic acids, which are used for special properties.

The most frequently used method to prepare fluorourethanes commercially is the well-known addition reaction of polyisocyanates with polyols. Fluorine is most frequently introduced through the polyol component, since fluorinated polyisocyanates are relatively difficult to obtain and considerably more expensive than the nonfluorinated kind.[34] Examples of fluorinated alcohols for polyurethane resins are listed in Table 8.3.[35]

Another manufacturing method involves irradiation by UV light, in which acrylic-modified polyurethane resins are used. Reactive fluorinated oligomers are reviewed in Reference 36.

Fluorinated polyurethanes may also be prepared by treating the surface of an unfluorinated material with cold plasma of elemental fluorine[37] or carbon tetrafluoride.[38]

8.3.1 APPLICATIONS

8.3.1.1 Surface Coatings

Because of the low surface energy, resistance to chemicals and corrosive agents, and resistance to weathering, fluorinated polyurethanes are very well suited for protective coatings. They can be deposited in a desired location and thickness with the added advantage of curing mostly at ambient temperatures.

Solvent-Based Coatings

The majority of surface coatings are solvent-borne and based on fluorinated ethylene vinyl ether (FEVE) polyol resins. These are readily dissolved in conventional solvents, such as toluene, xylene, or butyl acetate.[39] They are valuable for their resistance to abrasion, corrosion, staining, impact, thermal shock, water, ice, and weather and demonstrate a high gloss, gloss and color retention, durability, hardness, and adhesion to metals, glass, concrete, and many plastics. Their applications range from floorings to luxury automobiles.[40] FEVE polyols may be modified by acrylic resins

TABLE 8.3
Fluorinated Alcohols for Polyurethane Resins

Alcohol	Application
CF_3CH_2OH	Hard contact lenses
$CF_3CH_2CH_2OH$	Antifogging coating for glass
$(CF_3)CHOH$	Solvent
$CF_3CHFCF_2CH_2OH$	Water-based coatings
$F(CF_2)_nOH$	Oil-,water-, and soil-resistant textile finishes
[$n = 6$–12]	
[$n = 7$]	Leather substitutes
$(CF_3)_2CF(CF_2CF_2)_nCH_2CH_2OH$	
[$n = 3$-5]	Oil- and water-resistant textile finishes
$F(CF_2CF_2)_nCH_2CH_2OH$	
[$n = 3$–6]	Oil- and water-resistant textile finishes
[$n = 3$–7]	Emulsion polymers
$F(CF_2CF_2)_nCH_2CH_2SH$ [n unspecified]	Oil- and water-resistant textile finishes
$C_7F_{15}CH_2OH$	Rigid insulating foams
$HOCH_2CF_2CF_2OCF(CF_3)CF_2OCF=CF_2$	Elastomers
$C_6F_{13}(CH_2)_2S(CH_2)_3OH$	Cladding for optical fibers
$H(CF_2CF_2)_5CH_2OH$	Coating for magnetic recording tape
$C_8F_{17}CH_2CH_2OH$	Coatings for textiles and leather
$C_8F_{17}CH_2CH_2OCH_2CH_2OH$	Housings for office machines

Source: Brady, R. F., Jr., in *Modern Fluoropolymers*, Sheirs, J., Ed., John Wiley & Sons, New York, 1997.

to improve optical properties, hardness, and lower cost[41,42] and by other methods to achieve specific properties.[43]

Coatings based on hexafluoroacetone (HFA) are often modified by the addition of powdered polytetrafluoroethylene (PTFE). They exhibit toughness and hardness typical for conventional polyurethane coatings combined with low surface energy and ease of cleaning of PTFE. The optimum amount of PTFE added appears to be about 24% by volume.[44] Such coatings have been used successfully as anticorrosion and antifouling coatings on ships and small boats and as protective coatings on tanks and large structures.[45] Examples of such applications are in Figures 8.3. through 8.5.

Other coatings prepared from a variety of polyol resins, such as fluorinated acrylic resins, copolymers containing tetrafluoroethylene, vinylidene fluoride, hexafluoropropylene, exhibit generally high gloss, good gloss retention, high resistance to weathering, and water repellency.[46]

Water-Based Coatings

The addition of small amounts of fluorinated polyols to conventional aqueous polyurethane coatings can improve their water resistance and mechanical properties considerably.[47] FEVE resins can be applied as water-based coatings and cured at 160°C (320°F) for 25 min to produce coatings with high gloss and good water and weather resistance.[48] They may also be cured with water-based hardeners.[49]

FIGURE 8.3 Exterior protective coating on a Coast Guard ship. (Courtesy of 21st Century Coatings, Inc.)

FIGURE 8.4 Protective coating on a bridge. (Courtesy of 21st Century Coatings, Inc.)

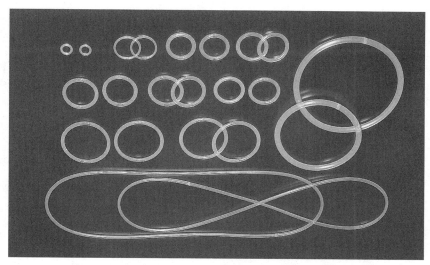

FIGURE 8.5 O-rings from thermoplastic fluoroelastomer. (Courtesy of Daikin.)

Powder Coatings

Fluorourethanes can also be applied using powder coating technology. Resins suitable for this should have T_g values between 35 and 120°C (95 and 248°F) to optimize flow out and cure at the annealing temperature. Blocked isocyanates, which form free isocyanates after being heated above certain temperatures, are frequently used.[50] Certain FEVE copolymers with hydroxyl and carboxyl functionalities combined with blocked isophorone diisocyanate are suitable for powder coating technology.[51]

8.3.1.2   Treatments of Textile, Leather, and Other Substrates

Surface treatment of textiles, leather, glass, wood, and paper is the second largest application for fluorinated polyurethanes. The coatings are applied in one-step treatment and impart resistance to soil, water, oil, and stains as well as a smoothness to fabrics and leather that resists removal by many cycles of laundering or dry cleaning.[52]

8.3.1.3   Medical and Dental Applications

Soft and hard contact lenses with good oxygen permeability, optical clarity, flexibility, and biocompatibility; dental composites; denture linings; surgical adhesives; catheters; and hydrophobic microporous membranes are examples of applications of fluorinated polyurethanes in the medical and dental fields.[53]

8.3.1.4   Cladding for Optical Fibers

Because of their low refractive index (less than 1.43), low permeability of water and weather vapor, very low water absorption, and good adhesion to glass and optical polymers, fluoropolyurethanes are suitable for cladding of optical fibers. A variety of specialty resins are used for this purpose, which are most frequently photocurable.

8.3.1.5 Elastomers

Elastomers based on fluorinated polyurethanes exhibit good mechanical properties and resistance to solvents, chemicals, cold, and heat.[54] Formulations for fluorourethane elastomers are frequently modified with siloxanes to optimize certain properties.[55] FEVE-based polyols are used to manufacture elastomeric automobile bumpers and interior trim components.[56]

8.3.1.6 Other Applications

The versatility of fluorinated polyurethanes is further demonstrated by the following applications:

- Electrical (printed circuit boards, recording media, insulations)[57]
- Printing (printing heads, thermal recording media)[58]
- Heat exchangers (coatings inside to prevent the formation of deposits)[59]
- Binders of explosives[60]
- Sealants (used, for example, for liquid-crystal display panels)[61]
- Protective coatings for concrete, stone, fibrous materials[62]
- Antifogging coatings for mirrors and optical components[63]

The subject of fluorinated polyurethanes is covered extensively by R. F. Brady, Jr. in *Modern Fluoropolymers* (Schiers, J., Ed.), John Wiley & Sons, New York, 1997, Chapter 6, pp. 125–163.

8.4 FLUORINATED THERMOPLASTIC ELASTOMERS

Considering the exceptional commercial success of hydrocarbon thermoplastic elastomers as a frequent replacement of conventional cross-linked (vulcanized) elastomers, it is logical that a similar concept is viable in the field of fluorinated elastomers. This is a particularly attractive concept, considering the rather involved chemistry of cross-linking fluoroelastomers (see Chapter 5). Currently, fluorinated thermoplastic elastomers (FTPE) are produced only in Japan. One is a block-copolymer type, composed of a central soft fluoroelastomer block and multiple fluoroplastic hard segments. This type has been available commercially since 1982 and is produced by Daikin under the trade name Dai-el® Thermoplastic.[64] The second type is a graft copolymer type comprising main-chain fluoroelastomers and side-chain fluoroplastics. This type was introduced commercially in 1987 by Central Glass Co. under the trade name Cefral Soft®.[65] Current estimated combined production of both FTPEs is about 100 tons (data from 1995).

There are essentially two methods used for the production of commercial FTPEs. The first is referred to as iodine transfer polymerization, which is similar to the "living" anionic polymerization used to make block copolymers such as styrene-butadiene-styrene (e.g., Kraton®). The difference is that this "living" polymerization is based on a free radical mechanism. The products consist of soft segments based on copolymers of vinylidene fluoride (VDF) with hexafluoropropylene (HFP) and optionally with tetrafluoroethylene (TFE) and of hard segments that are formed by fluoroplastics such as ETFE or PVDF.[66] The other method is a two-step graft copolymerization using unsaturated peroxides, such as [CH$_2$=CHCH$_2$OC(O)–O–O–tert-butyl] and the monomers involved are VDF and CTFE. In the second step, post-polymerizations mainly with VDF to form crystalline segments are repeatedly performed while successively raising the reaction temperature.[67]

Polyurethane-based FTPEs are produced by reacting fluorinated polyether diols with aromatic disocyanates. The resulting block copolymers contain fluorinated polyether soft segments.[68] Another possible method of preparation of fluorinated TPE is dynamic vulcanization. Examples are a blend of a perfluoroplastic and a perfluoroelastomer containing curing sites or a combination of VDF-based fluoroelastomers and thermoplastics, such as polyamides, polybutylene terephtalate, and polyphenylene sulfide.[69,70]

8.4.1 APPLICATIONS

8.4.1.1 Chemical and Semiconductor Industries

The most common applications for thermoplastic fluorinated elastomers are seals in chemical and semiconductor industries (O-rings, V-rings, gaskets, and diaphragms) because of their excellent chemical resistance and high purity.[71] These parts are often cross-linked by actinic radiation without adding any other components.[72] Other parts for these industries are tubing and liners of multilayer hoses for corrosive gases or ultrapure water, and liners for vessels for inorganic acids (e.g., HF).[73]

8.4.1.2 Electrical and Wire/Cable

Because of their flexibility, low flammability, and resistance to oil, fuel, and chemicals, FTPEs find use in electrical and wire and cable industries as wire coating and as sheathing and coating of cables.[74,75]

8.4.1.3 Other Applications

Other applications include tents and greenhouses, as laminates with polyester fiber-reinforced PVC, and as tubing, bottles, and packaging in food processing and in sanitary goods.[76]

8.5 COPOLYMERS OF CHLOROTRIFLUOROETHYLENE AND VINYL ETHER

Fluoropolymers offer several advantages, such as chemical resistance, resistance to UV and weather in general, and excellent dielectric properties. However, because of their poor solubility in solvents and high processing temperatures, their use as protective and dielectric coatings is limited. The method used for some applications and for substrates that can tolerate the high temperature for the film formation is powder coating.[77] PTFE, FEP, PFA, ETFE, and PVDF are applied as antistick and anticorrosion coatings. PTFE, FEP, PFA, and PCTFE are commonly applied as

TABLE 8.4
Commercial Fluoropolymers Used in Coatings

Polymer	Dispersion Type	Baking Temperature °C (°F) (Typical)	Use
PTFE	Aqueous	350 (662)	Non-stick cookware, wire coating, release coatings
FEP	Aqueous	280 (536)	Non-stick coating, wire coating, hot melt adhesive
PFA, MFA	Aqueous	330 (626)	Release coating, hot melt adhesive
PVDF	Aqueous, solvent	180 (356)	Architectural coatings protective coatings, paints, outdoor signs
THV Fluoroplastic	Aqueous, solvent	>150 (302)	Protective coatings, optical coatings
PVF	Latent solvent	>200 (392)	Weather resistant paints and coatings, outdoor signs
CTFE/VE*	Aqueous, solvent	RT	Weather resistant paints and coatings

* Copolymer of CTFE and vinyl ethers (e.g., Lumiflon®, Asahi Glass).

aqueous dispersions, and the coating after drying requires high temperatures. From this group, only PVDF is used widely in water dispersion or as a solution in an organic solvent for weather-resistant coatings.[78] Table 8.4 shows some of the conventional fluoropolymers used for coatings.

In an effort to find a fluoropolymer resin suitable for coatings, which is soluble in organic solvents and capable of forming a film at ambient temperature, Asahi Glass Co. Ltd. developed copolymers of CTFE and vinyl ether (PFEVE) and made them available under the trade name LUMIFLON®. PFEVE is an amorphous fluoropolymer, which is soluble in organic solvents, can form transparent films at ambient temperature, and is compatible with hardeners and pigments. All these characteristics make it suitable as a base resin for paints.[79] Compared with dispersion paints based on PVDF, PFEVE solvent-based paints have the distinct advantage of forming films at ambient temperature, as mentioned previously. PVDF requires temperatures of 250°C (482°F) or higher to form a continuous film. Moreover, PFVE can be cured chemically even at room temperature, while PVDF does not contain curable sites. The lower pigment compatibility of PVDF and the higher baking temperature restrict the choice and amount of pigments that can be used.[80]

The most recent developments are water-based dispersions of PFEVE,[81] some of them cross-linkable with waterborne isocyanates.[82] Another FEVE-based polymer, developed and commercialized recently by Asahi Glass Co. Ltd., has trade name LUMISEAL® and is used for high-performance sealants, similar to silicone sealants with the advantage of eliminating the staining problem associated with the latter.[83]

8.5.1 Applications

PFEVE-based coatings are used as protective coatings for large architectural structures, such as office buildings and bridges where on-site coating and curing are required. Other applications are in transportation (automobiles, trains, and ships) and as protective coatings on signs and solar panels.[84]

The subject of CTFE/vinyl ether copolymers is covered in detail by T. Takarura, in *Modern Fluoropolymers* (Schiers, J., Ed.), John Wiley & Sons, New York, 1997, Chapter 29, pp. 557–564.

8.6 PERFLUORINATED IONOMERS

This group of resins is based on copolymers of tetrafluoroethylene and perfluorinated vinyl ether containing a terminal sulfonyl fluoride group. After this precursor, which is melt-processible, is fabricated into a desired physical shape, the pendent sulfonyl fluoride groups are converted into sulfonate groups by reaction with a solution of sodium or potassium hydroxide. A conversion to other ionic forms is possible by ion exchange. Products developed over the last 15 to 20 years contain $-COONa$ and $-CF_2COONa$ group as an alternative to the $-SO_3Na$ group. The physical and electrochemical properties of perfluorinated ionomers are determined by the ratio of the comonomers used for their synthesis.[85] The commercial products are available mainly in the membrane form from du Pont as NAFION® membranes and from Asahi Glass as FLEMION® membranes.

Major areas of application are in the field of aqueous electrochemistry. The most important application for perfluorinated ionomers is as a membrane separator in chloralkali cells.[86] They are also used in reclamation of heavy metals from plant effluents and in regeneration of the streams in the plating and metals industry.[85] The resins containing sulfonic acid groups have been used as powerful acid catalysts.[87] Perfluorinated ionomers are widely used in worldwide development efforts in the field of fuel cells mainly for automotive applications as PEFC (polymer electrolyte fuel cells).[88-93] The subject of fluorinated ionomers is discussed in much more detail in Reference 85.

8.7 MODIFIED POLYTETRAFLUOROETHYLENE

Polytetrafluoroethylene has many remarkable properties (see Section 3.1.1), but it has several shortcomings, which limit its utility as an engineering material. It exhibits a significant cold flow (low creep resistance), is difficult to weld, and contains a large number of microvoids due to a rather poor coalescence of particles during the sintering process. The weaknesses result from the combination of a high molecular weight (extremely high melt viscosity) and a high degree of crystallinity.

Major research efforts resulted in the development of a modified PTFE, which contains a small amount (0.01 to 0.1 mol%) of a comonomer. The most suitable comonomer was found to be perfluoro propylvinyl ether (PPVE).[94] The comonomer reduces the degree of crystallinity and the size of lamellae.[95] The polymerization process is similar to that for standard PTFE except additives to control the molecular weight are used.[96]

The resulting polymer has a melt viscosity lower by an order of magnitude and because of that the particles coalesce better during sintering. Moreover, it has a markedly improved weldability.[97] All-important physical properties of commercial modified PTFE are significantly improved without any noticeable reduction of other properties.[98,101] Modified polytetrafluoroethylene is still processed by the same techniques as the standard polymer and no adjustments to processing techniques are necessary.[99] Because of the lower melt viscosity, modified PTFE performs better in coined molding, blow molding, and thermoforming.[100]

Currently, granular molding resins, such as TEFLON® NXT 70,[101] are readily available; however, at least one method of manufacturing a fine powder by aqueous dispersion method is known.[102]

Modifed PTFE can be used in practically all applications, where the conventional polymer is used. In addition to that, new applications are possible because of its improved flow and overall performance. In the chemical process industry, it is used for equipment linings, seals, gaskets, and other parts, where its improved resistance to creep is an asset. In semiconductor manufacturing, modified PTFE is used in fluid handling components and in wafer processing components. Typical applications in electrical and electronic industries are connectors and capacitor films. Other applications are in unlubricated bearings, laboratory equipment, seal rings for hydraulic systems, and antistick components.[103]

REFERENCES

1. Hung, M.-H., Resnick, P. R., Smart, B. E., and Buck, W. H., in *Polymer Materials Encyclopedia* Vol. 4 (Salamone, J. C., Ed.), CRC Press, Boca Raton, p. 2466 (1995).
2. Hung, M.-H., Resnick, P. R., Smart, B. E., and Buck, W. H., in *Polymer Materials Encyclopedia* Vol. 4 (Salamone, J. C., Ed.), CRC Press, Boca Raton, p. 2467 (1995).
3. Resnick, P. and Buck, W. H., in *Modern Fluoropolymers* (Scheirs, J., Ed.), John Wiley & Sons, New York, p. 399 (1997).
4. Resnick, P. and Buck, W. H., in *Modern Fluoropolymers* (Scheirs, J., Ed.), John Wiley & Sons, New York, p. 401 (1997).
5. Resnick, P. and Buck, W. H., in *Modern Fluoropolymers* (Scheirs, J., Ed.), John Wiley & Sons, New York, p. 415 (1997).
6. Hung, M.-H., Resnick, P. R., Smart, B. E., and Buck, W. H., in *Polymer Materials Encyclopedia* Vol. 4 (Salamone, J. C., Ed.), CRC Press, Boca Raton, p. 2474 (1995).
7. Sugiyama, N., in *Modern Fluoropolymers* (Scheirs, J., Ed.), John Wiley & Sons, New York, p. 542 (1997).
8. Resnick, P. and Buck, W. H., in *Modern Fluoropolymers* (Scheirs, J., Ed.), John Wiley & Sons, New York, p. 549 (1997).
9. Sugiyama, N., in *Modern Fluoropolymers* (Scheirs, J., Ed.), John Wiley & Sons, New York, p. 547 (1997).
10. Resnick, P. and Buck, W. H., in *Modern Fluoropolymers* (Scheirs, J., Ed.), John Wiley & Sons, New York, p. 417 (1997).
11. Sugiyama, N., in *Modern Fluoropolymers* (Scheirs, J., Ed.), John Wiley & Sons, New York, p. 552 (1997).
12. Sugiyama, N., in *Modern Fluoropolymers* (Scheirs, J., Ed.), John Wiley & Sons, New York, p. 553 (1997).
13. Cho, C.-C., Wallace, R. M., and Files-Sesler, L. A., *J. Electron. Mater.* 23, 827 (1994).

14. Chuvatkin, A. A. and Panteleeva, I. Yu., in *Modern Fluoropolymers* (Scheirs, J., Ed.), John Wiley & Sons, New York, p. 191 (1997).
15. Chuvatkin, A. A. and Panteleeva, I. Yu., in *Modern Fluoropolymers* (Scheirs, J., Ed.), John Wiley & Sons, New York, p. 193 (1997).
16. Chuvatkin, A. A. and Panteleeva, I. Yu., in *Modern Fluoropolymers* (Scheirs, J., Ed.), John Wiley & Sons, New York, p. 197 (1997).
17. Narita, T. et al., *Macromol. Chem.* 187, 731 (1986).
18. Pittman, A. G., in *Fluoropolymers* (Wall, L. A., Ed.), Wiley-Interscience, p. 446 (1972).
19. Chuvatkin, A. A. and Panteleeva, I. Yu., in *Modern Fluoropolymers* (Scheirs, J., Ed.), John Wiley & Sons, New York, p. 204 (1997).
20. Shimizu, T., in *Modern Fluoropolymers* (Scheirs, J. Ed.), John Wiley & Sons, New York, p. 507 (1997).
21. Ishikawa, N., *Fluorine Compounds, Modern Technology and Application,* Mir, Moscow (1984), translated from Japanese (edited in Japan 1981).
22. Chuvatkin, A. A. and Panteleeva, I. Yu., in *Modern Fluoropolymers* (Scheirs, J., Ed.), John Wiley & Sons, New York, p. 204 (1997).
23. Pittman, A. G., in *Fluoropolymers* (Wall, L. A., Ed.), Wiley-Interscience, New York, p. 446 (1972).
24. Kissa, E., *Handbook of Fiber Science and Technology,* Vol. II, Chemical Processing of Fibers and Fabrics, Functional Finishes, Part B (Lewin, M. and Sello, S. B., Eds.), Marcel Dekker, New York, Chapters 2 and 3 (1984).
25. Shimizu, T., in *Modern Fluoropolymers* (Scheirs, J., Ed.), John Wiley & Sons, New York, p. 517 (1997).
26. Ohomori, A., Tomihashi, N., and Kitahara, T., U.S. Patent 4,729,166 (January 19, 1988).
27. Shimizu, T., in *Modern Fluoropolymers* (Scheirs, J., Ed.), John Wiley & Sons, New York, p. 518 (1997).
28. Chuvatkin, A. A. and Panteleeva, I. Yu., in *Modern Fluoropolymers* (Scheirs, J., Ed.), John Wiley & Sons, New York, p. 203 (1997).
29. Shimizu, T., in *Modern Fluoropolymers* (Scheirs, J., Ed.), John Wiley & Sons, New York, p. 516 (1997).
30. Nomura, Y., Aoki, M., and Nemoto, S., Kokai Tokkyo Koho Japanese Patent 53-97435 (August 25, 1978); Shigeta, K., Takahashi, J., Ohmori, A. et al., Kokai Tokkyo Koho Japanese Patent 61-12069 (June 7, 1986); Yabuuchi, N. and Aoki, T, Kokai Tokkyo Koho Japanese Patent 62-39878 (February 20, 1987).
31. Koßmehl, G., Fluthwedel, A., and Schäfer, H., *Makromol. Chem.* 193, 157 (1992).
32. Shimizu, T., in *Modern Fluoropolymers* (Scheirs, J. Ed.), John Wiley & Sons, New York, p. 521 (1997).
33. Brady, R. F., Jr., in *Modern Fluoropolymers* (Scheirs, J., Ed.), John Wiley & Sons, New York, p. 127 (1997).
34. Brady, R. F., Jr., in *Modern Fluoropolymers* (Scheirs, J., Ed.), John Wiley & Sons, New York, p. 128 (1997).
35. Brady, R. F., Jr., in *Modern Fluoropolymers* (Scheirs, J., Ed.), John Wiley & Sons, New York, p. 130 (1997).
36. Head, R. A, Powell, R. L., and Fitchett, M., *Polym. Mater. Sci. Eng.* 60, 238 (1989).
37. Ozerin, A. N., Rebrov, A. V., Feldman, V. I., Krykin, M. A., Storojuk, A. P., Kotenko, A. A., and Tul'skii, M. N., *React. Funct. Polym.* 26, 167 (1995).
38. Benoist, P. and Legeay, G., *Eur. Polym. J.* 30, 1283 (1994).

39. Izumi T., Murakami, S., Inagaki, S., and Hirakuri, Y., Japanese Patent 03 281 611 (December 12, 1991).
40. Brady, R. F., Jr., in *Modern Fluoropolymers* (Scheirs, J., Ed.), John Wiley & Sons, New York, p. 144 (1997).
41. Nakao, I., Japanese Patent 06 281 231 (September 6, 1994).
42. Hirashima, Y., Maeda, K., and Tutsumi, K., Japanese Patent 07 76 667 (March 20, 1995).
43. Brady, R. F., Jr., in *Modern Fluoropolymers* (Scheirs, J., Ed.), John Wiley & Sons, New York, p. 145 (1997).
44. Brady, R. F., Jr., Griffith, J. R., Love, K. S., and Field, D. E., *J. Coatings Technol.* 59 (77), 113 (1987).
45. Brady, R. F., Jr., in *Polymers in a Marine Environment* (Goring, D., Ed.), The Institute of Marine Engineers, London, 191 (1989).
46. Brady, Jr., R. F., in *Modern Fluoropolymers* (Scheirs, J., Ed.), John Wiley & Sons, New York, p. 147 (1997).
47. Yang, S., Xiao, H. X., Chen, W. P., Kresta, J., Frisch, K. C., and Higley, D. P., *Progr. Rubber Plast. Technol.* 7, 163 (1991).
48. Okazaki, H., Fujii, S., and Tonomura, S., Japanese Patent 04 131 165 (May 1, 1992).
49. Kodama, S., Yamauchi, M., Hirino, T., and Kitahata, H., Japanese Patent 07 179 809 (July 18, 1995).
50. Sugimoto, K. and Saka, J., Japanese Patent 05 186 565 (July 27, 1993).
51. Yasumura, T., Kobayashi, S., and Komoriya, H., European Patent Application EP 556 729 (August 25, 1993).
52. Brady, R. F., Jr., in *Modern Fluoropolymers* (Scheirs, J., Ed.), John Wiley & Sons, New York, p. 148 (1997).
53. Brady, R. F., Jr., in *Modern Fluoropolymers* (Scheirs, J., Ed.), John Wiley & Sons, New York, p. 150 (1997).
54. Menough, J., *Rubber World*, January 9 (1989).
55. Koike, N. and Sato, S., Japanese Patent 06 234 923 (August, 23, 1994).
56. Maruyama, T. and Nakamoto, M., Japanese Patent 03 167 276 (July 19, 1991).
57. Brady, R. F., Jr., in *Modern Fluoropolymers* (Scheirs, J., Ed.), John Wiley & Sons, New York, p. 153 (1997).
58. Brady, R. F., Jr., in *Modern Fluoropolymers* (Scheirs, J., Ed.), John Wiley & Sons, New York, p. 152 (1997).
59. Brady, R. F., Jr., in *Modern Fluoropolymers* (Scheirs, J., Ed.), John Wiley & Sons, New York, p. 154 (1997).
60. Hoeller, R. and Rudolf, K., European Patent Application EP 316 891 (May 24, 1992).
61. Brady, R. F., Jr., in *Modern Fluoropolymers* (Scheirs, J., Ed.), John Wiley & Sons, New York, p. 155 (1997).
62. Brady, R. F., Jr., in *Modern Fluoropolymers* (Scheirs, J., Ed.), John Wiley & Sons, New York, p. 152 (1997).
63. Honda, T. and Kaetsu, I., Japanese Patent 06 172 675 (June 21, 1994).
64. Tatemoto, M., *Int. Polym. Sci. Technol.* 12, 4 (1985).
65. Kawashima, C., in *Fusso Jushi Handbook* (Satokawa, T., Ed.), Nikkan Kogyu Shin-bunsya, Tokyo, pp. 671–686 (1984).
66. Tatemoto, M. and Shimizu, T., in *Modern Fluoropolymers* (Scheirs, J., Ed.), John Wiley & Sons, New York, p. 566 (1997).
67. Tatemoto, M. and Shimizu, T., in *Modern Fluoropolymers* (Scheirs, J., Ed.), John Wiley & Sons, New York, p. 567 (1997).
68. Tonelli, C., Trombetta, T., Scicchitano, M. et al., *J. Appl. Polym. Sci.* 59, 311 (1996).
69. Logothetis, A. L. and Stewart, C. W., U.S. Patent 4,713,418 (December 15, 1987).

70. Goebel, K. D. and Nam, S., *Proc. 3rd Int. Conf. Thermopl. Elastomer, Mark. Prod.* 55 (1966).
71. Tatemoto, M. and Shimidzu, T., in *Modern Fluoropolymers* (Scheirs, J., Ed.), John Wiley & Sons, New York, p. 563 (1997).
72. Tatemoto, M., Tomoda, M., Kawachi, M. et al., Kokai Tokkyo Koho Japanese Patent 62635 (April 10, 1984).
73. Kawashima, C. and Koga, S., *Jpn. Plast.* 39, 98 (1988).
74. Cheng, T. C., Kaduk, B. A., Mehan, A. K. et al., U.S. Patent 4,935,467 (June 19, 1988).
75. Kawamura, K., Kawashima, C., and Koga, S., U.S. Patent 4,749,610 (June 7, 1988).
76. Tatemoto, M. and Shimizu, T., in *Modern Fluoropolymers* (Scheirs, J., Ed.), John Wiley & Sons, New York, p. 575 (1997).
77. Khaladkar, P. R., *Mat. Performance (MP)* 33, 35 (1994).
78. Takakura, T., in *Modern Fluoropolymers* (Scheirs, J., Ed.), John Wiley & Sons, New York, p. 559 (1997).
79. Munekata, S., *Progr. Org. Coatings* 16, 113 (1988).
80. Takakura, T., in *Modern Fluoropolymers* (Scheirs, J., Ed.), John Wiley & Sons, New York, p. 561 (1997).
81. Yamauchi, M. et al., *Europ. Coatings J.*, 124 (1996).
82. Takakura, T., in *Modern Fluoropolymers* (Scheirs, J., Ed.), John Wiley & Sons, New York, p. 563 (1997).
83. Takakura, T., in *Modern Fluoropolymers* (Scheirs, J., Ed.), John Wiley & Sons, New York, p. 564 (1997).
84. Takakura, T., in *Modern Fluoropolymers* (Scheirs, J., Ed.), John Wiley & Sons, New York, p. 562 (1997).
85. Grot-Grootaert, W. M., in *Encyclopedia of Polymer Science and Engineering,* Vol. 16 (Mark, H. F. and Kroschwitz, J. I., Eds.), John Wiley & Sons, New York, p. 641 (1989).
86. Dotson, R. L. and Woodard, K. E., in *Perfluorinated Ionomer Membranes,* ACS Symposium Series 180 (Eisenberg, A. and Yeager, H. L., Eds.) (1982).
87. Olah, G. A., *Synthesis,* July, 513 (1986).
88. Ralph, T. R., Hards, G. A., Flint, S. D., and Gascoyne, J. M., in *1998 Fuel Cell Seminar,* Palm Springs Convention Center, Palm Springs, CA, Nov. 16–19, p. 536 (1998).
89. Sugawara, Y., Uchida, M., Ohara, H., Fukuoka, Y., Eda, N., and Ohta, A., in *1998 Fuel Cell Seminar,* Palm Springs Convention Center, Palm Springs, CA, Nov. 16–19, p. 613 (1998).
90. Lee, E. H., Oh, T. Y., and Baek, K. K., in *1998 Fuel Cell Seminar,* Palm Springs Convention Center, Palm Springs, CA, Nov. 16–19, p. 620 (1998).
91. Passalacqua, E., Lufrano, F., Squadrito, G., Patti, A., and Giorgi, L. in *1998 Fuel Cell Seminar,* Palm Springs Convention Center, Palm Springs, CA, Nov. 16–19, p. 636 (1998).
92. Jung, D. H., Lee, C. H., Chun, Y. G., Peck, D. H., Kim, C. S., and Shin, D. R., in *1998 Fuel Cell Seminar,* Palm Springs Convention Center, Palm Springs, CA, Nov. 16–19, p. 695 (1998).
93. Wakizoe, M., Murata, H., and Takei, H., in *1998 Fuel Cell Seminar,* Palm Springs Convention Center, Palm Springs, CA, Nov. 16–19, p. 487 (1998).
94. Doughty, T. R., Jr. and Sperati, C. A., U.S. Patent 3,855,191 (December 17, 1974).
95. Hintzer, K. and Löhr, G., in *Modern Fluoropolymers* (Scheirs, J., Ed.), John Wiley & Sons, New York, p. 240 (1997).
96. Hintzer, K. and Löhr, G., in *Modern Fluoropolymers* (Scheirs, J., Ed.), John Wiley & Sons, New York, p. 243 (1997).

97. Hintzer, K. and Löhr, G., in *Modern Fluoropolymers* (Scheirs, J., Ed.), John Wiley & Sons, New York, p. 251 (1997).

98. Sulzbach, R. and Tschacher, M., *Angew. Makromol. Chem.* 109/110, 113 (1982).

99. Hintzer, K. and Löhr, G., in *Modern Fluoropolymers* (Scheirs, J., Ed.), John Wiley & Sons, New York, p. 2254 (1997).

100. Michel, W., *Kunststoffe/German Plastics* 79, No. 10, 984 (1989).

101. *TEFLON® NXT 70 Fluoropolymer Resin, Modified PTFE Granular Molding Resin,* Publication 2474696 C (4/98), DuPont Fluoroproducts, Wilmington, DE.

102. Treat, T. A. and Malhotra, S. C., U.S. Patent 5,731,394 (March 24, 1998).

103. *TEFLON® NXT* Publication 300445 A, DuPont Fluoroproducts, Wilmington, DE.

9 Recycling

As with any raw material, recycling of fluoropolymers is very important. Most melt-processible fluoropolymers can be reprocessed in a fashion similar to other thermoplastics. With PTFE the situation is more complicated. Because of its high melt viscosity, it is difficult to remelt and mix with virgin material, particularly if it contains mineral fillers. Nevertheless, a significant amount of PTFE production scrap is being reused by cleaning, grinding, and using in that form for ram extrusion.[1] Moreover, it is often compounded with glass fiber, carbon fibers, bronze, molybdenum sulfide, and other high-performance polymers, such as polyimides or polyphenylene sulfide (PPS).

Currently, most PTFE scrap (mainly residues from machining operations) is processed by radiation, being exposed to doses up to 400 kGy to reduce the molecular weight drastically and to obtain micropowders.[1] The most common process employs an electron beam processor, although gamma radiation can also be used. High-molecular-weight PTFE can also be converted into micropowders by thermal or shear degradation.[2]

Recently, a process involving chemical recycling of PTFE using fluidized bed has been developed and patented.[3-5] The optimum temperature is in the range of 545 to 600°C (1013 to 1112°F) and the main decomposition products are tetrafluoroethylene (TFE), hexafluoropropene (HFP), and cyclo-perfluorobutane (c-C_4F_8). The most important advantages of this process are that the monomers produced can be purified before repolymerization, which allows production of a more valuable product, and that the process is continuous.[1]

The use of reprocessed (reground) PTFE resin has limitations. For one thing, it exhibits markedly lower tensile strength and elongation than virgin PTFE. Reprocessed material creeps up to 25% more than virgin resin and contains twice the void content.[6] Because of porosity and larger number of voids, its dielectric strength is lower than that of the virgin PTFE. Thus, the use of reprocessed material is limited to such applications where cost is an important consideration and where lower performance is sufficient for the application.

At present, some 4000 metric tons of fluoroplastics are recycled annually.[7]

REFERENCES

1. Lyons, B. J., in *Modern Fluoropolymers* (Scheirs, J., Ed.), John Wiley & Sons, New York, p. 340 (1997).
2. Gangal, S. V., in *Encyclopedia of Polymer Science and Engineering* (Mark, H. F. and Kroschwitz, J. I., Eds.), Vol. 16, 597 (1989).

3. Simon, C. H. and Kaminski, W., *Polym. Degrad. Stab.* 62, 1 (1998).
4. German Patent DE 4334015 A1.
5. European Patent EP 0647607 A1.
6. Ebnessajjad, S. and Lishinsky, V., *Machine Design*, February, 82 (1999).
7. Korinek, P. M., *Kunstst. Plast. Eur.* 83 (11), November, 782 (1993).

APPENDIX 1
Registered Trade Names of Common Commercial Fluoropolymers

Trade Name	Company
Aclon	Honeywell
Aflas	Dyneon
Aflon	Asahi
Algoflon	Ausimont
Cefral-Soft	Daikin
Cytop	Asahi
Daiflon	Daikin
Dai-El	Daikin
Fluon	Asahi
Fluorel	Dyneon
Fluorobase T	Ausimont
Fomblin	Ausimont
Halar	Ausimont
Hylar	Ausimont
Kalrez	DuPont Dow Elastomers
Kel-F	Dyneon
KF	Kureha
Kynar	Elf Atochem
Kynar Flex	Elf Atochem
Lumiflon	Asahi
Neoflon	Daikin
Polyflon	Daikin
Solef	Solway
Technoflon	DuPont Fluoroproducts
Tedlar	DuPont Fluoroproducts
Teflon	DuPont Fluoroproducts
Teflon AF	DuPont Fluoroproducts

Trade Name	Company
Teflon FEP	DuPont Fluoroproducts
Teflon NXT	DuPont Fluoroproducts
Teflon PFA	DuPont Fluoroproducts
Tefzel	DuPont Fluoroproducts
THV Fluoroplastic	Dyneon
Viton	DuPont Dow Elastomers
Zalak	DuPont Dow Elastomers

APPENDIX 2
Glossary of Terms

ASTM — American Society for Testing and Materials is a nonprofit organization with the purpose of developing standards on characteristics and performance of materials, products, systems, and services and promoting the related knowledge.

Automatic molding — A PTFE molding technique for small parts in automatic presses, which is faster than standard compression molding.

Average particle size — The average diameter of solid particles as determined by various test methods.

Blow molding — The process of forming hollow articles by expanding a hot plastic element against the internal surfaces of a mold. In its simplest form the process comprises extruding a tube (parison) downward between opened halves of a mold, closing the mold, and injecting air to expand the tube, which is pinched on the bottom.

Blowing (foaming) agent — A substance that alone or in combination with other substances can produce a cellular structure in a plastic or elastomeric mass. It can be a compressed gas, a volatile liquid, or a solid that decomposes into a gas upon heating.

Coagent — An additive increasing the effectiveness of an organic peroxide used as a cross-linking agent.

Coalesce — To combine particles into one body or to grow together.

Coefficient of friction — A number expressing the amount of frictional effect, usually expressed in two ways: static and dynamic.

Coining — A PTFE compression molding technique for complicated parts. The sintered molding is quickly heated to the melting point, then quickly pressed into a mold cavity and held until it solidifies.

Cold flow (creep) — Tendency of a material to flow slowly under load and or over time.

Comonomer — A monomer reacting with a different monomer in a polymerization reaction, the result of which is a copolymer.

Contact angle — A measure of the ability of a liquid to wet solid surfaces. It expresses the relationship between the surface tension of a liquid and the surface energy of the surface on which the liquid rests. As the surface energy decreases, the contact angle increases.

Corona treatment — A method to render inert polymers more receptive to wetting by solvents, adhesives, coatings, and inks using high-voltage discharge. The corona discharge oxidizes the surface, thus making it more polar.

Cross-linking — A reaction during which chemical links are formed between polymeric chains. The process can be carried out by chemical agents (e.g., organic peroxides), reactive sites on the polymeric chains, or high energy radiation (e.g., electron beam).

Cryogenic — Referring to very low temperatures, below about –150°C (–238°F).

Crystalline melting point — A temperature at which the crystalline portion of a polymer melts.

Crystallinity — A state of molecular structure attributed to the existence of solid crystals with a definite geometric form.

Cure — A process of changing the properties of a polymer by a chemical reaction (condensation, polymerization, or addition). In elastomers it means mainly cross-linking or vulcanization.

Dielectric constant — The ratio of the capacitance assembly of two electrodes separated by a plastic insulating material to its capacitance when the electrodes are separated by air only.

Dielectric strength — Ability of a material to resist the passage of electric current.

Elasticity — The ability of a material to quickly recover its original dimensions after removal of the load that has caused deformation.

Elastomer — A polymeric substance with elastic properties. Such material can be stretched repeatedly at room temperature to at least twice its original length and upon release of the stress will return immediately with force to its approximate original length.

ETFE — Copolymer of ethylene and tetrafluoroethylene noted for an exceptional chemical resistance, toughness, and abrasion resistance.

Electron beam (EB) cure — A process using high energy (accelerated) electrons to promote reactions in a polymeric material (cross-linking, polymerization). The reaction is instantaneous. The voltage range used in this process is typically from hundreds of kilovolts to several megavolts.

FEP — Fluorinated ethylene propylene having excellent nonstick and nonwetting properties.

FEVE — Fluorinated ethyl vinyl ether.

FFKM — ASTM designation for perfluoroelastomers.

Film formation — A process in which a film is formed due to solvent, water, or chemical reaction.

FKM — ASTM designation for fluorocarbon elastomers.

FPM — ISO designation for fluorocarbon elastomers.

Friction, dynamic — Resistance to continued motion between two surfaces, also known as *sliding friction*.

Friction, static — Resistance to initial motion between two surfaces.

FTPE — Fluorinated thermoplastic elastomer.

Fusion — A process in which a continuous film or a solid body is formed by melting and flowing (coalescence) of polymer particles.

HFA — Hexafluoroacetone.

HFP — Hexafluoropropylene, a monomer used for the production of FEP and other copolymers, such as THV Fluoroplastic and fluorinated elastomers.

Ionomer resins — Modified polymers obtained by heating and pressing certain polymers containing carboxylic groups in the presence of metallic ions.

ISO — International Standard Organization.

Isostatic molding — PTFE molding technique allowing uniform compression from all directions. It uses a flexible mold, which is filled with free-flowing granular powder. It is used for parts with complicated shapes.

Laminate — A product made by bonding together one or more layers of material(s). It is frequently assembled by simultaneous application of heat and pressure. A laminate may consist of coated fabrics, metals, or films, or it may be different combinations of these.

Melt Flow Index (MFI) — The amount in grams of a thermoplastic resin flowing through a standard orifice at a specified temperature in 10 minutes. The higher the value, the easier the resin flows in extrusion or injection molding.

MFA — A copolymer of TFE and perfluoro(methylvinyl ether) with properties similar to PFA. It has about 20°C lower melting temperature than PFA.

Modified PTFE — Copolymer of TFE and a small amount (less than 1%) of other perfluorinated monomer (e.g., perfluoroalkoxy monomer) exhibiting considerably improved physical properties, moldability, and much lower microporosity.

Monomer — A relatively simple compound, usually containing carbon and of low molecular weight, which can react to form a polymer by combination with itself or with other similar molecules or compounds.

Perfluorinated resin — A polymer consisting of monomers where all main chain carbons are combined with fluorine atoms only (e.g., TFE, HFP).

PFA — Copolymer of TFE with perfluoro(propylvinyl ether), an engineering thermoplastic characterized by excellent thermal stability, release properties, low friction, and toughness. Its performance is comparable to PTFE except it is melt-processable.

PFAFA — Poly(fluoroalkyl-α-fluoroacrylates).

PFAMA — Poly(fluoroalkyl methacrylates).

PFEVE — Copolymer of fluoroethylene (TFE of CTFE) and vinyl ether.

PFPE — Perfluoromethyl vinyl ether.

PMDS — Poly(methyl siloxane).

PMTFPS — Poly(methyl trifluoropropyl siloxane).

PMVE — Perfluoro(methylvinyl ether) a monomer used for the production of MFA.

Polymer fume fever — An illness characterized by temporary flu-like symptoms caused by inhaling the products released during the decomposition of fluoropolymers, mainly PTFE. Tobacco smoke enhances the severity of this condition.

Postcure — A second cure at high temperatures enhancing some properties and/or removing decomposition products of the primary reaction.

PPVE — Perfluoropropyl vinyl ether monomer used for the production of PFA.

Prorad — A compound promoting the cross-linking reaction by high energy radiation.

Ram extrusion — A process to produce PTFE extrudates of continuous lengths from granulated resins.

Sintering — A process in which PTFE particles are heated, then soften and coalesce forming a continuous film or a solid body.

Skived film — A PTFE film prepared by peeling from a sintered billet using a sharp cutting tool in a similar fashion as, for example, wood veneer.

Substrate — Any surface to be coated by a coating or bonded by an adhesive.

Surface resistance — The surface resistance between two electrodes in contact with a material is the ratio of the voltage applied to the electrodes to that portion of the current between them, which flows through the surface layers.

Surfactant — A widely used contraction of *surface active agent*, a compound that alters surface tension of a liquid in which it is dissolved.

Terpolymer — The product of simultaneous polymerization of three different monomers or of grafting one monomer to the copolymer of two monomers.

TFE — Tetrafluoroethylene, a perfluorinated monomer used as a feedstock for the production of PTFE and as a comonomer for the production of a variety of other fluoropolymers.

Thermoforming — A process of forming a plastic film or sheet into a three-dimensional shape by clamping it, heating it, and then applying a differential pressure to make the film or sheet conform to the shape of the mold.

Viscoelasticity — The tendency of polymers to respond to stress as if they were a combination of elastic solids and viscous fluids.

Viscosifying agent — A substance used to increase the viscosity of a liquid, mainly by swelling.

Volume resitivity — The electrical resistance between opposite sides of a cube.

APPENDIX 3
Fluoropolymers —
General Biography

1. Blanchet, T. A., *Handbook of Thermoplastics* (Olabisi, O., Ed.), Chapter 40, Marcel Dekker, New York (1997)
2. Ebnessajad, S., *Fluoroplastics*, Vol. 1, William Andrew Publishing, Norwich, NY (2000).
3. Mazur S., *Polymer Powder Technology* (Narkis, M. and Rosenzweig, N., Eds.), Chapter 15, John Wiley & Sons, New York (1995).
4. Sanders, K. J., *Organic Polymer Chemistry,* Chapter 7, Chapman & Hall, London, (1988).
5. Scheirs, J., Ed., *Modern Fluoropolymers,* John Wiley & Sons, New York (1997).
6. Sperati, C. A., *Handbook of Plastics and Materials Technology* (Rubin, I. I., Ed.), Chapters 8 through 13, John Wiley & Sons, New York, (1990).
7. Wall, L. A., Ed., Fluoropolymers), Wiley Interscience, New York, (1972).

Index